The Only Game in Town

By

Peter Black

ISBN: 9798636188247
Imprint: Independently published

Acknowledgements

My fond and loving thanks are due to my wife Angela, who has had to put up with my sudden obsession with writing once I lost my Welsh Assembly seat in 2016, and who has always been patient and supportive in all my endeavours, even when it seemed that I had lost the plot completely.

Thanks too are due to my editor, David Lawlor, who once more helped me knock my story into shape, showed infinite patience with my inability to punctuate properly and used his invaluable experience to help me get a story that has been in my head for the best part of thirty years into a readable format.

I also owe profound thanks to Christoph Fischer, Melinda Moore, Rhian Vaughan, Joanne Foster, Helen Ceri Clarke and many others for their support, feedback, suggestions and assistance in putting this manuscript together and getting it published.

All the good things in this novel are there because of the assistance of those named above, any mistakes, inaccuracies, curiosities, or inconsistencies are entirely my own.

1

The Power and the Glory

Harry O'Leary awoke with a start. The room was unfamiliar. Bathed in the half-light of an as-yet unformed sunrise the walls and shadows cast by the furniture seemed alien. It took a few minutes to get his bearings. The persistent beeping of an adjacent machine jogged his memory and confirmed that he was still alive.

He had been dreaming again. The last few days had been haunted by one dream after another, each as vivid as the last; it was exhausting.

He tried to sit up, but fell back again in pain, yelping involuntarily. His chest was still sore from the first-aiders' efforts to revive him… efforts that had resulted in a broken rib.

As if to compound his discomfort, the scar from the by-pass was starting to itch – and he was thirsty. The surgeon had been at pains afterwards to tell him that he could have another heart attack if he didn't relax completely and let the operation wounds settle - easy to say he thought. He reached for the button to summon help, wincing at the effort.

An attractive young nurse appeared, plumped up his pillows, got him comfortable and placed a beaker of water with a straw in his hands. He slaked his thirst as she fussed around, tidying up the bed covers and checking the morphine drip.

He lay back and let his mind wander, afraid to go back to sleep. The last time he'd worried about failing to wake up in the morning was when he was a child. The heart attack had awoken an acute awareness of his own mortality. It wasn't helped by the fact that he could now hear said heart beating loudly. The doctor had explained that the cutting of the pericardium sac as part of the operation was responsible for that specific torture.

Looking around the room, Harry wondered if his best

years were behind. He reflected how, for such a long period, he'd stood like a colossus over Oldport, without challenge or dissent, as he had worked alongside others to transform his hometown into the modern powerhouse it had become.

Was that how it had happened? He was no longer sure about his own memories.

He let his mind drift back more than eighteen years to May 1969, when it had all started… picturing himself sitting in the half empty office he'd confiscated from the town's mayor. Leading a council was a real job with actual power, the mayor's role was ceremonial, lasted for one year at a time, and at best, involved just chairing council meetings and attending functions – as such, whoever held the position didn't really need the office…

It had been a slow day. He recalled sitting back in the large leather chair and placing his feet on the mahogany desk in front of him.

The surface of the desk was empty as were the drawers either side of him. This was his first day as council leader and he had not yet moved into the office properly.

Although there were pressing issues demanding his attention, he had decided that his first job should be to rearrange the furniture. The glass-fronted bookcases arranged against the wood panelled walls were stuffed with trophies that had been given to past mayors on official visits - presentation plates, pennants, glass ware, small porcelain dishes, trophies and engraved shields, all collected over a lifetime of civic visits and exchanges, most depicting the coat of arms of towns and cities around the UK and the continent.

There were pictures from the council's art gallery and photographs of past royal visits. The entire collection would not have looked out of place at a bric-a-brac sale. Perhaps that's where they should have been sent.

The office looked more like the hub of a social club than of a local authority charged with delivering vital services to its citizens. But he knew it was how business was conducted - good relationships, knowing the right people and helping them get what they want, expecting favours in return - quid pro quo.

He had made a note to get a drinks cabinet installed and, maybe one of those fancy colour televisions too, to keep track of the news. But the priority had been to pull together the reprobates that made up his Independent group, to force them to get behind his agenda.

Harry had always liked to think that he had been elected because of his natural ability and charisma, but it had been a messy affair involving lots of favours and promises. The real challenge was to drag Oldport into the 1970s.

* * *

Edwin Harry O'Leary, everybody called him Harry - was a stocky man, just five feet ten inches tall in his bare feet. He had never really been in the best of shape, even in 1969. Sweat patches tended to form under the arms of his shirts, his tie and collar were loosened to give his ample neck some breathing space, while the shirt buttons strained against a gut that pushed and spilled over his belt.

A good head of sandy-coloured hair and an ample beard compensated for his unhealthy demeanour, His piercing blue eyes and his quick wit were capable of disconcerting opponents, - together with his ability to get on with people, build alliances and choose influential friends, it was these traits that had enabled him to climb the greasy political pole and reach the top at Oldport council and would sustain him through the years ahead.

A knock on the door, pulled him from his reverie.

A woman in her mid-thirties, with long permed brown hair entered. She was wearing a tailored woollen jacket and a short skirt that accentuated her slim figure. She was classically attractive, more demure than sultry, but with good skin and an Audrey Hepburn-like elegance.

As she spoke, she peered at Harry over a large pair of spectacles, somewhat discomforted by the circumstances of his succession – an unexpected but carefully planned and brilliantly executed coup de grace against his predecessor - and his choice of surroundings.

'I hope you're settling in, Councillor,' she said in a stern, business-like manner. 'There's a Jerome Wilson to see you, from the local paper.'

Harry shuffled in his seat, hesitating over his first decision as leader. He could well do without a visit from Jerome Wilson. Why had he agreed to the meeting in the first place?

'Thank you, Sue. Would you show him in please?'

Sue stepped back and a large man in his early forties swept into the room. He was wearing his usual chequered cream jacket, black trousers, *red bow tie and plaid braces, nicotine-stained fingers grasping the stub of a pencil, the other holding open a grubby notebook, which seemed to be a permanent extension to his arm.*

Harry bit his tongue and greeted him like an old friend.

'Jerome, how good to see you. Can I get you a drink?'

The journalist's warm and fleshy grip was vice-like. His voice boomed as he spoke, little beads of spittle gathering on his upper lip.

'Good morning, Harry, congratulations on your new position. Your little woman is already seeing to my needs, thank you.'

Wilson squeezed into one of the red padded chairs in front of Harry's desk, as Sue reappeared with two cups of coffee. She placed two mats on the desk to accommodate them. Harry took the opportunity to try and size-up the Oldport Observer's council reporter.

Jerome Wilson had been born and bred in Oldport. A forty-fag-a-day man, fond of hot curries and the odd pint or three of Guinness, his main responsibility was relaying the ins-and-outs of council business to the good people of the town. It was a task he had fulfilled for the ten years Harry had been a member and for some time before.

Harry sipped some coffee.

'What is it I can do for you today, Jerome?'

'It's funny you should ask that, Harry.' He spoke loudly but carefully as if he were crafting each word individually, but not always in full sentences. 'My editor wants me to do a feature on our new council leader. Who are you? What makes you tick? What plans you have for our quaint little town? Paper of record and all that, keeping the people up-to-speed on all the news fit to print.'

Harry reflected that even now, nearly two decades later, the man still mostly spoke in shorthand, irrespective of his audience.

He knew that when somebody attained power, there was no more hiding on the backbenches – every misstep would be held to account. Probing interviews were one of the downsides of running a council, which was why Wilson had parked himself opposite Harry's desk that first day he took office.

'Okay, well you'd better get on with it then.' Harry had deliberately moderated his tone to convey the message that this intrusion was

unwelcome.

'Good. You're what, 45 years old? Have we had a council leader that young before?'

Wilson's tone was impertinent and disrespectful. Perhaps he was reacting to the clear reluctance in Harry's own voice to co-operate with this interview.

'Not that I'm aware of, and I'm 46 by the way.' Harry tried to hide his indignation behind an anecdote. 'You know Oldport, Jerome. It's always been run by independent councillors. It makes political decisions harder and leadership a nightmare. That's why in the past, they've opted to choose the oldest member as leader. It saved them having to agree on anything.'

'Yes, I'm aware of that. Like herding cats in thunder in my experience. Never make a decision today, when they can put it off until tomorrow, eh? What makes you different, Harry?'

'I suppose it was my natural ability and charisma, Jerome,' Harry said smiling. Wilson refused to acknowledge the self-deprecation.

'Seriously though, my colleagues saw that it was time for a change, time to drag Oldport into the 1960s, perhaps even the 1970s. It was an important part of the manifesto I offered them, and they were attracted by that."

'I heard that our local businessman and entrepreneur, John Baker, had a lot to do with your success as well - you're friends, aren't you?'

Not for the first time Harry checked himself before answering. He wanted to grab this son of a bitch by his lapels and sling him out of the office. Instead he decided to play it straight.

'We're both devout Catholics, who attend the same church and, yes we've done business together, but John has his own agenda. I'm interested in putting Oldport on the map — bringing better jobs here to replace the old industries like fishing that are going out of fashion and turning the town into a place where people want to come to enjoy themselves. That's my primary goal, my friendships and business interests are irrelevant.'

'Right. So, correct me if I'm wrong,' said Wilson, studying his notes. 'You took over the family shop straight from school, after your dad died, and built it up into a chain. What then?'

'I got involved with some local charities and that led to my interest

in politics.'

'I hear you're involved in the local Freemason's lodge. Did that help your rise to power?'

Harry ignored the question, instead he just glared at Wilson. The journalist took the hint and swiftly moved on as if the question had not been asked at all.

'And you have a wife and child. Your wife, Esther - her father is a long-standing councillor, I believe. David Kennedy isn't it? A former mayor and deputy council leader.'

'Yes, we have a son, Ian.'

'He's a bright boy I hear. You're a family man then? The voters will be pleased.'

'Have you always been this cynical, Jerome or did you need to practice?'

'I've been around a long time, Harry. I know how this town ticks. They say you're a breath of fresh air, but – and I hope you don't mind me saying this – I worry that perhaps you might have sold your soul to get where you are. I hear things, worrying things I can't print, but I'm sure you won't get caught up in those issues, like some of your predecessors.'

That was it. The interview was over as far as Harry was concerned. He wasn't going to pander to this rumour monger from the gutter-press anymore.

'I've no idea what you're talking about, Jerome,' the irritation was now showing in his voice. 'My duty is to Oldport and I will discharge that duty to the best of my ability. So, if you're finished, I need to get on.'

Even now, all these years later, thinking about the conversation from his hospital bed, Harry fumed. The sheer cheek of the man in storming into his office and implying that he was on the take continued to rankle. He remembered now why Wilson had been persona non grata amongst so many councillors and officers and had continued to be so up to the present day,

And yet, like chocolate and ice cream he was a necessary evil, offering the instant gratification of self-publicity to the greedy politician when it was needed, but always with a bitter after-taste.

Jerome Wilson liked to have the last word. He stood up and started to walk towards the door, pausing, he turned back to face the new council leader.

'A word to the wise, Harry, try and keep your political and business life separate. It's a slippery slope otherwise.'

Harry stood up without responding, and opened the door, resisting the temptation to aid the journalist's exit with a carefully placed boot. Waiting in the antechamber was another figure, with slicked-back hair, wearing a buttoned-up tan suit, dark-blue shirt and a beige tie.

John Baker was a well-built man in his late thirties. At well over six feet tall, he towered above those around him. Harry remembered thinking that all Baker needed to complete his outfit was a pair of two-tone brown spats. The businessman's appearance in the leader's office was not good timing.

Wilson looked at Harry and winked. Turning on his heel at a speed that belied his size the journalist was suddenly standing full-square in front of the new visitor with his hand out-stretched. Baker took it reluctantly.

'Mr Baker, how nice to see you. Have you come to get your feet under the table already?'

Baker fixed him with an icy stare before brushing past the grinning reporter. Harry shuffled Wilson into the corridor. By the time he returned, Sue had taken businessman into the office and had left him admiring the display cabinets. Harry turned to look at his secretary.

'Do we have any alcohol in this building,' he asked her. 'I could do with a stiff one, and I think we need to look after our distinguished visitors, don't you?'

'It's a bit early for me, Harry,' Baker said, 'I'll have a coffee though love, black with two sugars. Who was the freak in the clown outfit?'

'That was Jerome Wilson, from the Observer. He reports on council meetings. Nothing to worry about. He's a bit of a conspiracy theorist but nobody takes him seriously.'

'Have a seat, John. It's good to see you.'

Baker relaxed.

'Good, then I will put him out of my mind straight away. I came

11

around, so I could be the first to offer my congratulations.'

Harry knew that Baker had come to hold his feet to the fire, making sure he repaid all the favours that were owed in getting Harry into the leader's office in the first place. There was always a price, and Baker knew how to extract it better than most.

Sue brought in the businessman's coffee and set it down in front of him. As she left the room the eyes of both men watched her closely. Harry took a sip of his coffee. It was going cold. He should have asked for a fresh cup.

'It is a bit sparse in here at present,' he said. 'I only took possession this morning.'

Baker stood up and tapped his hand on one of the bookcases.

'These are pretty solid," he said, "must be worth a few bob."

'It all comes with being Mayor apparently, I'll have to send the contents on to his new office,' Harry said. "We've kept that junk in those bookcases for as long as I can remember. The office needs a bit of work, some comfy seats and a drinks cabinet for a start.'

'Very nice, let's hope you get to enjoy it for some time to come.'

There was a threatening tone that Harry couldn't ignore.

'What do you mean?'

'I need your help Harry. It's time to give back in return for me getting you into this office in the first place.'

Harry drank some more of his coffee and looked his backer in the eye.

'You know I'm here for you, John. What is it you need?'

'I think you already know that. My planning application for a night club has been languishing in your council offices for months now, with no sign of any progress. Now that you're the leader, I'd like it to be approved bloody damned quick.'

Harry sat up in his chair. He could see that this could get ugly. Baker had a quick temper and a reputation for getting his own way. But he was an important player in the town, and he could continue to open doors for Harry and the council. More importantly, his money could sustain Harry in power.

'You know that's beyond my control, John. Planning is non-political and there are far too many councillors on this authority with their head up their arse, who think their job is to protect people from themselves. The best I've been able to do up until now is to keep it away from committee to stop it being turned down.'

Baker pulled himself up to his full height and leant across the desk.

'None of that is my problem, Harry. I was rather hoping that now you're leader you could remove barriers like that. You know yourself how red tape is killing business in this country.

'We need a council leader committed to growing prosperity, someone who is going to stop his officers screwing it up. This project has the potential to rejuvenate the high street.'

He lowered his voice.

'More importantly, Harry, this club will make money for both of us.'

Harry grimaced at the unvarnished truth being uttered aloud.

'I understand all that. I just need a bit of time to sort the problem out. I've only been in this chair a few hours. You're right of course. We need a pro-business council and I'm committed to putting together a leadership team that will deliver that.

'In the meantime, getting your club through could be expensive. We're going to have to persuade enough councillors on the planning committee to our way of thinking. How about we work out how to do that rather than squabbling over details?'

'Good, just tell me who, when and how much and we'll fix this together.'

Baker picked up his coffee and downed it in one. He seemed much more at ease now that he had made his point.

'Not bad coffee,' he said, 'could have done with being a bit warmer. Listen, Harry, we're having a party at the house the weekend after next. Why don't you come up? And bring along those councillors who you think we need to persuade to our way of thinking. There'll be girls, so don't let them bring their wives, if you know what I mean.'

Harry smiled. He knew how the game was played, pull them in and take control. He had been to these parties at Baker's mansion, perched at the top of Pym Hill, before. The great and the good living it up while looking down on the town.

* * *

Harry pulled himself into a more comfortable position, bracing against the pain as he shifted his body. His rib really

13

hurt, but a smile came to his face as he recalled the many parties he had attended at Baker's place over the years.

There was a huge swimming pool and a games room, music, alcohol, girls, semi-naked and naked in the pool, illicit sex if guests wanted it, and many, many blackmail opportunities if other methods didn't work.

* * *

The two men shook hands. Harry walked his colleague to the door.

'You do know,' Baker said as if to underline his point, 'that this club is a big deal for me. I've needed to diversify for some time, and this is a good opportunity for both of us. I'm happy to bring you in as a partner if it helps.'

Harry nodded his appreciation.

'One thing at a time John. Let's get it done first. You know that you won't get a better council leader to work with than me. Nobody else here understands business as I do, nobody else has my vision for this town. We're going to be a great partnership.'

Baker opened the door and patted Harry on the shoulder. He looked across at the secretary typing away at a desk at the side of the small outer office.

'It's Sue, isn't it?'

'Yes sir.' He took her hand and kissed it.

'Well, thank you for my coffee. Perhaps we'll meet again.'

She blushed. Baker looked pleased. Harry knew the businessman liked to make an impression on women, especially if they were attractive. No doubt he would return to this challenge at another time.

'Harry, we have to talk about housing sometime. I have a scheme in mind for the Inchfield area. It could make a lot of money. We just need to sort out the planning side of things.'

'You do know that developing that area will attract a lot of resistance,' Harry said. 'We'll talk again, but not here.'

Baker nodded and then turned back to Sue to deliver his parting shot.

'You should come to one of my parties some time.'

She blushed again. Harry ushered him out quickly.

'I'll see you at church on Sunday. I'll have some key councillors with me at the party the weekend afterwards. That should create an

opportunity for us to get the result we need.'

'Just make sure you do.'

Harry strolled back inside, acknowledging the greetings of members of staff as he passed them, and into the antechamber to his office.

'Sue, can we get a sofa and an armchair into this office please and a fully stocked drinks cabinet? If we're going to grow this place, then we need to show that we mean business. Get a colour television as well. If this town is going to be put on the map, we have to know what's going on outside its borders.

'Oh, and don't under any circumstances go to one of John Baker's parties. I'm telling you for your own good. In fact, watch out for him. He's a lecherous bastard and can't be trusted.'

'Now, shall we get down to it? I want you to get Councillors Harris, Jacobs, Healy, and Kennedy in here to see me. We have work to do.'

2
New Kid in Town

It had been a few hours since Billy Jones had sought directions in a cavernous and bewildering bus station. Earlier still, he had sat and stared out of the window as his bus had wound its way down through the river valley into town, past several derelict factories, through rows of terraced streets, and into a bustling High Street.

It was a beautiful mid-summer day, with shoppers clad in shorts and shirt sleeves filling the streets. Hanging baskets bursting with blossoms adorned many of the houses, while those terraces with front gardens proudly showed off displays that would not have looked out-of-place at the Chelsea Flower Show.

Oldport with its seventy thousand population, nestled at the foot of a cluster of hills, around an estuary. For many years the town had served as a harbour for local fishing trawlers. Now, most of the business that came its way was from the commercial sea-going trade.

The arrival of the railway in the nineteenth century had led to a long period of prosperity for the port, and the small fishing village had grown into a full-sized settlement complete with busy storage units to store imported goods and those for export, built to take advantage of easy links to the continent.

However, the 1980s' recession had hit the town hard. Unemployment now impacted on one in five of the working population. But things were changing…

Billy's copy of the Oldport Observer reported that a new casino, live music venue and restaurant was planned near to a long-established nightclub. In addition, several new pubs and eateries were drawing in youngsters from the surrounding countryside every weekend, like moths swarming around a lightbulb. He reasoned that casual work should be easily available.

16

Despite the town's obvious ambition there was not much money about, and it was clear that local retailers were struggling to make ends meet.

As he reached the main street, Billy had been struck by the number of empty shops surrounding the bog-standard department stores. The area was busy, but it was also faded and shabby.

Vehicles clogged the street and pedestrians clung to the narrow footpath, struggling under the weight of their shopping; a middle-aged tramp with a long straggly beard, sat cross-legged on a flattened cardboard box at the entrance to W.H. Smith, pleading with passers-by for beer money.

Billy stood in front of the local newspaper offices, a rather ugly 1960s' building with aluminium window frames and pink plastic-panelled cladding. All the belongings he had in the world were stuffed into the backpack he carried with him.

He was hoping to find his brother, Simon, but the middle-aged receptionist appeared clueless. The journalist was not there, she said and suggested that Billy try the local council offices.

He must have looked as confused as he felt for the woman took pity on him. She rang the news desk to try and get a more precise location. Putting the phone down, she told him that his brother was covering a council meeting, but she would pass on a message to him when he returned.

She directed Billy to the Prince Albert Pub down by the harbour. All the journalists went there after work, she said. She promised to send Simon to meet him in the main bar as soon as he got back.

It was only three o'clock but already Billy saw small groups of young men gathering on street corners, smoking and joking. They were bored and just passing the day but, coming from a one-street village in the middle of rural England, it was rather unsettling for him. He chided himself for his over-active imagination.

The Prince Albert was a big sprawling giant of a building

with a red brick exterior, topped by two massive square chimneys, and commanded most of a ninety-degree bend in the road near to the harbour. Four huge, arched windows with green painted frames, dominated the ground-floor façade. They straddled two glass doors which were set back within an enclosed entrance below a large square bay window and a prominent high gable.

This was unlike any pub Billy was used to. There was no juke box. The plastic seats and wood veneer tables of his local, back home had no place here. This was a traditional establishment packed with solid oak tables, ancient wooden chairs, padded benches and a very substantial u-shaped bar fronted by wooden stools.

The clientele was mixed, too. In one corner a gang of older men in donkey jackets and jeans sat beneath a cloud of cigarette smoke, playing cards for money. At the other end of the bar, in a nook situated through an open archway, a group of young women were gathered in quiet union, all short skirts and skimpy tops, sipping half pints of lager and checking their make-up as if they were getting ready to go out on the town.

Elsewhere, small clusters of mostly middle-aged men in suits chewed the fat and knocked back half pints of bitter. A couple of regulars in jeans and check shirts sat on the stools, exchanging banter with a slim, attractive young, flaxen-haired woman with hazel-eyes, who was ministering to their needs from behind a row of towering enamelled beer pump handles, which towered over her slim figure.

Behind her was a huge mirror and an elaborate chrome coffee machine of the kind Billy had only previously seen in Italian cafés. He later discovered that it had been bought at a bankruptcy sale and was considered to be so difficult to clean and operate that it was rarely used.

The barmaid was wearing a simple, knee-length blue dress that accentuated her pert figure. A pair of flat black shoes may have been a practical aid in a busy pub, but they did nothing to give her more height or offer her greater leverage on the pump handles.

From the other end of the bar, just in front of the toilets, a vigorous discussion was taking place about horse racing. Four men in overalls, grasping bookies betting slips, were arguing about a nag called Lecky's Journey that some of them thought had been doped.

Billy walked up to the bar and asked for a pint of lager.

'How old are you?' the barmaid demanded. Billy imagined that her brown eyes twinkled as she spoke. Her voice though, did not deviate from its inquisitional purpose.

'Nearly nineteen, why?'

'You look like you should be in school.'

An older man behind him laughed loud and long.

'Give him a break, Jeanie. The boy's thirsty. He looks old enough to me.'

Jeanie shrugged and grabbed a glass from beneath the counter. She poured Billy's drink and took his money. He smiled and found himself a table near the entrance.

He had just sat down and taken the first sip of his pint when a door opened behind the bar and a bearded giant of a man with prominent tattoos, entered wearing a summer dress, a blonde wig, diamante earrings and high heels.

The man, who must have been in his early fifties, greeted several regulars like old friends and then reached for a rather worn enamel pump handle and pulled it back with sudden force.

He handed a pint of beer to a customer, took the money and rang up the sale on an old-fashioned till that looked like it belonged in a museum. He passed on the change and looked around for somebody else to serve.

The two men sitting on bar stools signalled for a refill. The barman moved over to serve them.

'Not such a traditional pub, is it?'

Billy jumped. He had been so fascinated by the scene in front of him that he hadn't seen his brother come in.

'Francesca has been the landlord here as long as I can remember. Nobody crosses him. They know better. How you doin', Bro?'

Simon Jones was a slight man in his late twenties. His blond hair had been cropped short, with no attempt to hide a recessive fringe. He was wearing a battered slim-fit navy suit, a creased white shirt and a thin plain tie, loosened at the unbuttoned collar. He had not shaved for a few days, but the resulting stubble was surprisingly neat.

The two men embraced. Simon went to the bar to get himself a drink.

'So, what brings you to Oldport?'

It had been some time since they had seen each other. Billy thought Simon looked older than his twenty-seven years, his face shadowed by sadness, his eyes world-weary and resigned. Town living had taken its toll. Were things so bad here?

'Got into a fight with Mum's new bloke and he threw me out,' Billy said matter-of-factly.

He was resentful that his brother had not spoken to anybody at home since their father had died three years previous. Simon had come to the funeral, headed back to Oldport and that was the last their mother had seen or heard from him. No explanation, not even a phone call.

'You're a hard person to find. I only knew you were here because of the birthday and Christmas cards passed on through Dave. Once I got thrown out, I threw myself on his mercy, borrowed money off him for the bus fare and begged him for your address. All he knew was that you work for the Oldport Observer. And here I am.

'I need somewhere to stay… and a job. It isn't for long. I'm taking time out before I go to Southampton University in September next year.'

Simon sighed. He had deliberately kept only his best mate in the know about his whereabouts, but Dave had blabbed.

'That seems a long time to me. What makes you think I can help you?'.

Billy's thick brown hair and pallid demeanour made him seem even younger than he was. His eyes had started to water at the prospect of rejection. He gulped down a mouthful of lager.

'I've got nothing to offer you,' Simon said eventually. 'You're welcome to the floor of my bedsit for a few nights, but it can't be permanent. I've built a life here and I'm trying to put our past behind me.'

Billy was desperate.

'I've got nowhere else to go, Si. You're my only hope.'

Simon put his hand on Billy's shoulder.

'I know, I know. But you've made a decision. You've come all this way and now you need to learn to stand on your own two feet. *I* had to. Wasn't it obvious that I wanted to be left alone?' He hesitated and seemed to relent.

'Look, I know some people. I can ask around and see if I can get something for you. But if I do this, you leave me be. I don't need to be constantly reminded of home by you hanging around me all the time.'

Billy pulled himself together.

'Why did you leave? You never told me. One minute you were there, the next you'd gone. What happened?'

'I don't want to talk about it. Have you eaten, because I'm starving? There's a takeaway curry place near my place. Drink up, we're leaving.'

Simon stood up, emptied his glass in one action and beckoned Billy to follow him.

*   *   *

It was a small bedsit, just ten minutes' walk from the pub. The wallpaper was faded and peeling in parts, and the dark green carpet had not been vacuumed for some time. In one corner was an unmade single bed; in another was a small kitchenette. There were two ancient armchairs and a television in the centre of the room.

Simon dragged a sleeping bag and a pillow out of a cupboard while Billy emptied the contents of several takeaway cartons onto some plates. He gestured to the space between the two armchairs.

'You can sleep there.'

Billy picked up the kettle, filled it with water and plugged it in. He pulled open a couple of cupboard doors, found mugs and teabags and set about making himself useful. They sat in the armchairs eating in silence. Simon looked deep in thought, as if he didn't want to be disturbed.

Something was troubling him. He cleared his plate, took a mouthful of tea, sat back and closed his eyes before, in a moment of candour that seemed to take even him by surprise, he blurted out:

'I had a big row with Mum and left. I didn't feel welcome there anymore. I just had to get away and never really felt inclined to come back until Dad died, and even then, I couldn't stomach it for longer than the funeral.'

An uneasy silence engulfed them.

'But...'

'I really don't want to talk about this. I've told you the situation. There's no more to say.' Simon was emphatic.

Billy fell silent. He had more in common with his brother than he had previously thought

'Look, I've been thinking,' said Simon, deciding to change the subject. 'This town, it's not a very nice place. Go back home, patch it up with Mum and her boyfriend.'

'And if I don't want to?'

'I don't know. Find something else. I really can't be responsible for you...for anybody if truth be told.'

'I'm not asking you to be responsible.'

His pleading was unconvincing, and he could see that Simon was sceptical. No doubt this was his brother's worst nightmare, having to look after his kid brother.

'This town will eat you alive, Billy. It really isn't a good place to be when you're still trying to find yourself.'

'I need a fresh start,' Billy said. 'And you're all I have.'

'So, what do you expect me to do?'

'Put me in touch with somebody who can offer me a job and leave me to it.'

'And where will you live?'

'I'll find somewhere.'

'And I suppose you want my help?' Simon repeated.

'I don't know Si. I'm not going to force you. You clearly don't want me here.'

'That's not it.' Simon sighed. 'Look, I'm sorry. I'll try to help, Bro. It's just that… 'He struggled to find the right words. '…I have a life here of sorts, but I'm struggling myself. It's not easy.' He studied his brother, grappling with his thoughts. 'But that doesn't mean I won't help you. I'm just concerned that it will all end badly.'

'It won't. I can handle myself… honest.'

Simon could hear the pleading tone in his brother's voice. It was something he couldn't ignore. 'Just so you know… the people who run this town are well dodgy, But I've heard Harry, our beloved council leader is looking for a gopher. It's not much, but it's all I've got, and even at that I'd prefer it if you said no.'

Billy suddenly felt exhausted, emotionally and physically. His limbs ached. He felt weak. He could barely keep his eyes open. Simon pointed at the sleeping bag.

'We're both knackered. Let's sleep on it. I've gotta go to work in the morning. We'll talk when I get home.'

Simon passed Billy the sleeping bag and pillow, then sat down on the bed and put his head in his hands. Billy thought he looked shattered.

Simon reached across for a book on a small bedside table. He found the bookmark and prised open the pages, reading for a few minutes but seeming to struggle to keep the words in focus.

He put the bookmark back and allowed the pages to swallow it up, then pulled off his clothes and climbed between the covers. The two of them drifted off to sleep within minutes of each other.

3
Dressed to Impress

The brush was held steady as it applied a faultless stroke of blood orange varnish to the nail. The colour worked well against the tanned skin of his hands. He dipped it back into the bottle and wiped the excess at the brim before applying the liquid again to another nail – slowly, lovingly… there was no rush. And so, the process went until all ten nails were covered. He wiggled his fingers slowly, enjoying how the daylight played on the colour.

Hands told you a lot about a person, and these told more than most. They were broad and strong, with sleek black hairs covering the backs and parts of the thick fingers. There were some scars, too, mementos of a life lived on the rolling wave, on ships that travelled the oceans, pitching themselves against all that Nature could throw at them. Yes, it had been an interesting life so far… a real voyage of discovery.

The tip of Frank McColgan's tongue ran along the bristles of his bearded lip as low winter light flooded through the pub window and flared against the floral orange design of his dress and his platinum blonde wig. He studied his handiwork, pleased with the manicure, then walked into the bar just as the door of the Prince Albert was pushed open and another customer entered.

The man ordered his usual – a pint of bitter and a sandwich – and Frank got what the man wanted. The sandwich was handed over, the money paid and that was it. No drama. It hadn't always been this way, of course… certainly not back in Seventy-Five, when he'd returned to the town leaner, meaner and determined to make a place for himself on his own terms, no matter what that reaction might be.

A full moon had illuminated the town's streets that night as Frank McColgan trudged from Oldport bus station towards the harbour, an enormous kit bag slung over his shoulder.

Frank barely had an ounce of fat on his body. Twelve years in the Royal Navy followed by eleven in the Merchant Navy had provided enough incentive for him to keep fit. Now, thanks to regular workouts, he hardly noticed the weight of the kit bag.

A thick woollen black jacket, weathered denim jeans above steel-toed doc martens and a woollen hat kept out the winter cold. A light rain fell as he picked his way through barely remembered streets.

At forty years-old, Frank felt as if this homecoming was a turning point in his life. It was so long since he was in Oldport that it had become an alien landscape to him, and yet so little had changed.

As he rounded a corner, the lights of the Prince Albert pub cut through the dusk like a beacon. He reflected that this was where he had grown-up, in the shadow of a father whose death had brought him back full circle.

Tom McColgan had been a legend in Oldport, a working-class boy from the harbour area, he had gone on to become a professional boxer and had fought for the British heavyweight title.

When his career ended prematurely in a car accident, Tom had returned to Oldport, bought the pub where he had spent his youth and built it up. His post-boxing life was not without controversy.

Tom had always liked a pint or two, and since leaving his boxing career behind him he indulged more frequently. The harbour area had become the place to do business and the pub offered a discreet but important watering hole for local journalists, businesspeople and leading politicians.

It helped of course, that there were other attractions in the pub as well. One night, Tom had discovered a prostitute discreetly pulling tricks in the bar. He had been about to throw her out but got talking instead. She described the benefits to be had for her and him if she kept her work on the premises Over time, a couple more of her friends also started to use the pub and began to rent out rooms there.

Tom did lay down conditions. He had created a haven for the girls, giving the best-looking one's rooms where they could take their clients, but in return he insisted that they clean up their act. Rent was to be paid on time and there were to be no drugs and no pimps.

The street trade moved elsewhere, unable to compete and suddenly the district felt much safer, as they took their pimps and drug dealers with them.

At first, the police had come down hard on the Prince Albert, but, recognising that Oldport's most famous citizen had done them a favour, they eventually turned a blind eye in return for a regular pay-off. The fact that important people who used the pub to strike deals had not been put off, and even availed themselves of the girls' services, helped to keep the local constabulary on board.

And if the forces of law and order and those running the town felt that they wanted to indulge in the delights offered by the Prince Albert, then who was Tom McColgan to argue.

Frank was Tom's only son. His mother had left shortly after Tom had taken on the pub. This was not an area in which she wanted to live. Nor did she want to be encumbered by a child while establishing a new life for herself, so she had left the boy behind.

Frank had liked the prostitutes – some of them would invite him to their rooms and even provide him with a free service or a blow job from time to time…a treat for the landlord's son.

When a girl Frank had grown up with, was murdered selling tricks by the harbour gates, he had resolved to do everything he could to protect the ones working from his father's pub. It was a resolution he brought back with him when he became landlord, after finding he couldn't persuade them to give up their trade altogether.

Frank looked forward to his encounters with the girls living in the Prince Albert, but not just for the physical release…he also enjoyed watching the hookers when they took off their clothes and revealed the underwear beneath. The sensuous touch and feel of it brought out a mix of emotions… and a curiosity about what it would be like to wear it.

One drunken night, one of the girls even let him try some on. After that there was no going back. Frank loved the sensation of the fabric on his skin…it brought with it a raging horniness combined with a relaxed sense of comfort that he couldn't quite define… it just felt right and calming.

It was his and the girls secret… until one of them blabbed and burly former top boxer Tom McColgan couldn't accept that his son was like that – 'a poofter'. The fact that Frank had sex with the girls didn't alter anything in Tom's mind – his son was an embarrassment and had to go…and that's exactly what he did, leaving at seventeen and heading straight to the Royal Navy.

The few times Frank had come back home, he found his father increasingly dependent on the bottle and on his two uncles to keep the business running. And now, the drink had finally killed Oldport's most famous son.

Frank was glad he had missed the funeral. By all accounts it had been a grand affair with thousands of well-wishers lining the streets to watch the coffin pass on top of a horse-drawn carriage.

No doubt the bill for that indulgence would be waiting for him when he got to the pub, along with the uncle who had been so keen to spend his inheritance for him in the final years of his father's life.

But this was a turning point in another way as well. It was an opportunity for Frank to live his life as he wanted and to hell with everybody else.

People living in the harbour area were largely unshockable however, it was a rough and ready community with a strong macho tradition.

Frank had been unable to indulge his preference for living in women's clothing up until now due to his profession. But if he was going to be his own man (or woman), living in the community he'd grown up in, running his own business, then he needed to take that leap of faith.

It was the 1970s for goodness sake, not Victorian times. He knew that it was not going to be easy and he would have to put down a mark quickly, but he was prepared for that. This was his time.

As he got to the door of the pub, he hesitated. The pub was full. He glanced through the glass. He didn't recognise anybody. He saw his father's whores sat, sipping half-lagers, waiting to be bought, and some younger men laughing and joking, daring each other to be the first to make an offer.

In a corner, a group of men in business suits sat, chatting earnestly, while behind the bar were a couple of barmaids, busily keeping the punters happy. Behind them a tall, well-built man, with receding white hair and a host of tattoos, emerged sucking on a pipe. It was his Uncle Jim.

Jim was Tom's elder brother. He had been quite handy in the ring himself, turned pro for a few years but gave it up to manage and train his sibling. When Tom retired, Jim supplemented his earnings with a *few gigs as a Lee Marvin impersonator. He could still do a passable rendition of 'Wandering Star' and was often called upon to perform at parties and occasionally in the pub.*

Frank pushed open the door and stepped inside. Slowly, the noise died down into silence as everybody turned to look at him, some because they recognised him, others because they were curious as to what their companions were so fascinated by.

'Well, it's about bloody time you showed up.'

Jim's voice boomed above the silence as he walked quickly to embrace Frank.

'I thought I was going to have to run this place by myself.'

Frank pulled himself away from his uncle.

'Don't you worry, Jim,' he said, 'you can enjoy your retirement at last. I'm back and I'm not going anywhere else for a very long time.'

Frank walked up to the bar and poured himself a brandy. He downed it in one.

'I'm going to drop my kit off and then you can get me up to speed on what's been going on around here,' he said.

*   *   *

The next morning Frank gathered the prostitutes in the bar. He wanted to make it clear where they stood and how things would be from now on. He looked at them for a few minutes, all devoid of make-up, in t-shirts and jeans. They were not used to being up so early in the morning. When he spoke, he did so slowly and deliberatively:

'I was in the Navy in one shape or another for over 20 years, and I've been in enough ports to see how girls like you can be mistreated. I didn't like it then and I don't like the idea of that happening now. Everyone's entitled to make a living – and as long as nobody gets hurt in the process, then what you do is your business.

Just like my Dad, I think that standing on cold street corners is no way to have to work. So, here's the deal – you can rent the rooms upstairs to do your work in, and you can pass the time in the bar here when you're in between customers if that's what you want; but if you're in here, you keep it low key and no flaunting your wares – I don't want you scaring off the locals who aren't interested in getting their leg over.'

'And what's in it for you, Frank? Tom didn't act as my pimp, why should I let you?' asked one of them.

'What's in it for me is I get rent on the rooms upstairs – and it'll be rent at a fair rate. I can also sleep easy knowing I'm not sending drunken customers out there to hassle working girls standing on street corners. As far as pimping's concerned; I don't want any part of that – what you earn is yours, like in any job. I'm a pub landlord, nothing else.'

'And there's one more rule: no drugs. My Dad didn't tolerate it, and neither will I. If I find anyone of you with that stuff then you are out of here…no second chances, no excuses. Am I clear?'

They nodded in agreement. The Prince Albert brothel was back in business.

*   *   *

It was two days later; a Saturday night and the pub was packed with regulars. Frank stood in front of a full-length mirror and smiled. He was clean shaven and wearing a bright red woollen dress buttoned up the front with a flower-patterned silk scarf around his neck.

His bare arms were distinguished by two prominent tattoos. On the right arm was a very elaborate old-fashioned ships compass, on the other an anchor intertwined with a wooden ship's wheel and the words 'Refuse to sink'.

He carefully placed a long blonde wig on his head and clipped a trailing crystal diamante earring to each ear. He applied some lipstick and looked down at his newly shaved stocking-coated legs and size 11, one-and-half-inch-heel silver-glittered shoes.

Frank had never felt more comfortable, but he knew that the real challenge was on the other side of the bar door. He had deliberately omitted to affix any false nails for that reason. He was expecting trouble, but he was ready for it.

Pausing just to adjust his bra, he turned and walked downstairs. At the bottom was his uncle. Jim had been forewarned but he was still taken aback by the overall effect.

'Fucking hell, Frank, you can't go out there looking like that. They'll lynch you.'

'This is my place now, Jim. They accept me for what I am, or they can fuck off.'

He took a deep breath, opened the door into the bar and walked through. There must have been fifty-or-so people there… a few *journalists, one or two local councillors, a dozen factory workers, footballers, youngsters who might or might not be under-age, three or four pensioners, some builders off a local site and the usual group of working girls.*

The pub was its noisy self. And then it was quiet. It was the second time in a week that he had reduced the place to silence. He felt fifty sets of eyes focus on him, their owners struggling to find words or even a suitable thought about the sight facing them.

A couple of the youngsters giggled and started nudging each other. One of the pensioners muttered 'bloody hell' under his breath, but loud enough for the whole bar to hear him. And then one of the builders emitted a loud wolf whistle.

Frank winked at him. The whole bar laughed but one or two of the regulars looked on stony faced. The laughter subsided into silence again as people waited to see what would happen next. And then one of a group of men by the bar spoke up:

'Who the fuck do you think you are? You fucking poof!'

Another joined in: 'You should go back to the Navy darling, with the other fairies.'

There was sustained laughter. Frank squared his shoulders, looked across to the group and singled out the biggest, toughest perpetrator, then walked over to him.

'Do you have a problem with the way I'm dressed?' he asked.

The man looked straight at him, his eyes unflinching, his muscles tensing.

'We don't want no poofs here,' he spat. 'You should fuck off back to the Navy.'

He opened his mouth to speak again, but before he could, Frank hit him with incredible force, knocking him backwards. The man picked himself up and then came back at Frank with fists clenched only to be pummelled by a combination of punches, collapsing in a heap on the floor.

One of his companions started towards Frank and threw a punch, only to hit thin air. Frank winded him with a blow to the stomach, dodged another punch and then proceeded to finish him off.

He looked around at the stunned customers.

'Does anybody else have a problem with the way I dress?'

Nobody said anything. The two men nursed their bruises on the floor, having decided that silence was the most sensible course for them at this stage.

'Well, this is how it is. Tom has gone. This is my pub now and I'm going to run it my way. That doesn't mean that much will change. We're not getting a juke box and if you want a live band you can fuck off into town.

'The girls are staying; the old-fashioned solid wood furniture is staying and we're going to continue serving good beer and the odd sandwich. The only change is me in a dress, and by this time next month you'll all have got bored of gawking at that.

'If you're okay with that then keep on coming here. If you can't cope, then fuck off and go elsewhere. Now, whose turn is it to be served next?'

He went back behind the bar and started to serve drinks. The pub settled back into its routine and the two refuseniks shuffled off to lick their wound, taking some of their mates with them. Only one or two of that group returned… it took six months before they felt able to.

As Frank served, his uncle cornered him.

'Well now you've gone and done it,' he said. Frank looked him in the eyes.

'The same goes for you, Jim. If you don't like it, you can fuck off.'

Jim hesitated. He wasn't sure himself what he should do next. He decided to stay, for now.

Over the next few months, the pub struggled to keep its clientele. There were poison-pen letters, people shouted insults at Frank from a safe distance across the street, homophobic graffiti was painted on the pub walls and, on one occasion, a brick came flying through a window shortly after closing time.

Frank tolerated it all. He wasn't going to give into bullies, and he knew that most of them would soon tire of the spectacle. He was right. The girls had continued to be busy throughout, and eventually the pub business started to pick up again. This was evidenced by the return of the local bigwigs to their favourite watering hole.

On the first night that the local councillors decided to patronise the Prince Albert again, Frank was serving in the bar with Jim. He was wearing a bright green dress, a brown wig and inch-high silver heels. He had painted his fingernails orange and was wearing matching lipstick.

The pub was fuller than it had been for some time, and both men were rushed off their feet. Frank noticed that this did not stop Jim from spending time chatting to the big wigs. He had just served a young couple when he was aware that Jim was standing in front of him on the customer side of the bar.

He was standing next to a shorter, fatter man in a suit. The stranger was clean shaven with sandy-coloured hair and piercing blue eyes.

'This is Councillor Harry O'Leary,' Jim said. 'He's the leader of the council and a regular here.'

The two men shook hands. Frank was wary, what was his uncle up to? Surely, he knew that his nephew was not one for mixing with the 'great and the good.' Nevertheless, the council leader seemed genuinely grateful for the introduction.

'It is good to meet you, Frank. I'm sorry about your father. He was a good man.'

Frank muttered his appreciation, while wondering what the hidden agenda was. At the same time, he knew that Tom had kept the pub afloat by encouraging those in power to use it as their local, to turn a blind eye to the prostitution and to exchange favours. He wondered how much all those bribes must have cost his father.

'I like this pub, Frank. I do a lot of business here and I can push some good things your way,' Harry said, clearly keen to renew this business relationship.' We should keep in touch.'

Frank nodded his agreement and they shook hands again. Jim took O'Leary back to his seat. As his uncle returned to the bar area, Frank pulled him to one side:

'Jesus Christ, do I have to suck up to politicians as well. Maybe I should go back to sea after all.'

Jim looked at his nephew's dress, wig, heels and make-up.

'Don't worry I don't think he's going to ask you to join the Freemasons.'

Frank smiled and went to serve another customer.

4
Called to the Bar

It was mid-morning when Billy awoke. He was alone in Simon's bedsit. The floor was surprisingly comfy, until he tried to move, at which point every bone in his body started to cry-out in protest.

He scoured the kitchenette area for some food. There was some cereal and half a pint of milk in a small fridge on the floor. He made himself a cup of tea, wolfed down a bowl of cornflakes, tidied up the remains of the previous night's curry, and left the dirty dishes in the sink.

Out of the corner of his eye he caught sight of a note from Simon; it read: 'See you at 6pm in the Prince Albert'. He looked at his watch, it was 11.30am. 'What to do for five-and-a-hours?'

Billy decided to explore the town. He had already seen the town centre, but he couldn't think of a better starting point. It was as bleak and as half-empty as he had remembered.

The summer sun was obscured by clouds, but it was still warm enough to walk around without a coat. He took off his bomber jacket and tied it around his waist.

In addition to the boarded-up shops and department stores there were quite a lot of pubs, many of them advertising live music. He paused outside Baker's nightclub. There was a picture of a DJ at a record deck displayed outside and lots of photographs of scantily clad girls dancing. A downstairs shop unit was packed with one-arm bandit machines, a Space Invaders console and another that seemed to involve shooting asteroids with a laser.

Further down the street, he noticed a building surrounded by a high wooden fence with a half-open door. Glancing inside, Billy could hear the whirr of a cement mixer and the muffled conversation of men hard at work.

A poster on the outside advertised that this was to be the

venue of the top-class restaurant, live music venue and casino heralded by the local paper. There was the promise of pole dancers, a top chef and artists catering to an older, richer clientele than the first venue.

The place was due to open in two months. Billy doubted that it would be ready but then what did he know?

As he walked through the high street, he found himself wondering what made a place like Oldport tick. It was obvious that, like many other similar English towns, it was still struggling to pull itself together after the recession earlier in the decade.

Despite that, Billy thought, Margaret Thatcher had won a third term only a few months ago and no doubt it was areas like this that contributed to her success.

He stopped outside the Job Centre. There were a quite a few jobs on offer, none of which paid very well. One caught his eye, though. It was work in the bar of the Prince Albert, with accommodation, if required.

Billy made a note to inquire about it that evening. He needed to get out from under Simon's feet and earn some money. It would also be nice to have a bed to sleep in at night.

He still had four hours to kill until he met his brother, fewer if he went to the pub early and asked about the job. He had come to the end of the high street. To his right was the road to the harbour, to his left he could see the entrance to a park.

He turned left and climbed up the hill towards the park entrance. There were some seats at the top of a slope which offered a good view of the harbour area. He was now looking down on the river inlet that was once the source of much of the town's wealth. That though, was in the past.

The harbour area seemed to have an abundance of Georgian-style houses, many of which had been converted into flats and offices. There was a shop selling boating equipment and clothing and a couple of CAFÉS, as well as the dominating presence of the Prince Albert pub.

Behind and above him he could see a relatively affluent district containing several large houses, while to his left, on the opposite bank of the river, was what looked like a council estate of a few hundred houses. To his right, beyond the town centre and the large sweep of traditional terraced homes, which formed the core of the town's residential area, there was a new estate leading onto green fields.

Above the terraced area on the edge of town was an industrial estate fringed by older, derelict units, though the newer buildings behind them seemed occupied and busy. Between the two areas he could just make out the campus of the town's technical college.

It was starting to get chilly. Having taken stock of the geography of the town, Billy pulled his jacket back on and headed towards the harbour. He had a book and the cafés looked very inviting.

* * *

Entering the Prince Albert for the second time, Billy was racked with nerves. Francesca, the cross-dressing landlord didn't look the most approachable of people. Nevertheless, he had to put his apprehension behind him.

The girl who had served him the previous night was standing behind the bar talking to a customer. Her hair was tied back in a ponytail. Her red summer dress stretched taut over her slim frame as she worked in the shadow of the huge enamel pump handles.

She came over to where Billy was waiting. He ordered a pint of lager, told her what he was looking for and asked to see the landlord.

Frank McColgan emerged from the back room in his customary outfit of dress, wig and high heels.

'You wanted to see me?' he asked Billy. 'I hear you're interested in working here.'

Billy nodded in assent.

'Do you have any experience? You don't look old enough to be drinking.'

'I worked in my village local for six months before I

came here.'

Frank looked sceptical.

'The Prince Albert is very different to any pub you might have worked in back in sheep-shagging country. How long have you been in Oldport?'

'I got here yesterday.'

'So, I suppose you want the accommodation as well, then?'

Billy nodded.

'The rent comes out of your wages,' Frank said. 'That is, if I decide to take you on.'

He paused to think for a few minutes while Billy steadied his nerves by sipping on his pint.

'Okay', Frank said finally, 'you can work a shift tonight and we'll see how you cope. Jeanie, can you show him the ropes?'

The barmaid ushered Billy behind the bar and talked him through the set-up. The biggest challenge was the old-fashioned till.

'This must be an antique,' Billy said. 'Does he know that you can get modern electronic tills nowadays?'

She smiled.

'Don't ruin the atmosphere,' she said. 'This is a traditional pub not one of those fancy places like they have in town.'

She didn't look happy at being put in charge of on-the-job training. Simon had warned him she had little tolerance for fools. Billy knew that he had better shape up quickly or he'd feel her wrath.

As they were checking over the optics, Billy felt he had to ask the one question that had been burning through his mind since he had first come into the pub the previous day:

'Jeanie,' he stuttered, 'there's one thing I'm not clear on, what do we call the boss? My brother says his name is Francesca.'

Jeanie looked appalled.

'For fuck sake, don't call him that,' she said. 'People only use that name behind his back. He may dress as a woman but that doesn't mean that he wants to *be* one.'

She shook her head in sympathy. 'No, I don't understand it either. Call him Frank if you must, but if you want my advice, when you're talking to him, just call him boss.'

Billy nodded. This was going to take some getting used to. Jeanie took him down the cellar and showed him how to change a barrel.

'From now on, this is your job,' she said. 'I bloody hate doing it.'

And with that she swept back upstairs to serve customers.

As Billy re-entered the bar, he saw his brother come into the pub. Simon looked startled to see him serving.

'What's up, Bro? Have you landed on your feet already?'

'I'm on trial, Si. And if I do okay then you can have your floor back as there's a room here for me as well.'

'You'd better give me a pint of bitter then,' Simon said, gesturing to one of the pumps. Billy grabbed a glass and poured the drink.

There was too much froth. Jeanie, who had been watching from a few feet away came over, took the glass off him and sorted out his mistake.

She took Simon's money, rang it up on the till and handed him the change.

'Sorry about that,' she said. 'He's new.'

'Yes, I know. He's my brother. Look after him for me, will you?'

Simon took his pint and went over to join a group of three journalists at a nearby table.

'There are too many country yokels in this town,' Jeanie said, speaking over Billy's head rather than to him.

The rest of the evening was busy, and it didn't take long for Billy to find his rhythm. Even Jeanie seemed impressed as they approached closing time.

'It's almost ten-thirty,' she told Billy. 'Whatever you do you let Frank ring the bell. He decides when we close, how much drinking-up time he is going to allow and whether we have a lock-in or not.

'As it's a weekday there won't be much leeway.'

She sent Billy out to collect glasses. Simon was still there. Billy asked him for a key as, even though he might get the job, he didn't envisage moving into the Prince Albert until the next day.

Simon looked up sympathetically: 'I don't have a spare, Bro. Just knock. If I'm asleep it doesn't matter especially as you're going tomorrow.'

'Don't get your hopes up just yet, Si, Frank hasn't offered me the job yet.'

Just then there was a loud clanging sound as the landlord reappeared and rang the bell with unnecessary gusto.

'Come on you fuckers, no dawdling. It's time to go home to your wives and sweethearts. Drink up your beer so I can get me beauty sleep.'

Billy grimaced, picked up some more glasses and made his way back to the bar.

An hour later it seemed as if the pub had never opened. Glasses had been washed and put away, ashtrays emptied, chairs had been stacked on tables and the floor swept ready for the cleaner to come and do it properly the next morning.

The three of them sat around one of the tables with mugs of tea. Frank and Jeanie were smoking. At another table four girls sat chatting.

Billy had been conscious of their presence during his shift and had even seen one or two of them through the corner of his eye disappearing into the rear of the pub with various men at different times of the evening.

He wondered who they were and why they were still here.

Frank stubbed out his cigarette in a large glass ashtray.

'I hadn't realised you were Simon Jones' brother,' he said. 'Jeanie thinks you did okay. If you want the job, it's yours.'

Billy murmured his thanks. He was too tired to get over-effusive about the offer.

'And the room?' he asked.

'Sure, come around tomorrow at 10am and we'll settle

you in. We can agree your wages then as well. You can work on our busy days and cover for Jeanie when she's at college.'

Jeanie finished her cigarette.

'My taxi will be here in a bit,' she said to Billy. 'But if you're staying you had better meet the girls.'

She stood up and gestured to him to come over to the other table.

Two of the girls were bottle blondes, one had dyed her hair black, while the fourth retained a natural brown colour. They were all wearing boob tubes and short skirts, heels and tights. Billy wondered if they had old-fashioned frilly suspenders to hold them up. It was not a question he was prepared to ask. He could just make out the faint odour of cheap perfume through the cigarette smoke, still lingering in the bar.

Jeanie introduced them one by one, Amber, Kitty, Heather and Serena.

'They're professional names,' she explained.

Billy stood open-mouthed. The girls laughed.

'I don't think he's met a working girl before,' Amber exclaimed.

Billy felt his face go bright red; he could feel the heat emanating off it.

'The girls live and work from the pub,' Jeanie said. She turned back to the table.

'Billy's starting work here and will be living here. So, don't keep him awake at night with all your grunting and groaning.'

They all laughed.

'I'm sure we can make him feel at home,' Heather mocked. 'Where you from Billy?'

'Thane Bridge. It's a small village about 100 miles from here,' he stammered.

'A country boy, eh? I've never had a country boy.'

Jeanie started to feel sorry for him.

'Okay, enough teasing for one night. I'm sure you'll have plenty of time to get properly acquainted.'

She led Billy away.

'Don't worry,' she said. 'They're nice enough when you get to know them. They'll leave you alone. Frank'll make sure of that.'

Billy felt a bit embarrassed at the way he had handled the situation.

'You need to work on your banter,' Jeanie told him. 'It's the only way you'll survive around here. My taxi's arrived, can you get back to your brother's place okay?'

Billy said that he could.

'It isn't far,' he added. 'And I could do with some fresh air.'

Jeanie smiled.

'It's been a tough day. I'll see you tomorrow.'

They left the pub together. Frank bolted the door behind them.

5
A Decade of Deals

A hospital orderly cleared away the breakfast tray and took it from Harry's private room. The past was ever present since he'd had his operation. A sense of fragile mortality hung about him like a musk, his thoughts always straying backwards, examining the key moments in his life as he tried to figure out how he had fallen from grace so quickly.

The first ten years had been a blur as, in partnership with John Baker, he had taken Oldport by the scruff of the neck and got it moving again. They had both benefitted, of course, each far richer by the end of that decade than at the beginning, and so John had thrown him a party to celebrate.

That first decade had left its mark on Harry, and not in a good way. The sedentary nature of his job had not been kind to his figure. His beer belly had grown substantially while, minus the beard, his podgy face had been showing how years of long boozy lunches had started to take their toll.

At 56 years of age, Harry had given up smoking on medical advice after suffering shortness of breath but had taken solace in alcohol and takeaways. He'd had a regular check-up scheduled in a few weeks and had been fully expecting to be told to lose weight. He'd been determined to make the most of it before the doctor's iron hand would come down on his lifestyle.

In truth, changing any part of his lifestyle would prove tremendously challenging.

His leadership of the council had enabled him to refocus his business activity. Harry had sold his chain of shops for a substantial sum and gone into real estate, in partnership with Baker.

It was a discreet partnership and a sensitive one. Harry's position as leader meant that it could not be an open relationship. He declared the relevant interests of course and did not take part in the public decision-making process when matters came before the council, but the rule of non-involvement was more observed in the letter than in the spirit.

Nevertheless, events elsewhere in the UK had been making him nervous. It was a matter he'd planned to raise with Baker at that party. There had been good reason to tread more carefully in the future. It all came flooding back…

As the council chauffeur pulled up to the massive iron gates of John Baker's mansion on Pym Hill, Harry looked down on the newly developed Inchfield Estate. It had been his greatest achievement as leader, bringing jobs and some prosperity to the town. He had also done very well financially from the development.

The gates opened, and the car swept up to the front of the house. Baker was there to greet him. He was wearing tan slacks, brown sandals and a multi-coloured shirt. He stepped forward and grabbed Harry by the arm.

'Congratulations on your ten years in charge, Harry. It's a cause for celebration and boy, do we have a party for you.'

'I'm looking forward to it, John. It's also ten years of our very successful collaboration but perhaps we should be more circumspect about that.'

Baker gave him a quizzical look.

'What's wrong Harry, are you getting cold feet?'

This wasn't a conversation he wanted to have right now.

'We should talk about this later,' Harry said. 'No big deal. We just need to be aware of the context in which we're now working.'

Baker smiled and put his arm around Harry's shoulder, leading him into the house and through to the back.

It was a hot summer's day and already there was quite a crowd gathered around the pool. One or two of the younger guests were in swimming costumes, but the majority wore chinos and cotton shirts.

Harry saw his father-in-law, Councillor Kennedy chatting to another Councillor, Fred Harris. He knew that Jacobs and Healy were on their way.

Sidney Nicholson, a local businessman, stood by a makeshift bar holding a drink.

Still in his thirties, Nicholson had made his money selling televisions, the new-fangled Betamax video recorders and music systems from his high street shop. His speciality was picking up new consumer technologies before they became popular and cornering the market.

He had a good head of long black hair and was wearing chinos and a t-shirt. He had so far resisted invitations to join the local Freemasons' lodge but had nevertheless done business with Baker, providing equipment for his nightclub. Harry reasoned that Nicholson had been invited today for that reason and so that Baker could tempt him once more into rolling up his trouser leg.

Next to Nicholson was another businessman, a local building contractor who had worked with them to develop the Inchfield Estate. Howard Fraser was a short, stocky man in his mid-sixties with a thick white beard, who had started off as a labourer on building sites before launching his own business… and going bald in the process.

Fraser wasn't coping well with the heat; the sweat was pouring off his forehead causing him to constantly mop it with a huge white handkerchief.

The two men were flanked by a couple of women, who Harry thought were in their mid-thirties. Both were wearing one-piece swimming costumes. He recognised one as Nicholson's wife and assumed that the other one was her friend. He couldn't imagine Fraser securing such a stunning companion.

Harry fielded the greetings and congratulations from the various guests as he made his way to the bar. He ordered a white wine and soda with plenty of ice. He was starting to feel the heat himself and half-wished he'd brought some swimming trunks, a move that would certainly have challenged the sensibilities of his hosts, he thought.

Nicholson approached, keen to ingratiate himself with the council leader.

'How are you, Harry? Keeping well?'

Harry nodded his assent.

'I'm fine, Sid. How are things with you?'

'Really good. Business is thriving. Technology is a wonderful thing. Say, how is that son of yours? Is he coming home over the summer?

43

Maybe he'd like a summer job.'

Harry appreciated the offer.

'He's doing well, thanks Sid. His head teacher says he's exceptionally bright and is predicting that he'll go up to Oxford. He's due to spend three or four weeks with me next month. I'll pass on the offer to him.'

Baker joined them at the bar as more guests started to arrive. He was holding a cold pint of lager.

'I thought we could do with some entertainment,' he said. Harry looked surprised. 'No, not that sort, this is a mixed audience after all. I've arranged for a local jazz band to play for us.'

The relationship between Baker and Harry - a strong bond built on common interest and respect - had evolved into one in which both men were more at ease in each other's company. It had been the basis of their success.

'You didn't need to do that for me, John.'

Harry was genuinely touched - he was a big jazz fan. He did enjoy these parties in Baker's mansion. They distracted him from his own personal problems. Now that his wife had left it was no fun going back to an empty house every evening. He tended to stay out as late as he could, whenever he could, just for the company.

'It's my pleasure, Harry. After all this is not just a celebration of your leadership; it's a celebration of our partnership.'

At that point Councillors Eamonn Jacobs and Sam Healy arrived accompanied by their wives.

Jacobs was the chair of the planning committee. He had had a very important role to play in the success of the O'Leary-Baker partnership and took great pleasure in the subsequent rewards that came his way.

He was in his early sixties, and sported a half-hearted comb-over, and a taste for light grey suits. He cut a diminutive but distinguished figure in any company.

Healy was almost the complete opposite. At forty-four years of age, his thin, gangling figure towered over his companion. He wore a bright green suit, a white shirt and a red tie. As chair of the council's economic development committee he, too, had played an important role in Harry's investment in his own and the town's future.

As Harry and Baker went over to welcome them, a van pulled up at the front of the house and the band started to unload their gear. They quickly set up their equipment in the pool area, next to the games room and began their set. A buffet was laid out nearby.

As the guests ate, Harry walked over with his plate and sat down next to Baker, reflecting on how they had got to this position in their lives.

Baker was the son of a door-to-door salesman and a dental receptionist. He had inherited a few thousand pounds from an aunt and invested it in property; and on the back of that initial investment he had built a small empire, gambling with property prices, buying and selling shares and opening his own entertainment venue.

He had moved from there into property development, conceiving and building the large Inchfield Estate. Corners had been cut and advantage taken of alliances, both temporary and permanent, to get his own way. He was not afraid to use the influence he had accumulated over the years, as well as some unconventional methods, to persuade people to his way of thinking. Simply put, Baker was ruthless and had a quick temper. Every room of the mansion may have been adorned with evidence of his seeming devotion to the Catholic faith, but Baker's definition of morals and ethics was entirely self-centred. His faith was an insurance policy, not a way of life.

'Can we talk?' Harry asked.

Baker gestured to Harry to follow him into the house to his study. There were filing cabinets in one corner, a prominent wall safe and a large wooden desk that dominated the room. Placed on top of one corner of the desk was a statue of the Virgin Mary. Baker invited Harry to sit opposite him.

'We have to be more careful, John.'

Harry's voice was hesitant. He was genuinely worried by recent events.

'Things are getting out of hand. The police are starting to clamp down on dodgy dealings. They sent T. Dan Smith to jail a few years ago after that fiasco in Newcastle, and now they've convicted a council leader in South Wales for accepting a free meal. Two years... for a fucking meal. What's the world coming to?'

Baker sighed.

'You need to calm down, Harry. These are isolated incidents. We've

always been careful. We're not untouchable but we have lots of insurance.'

Harry looked doubtful. He knew that he was in too deep to walk away now. More to the point John Baker would not let him go easily and Harry had learnt he was not somebody to mess with.

'I just think we need to be aware,' he said.

Baker walked around the desk and put his arm across Harry's shoulders.

'There's really no need to worry. We have it all covered.'

They discussed some future projects, deciding which councillors might need some additional persuasion. When they were both satisfied with their next moves in the grand chess game that was Oldport Council, they returned to the party.

Out at the pool area the band was playing at full throttle. Some of the guests were dancing to the music, others were sitting chatting and finishing off the food.

On a signal from Baker the band paused their set, and everybody turned in the direction of the door into the main house. Two men emerged wheeling a trolley on which sat a giant cake. The guests gasped. The band played a few bars of 'Congratulations' and suddenly a bikini-clad girl burst from the top of the cake.

'God, this is so hackneyed,' Harry thought. He smiled nevertheless, and everybody applauded as the girl wrapped herself around Harry and gave him a big wet kiss.

He was uncomfortable with public displays of affection, but he played along anyway. He got another drink and the girl sat on his lap.

The band resumed their set as. Baker looked on - the beneficent provider who pulled all the strings... the puppet master - and he loved every minute of it.

The party had well and truly got underway.

6
On the Town

It was a Friday and Jeanie had the night off. Her friend was celebrating her birthday and they were due to hit the town.

She stood in her bedroom at her parents' house. Although it was situated in the middle of the Millstream council estate, on the other side of the river from the Prince Albert, the house did not belong to the council. Her parents had bought it under the right-to-buy in the early Eighties. It was now part of her inheritance and that of her brother.

At the age of twenty-two, Jeanie Carter had already seen too much of life. Like her parents, Dave and Phyllis, she had grown-up on this council estate and knew many of its dirty little secrets.

Some of her contemporaries had secured apprenticeships in a nearby engineering works, others had just transitioned from school to dole, while one or two had escaped to college or university.

Tragically, she had lost several of her former school mates to drugs, motorbike accidents or even prison. She was determined not to follow them and had recently enrolled at the local Tech to continue her music studies from school.

Her father had served as an apprentice joiner with Jim McColgan. That friendship had led Frank to employ her as a barmaid when she came looking for a job.

Her mother still worked as a seamstress for a company that made flags and bunting. As a result, Phyllis ensured that the décor in the Prince Albert out-classed other establishments on royal occasions such as the wedding of Charles and Diana.

Jeanie had made friends with the girls who lived and worked in the pub as prostitutes, many of whom came from her community and some of whom she had been at school with.

She knew life was hard and that people had to do what they could to get by. If that involved the girls spending a few hours each night on their back, then so be it, but it wasn't a life she'd choose for herself.

Jeanie was expert at charming the important customers, the politicians and businessmen and the occasional senior police officer and she was aware that Frank's business depended on goodwill, so she helped him generate it.

Now, with the pub safely in the hands of Frank and the new boy for the next 36 hours, she stood in front of a full-length mirror and adjusted her blouse. She was wearing tight jeans and heels. It was not her usual outfit. She rarely wore trousers of any sort, but this was a special night out and the jeans looked exceptionally good on her.

She picked up her bag and went downstairs. Her friend, Cathy, was waiting for her, together with Maggie, the birthday girl. They had been drinking wine with her mother. There was a glass waiting for her. She picked it up and clinked with the others.

'Happy Birthday, Maggie,' she said. 'This is going to be a good one.'

It was a twenty-minute walk from the estate to the town centre, but the journey took longer and was more hazardous in heels. So, they had ordered a taxi. As it pulled up outside, the girls knocked back their drinks and piled in. They were heading into town intent on having a good time. First stop was the Admiral's Tavern on High Street.

Three hours later they staggered out, laughing and giggling, supporting each other as they queued to enter Baker's nightclub.

Inside, the music was loud and vibrant. They danced as a group, attracting the attention of every man on the dance floor. Two of the local lads sidled up and started dancing with Maggie and Cathy. The two girls smiled and turned towards them.

Another man started to dance with Jeanie. He was thin and tall, wearing black trousers, a shiny red shirt and a white jacket. He was clearly trying to model himself on Travolta in Saturday Night Fever, Jeanie thought, but without the moves.

It was quite dark, but she thought he must be in his thirties. She smiled at him and prepared to head off to the bar. He was having none of it though and insisted they have another dance. Cathy signalled that she would get the drinks in.

And then before Jeanie could react, he had his arms around her waist and was pulling her closer to him. She tried to pull away, but he was too strong. Jeanie looked around for a bouncer but could see none. Her friends had their backs to her at the bar.

'Will you get off me?' she screamed at him above the music. She struggled some more but he held on tighter and tried to kiss her. Jeanie tried to knee him in the groin, but he saw it coming and twisted out of the way. She was starting to panic.

Suddenly, a hand appeared on his shoulder and pulled him away. The man looked startled and then angry. He turned towards the interloper, swung a punch, missed and fell forward.

She moved away quickly and joined her friends. Looking behind her, she could see the groper being bundled out of the club by her saviour. Jeanie sighed loudly. The place was full of creeps who thought they could do what they liked.

She picked up her drink.

'You okay, babes?'

It was Maggie.

'Yes. Some creep thought he could take liberties,' she replied. 'You having a good birthday, love?'

Maggie smiled. She was quite drunk and not very steady on her feet. Just then Jeanie became aware of somebody standing behind her. It was the man who had intervened on the dance floor.

'I just wanted to check you were alright,' he said. 'I'm really sorry you had to experience that. He won't be coming back here if I have anything to do with it.'

Jeanie was curious. She stepped back to get a proper look at her white knight. He was tall and well-built. Quite fit, she thought. He had well-groomed blond hair and designer stubble.

He was wearing an expensive, beautifully tailored suit and an open-necked monogrammed shirt. She guessed that his shoes were expensive, too, but couldn't bring herself to look.

The man offered a hand.

'Apologies, my name's Ian O'Leary and I'm the manager here.'

She took it and smiled. Suddenly, she realised that she was also quite drunk. His accent was really posh, she thought, and his diction very correct.

'It's very nice to meet you Mr O'Leary,' she said, speaking slowly to avoid garbling her words. 'And thank you for coming to my rescue.'

'It was my pleasure. I hope that you and your friends enjoy your evening.'

Ian turned away but realised that Jeanie had tried to climb onto a stool and had missed, ending up in a heap on the floor.

He helped her to his feet. Jeanie had not been this drunk for some time. Her friends had moved away to give her some space with this good-looking man.

As Ian supported her, she used his elbow to keep herself steady.

'Nice shoes,' she slurred.

He smiled.

'Shall we get you a taxi? Where are your friends?'

Jeanie looked around. They were nowhere to be seen.

'I think they've pulled,' she said.

'Don't worry, I've got you,' he responded.

'Mmm,' she said wrapping her arm around him.

He helped her towards the exit, nodding at one of the bouncers to summon a taxi; then supported her to the street and put her in the car. He asked her address, passed it onto the taxi driver and gave him some money.

As he closed the door, he told the driver to make sure she got into her house safely. The man nodded.

'You're a real gentleman,' Jeanie said. But the taxi had already pulled away and Ian was heading back into the club.

*   *   *

The next morning, Jeanie had a hangover that was so bad she feared it might be fatal. She sat at the kitchen table in her a dressing gown. Her hair was dishevelled, her makeup was smeared. Her father was completely unsympathetic.

'Fry-up?' he asked, brandishing a pan.

She paled and had to restrain an urge to be sick.

'Don't,' she groaned.

He handed her a strong black coffee.

'What have I told you about drinking water before going to sleep? You feel worse because you're dehydrated.'

She took this piece of paternal wisdom under advisement as she sipped her coffee. He handed her a plate with a piece of dry toast on it. Jeanie pushed it away.

'I think I'm going to go back to bed,' she said. 'I don't have to be in work today. Frank and Billy are in charge.'

She picked up her mug of coffee and walked back upstairs for more sleep.

A few hours later she was awake and remembering disjointed events from the night before.

'Oh my God,' she thought, 'what had happened to Cathy and Maggie? She must have left them behind. Were they looking for her?'

She had a long, reviving soak in the bath, towelled herself dry and got dressed. Her mother was in the kitchen preparing tea.

'Did anyone call earlier when I was sleeping?' she asked.

Her mother shook her head. Then Jeanie remembered her knight in shining armour. She had to thank him and give him his money back.

'Did you have a good time, love?'

Her mother had put the pie she had been making in the

oven and was now able to talk properly.

'Yes, lovely,' Jeanie replied. 'Though I got separated from Maggie and Cathy and ended up being put in a taxi by a strange man.'

Her mother raised an eyebrow. She knew better than to ask too many questions.

I'm just going to pop into town for a few hours,' Jeanie said, grabbing her coat.'

'Be back for six or you'll miss your tea,' her mother ordered as the door closed behind her daughter.

*   *   *

It was about four o'clock when Jeanie finally got to Baker's nightclub. She had walked from the Millstream Estate to clear her head and was starting to feel the heat. The club was closed but there was a bouncer smoking a cigarette outside the entrance, who she recognised.

'Andrew Thomas,' she said out loud, 'How are you?'

He looked around. They had been at school together and still lived only a few streets away from each other.

'Jeanie. How are you? What're you doin' here, luv?'

'I was looking for your manager. I think I owe him some money.'

'What, Mr O'Leary?'

'Yes, that's the one, unless you have other managers tucked away in there.'

'Don't be so cheeky.'

He opened the door and pointed her to an office at the end of a long corridor.

'He's in there. Just knock and go in. Should be okay.'

She followed the instructions. As she opened the office door, she saw Ian sitting behind a desk scrutinising an account book. He looked up and then jumped to his feet.

'Oh, hello again, I wasn't expecting to see you so soon.'

He had a deep tan and was wearing a neatly pressed, beige suit, a light blue monogrammed shirt and a pair of brown, possibly hand-sewn leather shoes. She thought he looked like a younger version of Don Johnson from Miami

Vice.

'I think I owe you some money, and my thanks for rescuing me last night.'

'You don't owe me anything,' he said. 'It's my duty to look after my customers, especially the good-looking ones.'

She smiled. This one was going to be a handful.

'Have a seat. Can I get you a coffee?'

She assented, reluctantly, and he walked over to a table where a glass percolator of coffee was simmering.

'I hope you don't mind using a mug,' he said. 'I'm afraid I haven't been able to get any china yet. I've only been here a few weeks.'

Jeanie took the mug and sipped it slowly. She pulled out a ten-pound note and put it on the desk. He left it there.

'You really don't have to pay me back,' he said.

She ignored him and changed the subject.

'So, you've just moved to Oldport then?'

'Yes and no. To be precise, I moved *back* here. I was born in Oldport but moved away with my mother when I was young. I went to a boarding school in Surrey.'

'So, what brought you back?'

'My father is still here, and he got me this job.'

'So, it's not *what* you know, it's *who* you know.'

'Perhaps, how did you get *your* job?'

Jeanie looked startled.

'Do you know what I do?'

'No, of course not, how would I? I meant it's common for people to get jobs in that way, at all levels. It's not just reserved for the better-off.'

'Fair cop. I work in a pub. My father knows the family.'

'Well there you are, then. You make my point for me.'

Jeanie was warming to this man. He was clearly intelligent, and very good looking. The posh accent was a problem, but then it also made her go a bit weak at the knees.

'So, you have a lot of experience of managing nightclubs, then?'

'No, but how hard can it be? My job is to keep the books straight, keep the punters coming through the door and to stop perverts pawing beautiful young ladies on the dance floor.'

She laughed. Where was this conversation going, she wondered? She felt relaxed and happy and didn't really care.

'You really are too smooth for your own good,' she said. 'I think you'll find that it's the bouncers' job to protect us ladies.'

'Well, yes, but, where were they?'

'Isn't it your job to make sure they're watching out for trouble on the dance floor?'

'Touché.'

'You speak French?'

He ignored her question as he was meant to. Jeanie felt a small spark of attraction as they indulged in banter.

'Okay, I admit that my main interest up until the incident had been you, rather than the dance floor.'

'Do you make a habit of watching the talent?' she asked only half-seriously. 'This is quite a little honey pot for a man of your breeding.'

'It is not something I make a habit of.'

Jeanie looked sceptical.

'Honestly, I promise you.'

They were both laughing now. Jeanie glanced at a clock on the wall.

'Oh, God. I must go. I need to be home for six.'

'Let me give you a lift?'

'Do you have a Ferrari Testarossa?'

'I wish.'

'Don't worry, then. I'll get a bus.'

She stood and walked towards the door.

'Wait, how will I find you again?'

Jeanie walked back to the desk, picked up a pen and wrote her name, address and telephone number on the blotter.

'You won't be able to avoid me. I'm everywhere in

Oldport' she said.

And with that she swept out of the door, closing it behind her.

7
Amber Alert

It was ten o'clock on a Wednesday morning when Billy awoke. He had been working in the Prince Albert for just over a week now and was enjoying it.

His attic room was sparse, just a bed, an old-fashioned wardrobe with a stained mirror on the door and a big chest of drawers. The carpet was old and threadbare, and the cream-painted anaglypta wallpaper had seen better days. The paint on the door and skirting boards was yellowing, while the paper covering the high ceiling was peeling away in the corners and around the bare light fitting.

The bed had a metal frame and headboard and was too high off the floor for his liking. The mattress was lumpy and had taken some time to air properly. Still, it was a comfortable and welcoming sight in the early hours of each morning, after he had climbed the stairs exhausted at the end of his shift.

Billy stretched his arms and yawned. He felt that he had properly fallen on his feet with this job. It had been strange at first working in a pub and brothel, but he was beginning to get used to it.

There was a knock on the door and before he could respond, it opened and Amber walked in. Billy quickly pulled the sheets up to his neck to hide his nakedness.

'Don't you people wait to be invited in?' he asked indignantly.

She was wearing a very short nylon robe, tied loosely at the front, that rode up slightly as she walked. She had no make-up on, and her bottle-blonde hair was tied up at the back with an elastic band. Her legs were long and bare. Billy struggled to take his eyes off them.

'Thought you might like some company,' she said perching herself on the end of the bed.

'The other girls are asleep, and I'm bored. I've not got any clients booked in until this afternoon.'

Billy was indignant, and a bit embarrassed. He could feel his face reddening.

'Amber, I haven't got any clothes on. Could you at least wait until I'm dressed?'

She laughed and tugged at the sheets. He pulled back on them. A playful tug of war ensued.

'You've found me out. I came in here to seduce you.'

Billy pulled the sheet closer around his body. This girl was very scary, but he thought that he wouldn't mind if she took off the robe and got in with him. Why didn't he say so? He blushed again as he realised that he had become aroused.

'So, tell me something about yourself, country boy. I'm curious.'

He flinched at the use of the nickname, but he had taken to heart Jeanie's instruction to get better at banter, so he did not react this time.

'There isn't much to tell really. I'm eighteen and I came here after a row with my mother and my stepfather.'

'Did you have a job before you left?'

'Worked in the local pub for a bit, did some driving for a local delivery company, had a paper round, nothing special. What about you?'

Amber hesitated.

Perhaps this kiss-and-tell game was not such a good idea after all. She hadn't anticipated having to answer questions herself.

'What do you want to know?'

'Well, how did you end up working as a prostitute?'

'Ah, you're looking for a hard-luck story. You won't find one here.'

'So?'

'This town is my home,' Amber said hesitantly. 'I grew up on the Millstream Estate in a two-up two-down council house, I went to school here with Jeanie as it happens. My parents split up when I was twelve, my mother brought my

57

brother and me up on her own.'

'Where's your brother now?'

'In prison. Is this story starting to sound clichéd?'

Billy looked surprised at the use of a familiar adjective. She was as sharp as a tack and picked up on his astonishment.

'What, you don't think I've had an education, that I don't read or watch telly? I know words.'

'Not at all, I mean I'm sorry, I mean...'

She was laughing, revelling in his discomfort.

'So, what got you into this business?' Billy asked, genuinely curious.

'I needed the money,' she said in a matter-of-fact tone that startled him.

'How did this become a brothel? How are we able to operate without the law coming in and closing us down?'

Suddenly he was blurting out a stream of questions, asking about matters that had been bothering him ever since he had first walked into the pub.

'Oh, the police have been here, and they've closed us down in the past,' she responded, 'but they know that if we can't do it here, we'll be on the streets. And besides some of our best clients are police officers.'

Billy was shocked and let it show on his face. She laughed again.

'You really are an innocent, aren't you?'

'There weren't any prostitutes in my village.'

'Working girls,' she corrected him. 'I guess you had the sheep instead?'

'Now who's using clichés?'

'Sorry, darling.'

She smiled at him in a blatantly flirtatious manner and started to fiddle with the tie string on her dressing gown. He ignored her.

'Don't you want to do anything else?'

'What do you mean?'

'Well you can't be a working girl all your life.'

'One day at a time, Billy, one day at a time.'

'Tell me about Frank and Jeanie,' he said.

'Well Frank is a local legend. Jeanie is my best friend. To be honest she's a bit wasted here. Did you know that she plays the violin?'

'No, I didn't. Does she still play?'

'Yes. She lost interest for a bit and then decided to take it up again. She goes to the Tech twice a week for music lessons, trying to play catch-up, she says.

'We hung out a lot as teenagers and I guess we didn't go to school that much, but she has the brains…and the talent. She saved my life.'

Billy wanted to know more, but Amber was in full flow and had moved on to how Jeanie ended up at the Prince Albert.

'After we dropped out of school, Jeanie went to work with her mother for a few years in the flag factory and then came to work here. Frank is an old friend of her family; he was happy to give her a job. I don't know what he'd do without her.'

She stood up and walked towards the door. Her robe clung to her body as she paced away from him. He could see the lower part of her buttocks poking out below it as she walked. He watched every move in silent fascination. She stopped, turned to face him and smiled.

'Got to go Billy-boy, got to make myself beautiful for Mr Right just after lunch, and all the other Mr Rights that come after him. A girl has to make a living.'

'I do enjoy our little chats,' he shouted after her, half hoping she would take it as an invitation to come back and seduce him sometime.

As she closed the door behind her, Billy realised that it was getting late and that he needed to get dressed as well.

A few hours later he was in the bar, washing some glasses. Amber was sitting at her usual table with Kitty and Serena. Frank was chatting to some customers at the far end of the bar. Jeanie was not in work until a bit later.

A middle-aged man walked through the door wearing black trousers and a plain white shirt. He had short brown hair with a bald spot on the back of his head and was carrying a battered leather briefcase. Billy thought he might work in one of the nearby offices.

The man walked over to the table and invited Amber to join him. There were no formalities, not even a quick drink, or a peck on the cheek. It was a straight business transaction. Billy watched intently as they walked to the back of the pub and up the stairs, the man's hand resting on the small of her back.

He couldn't take his eyes off her as she disappeared into the interior of the Prince Albert. All he could feel was jealousy that this punter was going to have her, and he wasn't.

Billy wondered if he could ever overcome his distaste for her profession. She was cute, but she was a whore. She'd had hundreds of men, why would she settle for just him? This was her life and her work, but it was not something he felt he could ever get used to.

Just then Jeanie appeared in front of him.

'I saw you,' she teased. 'I don't think you're Amber's type.'

He flushed bright red and looked at her, puzzled. She held her hand in front of his face and rubbed her forefingers together.

'Money, dear. You have no money. Besides which I just wouldn't recommend it. She'd eat you alive and spit you out. More to the point you shouldn't sleep with your workmates. Things can get awkward.'

'She's hardly a workmate.'

'We're a team or nothing, Billy. Even if part of that team spends their working life underneath a sweating middle-aged pig.'

'You don't approve?' he asked.

'I try not to judge. Well, not the girls anyway. They do what they must to survive. And they're friends of mine. The men though are a different matter.'

He shrugged.

'I guess they have their reasons.'

'Oh, are you defending them now?'

'No, I just think that there are two sides to every story.'

Jeanie threw her head back in despair.

'You men are all the same,' she said. 'One track, sex, sex and more sex.'

She cast him a wicked-looking smile.

'You may find out when you get some,' and with that she flounced into the back room.

Billy thought he had got used to the girls and their clients trudging up and down the stairs. He had begun to barely pay them any attention, but his conversation with Amber that morning had piqued his interest in her, and that was distracting him from his work.

Jeanie noticed that he was not his usual efficient self. Frank was occupied talking with a group of men at the far end of the pub, in a long Laura Ashley dress and a short brown wig. As the two of them cleared up after the lunchtime rush, she broached the subject with him.

'You okay, country boy?'

'Don't you start,' he said indignantly. She ignored him.

'You don't seem yourself today?'

'I'm fine,' he said. 'This stuff takes some getting used to. Who'd have thought a few weeks ago that I would be friends with a prostitute?'

'Don't forget the sassy barmaid,' she said.

'Yeah, as if I didn't have enough problems.'

She punched him on the arm.

'Hey, that's no way to treat a friend.'

'Act like one, then.' She grinned.

She sat down and invited him to join her.

'What is it with you girls today? Maybe I should get you a lamp, so you can interrogate me properly.'

She laughed.

'So, Amber gave you the tenth degree this morning, did

she? That would explain many things.'

'She does it a lot then?'

'Yes. She misses her younger brother, I guess. You're the latest surrogate.'

Billy was genuinely curious.

'She says he's in prison.'

'Yes, got into a fight and killed somebody.'

'That must have been very traumatic for her.'

Jeanie explained how she had been there to support Amber through the trial. How they had become close and how she had helped her clean herself up and establish herself in the Prince Albert.

'Amber was already on the game when it happened and was messing around with drugs. Terrible drugs like heroin. I was afraid that the trial would send her further over the edge. I was worried that she'd end up dead in a gutter with a needle sticking out of her arm.'

'It must have been difficult.'

'It was. Her mother fell apart. Amber didn't seem to care anymore but I managed to convince her that she needed to pull herself together for her family. Her mother needed her if she was going to see the thing through. And her brother needed support on the inside.'

Billy reached out and touched her hand in what he thought was a sympathetic gesture. She pulled it away but didn't allow the attempt to break her flow.

'Frank and I got her into a rehab place where she could go cold turkey. Got her checked over and cleaned up and then Frank installed her here. He even tried to get her off the game, offered her bar work, but she wasn't interested, a step too far I suppose at that point in her life.

'It was terrifying watching somebody you know, and love, go through something like that. There were times when I thought we wouldn't get there. I still worry about her every time she goes to visit him, just in case it knocks her back.'

Tears welled in Jeanie's eyes. Billy was shocked at how the story was affecting her.

'Can I get you a drink?' he asked.

'No, it's fine. I thought you should know.'

'Does she still do drugs?'

'I hope not. Frank doesn't allow it. She's been clean for nearly two years now. I'm very proud of her. But you never know what might send somebody over the edge. We just have to take one day at a time.'

'We? You mean she?'

'Yes, of course. Amber's like a sister to me. I tend to use the royal 'we'.'

Frank reappeared.

'Are you girls doing any work today?'

He was directing his inquiry towards Billy and Jeanie.

'Not much left to do, boss,' Jeanie said. 'We're all set for the evening shift.'

Frank smiled.

'Do I look like I have a cup of tea in my hand?'

Jeanie smiled back.

'You know where the kettle is Frank,'

He ignored her and pointed at Billy, who taking the hint walked into the kitchen and put the kettle on. Just then Amber reappeared with Serena.

'Is there any tea for us working girls?' she asked. 'It's thirsty work all this whoring.'

Frank joined him and helped him set up the refreshments. He made a pot of tea put it on a tray and took it out into the bar with Billy trailing behind. Frank had laid out cups and saucers as if they were at a formal tea party together with a plate of biscuits.

Jeanie picked up the pot and poured. Billy stopped her so that he could put the milk in first. She looked at him indignantly and then carried on pouring.

'That's very English of you, country boy.'

They all laughed. Frank patted Billy on the back.

'Don't you worry about these girls, Billy, us men have to stick together against their bullying ways.'

Jeanie threw her biscuit at him. 'Don't you start,' she said.

8
Making Headlines

The court and council beat require a special sort of journalist, one with a high boredom threshold, an encyclopaedic knowledge of procedure and an understanding of the context in which decisions are taken.

Simon Jones had been initiated into this specialism very early on in his journalistic career and over the last two-years, had made it his own through an outstanding grasp of detail and the fact that nobody else wanted to touch it with a bargepole.

In truth, he enjoyed reporting on the human stories involved with this work but hankered after a more exciting assignment in which he unveiled political scandals and competed for the Pulitzer Prize like Woodward and Bernstein.

He knew that he was unlikely to achieve this ambition at the Oldport Observer.

It was the second Wednesday of the month and that meant a meeting of the Planning Committee at Oldport Council. Simon did not want to be late; there was a controversial application on the agenda to extend the Inchfield Estate onto land that had previously been protected as environmentally sensitive.

Simon knew several councillors were opposed to the proposal, which had been submitted by local bigwig John Baker, and he was fully expecting it to fail at the final hurdle.

As it was, he had been astonished by the report before councillors that recommended approval for no other reason than it would enable the town to grow. Objections from residents about how their quality of life would be diminished had been dismissed out of hand.

Simon had carried out some research and had found irregularities and uncanny similarities between this application and that for the original estate in the way they were treated. It was also suspicious that the first application had been approved at all given the level of opposition it had generated. His intention was to keep an eye on those councillors who were known to oppose the development and see if there was anything fishy going on.

The town hall was an imposing building. It had been built at the turn of the century when Oldport's denizens had ambitions and an expectation that they would be realised. The front entrance boasted a huge oak door beneath a rounded clock tower which was dressed in large limestone blocks like the rest of the building.

As Simon walked up the steps to the main door, he saw Eamonn Jacobs, the veteran councillor and chair of the planning committee. He greeted him enthusiastically causing Jacobs to stop in his tracks.

'Sorry, boy do I know you?' Jacobs had grown increasingly short-sighted of late, a fact that he occasionally used to gain advantage by demanding people identify themselves to throw them off-track, when he knew full-well who they were.

'Simon Jones sir, reporter with the Oldport Observer.'

'Ah, yes. I thought you looked familiar. You're here to report on my planning committee, I take it?'

'Yes, that's right. How do you expect the vote on the Inchfield Estate extension to go?' Jacobs paused as if to fully absorb the audacity of the question. His tone in response was abrupt.

'You know the rules don't allow me to comment on these things in advance. No doubt the planning committee will act with great wisdom as usual.'

Simon smiled as he watched the familiar figure walk away, clad in his usual light grey suit.

The council chamber was as imposing as the building that contained it, all wood and tapestries. The seats were padded leather, the desks made of the finest oak.

Councillor Jacobs sat high above the assembled

councillors surrounded by officers. The proposal had generated massive opposition and the public gallery was packed with protesters. Simon inspected their ranks and was surprised to see John Baker there, sitting next Harry O'Leary's agent.

He recognised Gavin Phillips from the last election count where he had been seen marshalling volunteer counting agents into ensuring that the right ballot paper was put into the correct pile. Phillips had stood next to O'Leary as he inspected the spoilt ballots and again when he had been told the result.

Simon vaguely remembered that Phillips was a former bouncer. He certainly had the physique for it, though his fifty-or-so years had seen him pay rather less attention to his fitness. He was a sturdily built man with very little hair apart from a thin, greying moustache, and a rather large beer gut.

Were Baker and Phillips so complacent that they thought they were untouchable, he wondered? There had been rumours for some time about Harry O'Leary and John Baker, but this brought a new dimension into play.

Just then, O'Leary walked into the chamber and took his seat. Simon wondered just what this property development was worth to Baker and his chums. There must be a substantial profit in turning cheap agricultural land into a prime housing estate at the height of a property boom.

As the debate went on passions in the chamber ran high. On several occasions the chairman had to call the public gallery to order, and once he even threatened to have them all thrown out.

And then O'Leary rose to his feet. He spoke with the certainty of a man who knew he was going to get his way, reminding councillors that the planning officials had recommended this development for approval.

He spoke of the need to revitalise the town, to attract new companies and to house their workers. And he underlined his main point that the council could not stand in the way of progress.

The anger in the public gallery was palpable and once the vote was taken and the development approved, the crowd became a jeering mob.

Jacobs closed the meeting and led the councillors from the chamber. The residents of Oldport who had attempted to sway the decision the other way hung around in small groups muttering.

Simon should have stayed to speak to them, but he was intent on pursuing Baker and his companion. They had left once the outcome was announced. Simon was hot on their heels.

'Mr Baker', he shouted after them. 'Do you have a moment.'

Baker turned to see who was trying to delay his departure. Phillips waited a few feet away. Simon reached them, breathless.

'I'm sorry to interrupt, Mr Baker. My name is Simon Jones. I'm with the Oldport Observer. I was wondering whether you would like to comment on your successful application to extend the Inchfield Estate.'

He had his notebook out in front of him, a pencil in his right hand. Baker looked disconcerted. He was not used to being put on the spot in this way.

'I think this development is good for the town,' he said. 'I agree with Councillor O'Leary that it will help to attract new companies to set up here.'

'Isn't it true that you will make a tidy profit from this development and that that's the real reason for building it?

Simon had decided to go for broke.

'What's wrong, boy? Are you against people making money? Are you saying that I shouldn't be rewarded for my efforts to bring jobs to Oldport?'

'Not at all, Mr Baker. But can I ask what your relationship is with Councillor O'Leary? I note that you have been sitting with his agent today.'

Baker went bright red. He put his face inches from Simon's and barked his displeasure.

'Listen here you little pipsqueak. If you go spreading rumours of that sort, I will break you and your sordid little rag.'

Simon pulled back from the physical confrontation, but he was not going to let the point lapse.

'There are a lot of angry people in that chamber, Mr Baker, who will not take kindly if they think there has been foul play.'

Baker clenched his fists and then thought better of it. He signalled to Phillips to go on ahead, almost as if he didn't want any witnesses.

'If you publish any of that,' he said, 'then you had better have a good lawyer and deep pockets.'

He turned and stormed out of the building. Simon put his notebook away and went to talk to any protestors that might still be hanging around. He didn't expect that they would have rushed off without having their say to the local press.

An hour later he was back at the office and in conference with his editor.

Time had not been kind to Jerome Wilson. He had finally taken on the editor's chair five years previously and was seen as a safe pair of hands. His rotund figure, ruddy face and taste in distinctive suits, always worn with a bow tie, set him apart from his peers. His love of foreign beers and cigars marked him out as a heart attack waiting to happen.

He listened carefully to everything his reporter had to say and mulled things over.

'You need to verify this stuff,' he said finally. 'For a start do some digging into the applicants, Inchfield Holdings Limited, and then when you have all your facts you need to get a comment from Harry O'Leary.'

Simon nodded. He stood up ready to start work.

'Oh, and you have three hours to deadline.'

Simon was straight on the phone to Companies House. Inchfield Holdings Limited had three directors, John Baker, Gavin Phillips and Ian O'Leary. The land was registered in the Land Registry to the holding company.

He scratched his head. Who the hell was Ian O'Leary? As far as he knew the council leader was single. Jerome Wilson, however, had an encyclopaedic memory.

'Harry was married,' he told Simon, 'to the daughter of a prominent councillor. David Kennedy, a former mayor. His daughter Esther was quite a bit younger than Harry and didn't take well to public life, despite her parentage.

'Quite a wild child I believe, there were affairs and then she upped sticks and left him. Took their son with her.

'The last I heard the fifteen-year old Ian O'Leary was at a boarding school somewhere in Surrey. That was ten or so years-ago. I remember Harry complaining that it was costing him an arm and a leg in fees. Ian was just starting his O-level year and was tipped for big things.'

Simon nodded. A few minutes later he was on the phone and asking to be put through to Harry O'Leary.

'Mr Jones, what can I do for you? Did you enjoy our little planning committee this morning?'

'Yes, thank you, Councillor. It was very educational.'

'How can I help you?'

Simon decided to get straight to the point.

'I'm writing a story linking you to the extension of the Inchfield Estate,' he said.

Harry laughed.

'Are you writing fiction nowadays, Mr Jones?'

'Just the facts, Councillor. The land you discussed in planning this morning is owned by a holding company, which has just three directors, John Baker, your agent and your son.'

'Believe it or not,' Harry said indignantly, 'I don't own my agent or my son. They are free to do what they like. There's no connection between them and me regarding this land.'

The denial was expected.

'So, I can take it that you deny any involvement in this development.'

'Absolutely!'

'Okay, but should you not also have declared an interest in the application and excused yourself from speaking on it?'

Harry seemed a bit thrown by this question but recovered quickly.

'I only need to declare an interest,' he said, 'if I stand to benefit from the scheme or it benefits a dependant of mine. Neither is true in this case. Ian does not live with me and is not dependent on me.

'Now if you don't mind, I am very busy and have to get on with my work.'

Simon was not convinced by any of these explanations. He spent the next twenty minutes trying to get hold of Gavin Phillips, but without success. This was not a major problem. He had his story for the time being and so got down to writing it.

A few hours later he had his front-page by-line. He scanned the early proofs. The main headline reported 'Council leader linked with developers' by Simon Jones.

Below it was another piece reporting that the Inchfield Estate extension had been approved. It quoted from Harry O'Leary's speech and various angry denunciations by residents.

Simon grinned. Jerome was pleased.

'Come on,' he said. 'You can buy me a drink.'

9
Right-hand Man

Harry O'Leary was furious. 'I've been publicly humiliated', he said, holding his copy of the Oldport Observer tightly and waving it above his head. 'This is a terrible slur on my character,' he raged.

He was not used to headlines criticising him personally.

'I'm going to sort that editor out,' he said. 'He should know better.'

Phillips sat there calmly, allowing the invective to pass over his head. He had been listening to his colleague complain about the great injustice that had been done to him for the past ten minutes.

The paper had gone on sale the day before and almost immediately the council switchboard had lit up with calls from residents demanding that the planning application be reopened.

Harry was apoplectic. 'My home phone hasn't stopped ringing about this. I tried to explain that there was no conflict of interest and that the new development would help attract jobs, but to no avail. They didn't want to know!'

Phillips stopped him in mid-flow.

'Harry, you need to calm down. This is helping nobody. That journalist was just doing his job. And there's nothing in the article that's not already in the public domain.'

'I know Gavin. It's just that I don't like being personally targeted.'

'For fuck's sake, Harry, you're a grown man. You've been in this game for nearly twenty years. You know how these things work. You have to take some heat to get things done.'

Harry went over to the mini-bar and poured himself a whisky. He offered a drink to Phillips,

'No, it's too early for me.'

'We were careless, Gavin. You shouldn't have been at

that meeting with John. You showed this fellow, Jones, a chink of light and he kicked the door in.'

'Yes, you're right, we got careless. But he doesn't have anything. This thing will fizzle out.'

'What if they go after Ian?'

Phillips thought Harry was starting to look his age. His hair had thinned and turned white. He'd lost weight and was looking drawn. For a man of sixty-six the council leader was in remarkably good health, but Harry was drinking more and earlier each day.

'Ian works for John. He'll back up our story. It might be a good idea if you brief him though… after all, you got him to sign up as a director without fully explaining what he was getting into.'

'Yes, I'll speak to him tonight,' Harry said. He took a large swig of his whisky.

'Are you sure you don't want a drink, Gavin?'

Phillips demurred.

'Have you spoken to John about this article?' he asked.

Harry hesitated. Phillips already knew the answer.

'No, no I haven't. There's something else, Gavin. The journalist asked me if I should have declared an interest and excused myself from the debate. Technically, I think I was right not to do so, but if he pushes it and opposition councillors latch onto it, there could be trouble.'

Phillips was getting very tired of this handwringing.

'I think you need to stop worrying, Harry. We're fireproof. I didn't come here to listen to you have a meltdown. Shall we talk about more important matters?'

Harry stopped pacing the room and sat down behind his desk. Phillips continued.

'The casino opens in a few months and we need to sort out the licences. Are you envisaging any problems?'

'That's Fred Harris' territory,' Harry said. 'I believe that there are some jitters about the pole dancing, but I'd hope it won't be an issue. The big problem was getting the planning application through. It's getting so that some councillors expect a backhander as of right nowadays and have stopped looking at applications on their merits. Who's going to be the licensee?'

'Initially that's going to be me. That way we have somebody there who has done the job before. It takes away any grounds for objections.'

Harry nodded.

'That seems sensible, but I was rather hoping you'd consider putting Ian in there. I think he's proved himself and he would thrive on the challenge.' he said.

'Okay, I'll talk to John about it and consult with the other stakeholders.'

'Thank you, there's something else I want to raise with you.' Harry poured a substantial amount of whisky down his throat before making his point.

'Some councillors have come to me concerned at the number of drugs that are turning up in Oldport. I'm told that heroin is starting to appear on the streets. I want to find a way to keep it out of the town's pubs and clubs.

'There are suspicions that some of the bouncers in town are turning a blind eye to what's going on or worse, profiting from it. In addition, there have been incidents in town which indicate that some bouncers are out of control.

'It's been suggested the council introduce a licensing scheme for bouncers… we can have compulsory training and if they step out of line then we can pull their licence and stop them working in Oldport.

'What would John and you think of such a proposal?'

'To be honest Harry, I think we'd look upon it as a restraint of trade. We should be free to manage our own staff. It isn't for the council to do it for us.'

'Well, if that's what you think then we'll shelve the idea for now. But if things continue to get out of hand then we'll come back to it. It has good political mileage for us, looking after the public's safety, weeding out the bad bouncers and improving people's experience when they're on a night out.

A lot of councillors want to press ahead with it.'

Phillips nodded.

'We'll get our house in order, don't you worry Harry. You won't have to do this, but if you do then you know that we'll fight it.'

'Yes, of course you will. Let's hope that it won't be necessary.'

Phillips sat back in his chair and reflected for a moment on how far they had all come. He had started out as a bouncer at Baker's and had caught the eye of the boss for his organisational ability.

He had quickly established himself as indispensable, teaming up with Harry O'Leary and becoming his election agent. When the Inchfield Estate project started he took charge, liaising with the council and other agencies, thus allowing O'Leary and Baker to put some distance between them and the development. They had all become quite rich together.

He was starting to feel thirsty.

'Do you have a beer in that fridge?' he asked, pointing at the drinks' cabinet.

'Help yourself.'

Phillips pulled out a bottle, opened it and drank straight from the neck. He took a cigar from a metal case in his inside pocket, turned it on its side and slid it along his upper lip, inhaling the smell of the tobacco. Searching in another pocket he found a pair of clippers and was just about to cut off one end of the cigar so that he could smoke it, when Harry stopped him.

'Not here, please, Gavin. I can't bear the smell of stale smoke in my place of work. It's bad enough in pubs and restaurants.' Phillips put the cigar away, noting to himself that the stink of whisky didn't seem to bother O'Leary's sensibilities.

'Are you going to be in the Prince Albert on Saturday night?' he asked. 'We should celebrate the new development properly, maybe go up to Baker's afterwards.'

'Have you been listening to anything I have said in the last half hour?' Harry asked, the exasperation evident in his mouth.

'You've got to front it up, Harry.'

Harry shrugged.

'I'll be there,' he said, 'but let's give John's club a miss for now. No point in taking unnecessary risks while things are so public.'

Phillips took another swig of beer and nodded. Just then there was a knock on the door. Harry's secretary, Sue came into the office.

'Excuse me, Councillor O'Leary, but there is an Inspector Anderson to see you.'

Harry asked her to send him in. Phillips got up to go, but Harry indicated that he should stay. A uniformed police officer was shown in by Sue and greeted them like old friends. Harry ordered coffee and the three men sat down in the easy chairs in one corner of the office.

'How are you, Ollie?' Harry asked.

'I'm fine thanks, Harry. However, this isn't a social call. There's been a complaint and I've been tasked with investigating it.'

Inspective Oliver Anderson was a native of Oldport. He had started as a beat constable on the Millstream Estate twenty years earlier and had become an inspector within the past five years. Harry and Phillips knew him well from the lodge.

Not yet forty years old, Anderson prided himself on his fitness. Gavin was aware that he regularly worked out at a local gym. With a head of jet-black hair, a full, well-groomed moustache and a taste in flowery shirts, Anderson liked to model himself on Tom Selleck in Magnum P.I.

He was very much a ladies' man, despite having a wife and three children at home. It was a weakness that Phillips and Baker had exploited before and would no doubt do so in the future.

Harry feigned puzzlement, a look that Phillips had seen

him adopt many times in the past when he needed to get out of a difficult situation. The inspector continued.

'You saw the news story in the Observer yesterday, Harry? Well we have now had a formal complaint?'

'A complaint?' Harry seemed genuinely affronted.

'Yes, a couple of people have alleged that you failed to properly declare your interest in the Inchfield holding company when you spoke and voted in the meeting on Wednesday.'

Harry laughed.

'I had no interest to declare, Ollie.'

'Well, it seems to the complainant that you did, due to your close relationship with at least two of the directors, including Gavin here and your son.'

Phillips interrupted.

'What close relationship is that, Ollie? Harry and I may be political colleagues but that Inchfield holding company is all me. Harry has no financial interest in the development,' he lied.

'I think the real concern is the fact Harry's son is a director.'

Harry stood up and pulled a small booklet from the nearby shelves.

'This is the council's standing orders,' he said. 'If you see here, it quite clearly states that a councillor only has an interest in a matter before the council if he or a dependant has a direct financial stake in it. Ian is not a dependant; therefore, I did not have an interest to declare.'

Anderson took the booklet from him and read through the passage. He handed it back to Harry.

'This seems to be rather a grey area.'

'You bet,' said Phillips.

Harry seemed rather more certain.

'I've been on this council for thirty years now, Ollie. Do you think I don't know the rules?'

Anderson nodded. He smoothed his moustache with the forefinger of his left hand.

'That's what I thought, Harry. But I had to ask the questions otherwise I wouldn't be doing my job. I think I've enough now to write my report and close this inquiry.'

Harry and Phillips smiled. The 'inquiry' had been as cursory as they had expected.

The three men stood. The inspector shook hands with each of them. Harry escorted him to the door and then stopped.

'We're going to the Prince Albert for drinks on Saturday night, Ollie. Why don't you join us?'

'Yes, that would be good.'

Phillips watched as the two men walked out of the office. He needed to report this to Baker. He knew that Harry had got cold feet before, around the time of the Poulson trial. They couldn't afford to lose the council leader at this stage of the project.

He was thankful that the favours and benefits-in-kind Ollie Anderson had received from them over the years had paid off with a less than thorough investigation of some legitimate complaints.

Oldport was a small town where everybody knew everybody else, and that included the police. The fact that the business Gavin was in with Harry and John Baker had been built on close relationships and favours made them vulnerable to prying eyes.

The one loose end though was the nosey journalist. Phillips needed to keep a close eye on the activities of the local paper. Investigative journalism had not been their strong point when he and Baker had started in this business, years before, so there was no reason why it should be now.

Harry re-entered the office, having escorted the inspector out of the building. Phillips got up to leave. As he got to the door he turned around.

'What the fuck did you think you were doing inviting Ollie out on Saturday? He may be part of the wider team, but we don't want to be seen socialising with him in public at this stage, or some of those busy-bodies who've got it in for us will be taking their complaints higher up the chain.'

'It'll be fine,' Harry said. 'The Prince Albert is a discreet sort of place… it has to be. And we have our little nook, so we will be mostly out of sight. I mean, why else would you go there. Besides, Ollie often joins us for a pint. There's no reason to change the way we normally behave. That would be suspicious.'

Phillips shrugged.

'If you're sure,' he said.

Harry nodded.

'See you Saturday,' he said.

10
Inchfield Cove

The area to the west of Oldport is quite lovely. The fields beyond the Inchfield Estate roll down to the coast and a series of small bays and coves. Wildflowers clump together across the run of the cliff, nestling against blackberry bushes and purple-flowering heather, while some twenty or thirty feet below, the sea slowly fills in gaps between the rocks with white foam and dirty green water.

A narrow footpath winds its way along the top of cliffs, carefully avoiding the unguarded edge, transporting walkers and other adventurers to the rocks and sand below by way of its many branches and offshoots.

Ian and Jeanie strolled along this path, deep in conversation. It was a fine summer's day and the sun was beating down unrelentingly. A cooling breeze blew in off the sea, as seagulls wheeled and soared on its currents above them, squawking, chirping, wailing and listening to the distant caws of other birds.

Ian wore expensive walking boots and what looked like new jeans. An open-necked white shirt with rolled up sleeves, seemed to be moulded to his torso, highlighting a well-sculpted figure.

Jeanie was wearing a simple skirt and top over bare legs and trainers. Her hair was loose, so that it softened her face. She was enjoying the opportunity to get away from the hustle and the grime of the town, to take in some fresh air and discover new horizons. Her skin tingled every time a light breeze blew in from the sea.

They walked side by side, Ian placing himself between her and the cliff edge.

'I really didn't know it was so beautiful out here,' Jeanie said. 'I've lived my entire life in the town surrounded by buildings and motor cars, hardship and graft. I never dreamt that there was something beyond all that.'

Ian smiled. 'I used to come out here all the time as a boy. That was before the Inchfield Estate was built. We lived on Pym Hill. You can still see these cliffs from my parents' bedroom window.'

'It's strange how we always destroy the beauty around us,' she said. 'Give us some green fields and somebody will build houses on them.'

'Yes,' Ian said thoughtfully. He spun her around. 'Do you see those fields at the edge of the estate?'

She nodded.

'Those fields are the subject of the latest controversy, seventy-five executive-style homes, now approved by the council.'

'Really?' she said horrified. 'When did that happen?'

Ian sighed. 'Just this week, don't you read the local paper?'

'No, not really. Life's too short to spend it reading boring newspapers.'

'And so, you let these changes happen by default. That is why men like my boss get away with these things. And now they're using my name as a proxy for my father, without my full consent.'

'And do you challenge them?' she asked. 'Surely, they can't mess you about like that.'

'No, I'm a coward. I let them bully and use me. I just get on with my job and keep my head down.'

She squeezed his hand.

'Maybe it's time to stand up to them, or else walk away and start again elsewhere.'

'I don't know if I'm strong enough. Jeanie. I'm not sure how deeply they've caught me up in their affairs. And it's family as well. Harry may be the council leader, but he's also my father. I can't just walk out on him.'

She tried to be sympathetic.

'You have to stand up to them, Ian.'

'I know, and I will, in my own time.'

They turned and walked down towards a nearby cove. The well-worn path twisted and plunged at an awkward angle. It was covered in sand and loose stones so that Ian had to steady her as they descended.

They brushed past some gorse bushes, trying not to catch themselves on the sharp bits. Jeanie slipped on some pebbles, but Ian caught her and supported her past that section.

'Do people actually come down here?' she asked.

He laughed.

'Every now and again,' he said. 'This is actually a popular little cove.'

'For mountain goats, perhaps.'

'Shall I call you Heidi?'

'You can call me what you like, just don't do it anywhere near a cliff edge.'

They reached the bottom of the path and clambered over some stones onto the sand. Ian pointed out a blackthorn bush. He picked some of the half-formed fruit and held it in his hand in front of her.

'You're a barmaid. What do you think people do with these?'

'Don't you patronise me,' she joked. 'Give them to me so I can throw them back at you.'

'Have you never heard of Sloe gin?'

She shook her head.

'Well traditionally, you pick these near the end of October, prick them and then soak them in gin in a sealed jar. You store the jar in a cool, dark place and three months later you have a deep red liqueur. You remove the sloes, filter away any stuff that is left and voilà, a lovely alcoholic drink.'

'It sounds like a lot of fuss and effort if you ask me,' she said. 'What's wrong with just going to the off-licence and buying some?'

'You really are a lost cause,' he laughed.

They were now at the sea's edge. The cove was quite

small, narrowing into a cone at the rear. They walked along, dodging waves until they came to the cliff wall.

'When the tide is out you can walk around the headland to the next cove,' Ian said, scrambling over some rocks while pulling Jeanie behind him.

'Well, I'm not really equipped to do it now the tide is in,' she said. 'Maybe you should have told me to bring my swimming costume.' He gave her a mischievous look. 'And no, I am not skinny-dipping with you.'

They settled to sit on an outcrop of rock. Jeanie pulled out a packet of cigarettes and lit one. She offered him one, but he declined.

'This is the original Inchfield Cove' he told her. 'In the old days, it was used by smugglers.'

He pointed at a fold in the rocks near to the path.

'They used to store their contraband in that cave over there and then take it into town to sell it. This cove was the scene of a pitched battle between the smugglers and customs officers in the nineteenth century, all over half a dozen barrels of brandy.'

'How do you know all this stuff?' Jeanie demanded indignantly. 'I was born and brought up in this town as well, and nobody ever mentioned any of this to me. In fact, I've lived here longer than you. How dare you know more than me.'

'I know this stuff because I've been living away. When you've settled in a place all your life, you tend to be less curious. I guess I want to know more because I've been trying to find some roots. Boarding school can be quite disorientating.'

Jeanie, stubbed out her cigarette, leaned across and kissed him on the mouth. He responded enthusiastically. They lay down on the rock and cuddled, soaking up the summer sun.

After half an hour or so, Jeanie stirred.

'I need to get back,' she said. 'I have to work a shift tonight.'

He helped her off the rock ledge and they walked hand in

hand to the winding, rock-strewn trail that had brought them down to the sand. The climb up to the cliff path was easier than they had anticipated, with Ian dragging Jeanie over the tricky bits, occasionally pulling her closer to him so they could kiss again.

They made their way along the cliff path in the direction of his car. Ian had his arm around Jeanie's waist. She snuggled into his body.

'You really are lovely,' he said. 'But why do you carry on working in that awful pub when you could have a job anywhere?'

Suddenly, Jeanie was acutely aware of the gap that existed between them. Him, a public-school boy, who had been to university and whose parents had brought him up in luxury, not wanting for a thing. Her, an ordinary working-class girl from a council estate, whose parents had had to struggle to put food on the table, and who still had to work hard for every little luxury, even for the basics.

She resented the fact that Ian was asserting his superior upbringing, as if he was trying to mould her into somebody who might be more acceptable to the circle he moved in. And she resented it.

'You don't approve of the Prince Albert?' she asked.

'It's a brothel, Jeanie. Of course, I don't approve of it.'

'What are you implying?'

'Nothing. I know you aren't involved in that side of the business, but there are so many better places you can work.'

'You mean Baker's, of course?'

'Well, yes.'

She pulled away from him.

'You're such a snob, do you know that? The Prince Albert is like a second home to me. Frank was there when I needed him, I wouldn't let him down by walking away because his pub isn't posh enough.'

'But what about the prostitutes? Don't you feel threatened by the sort of people they attract?

Now she was angry.

83

'Those girls are my friends. I grew up with them. They're doing a job like any other and Frank makes sure that they stay clean and safe.'

She paused and then let fly again.

'And who are you to lecture me on morals. These girls earn their money because men like you can't keep their trousers zipped up. It's not them who deserve your condemnation, it's the men who use and abuse them.'

Ian tried to calm things down.

'It's your right to choose where you work and who you work with, of course it is. But I'm not judging you or them. I just worry about you.'

'Well there is no need for you to worry. God, you've got a cheek. We're on our first date and already you're trying to tell me how to run my life.'

'That's not it and you know it.'

'Isn't it?' she snapped.

They had reached the car. Ian opened the passenger door for her and then climbed into the driver's seat. They drove back in silence, Jeanie seething, Ian not knowing how to come back from his faux pas.

He turned his car into Millstream Estate. He was shocked by the condition of the streets and houses.

The estate itself had been built just after the Second World War for homecoming heroes. It consisted of a few hundred houses spread up a long slope leading from the river below. In recent years though, it had suffered from neglect.

Many of the homes no longer met modern standards as the council had failed to invest in repairs and modernisation, preferring to use rent income to subsidise the rates instead. Those homes which had been bought by the tenants stood out as models of good housekeeping by comparison to their neighbours.

Unemployment was high, and Ian knew from what his father had told him that drug dealers were active on the estate. Communal areas looked overgrown, fly-tipping was rife and every now and again he caught sight of an abandoned or burnt-out car, the victim of some joy-riding incident.

'Why don't the council invest in this estate?' he said out loud.

Jeanie turned her head to look at him, not entirely sure what point he was trying to make.

'Is it too common for you?' she asked.

'No, of course not, but it's evident that this community has been abandoned by the council when they should be investing in it and creating jobs for local people.'

'This isn't Pym Hill,' Jeanie replied. 'We don't get the money spent on us that you lot do. We're the forgotten estate.'

'Yes, I can see that. It doesn't make it right though.'

Ian was relieved that she was talking to him again, but he could see that she was still wary. He followed the directions to her home and pulled up outside. She reached for the door handle.

'Can I see you again?' he asked more in hope than expectation.

'I don't know, Ian. I'm not interested in getting involved with somebody who wants to dictate how I live my life.'

He went to speak but she put her finger on his mouth.

'You have to accept me as I am or not at all. I don't want to be told where to work, I don't want to be with somebody who slags off my friends, and I don't want a man who is going to try and change who I am.

'I'm not like the girl in that film, the one where that professor teaches her how to speak and behave properly.'

'Pygmalion,' he offered'.

'No, I was thinking about My Fair Lady' Ian bit his lip and said nothing as she continued. 'I'm my own person and I was very disappointed with you for being so judgemental. You're lucky I'm speaking to you at all.'

He didn't know what he could say to make this right.

'I need some time,' she added, 'and you need to think

what it is you want. Maybe you would be better finding some debutante from Pym Hill.'

'No, that is definitely not what I want.'

'Well then, if you want a bit of rough, you're going to have to buy into the complete package.'

Now Ian looked affronted.

'I think you do us both an injustice. I'm not looking for a bit of rough and if I were you would not be it, Jeanie. You're a remarkable person, more so than you realise. I'm staggered by your intelligence and your beauty and I'm sorry if I've ruined it between us so early on.'

Jeanie looked a bit stunned at this declaration. She opened the car door.

'You're such a bull-shitter,' she said as she got out of the car. 'Give me a week and then ring me. No promises mind.'

She closed the car door firmly behind her and walked up the path to her home.

11
That Friday Feeling

Simon had spent the past week sampling Oldport's nightlife. He had become a permanent feature at Baker's and in the surrounding bars, talking to people informally and finding out everything there was to know about the club scene.

Although he had been in Oldport for a few years this was not a subject that he was familiar or comfortable with. He had been out with friends in Baker's, of course. He'd also visited some of the other pubs and enjoyed live bands, but unlike a couple of his friends, he'd avoided getting caught up in the drugs culture.

Back home the local pub had been a comparatively tame affair, a few regulars mixing with the local farmers and the younger element getting drunk on cider and a few real ales. In Oldport, alcohol mixed freely with drugs amongst underage kids.

The police had reported an increase in heroin use as dealers moved in to take advantage of the fact the town attracted so many young people at weekends from the surrounding villages.

There was widespread concern amongst those who saw these trends. People sharing needles, and infections such as HIV and hepatitis C were taking hold.

Jerome Wilson had heard all of this. In the time left to him in the hot seat, he had ambitions to become a crusading editor. With a casino and live music venue about to open, now was an opportune time to feature these issues in a sensational scoop, if one was available.

It was a Friday night and Baker's was packed with young people having a good time, many of them from out-of-town. Simon drifted over to the bar and ordered a pint of lager. As ever, he blanched slightly at the price. It would have been too conspicuous to ask for a receipt, he thought.

He stood on the edge of the dance floor observing the mass of writhing bodies. There was quite a cross-section of society there, including a man who he recognised as Fred Harris, the chair of the council's licensing committee chatting to a younger woman at the far end of the dance floor.

Simon hadn't been in this club since he had broken up with Hannah, his girlfriend of two years. She loved getting down on the dance floor, and often dragged him to Baker's on a Friday night to dance until the early hours. However, she had wanted more from him, something he wasn't ready to give. Now, back in the club for the first time in six months, he felt some painful memories stirring.

Gavin Phillips appeared and went over to greet Harris. The two of them moved over to the bar, deep in conversation. Simon had heard that the licensing committee chair was a bit of a lad but had not realised he ventured onto the dance floor when he was in Baker's.

Just then he saw a man moving amongst some of the young people on the dance floor distributing what looked like tablets in exchange for cash. The pusher was wearing a black T-shirt, black chinos and a white jacket. He had long, well-groomed dyed-blond hair and was clean-shaven. Selling tabs of ecstasy was clearly a lucrative business; at least Simon presumed it was ecstasy, which was the drug of choice in clubs nowadays.

He noticed that the bouncer, a muscle-bound man who was as tall as he was broad, had a clear view of the transactions but was ignoring them.

He was dressed in the standard uniform of his trade, a cheap black suit and a white open-necked shirt. He wore a single earring in one ear and a tattoo on his substantial neck, above which was a head of thinning long brown hair, held in a ponytail.

Clearly not a man to mess with, so why was the drug pusher being allowed to trade so openly on the dance floor?

Simon was tempted to intervene, but it wasn't his job and

doing so would have given away his purpose for being in the club. There was more to this than met the eye.

Drug dealing was rife in the clubs but those charged with managing them were not meant to be part of the problem.

He sipped his lager and watched the dealer at work. Ecstasy was the drug *du jour*; it heightened the senses, making the music sound better. No dance scene was complete without it. But there was a downside. He'd read stories in the tabloids about fatalities and of how it caused liver failure, but like other residents of Oldport he'd not imagined that these things were happening on his doorstep, in what was after all, a remote coastal town.

Simon realised that it was not good enough to just observe the deals, he needed more proof. He put his drink down and edged his way across the dance floor to the dealer and bought some of the drugs. He put it into his pocket and moved back to retrieve his pint.

When the man had sold all his tabs, he headed towards the stairs. The bouncer followed him, careful to stay some distance behind, and indicating to another employee to take his place at the dance floor. Simon finished his drink and went after them, also keeping far enough behind not to be noticed.

The dealer stopped outside a door marked 'Private' and the bouncer joined him. He watched as the dealer stuffed a wad of notes into the bouncer's jacket pocket. Simon had his story.

He waited until the bouncer had moved on and then went back up to the dance floor. He ordered another drink and sat down to watch proceedings. It was 1am and things were only just getting underway.

He joined a group of girls on the dance floor. They seemed very happy but a bit out of it. One of them popped a pill into her mouth and carried on dancing. She offered him a tab, but he declined.

After half an hour or so he'd had enough. He needed to get home to write up his notes while events were still fresh in his mind. As he left the club, he saw the bouncer chatting to his workmates by the door.

Gavin Phillips was among the group. Simon turned his head away in case he was recognised. No doubt they would have just put him down as another punter enjoying his Friday night out, but it was difficult to play casual when he was effectively undercover.

He strode quickly back to his bedsit.

12
The Prince Albert

Billy's chats with Amber had become a regular feature of his residence at the Prince Albert. Sometimes she brought Kitty or Heather with her but never the two of them at the same time.

They talked about their customers, those they had picked up when they had come into the pub for a drink and the regulars who pre-booked, many of whom were married. They discussed Oldport and its secrets and they speculated on the morals of those elders and businessmen who had not yet availed themselves of the girls' services.

Billy regaled them with tales of country life, how he had learnt to drive in his cousin's farmyard in between milking the cows and the time he had ended up knee-deep in mud while trying to build a fence alongside a nearby stream.

It was an attraction of opposites, a friendship built on the need for security and reassurance as each sought to find their way in this complicated town.

Billy had started to feel much more at ease in the girls' presence. He was still shy and a little afraid of who and what they were, of their experience and their edginess, but he also saw Amber's vulnerability and, to some extent, that of the other girls as well.

This whole scenario was alien to him, but it was exciting and challenging, too. He was particularly intrigued by Frank and the way many in the community had accepted him for what he was.

'People here are really down to earth,' Amber had told him as she sat on the end of his bed during one of their chats. 'Not everybody has accepted him of course, but those who have don't care who or what you are, providing you don't try and pretend you're better than us. It helps that Frank was born and brought up here and that he earned our respect, as his father did before him.

'He was there for me when I needed him, as he's been for lots of others.'

'Surely you don't remember his father?'

'No, I was just twelve when Tom McColgan died. It was a heart attack, I think. But my parents talked about him all the time, at least my father did before he upped and left.'

'I read about Tom McColgan,' Billy said. 'He was a boxer, a contender for the British title.'

Amber smiled. It was time for them to get moving. She stood up and her robe slipped open. She casually pulled it closed. It was best not to excite an eighteen-year-old boy too much, she thought.

Billy pretended not to have noticed. He pulled on his pants as the door closed behind her and went into the bathroom to freshen up.

Half an hour later he was in the bar setting up for the day. Frank was sitting in a corner reading a newspaper. He was wearing a plain long-sleeved dress and a blonde wig.

The Saturday lunchtime trade started to arrive and with it, Jeanie. She took charge straight away, pulling pints, fetching the odd glass of wine and delivering an entire round of whisky chasers to a group of casually dressed businessmen who had breezed in from one of the offices in a nearby converted Georgian residence.

Billy played his usual supporting role, collecting and washing glasses, changing one of the barrels and fetching sandwiches from the kitchen.

Frank had made up a large pot of his favourite soup. It sat there simmering on the stove, a large ladle standing proudly embedded in its murky depths. Billy didn't much like the look of it, but it tasted incredibly good and proved to be very popular with the customers.

He half suspected that Frank had added some narcotic to encourage his customers to come back for more, but then dismissed the idea. Still, it was bloody good stuff.

A couple of the girls had lunchtime clients booked and

one or two casual customers turned up as well. Frank marshalled them towards the area where the girls were sitting as if he were Dolly Parton in the Chicken Ranch in the film, '*The Best Little Whorehouse in Texas'*

Billy quite enjoyed the analogy even though he'd been too young to watch the film at the time. ET had been his film of choice in those days, but he was a big fan of films and voraciously consumed magazines about them whenever he had the opportunity.

The nearby betting shop was doing a roaring trade, and men would come into the pub clutching betting slips and sit over pints watching TV coverage of the Saturday race meeting before going out again later for another flutter of their hard-earned cash.

Billy had started to get to know some of the customers by name, greeting them like old friends and remembering what they liked to drink. He caught Jeanie looking on approvingly as he dealt with a couple of regulars effortlessly and even managed to pull two flawless pints.

Realising that her hands-off management had been rumbled she pulled a face, stuck out her tongue at him and then turned her back on him to serve another customer.

Before he knew it, the lunchtime shift was over and the three of them were tidying up, ready to re-open, four hours later, at 6.30pm. There was talk of the government relaxing licensing laws to allow pubs to effectively choose their own opening hours, but Frank dismissed such speculation out-of-hand.

'They'll never do it,' he told Billy and Jeanie. 'They're too afraid of turning us into a country of alcoholics.'

There was no sign of the girls. Either they were working, or they had gone AWOL. Billy knew they would be back, but he was missing Amber's company.

With the pub set for the evening, he went back to his room to read a book. Jeanie had gone for a walk. She needed to get a few things from the shop she'd said.

It hadn't occurred to him to offer to accompany her but

then she hadn't looked like she'd wanted company either. In retrospect, he felt that he should have offered, if only because he needed some fresh air.

He couldn't remember the last time he'd left the pub. He was grateful for the job and had quickly established himself as a fixture, but perhaps it was time to expand his horizons.

A few hours later Billy and Jeanie were unbolting the doors for the Saturday evening shift. Frank had put a 'Reserved' sign on a table in the half-hidden nook at the back of the bar. Billy thought this was unusual, but Jeanie knew better.

'We're clearly expecting the local bigwigs,' she told him. 'Frank likes to make them feel special. It's quite important. If we piss them-off, then they can make our life very difficult.'

The pub started to fill up and Billy was so busy he didn't notice the arrival of the VIPs. The Oldport football team had rolled in and were in a celebratory mood. They'd won a local derby game two-nil that afternoon and they were going to make sure everybody knew it.

Pints and chasers by the dozen were the order of the day. Billy thought the team might need extra training to **work off** this session. The footballers didn't care. As far as they were concerned their season was complete.

At one point there was a kerfuffle at the far end of the bar as one of the players started to take liberties with Heather. He either didn't like the price he'd been quoted, either that or she'd decided that he was too drunk to risk taking on.

He was gripping her wrist and she was clearly in pain as she struggled to pull away, his other arm raised to strike her. At that point Frank stepped in and dragged the man away. The footballer looked accusingly at Heather:

'That's right, get your pimp involved, why don't you.'

Frank pinned him against the wall and moved his face within an inch of the perpetrator.

'I'm no pimp, mate, just someone who won't sit back and let a girl be bullied just for trying to do her job. If you don't like how she treats you or what she charges, then take your business elsewhere – but don't act the heavy with her, otherwise there's plenty of blokes here, me included, who'll see that you get the same treatment right back – and by the looks of you, I think I might hit a lot harder.'

He frogmarched the footballer to the door and deposited him on the pavement.

'Go home and sleep if off, and don't come back here unless you're going to apologise.' Frank closed the door on the street and within minutes the pub had settled back down.

The one person Billy hadn't seen in the pub for a few days was Simon. Some of the other journalists had settled around a table by the door. Billy inquired after his brother but none of them knew where he was.

Jeanie was run off her feet serving a stag party. They were following the standard Oldport stag run, getting drunk in the Prince Albert and then hitting Baker's afterwards.

She kept looking around for Frank to give her a hand, but he was busy talking to the VIPs. Finally, she lost patience and went and got him. He protested that he needed to work the table but even he could see that he was needed.

He went and got Billy instead.

'Listen carefully,' he said. 'Do you see that table over there?'

Billy nodded.

'Well the man with the white hair is Harry O'Leary. He's leader of the local council. The old bald fat man next to him is Eamonn Jacobs, he's chairman of the planning committee, and the tall thin younger guy is Sam Healy. He chairs the economic development committee.'

'Who's the stocky guy with the beer gut,' Billy asked.

'That's Gavin Phillips. He's a nasty piece of work. You watch out for him. He's Harry's election agent…a kind of fixer or something like that, but his main role is as an enforcer for John Baker, who owns the nightclub.'

Billy nodded.

'I want you to look after them. Make sure that they

get what they need. Table service, do you understand? And they have a tab, so keep a record. They'll settle up with me afterwards.'

Billy said that he understood. Just then another man approached the table. He looked familiar, a bit like one of those television detectives. He had long dark hair and a full moustache.

Billy noticed that the patterned printed shirt he was wearing was slightly too small for him as if he was trying to showcase his muscles.

'That's the local police Inspector, Ollie Anderson', Frank explained.

Anderson spotted Frank and walked over, whispering something in the landlord's ear before going to sit with the others on the reserved table.

Minutes later, Frank went over accompanied by Amber. Anderson smiled, passed her some money and she sat on his lap, draping her arm over his shoulders.

Billy felt a tinge of jealousy but pulled himself together. He remembered what Amber had told him:

'It is a job like any other,' she'd said, 'a transaction between two consenting adults. It doesn't mean anything.'

13
Pym Hill

For the rest of the evening Billy tended to the party's every need, while attempting to manage other customers as well. He collected their glasses, brought fresh pints and served whisky chasers when demanded. Gavin Phillips had been feeling quite relaxed as he puffed on an oversize cigar and watched the young barman at work.

Phillips and Harry O'Leary had worked closely with Jacobs and Healy over the years and trusted them implicitly. The four men had pints of bitter in front of them and were discussing the planning committee and the headlines it had generated. Then Ollie Anderson had joined them, but was far too busy pawing the hooker to engage in any meaningful conversation.

'Apparently, some people lodged complaints with the local police,' O'Leary said. 'and naturally Ollie has had to investigate. They've got nothing though, just innuendo and speculation.'

'Still,' Phillips interjected, 'we need to be careful. We can't have people putting two and two together too often and getting the right answer.'

'That would be four, Gavin.'

Councillor Sam Healy was a literal sort of person. He enjoyed speaking bluntly as he felt it earned him respect. In fact, it often irritated his companions. Phillips looked put out by the interruption.

'Yes, Sam, I know. Have another drink.'

Healy had started as a mortgage broker but then moved on to invest other people's money. He wasn't as rich as John Baker, but comfortable nevertheless and far more discreet in the way he spent his money. He looked much younger than his fifty-six years, with a good head of brown hair, a thick moustache and a youthful complexion.

He had married late. His wife was fifteen years younger

than him and they had a young family. She was rarely seen in public with her husband, preferring instead to socialise with close friends in book clubs and sewing circles.

Frank had joined them at the table and was busy chatting to Harry about the need for the council to invest in the harbour area.

Phillips turned to Eamonn Jacobs and solicited his view on the launch event for the new club. Healy, impervious to the earlier put-down, joined in. He was excited by the possibility of pole dancing, but Jacobs wasn't so sure.

'I'll tell you later. But there may well be trouble from our more upright citizens who aren't so keen on this part of the plan.'

Looking at Anderson's antics with the girl, Phillips wondered whether he should have ordered company as well but had decided that such an indulgence was best enjoyed in private. Anderson didn't seem to care who saw him groping the girl. One of his hands was on her left breast, the other rested in her crotch. Thank God, they were partially out-of-sight in the little nook.

Phillips may have worked his way up from bouncer, but he was well-read and liked to think of himself as sophisticated with strong sensibilities. He was offended by the way that Anderson was treating the girl but kept his feelings to himself. This was not the time to upset the local police.

He'd ordered another round of drinks from the boy who was now looking after their needs. Harry had started to look the worse for wear, having already drunk several whiskies at the town hall and was well ahead of the others in consuming several pints and whisky chasers.

Phillips had suddenly felt exposed in this pub. He'd wanted to take his companions somewhere more private to discuss their business. He'd also been keen to catch up with Fred Harris, who chaired the Licensing Committee and who he knew tended to spend Saturday nights in the late bar upstairs at Baker's. Now might be the time to head there.

Billy noticed that the council leader was slurring his words quite heavily and struggled to stand upright as he made his way to the toilet. Meanwhile, the inspector was failing to keep his hands in check and was groping Amber in some intimate places.

She tolerated it; after all Anderson was paying generously for the privilege.

As closing time approached, he realised that Gavin Philips had made his excuses and left early, taking Healy and Jacobs with him. Clearly, they had business elsewhere.

Anderson lifted Amber off his lap, stood up and then grabbed her hand. She gave him her best hostess smile as he whispered something in her ear, and they walked off together towards the stairs.

Billy grimaced. There was just the council leader left now. He was looking much the worse for wear. Frank went over, looking concerned.

'Harry,' he said. 'how are you getting home? Do you have your chauffeur?'

Harry shook his head.

'Don't you worry about me, Frank.' He brandished a set of keys. 'I've got my car.'

'No, Harry, you're not in a fit state to drive. Let me get you a cab.'

'Wouldn't hear of it, Frank. I'll be fine.'

Frank took the keys off him. He turned to Billy.

'Can you drive?' he asked. 'Do you have a licence?'

Billy nodded. It was the only way to get around in the country. Frank handed him the keys.

'You're going to have to drive him home.'

Billy protested. He didn't know his way around Oldport.

'Don't worry about that,' Frank said. 'He lives on Pym Hill. You can't miss it. He'll tell you which way to go.'

Billy looked sceptical. Frank gave him rough directions and wrote the address on a piece of paper.

'This man is a valuable piece of real estate,' he directed as a parting shot. 'For fuck's sake don't break him.'

Billy nodded. He went over to Harry and helped him out of the pub.

*   *   *

Phillips and the others had left O'Leary talking with Anderson, and after a five-minute taxi ride they were at Baker's.

The bouncer had greeted the three men like old friends and showed them into the bar. Ian O'Leary had joined them to say hello, but he was busy and had to get back to looking after the club. Phillips ordered drinks, and they'd got down to business.

'The casino and club are due to open in a few weeks,' he told them. 'You both have a stake in it and I just wanted to make sure you're comfortable with the way things are going. We want to ensure everything goes smoothly on the day.'

Healy nodded.

'I've got the council's economic development officer working on some promotional material,' he said. 'This is a big event for the town. A casino can bring in plenty of business and put Oldport on the map.'

Jacobs agreed. 'I've done my bit, Gavin. Made sure it went smoothly through planning. What do you need of me now?'

'Don't you worry, Eamonn, John has noted your contribution. But you're both partners in this venture so you have a right to know what we're doing.'

'The big question,' he continued, 'is who we're going to get to run it. Harry wants to hand the job to Ian O'Leary. That's why I was hoping Harry would be here. Personally, I think the boy has got his hands full and John is keen that I do it. He wants a safe pair of hands in charge.'

Healy and Jacobs indicated their agreement. Phillips was so used to dealing with politicians that he often wondered whether they had an opinion or were just trying to keep him happy. He was only consulting them because he'd been told to and because the boss needed to keep them on board and to make them feel valued.

Baker reminded him constantly that there were just three things that made Oldport tick money, self-interest and the egos of those elected to preside over its future. Pay attention to all three he had told him, and you will become a very rich man.

Sometimes, Phillips thought it would be nice to find a council committee chair who put principle before his own self-interest. He dismissed the thought immediately. Harry O'Leary would never let such a person run one of his committees.

* * *

Harry had parked his car directly opposite the pub. It was a brand-new black Rover 800 with a big two-litre engine, leather seats and five gears. Billy was impressed.

'Nice car,' he said out loud.

'I always buy British,' Harry slurred, barely able to stay on his feet. 'Got to set an example.'

Billy unlocked the car and bundled Harry into the passenger seat. He fastened his seatbelt and fumbled to get the key into the ignition while trying to work out the other controls. A few minutes later they were on their way, headlights and windscreen wipers on, even though it wasn't raining.

* * *

Phillips had been proved right in doubting that O'Leary would make it to Baker's. He worried that the council leader was drinking much more frequently and often struggled to stay awake past closing time.

Healy had ordered a further round of drinks. Phillips noticed another councillor approaching them. It was Fred Harris, the chair of the Licensing Committee.

Harris was an ambitious man in his mid-fifties. He was distinguished by being one of the tallest members of the council, and by a head of coarse ginger hair and an unruly beard to match. It was little wonder that he'd been invited to dress up as a Viking in the recent town carnival.

He wore a pair of thick, dark-rimmed glasses that helped to hide a small scar above his left eyebrow. He was frequently seen in the upstairs bar in Baker's, drinking and chatting into the early hours of the morning to anybody who would talk to him.

The owner of a large chicken farm at the edge of the town, Harris had fought off local protests to establish it fifteen-years ago and still dealt with the occasional protestor against factory farming. He was known as a man with the ability to think outside the box and propose novel solutions to difficult problems. His potential had become apparent after he was elected to the council. Harry O'Leary had brought him into the group pushing through planning for Baker's nightclub nearly twenty years previous. He had subsequently joined the ruling cabal.

Phillips had stood up to greet him. Harris was nursing a large whisky.

'Fred, it's good to see you. I see you're continuing to contribute to John's profits.'

Harris smiled and acknowledged the presence of his fellow councillors.

'Eamonn, Sam, this is an unexpected pleasure. Surely it's past your bedtime.'

'You know how it is Fred, we like to get out every now and again,' Healy said.

Harris had sat down next to Phillips and ordered a top-up from a nearby waiter.

'Now, listen Gavin, we're going to have a problem getting a music and dance license for this new club of yours. Did you have to throw in the pole-dancing and live-music venue? Couldn't you just have kept it as a casino and restaurant. There are a lot of people upset by it and my committee are very jittery.'

'Surely, you have it all sewn up, Fred,' Phillips had soft-soaped him.

'Well normally I do, but this is a God-fearing town, a lot of voters don't like having semi-naked girls halfway up a pole thrust into their faces.'

'They don't have to go in there if they don't want to,' Phillips said. 'But there's a demand for it from our business clients and we want to meet that demand.'

'Yes,' said Healy. 'What's the problem?'

'Well. I don't know about you,' Jacobs interjected, 'but my missus is not very amused by the pole dancing and a lot of her friends in the bridge club are talking about picketing the town hall when Fred's committee meets to consider the licence.'

Phillips sighed, giving Jacobs an irritated look. It was going to be a long night…

*   *   *

Within minutes Billy was lost. He had found his way to High Street and pointed the car up the hill but had not counted on the roads following the contours of Pym Hill rather than climbing straight up.

He found himself crawling along trying to identify the correct side street in a 1930s-housing estate of detached and semi-detached dwellings, their doors hidden at the end of long driveways behind trees and bushes.

He turned to Harry for assistance, only to find the council leader snoring alongside him, dead to the world. Just then he caught sight of the correct road sign and turned into a cul-de-sac. Remembering that Frank had told him to aim for the house at the very top of the road, he swept into a tree-lined drive and pulled up outside the front door.

The house was in darkness. He hoped that he had chosen the correct property. Harry was still fast asleep. As the house and car keys were on the same key ring, Billy decided that he needed to explore a bit before depositing his passenger in a strange house.

He walked purposely up to the heavy wooden front door and inserted the key. It turned, and the latch clicked open. He breathed a sigh of relief. He found a light switch and took in the cavernous entrance hall and the imposing wooden staircase running up from it.

Billy left the door open and went to get Harry. He struggled to get the older man out of the car. He was a dead weight. Thankfully, Harry woke long enough to allow Billy to walk him up the stairs but slipped back into a comatose state once that obstacle had been overcome. Billy found the master bedroom and deposited him on the bed.

He removed Harry's jacket, and shoes and pulled a blanket over him, remembering to turn him on his side as his mother often did with his stepfather, so he would not choke on his own vomit.

Billy removed the car key from the key ring, left the remaining keys on the bedside table, pulled the front door behind him and set off back to the Prince Albert.

* * *

A retired accountant in his seventies, Jacobs and his wife were natural members of the moral majority in Oldport, though those scruples didn't seem to apply to his own private activities. His wife was involved in a few groups who were likely to be at the forefront of any protests.

As a church elder and prominent member of the town's rotary club, Jacobs was considered by many to be the respectable face of the council administration. His objection to the pole dancing threatened to throw a spanner in the well-oiled and malleable machine that was Oldport council.

'You only felt able to mention this now, Eamonn? I thought you were a team player?'

'I am and I did say to you when we were in the Prince Albert that there was trouble ahead. You know what women are like.'

'Look,' said Harris, 'you don't need to introduce the pole dancing straight away. Tell the public you've changed your mind after listening to all the objections. Come to us with an application for a straightforward club with live acts.

'Once we've given it to you and things have settled down, unveil the dance poles. You won't need any more licences off us. It'll be a fait accompli.'

Phillips liked this scenario. There was no need for conflict if it could be avoided.

'That's very helpful, Fred. I'll brief John tomorrow. Now, I was discussing with the other lads the position of inaugural manager. We agreed that Ian O'Leary had his hands full and that I should do the job for the time being. I take it that will be acceptable to your committee.'

'John doesn't want the new place to be too closely associated with Harry, especially after that newspaper article on the Inchfield Estate. And Harry is getting twitchy again.'

'Well, strictly, none of us should be involved at this level,' said Healy. 'But then who's really asking questions? The local paper is toothless, and the police are hand-in-fist with us.'

Jacobs was a bit more cautious.

'That may be so, but when people are kicking up a fuss, we start to attract attention from outside. That's something we need to avoid.

'We're not untouchable. Discretion is the order of the day.'

Harris agreed.

'Ollie has been starting to get a bit careless recently. There's a danger that some of his bosses may start to take an interest. We need to step carefully so as not to invite too much scrutiny. I think you should do it Gavin. It will certainly be easier to get through committee that way.'

'We're agreed then,' Phillips said. 'I'll suggest to John that I'll look after the new club for the time being.'

Harris called over to the bar for refills. As they were brought, he picked up his drink and stood up.

'This evening has been far too serious,' he said. 'I'm going to do a bit of dancing. Are any of you boys up for that?'

There were no takers, so he took his whisky and headed downstairs. Phillips knocked his drink back.

'I'll be in touch,' he said to Healy and Jacobs as he headed to the exit.

14
Law and Disorder

Billy had been gone for nearly an hour and was quite exhausted – he was looking forward to his bed when he returned to the Prince Albert. As he ascended the stairs of the pub, he saw a light shining beneath the door of Amber's room. He heard muffled voices from within, and assumed the policeman was still there. It was an animated discussion.

Billy turned to go to his room when he heard a scream. It was Amber, she was now shouting at her visitor to leave. There was a crashing sound. Billy turned on his heels and opened the door.

Anderson was standing over Amber, his arm raised. They were both partially clothed. A lamp lay in pieces on the floor besides her. The police inspector grabbed her with both arms as if to lift her up. Billy strode across the floor and pulled him away.

Amber looked shocked. She shouted out at Billy but before he could react Anderson had picked himself up and swung a punch into the younger man's face. Billy fell to the floor. Amber shouted 'No!' as Anderson went to hit him again. But he didn't reach his target.

Frank had appeared wearing a long-sleeved winceyette nightdress, straight out of a Victorian melodrama. Without his wig he was completely bald. He grabbed Anderson's arm as it swung down on Billy and pulled the inspector away.

'I think it is time you went home, Ollie,' he said calmly.

Anderson shook himself away and took stock of the situation. He smoothed his hair back and gathered up his clothes.

'This isn't the last you'll hear of this, Frank,' he said as he walked towards the door.

Frank moved to block his exit.

'I think Ollie, that in the cold light of day, you will realise that your judgement was not at its best, and that this whole episode should be put behind you.

'I'm sure that the three of us can forget your behaviour tonight if you're prepared to accept that this ends here.'

Anderson looked a bit sheepish. In the seconds it took him to consider the offer, his face changed as his anger dissipated. He nodded his agreement and Frank stood aside to let him leave before turning his attention to Billy.

Amber was kneeling at his side trying to inspect his bruise. Billy rubbed his cheek ruefully.

'You should learn to keep your nose out" Frank said to Billy. He nodded at Amber and went back to bed.

'He's right,' Amber said. 'You could have been seriously hurt.'

Billy wasn't in the mood to argue. She continued admonishing him: 'He was just getting a bit excited. I had the situation under control. It happens occasionally, we learn to deal with it.'

Billy felt a bit groggy. Amber helped him to his feet and upstairs, into his room. He sat down on the edge of the bed and put his head in his arms. She sat down next to him, her arm around his shoulder.

'Are you alright, country boy? Shall I go and get Frank?' Billy shook his head.

'You working girls will be the death of me,' he croaked. She smiled and kissed him on the cheek.

'Now you're talking like an old man.'

She stood up and moved towards the door, still in her underwear, then stopped, turned and walked back towards him.

'Thank you for what you did,' she said, cupping his cheek in her hand and kissing him on the forehead. She left him alone to sleep.

* * *

Billy woke the next morning with a splitting headache. The sunlight hurt his eyes. He struggled to get out of bed, staggered over to the mirror and groaned. His left eye was half-closed.

He put his hand to the purple bruising and then pulled it away quickly as a stabbing pain shot through his head. Washing himself as best as he could, Billy pulled on his clothes. It was 10am but there was no sign of Amber.

Slowly, he eased himself down the stairs and poured himself a mug of coffee from the percolator at the back of the bar. Frank was sitting at one of the tables reading a newspaper. He was wearing a skirt and a simple top. He looked up as Billy came in.

'Good morning, hero. How're you feeling today?'

He noticed the black eye.

'Fuckin' hell Billy that is one big shiner. I'd better find you a steak to put on it.'

He went to the kitchen and re-emerged a few minutes later with a limp looking piece of meat.

'Here, put that on your eye for a bit. It will draw out the bruising.'

Billy obliged. The cold meat felt soothing. He was starting to feel human again.

'You can't serve behind the bar looking like that,' Frank said. 'You'll have to sit out the lunchtime shift.'

Billy nodded.

'How was our illustrious council leader last night? Did you get him home safely?'

'Yes, eventually,' Billy said. 'That Pym Hill estate is like a maze.'

Frank nodded.

'Where did you leave the car?'

'Just outside.'

Billy fished around in the pocket of his jeans for the key and offered it to Frank, who declined.

'You hold onto it.'

'Will he come and get it?' he asked.

'Eventually, or he'll send somebody. When he remembers where it is that is.'

'Frank, about last night, I hope that I didn't ruin anything with that policeman.'

'Don't you worry about Ollie. He'll see sense when he realises that he overstepped the mark. Just because he's paying for a girl's company doesn't mean that he owns her.'

'Don't you rely on him turning a blind eye to keep this place going?'

Frank smiled.

'The only person with a blind eye around here is you. Ollie knows a good thing when he sees it. And besides he needs a bolthole away from his wife and kids… quite a sad case really.'

Billy nodded.

'Is Amber okay?'

'I don't know. Haven't seen her today. Didn't she pay you a visit this morning as usual?'

'How do you know about that?' Billy demanded.

'Nothing happens in this pub I don't know about Billy. You should be careful there by the way. She's a lovely girl but don't fall for her whatever you do. You'll get hurt. Besides she looks on you as a brother not a lover.'

Billy nodded and told him that Jeanie had already made that clear.

'Good. It's easy to mix these things up when you're young. I know, I've been there. There was a girl in Singapore, I was besotted with her, but she wasn't interested. Nearly topped myself over that one, until my mate knocked some sense into me.' He clammed up, as if conscious he had revealed too much about himself.

'Jeanie said that you used to be in the navy,' Billy ventured attempting to get the conversation moving again.

'That girl talks too much. Yep, twelve years in the Royal Navy as an engineer and then eleven in the merchant fleet. I was glad to get out of there to be honest.'

'How come?'

'I needed to express myself, kid. You know how it is. At some stage in your life you need some space for yourself. When I inherited this place, I jumped at the chance.'

Frank looked at his watch. It was almost time to open the pub. The door opened, and Jeanie walked in, then stopped in her tracks.

'Fucking hell, Billy who've you been scrapping with?'

Frank left him alone to explain. He went about setting up the pub. Heather and Serena appeared and helped themselves to some coffee. Without acknowledging Billy and Jeanie, they went over to their usual table and chatted quietly. It had clearly been a heavy night for them, too.

Amber emerged looking subdued She got herself a coffee, walked over to Billy and kissed him on the forehead. She touched Jeanie's arm in greeting.

'Are you okay, country boy? God, that looks nasty.'

Billy removed the meat from his face and grimaced.

'I'll survive Amber, what about you?'

She nodded.

'I think I need a new lamp,' she said.

Jeanie felt the need to intervene.

'Maybe I should get Frank to put an alarm button into your rooms.'

Amber demurred.

'You know, this is a safe place, Jeanie. Much safer than the streets. Besides I have Frank on hand, and my boy here.'

'It's Billy I was worrying about. It's getting so that I'm afraid to leave him here each evening in case you break him.'

'Oi, I am *here* you know,' Billy said indignantly, wincing as a pain shot through his face. Perhaps it was not such a good idea to talk too much.

Heather and Serena came over to see what was going on. The four girls fussed around him for ten minutes until Frank came over.

'Girls, it's time to put your mascot away, we have work to do. Billy, put that meat back on your eye and go and sort out the kitchen. Just because you can't work in public doesn't mean you can't work.'

He unbolted the door and invited the few people outside into the pub. Sundays were always quieter, despite the influx of men trying to get away from the weekly ritual of cooking roast dinners.

Billy got down to cleaning up the kitchen. The previous night's drama was behind him and another week lay ahead.

15
Read All About It

It was Monday morning and Simon was looking out through the large glass window of Jerome Wilson's office out onto the open-plan newsroom while his editor studied a piece of paper.

There were half a dozen journalists and photographers hard at work at their desks. Beyond them was the commercial section which handled all the birth and death notices, advertising features and subscriptions.

The paper was part of a larger group of dailies spread out across the south coast, all of which covered community events, local news and sport. But there was nothing like a good scandal or campaign to boost circulation and profits.

Simon looked back to his editor, who was animated and quite indignant.

'They charge *how much* for a pint of lager? That's a national disgrace. No wonder these kids are popping pills, they can't bloody afford the booze.'

He signed the expenses chit, reluctantly, tutting loudly, and then examined the drugs that Simon had bought in the club.

'So, you're sure that the bouncer is involved in this drug dealing?'

Simon said he was. He was used to being quizzed in detail by his editor. He understood that there were legal implications to anything he wrote. Jerome sat in silent reflection for a moment before taking a decision on the way forward.

'Our problem is that we don't have any proof. It's your word against his. We do have a story though. You were clearly able to buy drugs in the club. I want you to ring the manager and ask him to comment.

'Tell him that you saw a bouncer take a backhander and ask him what he's going to do about it. We can't prove that, of course; as I said, it's your word against his, but it will be good to get a reaction. And then get onto to that useless police inspector, Anderson his name is, and ask him why he's letting this sort of stuff go on without doing anything about it… and make sure you hand that ecstasy over to him – we don't want to be accused of keeping the stuff for ourselves.

'It's time that this paper stood up to the buffoons who are running this town.'

Simon said he would get onto it straight away. He went to his desk and telephoned the club. It was mid-morning, but he had found out that the manager would be in early to sort out the weekend's takings. A few minutes later he was speaking to Ian O'Leary.

'We're running a story, Mr O'Leary, about drug dealing in your club and I wondered if you wanted to comment.' There was brief silence before Ian responded.

'I think that you will find that my club does not allow that sort of activity, Mr Jones.'

'I'm not making this up, Mr O'Leary. I was there on Friday night and I witnessed it myself. I have a sample of the drugs on sale, which I will be forwarding to the local police. Furthermore, one of your bouncers was not only turning a blind eye but taking a cut of the proceeds.'

'Those are very serious allegations. I will of course, require the name of this bouncer you allegedly saw commit this crime and some proof, so I can investigate. In the meantime, I deny categorically that any of this went on.'

Simon said that he did not have the name of the bouncer but could point the man out if required.

'Well then perhaps we should have an identity parade at which you can confront the man yourself.'

Simon said he would take that suggestion under advisement. He rang off and sought to speak to Inspector Anderson. He didn't have much joy there either. The best he could get out of him was an arrangement for the drugs he had bought to be sent over for further examination.

When he went back to Jerome, he found him talking to the paper's lawyer. The editor was clearly frustrated. He glanced up at Simon as he entered.

'Our brief here, has confirmed my suspicions that we can't run this as a news story without more evidence. Apparently, the bouncer will sue, and the club will take us for every penny we have in damages.

'Unless the police prosecute, we don't have a case, and we all know that the police will continue to turn a blind eye while Anderson is in charge.'

Simon looked downcast. He was disappointed that his big story was going to amount to nothing. Jerome, though, had a solution.

'So, here is what we're going to do. I want you to write a 1500-word feature on the drug crisis facing Oldport.

'You can talk about ecstasy being available in clubs, the growing availability of heroin, the dangers of hepatitis C and HIV and how our young people are being put in jeopardy by this epidemic.

'Get some reaction from local youth groups and the doctor's surgery and see if you can find some expert counsellors. There is a support group, Oldport Action on Drugs and Alcohol, who help addicts. What's their take?

'And get back onto that police inspector and ask him to comment on how his force is dealing with this problem. We'll let people draw their own conclusions.'

Simon looked at the lawyer, who nodded his agreement.

'Well get on with it then,' Jerome said impatiently. 'You don't need his say so.'

Simon went back to his desk and started the piece. He had all his notes about drugs scattered on pieces of paper around him.

He wanted the article to be both informative and hard-hitting but was feeling constrained by the fact that he could not include specifics. He was starting to feel much older than his twenty-eight years, writing an article urging parents to check what their kids were up to.

He smiled, inwardly. He had often thought that the kids should be the ones checking up on their parents.

The research and writing took most of the day. When he finished, Jerome read through it carefully. He looked up smiling.

'Bloody good job, Simon. We'll run it tomorrow. We'll headline it something like "Drug menace threat to Oldport's youth". That'll shake them up.'

Simon was pleased, but he couldn't understand why Jerome was looking so despondent. His editor picked up on Simon's unease.

'Christ, Simon, I've got grandkids. I don't want them taking this stuff in a few years' time. These club owners need to take some responsibility and so do the parents.

'It's only a matter of time before we get a death in Oldport.'

Simon hesitated to interrupt, but he wanted to ask about some wider implications.

'Do you think this publicity will have an impact on the new club and casino?'

'I don't know, Simon, isn't that a done deal?'

'Yes, and no. It's due in front of licensing the week after next. There's already the opposition over the pole dancing and many people don't like gambling. Once you throw in drugs as well the protests could well grow.'

'Well let's see what happens. Small stones can cause big ripples. Maybe the bastards are not going to get it all their own way after all.'

'Okay boss – but I think I need a pint.' It was coming up to opening time.

'You go on boy. I have work to do. But take care. We've already stirred people up. They won't like it one little bit.'

As he left the office Simon saw a man out of the corner of his eye standing a few hundred yards away watching him. He ignored him and set off towards the harbour area.

As he walked, he was conscious that the man was

following him. He speeded-up but the man was gaining on him, Unsure what exactly was going on, he turned into an alley, hoping the man would walk past, which he did.

Simon sighed with relief, then walked back onto the street straight into his pursuer. He was tall and solid, muscle upon muscle, a temple to steroid abuse.

'Do I know you?' he asked. The man looked familiar. It was the bouncer.

'Are you Simon Jones?'

'I may be. Why?'

The bouncer hesitated. He looked behind him at a man standing some distance away. In the half-light of the early evening Simon could not make out who this second person was, but he suspected it was Gavin Phillips. The man gave a thumbs-up signal.

Simon slipped past the bouncer hoping to put some distance between them and to find a place where there were more people about, but the bouncer was too fast and pulled Simon back, pinning him against the wall.

'You nearly lost me my job, you fucker.'

Simon feigned innocence.

'I don't know you.'

The bouncer tightened his grip on Simon's collar.

'Don't fuck with me. You were at the club on Friday night. You told my boss that one of the bouncers was turning a blind eye. We've all been given the third degree. If I was you, I wouldn't hurry back. The stairs can be very slippery.'

Simon found some strength he didn't know he had and pulled away from the bouncer.

'Don't threaten me. You may be holding onto your job now but you're going the right way to lose it.'

He looked across the street at the other man. He still couldn't make out who it was.

'And don't think Gavin Phillips will help you. He has a substantial investment in that club. He isn't going to jeopardise it just to protect you.'

The bouncer hesitated; he clearly wasn't the brightest tool in the box.

'Listen, this is my word against yours. I'm not the police, I'm just a journalist doing my job. This is a free country, not a police state. And no matter how much your bosses think they own this town, they don't own me, or my newspaper.'

The man recovered his poise. He put his face just inches away from Simons.

'This isn't a game, chum. You and your paper need to keep your nose out of our business. This is your final warning. No more chances.'

Simon was shaking as the bouncer walked away. He watched him re-join the man he had half-identified as Gavin Phillips and disappear around a corner in the direction of Baker's.

Should he report this incident to his editor? But then what could Jerome do? He'd warned him to be careful, but it was his boss's crusading zeal that had also put him in this position in the first place.

He reached the Prince Albert and tumbled inside the door with some relief. Jeanie was behind the bar. He ordered a pint of bitter and a whisky chaser.

'Are you okay?' she asked. 'You look as white as a sheet.'

'I'm fine, Jeanie. It's just been a bit of a rough day.'

'Do you want me to get Billy? I'm sure he would be glad to see you.'

'No, it's fine. Where's he hiding anyway? Is it his day off?'

'He's skulking in the kitchen,' she replied, 'nursing a black eye.'

Now Simon was curious.

'Has he been fighting?'

'In a way, he got into a scrap with the local police inspector over Amber.'

Simon looked puzzled at the mention of Amber's name. Jeanie gestured over to the table where some of the prostitutes were sitting. He nodded his understanding.

'Frank's told him to keep out of sight until the swelling

goes down.'

Simon looked amazed. He didn't know his brother had it in him. He was also a little worried. The harbour area was a rough district and Billy was young and green. More to the point, both brothers appeared to have made it their mission to upset the movers and shakers in this town.

'I'd better see him then. Can I go through?'

Jeanie looked across at Frank who had not heard the conversation but picked up the gist almost straight away. He indicated to go ahead.

As Simon and Jeanie entered the kitchen, Billy had his back to them, washing some glasses. He turned to see who was there.

'Christ, Bro that's a whopper'. Simon couldn't help himself.

Billy grimaced.

'It still hurts. For God's sake, don't make me laugh.'

Simon walked over and embraced his brother. He started to hum an old Clash song. Jeanie laughed.

'I fought the law and the law won,' she sang. 'Nice one Simon'

Simon looked concerned.

'Are you okay here, Bro? This is a very different neighbourhood to what we're used to. You can't go around challenging police officers to a fight.

'It's fine, Si. I love it here. Frank is great, and the girls look after me. I'm really settled in.'

'It's time you got out a bit though,' said Jeanie, smirking. 'You can't lurk in here the rest of your life.'

'Is that an offer?' Billy asked.

'Cheeky! But you know that you'd rather Amber showed you around.'

'Yes, what is it about you and this girl? I've been hearing all sorts of stories,' Simon teased.

Billy went red.

'We're just friends, nothing to write home about. Jeanie knows that.'

118

Simon and Jeanie were smiling at him.

'Look, Bro, if you need anything you know where to find me. I'm sorry if I sort of put you off when you first got here. I was feeling a bit crowded.'

'It's no problem, Si, you did me a favour.'

'Ah, this is sweet,' Jeanie mocked. 'I do love family reunions.'

Simon grinned at her, He embraced Billy again and headed back out into the bar, Jeanie following behind.

'About time,' Frank said to them as they reappeared. 'I've been run off my feet here.'

'It's about time you did some work,' Jeanie retorted. 'You okay for a drink, Simon?'

'Yes, I've got my pint over there.'

He pointed at a table occupied by a couple of staff from the Observer. He went over to join them. Charles, the arts editor, was steeling himself for a production of Iolanthe by the local Gilbert and Sullivan society later that week. Jonathan, the paper's sports correspondent, was recovering from a busy weekend covering Southampton's home game against Chelsea.

All the talk at the table was about the upcoming international football friendly. Simon was relieved to be part of a normal conversation for a change. He had begun to feel like he was drowning in council agendas, conspiracy theories and politicians.

He joined in with the chat enthusiastically. He was not a big football fan, but he knew enough to be able to offer an opinion about Bobby Robson's tenure as England manager.

About half-an-hour later, Jeanie noticed they were joined by a woman in her late twenties - Sally, one of the other reporters. Slim and attractive, with long brown hair and glasses, she was smartly dressed in a skirt and jacket over a frilly beige blouse. Within a few minutes, she was monopolising Simon's attention.

The small group grew as the evening went on, chatting amongst themselves until it was almost closing time, stacking up the drinks between them. The chat grew more animated and the laughs got louder as the empty glasses filled the table. Sally accepted a lift home from one of the sub-editors and left the others to it. It wasn't long after that Simon realised just how tired he was and needed to get to bed. He stood up and said his goodbyes, nodding to Jeanie as he stepped out into the street.

The night was warm and comforting. Streetlamps cast pools of light on the deserted harbour streets as if to guide him home. Residents' cars and work vans lined the road, trees planted along the kerb, swayed slightly in the breeze blowing off the sea as Simon steered himself around the dustbins that sat outside people's houses, awaiting collection the following morning.

He could hear the creaking of fishing boats in the harbour as they moved against their moorings, the smell of fish lingering in the air from that day's catch. A three-quarter moon illuminated the old Georgian houses in front of him, many now converted to flats and offices.

Simon walked at pace. He was always nervous in this area. He turned a corner and headed down a small side street. It was the shortest way back to town and was a well-used route. Tonight, though, it was deserted.

Suddenly, he felt a searing pain in his head as something hit him hard from behind. He fell to the ground. The pavement seemed to sway and then blur. He could vaguely make out a figure standing over him.

There was another sharp pain, this time in his ribs, and then a second one, as someone kicked him again and again. Simon curled up into a ball to protect himself against the onslaught. And then everything went black.

16
The Inner Sanctum

Billy had almost finished washing the glasses when he became aware of other people in the room. He assumed that Simon and Jeanie had returned and turned around to chide them.

Frank was standing there with Harry O'Leary. Billy thought that the council leader was looking paler than usual and his jowls were more pronounced. His eyes were bloodshot, too, defined by a decade of bags below them.

'I hope I didn't give you that black eye,' Harry said. Billy hesitated before responding.

'No, sir,' it happened after I drove you home.' Harry smiled, having somebody drive him home after a night's drinking was not an unusual experience for him. Nevertheless, he seemed grateful.

'Yes, thank you for that. I appreciated the care with which you looked after me.'

Billy acknowledged his gratitude.

'Harry has come to collect his car,' Frank said. 'I believe you have the key.'

'Yes, I would have come earlier but I wasn't feeling too good yesterday, and I've spent most of today in meetings and an evening event.'

Billy fumbled in his pocket and then passed it to him. Harry was about to leave but paused in the kitchen doorway.

'Do you work full-time, Billy?' he asked.

Frank answered for him.

'He does half a dozen shifts a week for me, mostly around the weekend and stands in when I need him, Jeanie is full time. I don't do enough business to justify two full-timers.' Harry rubbed his chin thoughtfully.

'Well, here's the thing, I need an assistant, somebody to carry papers, drive me when I don't have an official car, run errands for me...'

'A gopher,' Frank said.

'That's a bit harsh, Frank, but if you want to call it that then who am I to argue? Are you interested, Billy? I'll pay you, not a lot, but a bit more than you earn as a barman. You could fit it around the work you do for Frank.'

'And if I need him at the same time as you?'

'Then you have first pick, Frank. I don't want to tread on your toes.'

Billy was torn. Simon had said that Harry was looking for an assistant on his first night in Oldport but had warned him off. Nevertheless, Harry seemed respectable, apart from being a bit too fond of his drink.

'I don't mind giving it a go,' he said.

'Good. Well if Frank doesn't need you tomorrow could you come to the town hall for eleven o'clock? Go to the reception and ask for me. We can thrash out the details then.'

'Yes, of course, I'm sure I can find the town hall.'

'Good. I'll see you then.'

Harry and Frank left together, an unlikely couple, Billy thought. Harry dressed in a grey suit, white shirt and conservative blue tie, Frank wearing a long red dress, silver-coloured high heels and his favourite blonde wig.

* * *

The next morning, Billy set off early. The town hall was located at the far end of the high street, dominating its surroundings as it had been designed to do. Billy could not help but be impressed by the large oak door and the rounded clock tower.

He walked into the building and approached the reception desk; they were expecting him. He sat on a long marble bench waiting to be collected, feeling overawed by the history that oozed from every one of the building's dressed limestone blocks.

In the foyer were two wooden scrolls, one listing all the Mayors of Oldport in neat gold leaf lettering; the other was a list of council leaders. Harry O'Leary was prominent at the bottom of the list, his leadership commencing in 1969 but with no end date.

There was a third board above the glass doored entrance to the council chamber that appeared to list High Sheriffs and Lord Lieutenants. This was a town, he reflected, in which the highest ambition of its dignitaries was to be remembered in gold leaf.

Just then a woman approached him. Billy thought she was in her late forties. Her hair was tied up in a bun and was streaked with grey. She wore a pair of severe spectacles perched atop a large nose. Her buttoned up blouse and long A-line skirt gave her a business-like air.

'My name's Sue Evans,' she said. 'I'm Councillor O'Leary's personal secretary. I believe we'll be working together.'

Billy sensed a trap. He decided on the diplomatic route and held out his hand.

'It's a pleasure to meet you. I believe my role is to be Councillor O'Leary's errand boy. I suspect that means that I will be working *under* you.'

Sue smiled. She clearly approved of this answer.

'If you come with me, I'll take you to the leader's office. He's in a meeting at present so you may have to wait.'

She turned on her heel and headed off down a long corridor, with Billy following as best he could, trying to take in his surroundings as he went. He was impressed by the wood panelling in the corridor and the high carved plaster ceilings.

They came to a plain wooden door, behind which was an antechamber where Sue was established as gatekeeper, deciding who did and who did not have access to the council leader.

A large electric typewriter was on her desk, as well as some trays containing different coloured papers, and a large bottle of Tippex. Sue pointed to a side table and chair.

'You can base yourself there when you're in the town

hall. I understand that you're serving Councillor O'Leary on an ad hoc basis, so you won't be here all the time.'

'I won't get under your feet, Mrs Evans.'

'Good. Councillor O'Leary is with his son at present. They've been in there for half an hour or so. I don't expect that they'll be much longer.'

Billy sat down at the side table and picked up the Observer. He turned to the sports pages and immersed himself in news of the local football team, Oldport Albion.

The inner door opened, and Harry appeared in shirt sleeves deep in conversation with a tall, well-built younger man with blond hair, wearing a very expensive looking suit and a smart shirt. Harry was very much on the defensive.

'I thought you would appreciate being put forward to run the new casino,' he was saying. 'I was just looking out for you.'

'Well, don't. Let me make my own decisions in future and stop trying to do things for me without asking first. It was bad enough being bundled off to boarding school and having you ignore me, without you trying to make it up to me now with unwelcome gestures.'

Harry was just about to reply when he noticed Billy standing in the office, expectantly.

'Ah, Billy,' he said. 'I'd forgotten what the time was. Can I introduce you to Ian, my son?'

Ian shook Billy's hand and mumbled something about being pleased to meet him before making his excuses and leaving. Billy followed Harry into the office where he was handed a piece of paper.

'Sign that,' Harry demanded. 'It's a contract. It tells you how much you'll earn for each hour you work for me. We'll negotiate what you work on a week-by-week basis depending on what I have for you to do and when Frank needs you.'

Billy sat down on one of the chairs reserved for visitors at Harry's desk. To his left were several stacks of neatly arranged papers, to his right some writing pads, pens, and a couple of reference books on local government. He read through the document and signed it.

'Right, we have an engagement shortly. I'm to visit a local factory to discuss their expansion plans. We're hoping that they might be creating a lot of jobs. I need you to carry my bag and to take notes. This time we'll be driven in an official car.'

He handed Billy a briefcase and grabbed his jacket. Billy hesitated.

'Come on then, we need to get a move on.'

As they walked to the car Harry outlined Billy's obligations in his new job.

'You have to understand that everything you see or hear in this job is confidential. Is that clear?'

'Yes, of course.'

'Frank said you were a good boy who could be trusted. You don't want to let him down.'

Billy felt that this was getting a bit patronising, but it seemed to be important to Harry, so he went along with it.

'Absolutely, Councillor O'Leary I can keep my mouth shut.'

'Not that there's anything to hide, of course, but I deal with a lot of sensitive information some of it, like today, is commercially sensitive. People's jobs depend on things not getting out prematurely.'

'I understand.'

'And you will be party to private conversations about politics that I wouldn't want my opponents to hear about.'

'I'm not going to talk to anybody about this stuff. I only know a couple of people in Oldport anyway, so I have nobody to talk to.'

'Good. One more thing, that piece of paper you signed is a legally binding contract. It ties you into everything I have just said. Just so we're clear, if you do break it you could be breaking the law, like breaching the Official Secrets Act. You could go to prison.'

Even Billy could see this was bullshit, but he played along. Perhaps paranoia was an occupational hazard for a council leader, or maybe Harry had more to hide than he was letting on.

'What like that civil servant, Clive Ponting?'

'Good, you take an interest in current affairs. No, I was thinking about the other one, Sarah Tisdall. She went to prison."

'Sorry, I'm not familiar with that case. But you've made your point.'

Harry acknowledged the concession. They had reached the town hall steps and Billy could see a black limousine waiting. A man in chauffeur's livery waited to open the door for them.

Harry climbed into the back, indicating to Billy that he should sit up front next to the driver, who introduced himself as Cyril.

A few minutes later they were driving onto the industrial estate and up to a new factory unit. A man in his mid-fifties, about six feet tall and with long, thinning black hair stood outside waiting to greet them.

The chauffeur opened the door for Harry, who greeted the factory owner like an old friend. Billy joined them.

'Billy, I want you to meet Sidney Nicholson. He and I go back a long way.'

Nicholson shook Billy's hand.

'Billy's my new personal assistant. This is his first day.'

'Well it's nice to meet you, Billy. And welcome to my new factory.'

'Sid has expanded his retail operation to include manufacture,' Harry explained. 'As well as selling all the latest gizmos and gadgets, he's now going to be assembling CD players under licence.'

'Let me show you both around.'

Nicholson led the way as they toured the factory unit, chatting to some of the workers and inspecting the assembly line. Billy was impressed. At the end of the tour Nicholson showed them into an office and arranged for tea and coffee to be brought in.

Billy got out a notebook. Harry signalled to him to put it away.

'This is a big risk for me, Harry.' Nicholson seemed nervous. 'I think I can create a lot of jobs, but I need help from the council. The start-up costs are crippling, and the banks are bloody impossible because of the economic situation.'

'I know Sid. Don't you worry, as you know the council have an economic development fund which we can use. But it'll have to be a mixture of grant and loan.'

'That's a relief.'

'I can justify this because of the jobs, but I'll still need to get Sam Healy's economic development committee to rubber stamp the deal.'

'That's just a formality, right?'

'Effectively, but we might have to grease the wheels, if you know what I mean.'

Nicholson nodded.

'I hear John Baker might have a stake in this little venture of yours,' Harry said.

'He's a sleeping partner. Yes.'

'Can he put up any of the money?'

'He has done already. He told me to come to you for the rest.'

'That's nice of him. Okay, we have a way forward. You need to get your people to sort out all the paperwork with our officers and then I'll speak to Sam.'

The two men shook hands.

'I hear that you're still holding off joining our lodge,' Harry added as a parting shot. 'That's a shame.'

'You know me, Harry. I've never been the clubbable type.'

'Yes, but surely you can make an exception,' Nicholson looked doubtful, Harry demurred and tried another tack. 'John is having another of his parties soon. No doubt I'll catch up with you there when we can discuss this again.'

'Almost certainly,' Nicholson said, taking the line of least resistance.

They were now at the car. Cyril opened the door for Harry, and Billy climbed into the front seat. He was not sure why he had been brought along. Harry seemed to read his mind.

'I'll have things for you to do, Billy, but today has been about appearances. It looks good to have a personal assistant, adds to the gravitas if you know what I mean.'

Billy didn't. Harry reached into his pocket and pulled out a wad of notes.

'Here's a hundred and fifty quid, buy yourself a suit. You need to look the part. There's a shop in High Street, Thomas Bros. Tell them I sent you. The owner's a friend of mine.'

Billy took the money and stuffed it into his pocket, smiling This job was going to be an adventure and a half.

17
St Theresa's

When Simon opened his eyes, he was lying in a bed in a six-person ward in the local hospital. The curtains had been half drawn around him and a nurse was engrossed in her work at a medicine trolley just a few feet away. He had some difficulty focussing and his mouth was dry. His head hurt, and he could barely move without a sharp pain shooting through his chest.

The nurse saw that he was awake and approached.

'How're you feeling?' she asked.

Simon tried to talk but could only manage a groan. She poured a glass of water and helped him sip from it.

'I'm just going to get the doctor. Don't try and move, you've got two cracked ribs and we've had to bandage your chest quite heavily.'

A few minutes later, she returned with a doctor, who introduced himself and inspected Simon's eyes.

'We carried out a scan earlier,' he said, 'just to make sure that there are no internal bleeds. You have a very tough skull, Mr Jones. No sign of any fracture but we had to check just to be on the safe side.

'You'll need to stay here for a few days while we monitor your condition, though I doubt you'll want to do much until those ribs heal.

'You may want to sleep a lot; don't be afraid to do so, that's a good sign. Sleep helps you heal. We'll wake you every now and again just to make sure you're okay.'

Simon tried to take all this in.

'Where am I?' he asked. 'What happened?'

'You're in St Theresa's Hospital. You had a blow to the head. They brought you here in the early hours of the morning. We patched you up as best as we could, but I'm afraid the rest of the healing process is down to you.'

'Have I been out all this time?'

'No, you were awake when they brought you in, but you've been drifting in and out of consciousness ever since. I'm glad to see that you're now properly awake.

'Do you feel up to talking? There's a policeman who's waiting to speak to you.'

'Yes, that's fine. I'm not sure I'll be able to tell him much though.'

The doctor left the room and a few minutes later a uniformed policeman entered. He introduced himself as P.C. David Cowley. He was young and fresh-faced. Simon wondered whether he was even a proper policeman; surely, he hadn't yet reached the age when all policemen start to look young.

'Can you tell me what you can remember?' Cowley asked

'Not a great deal. I left the pub and was walking home when somebody jumped me.'

'Did you see who did it?'

'No, it was dark, and he hit me from behind.'

'Do you know for certain it was a man?'

'Sorry, I just assumed.' Cowley shrugged and wrote something in his notebook.

'Is there anybody who might want to harm you?'

Simon laughed and then stifled it. The pain was too much.

'I'm a journalist. I report on local politics. I think there might be a long list.'

'Anybody threatened you recently?'

'Yes. I've just finished a feature on the local drugs scene for today's paper. I did some research in Baker's and found that one of the bouncers was taking a cut from a dealer selling ecstasy. I confronted the manager about it and the next thing I know the bouncer paid me a visit.'

'Do you know this bouncer's name?'

'No, but I can describe him. He was a big bloke, about six-feet tall. He had an earring in one ear, a tattoo on his neck and brown hair, which was thinning on top.'

Cowley wrote all this down. As he did Simon thought he saw Billy chatting to the nurse just outside the room. He wanted to call him in, but the nurse had sent him away. She came into the room.

'Have you finished,' she asked the policeman, 'he needs his rest.'

'Yes, I think I have what I need for now. I may be back.'

He packed up his notebook, took his helmet and left. The nurse tidied up Simon's bedclothes.

'Was that my brother, I saw talking to you just now?'

'Yes, I told him you needed your rest and suggested he comes back tomorrow. I think you've had quite enough excitement for one day, don't you?'

Simon yawned. He really did feel tired. He lay back onto his pillow and within minutes had fallen asleep.

When he awoke, he was aware of two people sitting at the side of the bed. It took time for him to focus but when he did, he saw that it was Billy and Jeanie.

'What time is it?' he asked.

'Ten o'clock. It's Wednesday,' Billy replied.

'Have you two been here long?'

'We got here about an hour-ago.'

Simon tried to move. A sharp pain shot through his body and he groaned loudly. His head felt like it was stuffed with cotton wool.

'You've got a couple of cracked ribs,' Billy said.

Simon gave a wan smile.

'Yes, I remember,' he whispered. 'They told me yesterday.'

'It's lucky that they hit your head,' Billy said. 'It's clearly the hardest part of you.'

'Cheers. Bro.'

'So, what did the police say?'.

'I can't really remember.'

'The police said you were threatened by one of the bouncers in Baker's club,' Billy said.

'Yes, I think they're going to investigate.'

The pain in his ribs was still restricting his ability to sit up unaided. He signalled to his companions to help him. Billy supported him in an upright sitting position while Jeanie positioned the pillows behind. They sat in silence for a few minutes.

'So, do you think it was the bouncer?' Billy asked eventually.

'I don't know Bro. The guy was clearly out to get me because I saw him take a backhander from a drug dealer at Baker's. That's why he threatened me. It might have been him who attacked me, it could have been somebody else. I guess I must have upset some people. Maybe it was just random. I'm sure the police will come up with some answers.'

'You have more confidence than me then,' Jeanie said.

'Hey,' Simon responded. 'I almost forgot you were there. Not like you to be so quiet. You didn't have to come.'

'I think she fancies you,' Billy said.

Jeanie hit him hard on the arm causing him to yelp in pain.

'Ow, that really hurt.'

'Good. I came to keep you company, you moron. That's what friends are for.'

Billy rubbed his arm ruefully.

'Oi, you two, stop making me laugh it really hurts. And if you're going to flirt get a room.'

'It will hurt a lot more, if you're not careful,' Jeanie threatened.

Simon grimaced.

'It's nice to see you too, Jeanie. What have you been up to then, Bro?'

'I have another job.'

'Yes, he's become much more disreputable since you last saw him,' Jeanie interjected.

'I'm working as a personal assistant to the council leader.' Jeanie nodded knowingly.

'Ah, I see what you mean Jeanie. Didn't I warn you about

him, Bro?'

'In a roundabout way, yes. But you told me about this job my first night here.'

'Well, be careful. He's a slippery bastard and rumour has it that he's involved in some very dodgy dealings, not least over the Inchfield Estate.'

'I really have no idea what you're talking about, Si.'

'I think *I* do,' Jeanie said. 'You're still new around here, Billy. This town is rotten. It's been like that for years. You need to keep your distance, if you can. And if you are going to deal with Harry O'Leary then hold your nose and try not to get drawn in.'

'Is it really that bad, Jeanie?'

'So, I've heard. Of course, us ordinary people don't get to mix in such high-falutin' company.'

'I watch the council for a living,' Simon said. 'There certainly is some fishy stuff going on down there.'

'Okay, enough. Let me find my own way. But don't you two worry, I've made a note for future reference.'

'Just make sure you have,' Jeanie said.

Simon felt tired again, he yawned loudly.

'Do you want me to get the nurse?' Jeanie asked.

'No, I'm told that sleep is good for me. It helps me to recover.'

They stood to leave.

'We'll let you get some rest then,' Billy said.

He patted Simon gently on the shoulder.

'I'm glad that you're okay, Si. And next time you lecture me about getting involved with the wrong people I'll remind you which one of us ended up in hospital.'

'Touché. But you take care, Bro. I don't want to end up visiting you here in the future.'

Jeanie dragged him away. 'Come on country boy, your brother needs his rest.'

As they moved away from his bed, Simon felt himself drifting off again. He closed his eyes and fell asleep.

When he next awoke, Jerome Wilson was sitting there.

Simon took in his portly figure, unshaven face and nicotine-stained fingers. He was wearing a very loud large-checked woollen suit, white shirt and red bow tie.

Simon groaned as he tried to move to make himself more comfortable. He imagined he had been asleep for some time and that, combined with his restricted movement, meant his whole body was quite stiff.

Wilson looked up.

'Ah, awake, are you? I told you to take care, didn't I?'

'Yes, you did. What do you know, Jerome?'

'Only that there are some men in this town desperate to hold onto what they have and ruthless in the way that they go about holding onto it.'

'And you think they're responsible for this attack on me.'

'I don't know, boy. It seems likely. And yet I've spoken to the police today and they've drawn a blank.'

'The bouncer?'

'Has a watertight alibi it seems, so much so that they can't even place him with you at the time he threatened you.'

'That alibi wouldn't be Gavin Phillips, would it?'

'They're not saying so, but for my money it's the very same.'

'Can you help me sit up please Jerome?'

Wilson supported Simon, while at the same time adjusting the pillows behind him. Simon gritted his teeth from the pain, then reached over and rang for the nurse.

'I need a pee, do you mind?'

Wilson absented himself while the nurse attended to Simon's needs. When he returned, Simon had more questions.

'What exactly is going on in this town, Jerome?'

'It's difficult to say, but what I do know is that Oldport is corrupt from head to toe. You think I exaggerate. That may well be the case, but it's hard to draw any other conclusion.'

Wilson was passionate and angry.

'It's not just the council, Simon, it's the police as well… the magistrates, local businessmen. They work together, they profit together and they close ranks to protect their little conspiracy.

'As I've told you many times, this is a rotten borough, a rotten town and those who run it are rotten to the core. They enjoy their privileged status like the Romans of old… depraved, immoral, untouchable.

'And do you know what, I want to use my short spell as editor, before I retire, to prick their bubble. I may not be able to deconstruct the network of self-interest they've built up, but I can at least peel away some of the veneer that hides it.

'It won't be easy. I have obligations and legal boundaries, but I'm going to do my damnedest to publish what I can, to tell the good people of Oldport what sort of town they're living in.'

Simon sat open-mouthed while he tried to find the words to respond.

'I understand your passion, Jerome, and I'll support you in what you need to do, but is it really that bad? I've seen some strange goings on and some suspect behaviour, but I'm not sure that it amounts to a mass conspiracy to defraud the public and subvert our democratic processes.'

'You think I'm exaggerating?'

'I think I want to see more evidence before I draw that sort of conclusion. I find it difficult to believe the town is as bad as you paint it. There may be one or two rotten apples but ultimately people go into public life to serve not to feather their own nest.'

'Yes, there are rotten apples. The problem is that we have more than most. So much in this town is unsaid. People keep things to themselves. Nobody talks about the corruption, the you-scratch-my-back, I'll-scratch-your-back culture. It's accepted as the norm. It's almost as if people think that's how politics and business should be conducted. It's time all that changed.'

Simon looked sceptical. Jerome checked himself.

'No, I'm sure you're right. I didn't come here to argue. I

came because I feel guilty about what happened to you.'

'There's no need. It wasn't your fault.'

'Still, I shouldn't have put you in the firing line in the way that I did.'

'I did what I needed to do. You always taught me that the first duty of any journalist is to tell the truth. That's my mission and I'm not going to let a little bump on the head stop me doing that.'

'This isn't your fight, Simon. It's mine. This isn't even your town. The assault on you was a direct attack on the Oldport Observer, on freedom of speech and our right to publish news.'

Simon demurred.

'This is my home now. I care about Oldport as much as you do. And with all due respect, Jerome I'm the one with the cracked ribs and a god-awful headache, not the Observer.'

'Yes, I'm sorry about that,' Wilson replied, looking abashed.

'I've wanted to be a journalist all my life, Jerome. I'm in the early stages of my career. What sort of career would it be if I started off by failing to take risks?'

'You can take risks, Simon, just don't get reckless.'

'Well, as long as you don't forget that none of this is your fault.'

Wilson nodded.

'I got the message. Listen, how will you manage when you get out of here?'

'I'll be fine, Jerome. Honestly. I have a few cracked ribs, I'm not a cripple.'

'Okay, but if you need anything please ring me.'

Simon promised. Just then a nurse entered.

'I'm sorry but visiting time is over. Mr Jones needs to rest now.'

Wilson gave a half-wave and then paused.

'Oh, I forgot to mention, Sally asked whether she could visit you. Are you okay with that?'

Simon smiled. 'Of course. Tell her I'll look forward to it.'

Wilson nodded. 'I bet you would. You take care, son. I'll see you back at work very soon.'

18
Pressure Points

Gavin Phillips and Fred Harris sat in silence in the front of a red Ford Escort. Phillips was driving. It was raining, not hard but a fine, insidious rain, the type that seeps through every seam of even the most waterproof of clothing.

The windscreen wipers swung back and forth hypnotically, creaking as they brushed the glass, the only noise to break the tension that hung heavily between them.

Phillips was quietly fuming. By contrast, Harris was just thoughtful. They had been summoned and he knew that neither was looking forward to the conversation that awaited them.

The car climbed Pym Hill, past the 1930s estate to the big house that presided over it. As they approached the entrance, the large iron gates were opened electronically to allow them to pass.

The car crunched over the gravelled drive towards the heavy, brightly glossed front door. They parked at the side of the building and walked back to the main entrance.

John Baker was standing there, a crunched-up newspaper grasped in his hand. He looked furious.

As the men approached, he turned and walked back into the house, indicating that they should follow him. The three gathered in a spacious sitting room, Phillips and Harris sitting on a large sofa, Baker standing over them still clutching the newspaper before anger got the better of him and he threw it down on the coffee table in front of them.

'This is a complete fucking mess,' he seethed. 'They've all but said that we're dealing drugs in the club.'

'If they had said that we would have sued the arse off them,' Gavin retorted.

'Maybe, but it doesn't help our cause. What about this bouncer? Has he been working with these dealers?'

'He denies it emphatically. But Ian and I are keeping an

eye on him. We need some proof if we're going to fire him.'

'Bollocks. If we even have a hint of suspicion, we need to kick him out.'

'It's not that easy John. He's been with us a long time. He's a key member of staff. We have it under control.' Harris could see that Phillips was reluctant to relinquish any ground to his boss. He controlled the bouncers, almost as his own private army, Baker should know better than to interfere in that arrangement.

'And is it true that he paid the journalist a visit? Is he fucking stupid?'

'Yes, it is. I tried to talk him out of it, but he thought he could intimidate the boy into leaving us alone.'

'For fuck's sake, Gavin. You should have physically stopped him. We may run this town but there are limits. And I hear the journalist is in hospital. Was that him as well?'

'No, I swear. I told him to leave the guy alone. I told him that a warning was enough. There was no need for violence.'

Baker rubbed his chin. He didn't know whether to believe Phillips or not. He pressed the point.

'So why is this journalist…this Simon Jones lying in a hospital bed? Are you sure your man didn't go back and finish the job? Because now we have the police sniffing around the club asking questions.'

'Look, John, I've dealt with that. I gave him an alibi to get the police out of there. I really don't know if he went back and battered Jones, but we couldn't afford to have the club involved with a scandal on top of this drug story.'

Baker kicked the table in frustration.

'I can't believe what a fuck-up this is, Gavin. It's almost as if you're trying to sabotage our operation.

'I trust you to look after these things for me. You're meant to be a safe pair of hands.'

Phillips looked chastened. It was obvious to Harris he'd taken his eye off the ball.

'We got complacent. John. I'm sorry. But we've managed

the damage. I don't believe there'll be any further consequences.'

Baker looked incredulous.

'Do you know this editor, Gavin? He's the real problem. He's obsessed with conspiracies.

'I've known him for over twenty years and all he cares about is pulling down people who have worked hard to make this town a success.

'He's not going to let this rest, not when one of his reporters is occupying a hospital bed.'

'Well, we'll just have to avoid feeding him any more stories, then won't we?' Phillips was keen to move on.

'Just make sure that you do.'

Baker turned to Harris.

'You're quiet, what's your take on this mess?'

'None of my business. John. You manage your affairs; I look after mine. But I'll tell you this, that newspaper article is going to make it bloody hard to get the licences sorted for the casino.'

'Yes, that's why I asked you up here.'

Baker stopped pacing about and sat down opposite the two men. Harris knew that look. Baker was not going to compromise for anybody. As far as he was concerned it was win or bust.

'I know you're going to tell me to back off, Fred, but I don't want to. I've a huge amount of money invested in this casino and I need to get it open as soon as possible. What do I need to do to make that happen?'

'For once, John, I think you're asking too much. The whole committee is spooked after this drugs article. Some of them already had a thing about gambling. Many of them feel that they must be tough on the whole club scene to reassure people. Your casino is going to be a casualty of that because it needs a music and dance licence.'

'For fuck's sake, Fred, they're always getting cold feet. It's like nursing children. These bloody councillors need to grow a pair.'

'That's easy for you to say, John but none of them have a stake in this casino like we do. As far as they're concerned this is just another application for a music and dance licence.

'Dropping the pole dancing up front helped, but now we have the moral majority, the busy bodies and hundreds of parents up in arms about drugs. Many of them have kids who use your club.

'For fuck's sake John, I have a daughter and a son who'll be using your clubs in a few years' time. We want them to be safe, not subject to predatory drug dealers.'

'I get all that, Fred, but that doesn't help me in any way whatsoever.'

'What do you want me to say, John?'

'I want you to tell me how to fix this!'

Harris worked his jaw muscle in frustration. What did he have to do to get through to this pig-headed man? He knew a brick wall when he saw one. And he didn't feel like being John Baker's bulldozer.

Phillips jumped in.

'We need a plan,' he said.

Harris shrugged his shoulders. He looked at the floor as though for inspiration.

'It's not like you to be so negative, Fred', Phillips said. 'You're normally so can-do.'

'And if I saw a way through this, I would be the first to say let's put together a plan. But every single councillor has been fielding calls over the last 24 hours demanding we stop this application. They're spooked. We need time.'

'Time is the one thing we don't have, Fred.' Baker was emphatic.

'Look,' every member of your committee knows that this application has to be treated in a certain way.'

'Quasi-judicial,' Harris interjected.

'Yes. They must consider it on its merits, within strict legal criteria. They can't let irrational fears interfere with that or they'll find the decision appealed in court.'

'Well we're going to go to court then, because at present,

I can't see us persuading these councillors to buck public opinion.'

Phillips had been doing some sums.

'There is what, nine members of your committee, including you Fred?'

'Yes.'

'So, we just need five votes. We don't need them all.'

Baker saw where this was going.

'And the council officers will recommend we approve it because of the strict legal criteria that is applied to these applications, they have no reason to do otherwise.'

'I'll make sure of that,' said Harris.

'Okay, we have a plan. Let's identify the four most likely and find their price.'

'Our priority has to be countering this publicity,' Harris said. 'You need to persuade the local rag that you've cleaned up your club. And then you have to show you have processes in place to keep it clean.'

'If you can do that, we might have a chance. But you'll have to make it worth my colleagues' while to piss so many people off.'

'Okay, so this is going to cost us,' said Baker. 'It'll be worth it to get this bloody casino finally opened.'

'Where are my manners? Let's have some drinks while we discuss this.'

He walked over to a large cabinet and filled glasses for them all. As they sat nursing their drinks, dissecting the careers and prospects of each individual member of the licensing committee, they were disturbed by the sound of a car crawling over the gravel drive.

Baker went to see who was there and returned a few minutes later with Inspector Oliver Anderson, dressed in full uniform.

Harris and Phillips greeted him like an old friend. Baker offered him a drink.

'No, sorry John, I'm on duty.'

'Is this an official visit then?'

'Not really. Well, yes, in a way. It's meant to be a helpful visit.'

'Oh? '

'I reckoned that you might need somebody to clean up your club or at the very least offer assurance that it's clean.'

Baker patted him on the back.

'See,' he said to the others, 'here is a man who brings me solutions not problems, a man who can work on his own initiative.'

'You know I value your friendship, John.'

'Yes, we both profit from it, Ollie. What do you suggest?'

'I want to catch these dealers. The police force wants to catch these dealers. It's in all our interests. This newspaper article has stirred things. It's embarrassing for us, too, and my bosses want results.

'We want to work with you, put some surveillance in and identify who's doing this. A quick arrest might do us all good.'

Baker looked thoughtful. He sat down in an armchair and chewed on his lip. Anderson stood at the far end of the room. Harris noticed that he had a clear view of a large mirror on the opposite wall and that every now and again checked his own image. '*Vain bastard*,' he thought.

'I like the idea, Ollie, but if we're to work with you on this I don't want the dealer arrested in my club. In fact, if you can keep the club out of it as much as possible it would help me enormously.'

Anderson looked perplexed; Baker continued.

'There's a danger that a high-profile arrest will just focus attention back onto the club. We need to calm things down, and yes, an arrest will help that, but I don't want to give the impression that my club is where all the action is.'

'You don't make things easy, do you John? But we'll do our best, if you can work with us on this.'

'Understood.'

Harris invited Anderson to sit down next to him.

'I hear that you were out with Harry at the Prince Albert

a few nights ago, I thought I might have seen you at Baker's afterwards.' Anderson blushed.

'You know how it is, Fred, I had a bit of business to attend to.'

'Indeed. We'll have to get together one night, maybe spend a couple of hours in the new casino when it opens.'

He could see Anderson was flattered by the attention.

'Yes, that would be good.'

Phillips indicated to Fred that it was time to leave.

'We've got a lot of work ahead of us, Fred, if we're going to persuade your colleagues of our point of view.'

The two men stood up and headed to the door, closely followed by Anderson and Baker. As they got to the car, Baker joined them, taking Harris to one side.

'We can't afford to lose this, Fred. You'll keep me in touch with how things develop won't you?'

Harris gave him a reassuring tap on the shoulder.

'Don't worry. Between us I think we'll be able to sort it out.'

19
Class Lessons

Jeanie sat in one of the many cafés on High Street nursing a cup of coffee. It was ten-past-eleven in the morning. She knew this because she had already looked at her watch five times. Patience was not one of her virtues.

A young couple sat on a table opposite attempting the task of eating a toasted sandwich and drinking tea while coaxing a young child to consume orange juice from a plastic container.

A waitress in a black dress and pinafore was wiping down tables. A middle-aged man with thinning hair and a significant paunch, perused a menu. There were three well-dressed women sitting at the back of the café, enjoying a good gossip over coffee and cake.

Jeanie eyed a chocolate cake sitting on the counter under a glass container, fighting the temptation to order a large slice as compensation for having to wait so long. Ian was only fifteen minutes late, but seemed longer. She decided that he was five minutes away from blowing his second chance.

There was just one-minute left to run before this deadline when the café door opened, and he fell through it, breathing heavily. He spotted her straight away, her dress taut across her body, the hem slightly too high, revealing a shapely-length of leg.

'You're late,' she said.

'Yes, I'm really sorry. All hell has broken out at the club since this newspaper article and I've spent much of the morning fire fighting.'

Jeanie looked sceptical. She considered that Ian might look like Don Johnson, but Don would never have kept a good-looking girl like her waiting, unless of course he was chasing drug dealers with Tubbs. It was clearly her fault for settling for a lookalike instead of shooting over to Miami and stalking the real thing.

Ian was wearing his beige suit again. The shirt underneath had one too many buttons undone, a couple of blond hairs poking through the open collar. She approved but was less certain of the man himself… his status, his background and his views about her friends and the community she had called home all her life.

The waitress came to take their order. Ian asked for coffee for the two of them. Jeanie succumbed to temptation and asked for some chocolate cake.

'So, what's going on at the club?' she asked.

'Did you see the newspaper article?'

'For once I did. One of our regulars wrote it and has ended up in hospital for his trouble.'

'Really?'

Ian seemed shocked. Jeanie told him about the attack on Simon.

'How can you be certain that the two are related?'

'I can't be certain, but it seems a strange coincidence that just hours after one of your bouncers threatened him, he's assaulted from behind.'

'I'm aware of that accusation, but not of the assault. However, the police have been around to talk to the bouncer, and he has an alibi. If that holds up then the alleged threat must have been a case of mistaken identity, and he certainly could not have assaulted your friend.'

Jeanie found this hard to swallow.

'So, he's found somebody to vouch for him? Do you believe him? It sounds like you're defending him.'

'No, I'm not. I've given you the official version. Personally, I think the whole episode stinks, but at present I'm not able to do anything about it. This incident didn't take place in the club and he's not been charged with anything. I can't touch him.'

'Well, I hope you'll be keeping an eye on him especially as Simon believes he's in league with the drug dealer.'

'Mr Jones did make that allegation to me, however, you

will notice that he didn't publish it, nor did he include it in his feature on the drugs scene, as he has no evidence. It's his word against my employee. And I need evidence if I am to act. The man is on a warning and I'll be keeping an eye on him. And we're taking steps to stamp out the use of drugs in the club.'

Jeanie snorted. 'Another 'official answer'? Come on, Ian. Surely you can do better than that. And as for stamping out drugs, you know that you'll never manage that, don't you? There've always been drugs on the club scene. God, when I was younger, I even took the odd tab myself to give the night a bit of an edge. All the youngsters do it. You know that.'

'It's something I've learnt since I took over running the club. You don't get much direct experience of these things at boarding school. But if I find evidence of collusion between drug dealers and my staff, then I'll act. You have to believe me on that, Jeanie.'

Jeanie took a mouthful of chocolate cake. She was beginning to think that she was taking on too much with Ian. There were so many issues.

'So how can you manage a club like Baker's when you have so little experience of these things?'

'I'm a quick learner. Seriously though, the job is management; I manage people who do know what is going on and have long experience of it.'

'But isn't that the problem? These people could be running rings around you for all you know. Maybe that's why that bouncer is getting away with taking his cut from the drug dealer.'

'You may be right, but as I said, I'm onto him now and if that's his game, he won't be getting away with it again. The stakes are too high.'

'Stakes, what stakes?'

'The new casino. Mr Baker wants it open as soon as possible, He can't afford the bad publicity. We need to get things under control and I'm working with his team to do that.'

Jeanie assumed an incredulous look. She was sceptical, but she knew she wasn't going to get any further with this line of questioning. Maybe she should give him a break.

'Have you always talked like that?' she teased.

'Like what?'

'Like you swallowed a book on management, I feel like I'm in class or something.'

'And yet you can follow it all without breaking sweat,' Ian mocked.

'Tell me about boarding school. Are all the rumours about these schools true?'

'Well that depends, Jeanie, on which rumours you're referring to.'

They both laughed.

'I was sent to boarding school as a sort of compromise when my parents split up. My mother wanted out of Oldport, but my father didn't want to lose touch. So, they found a school halfway between Oldport and London, where mother had moved, and enrolled me.'

How old were you?'

'I was ten. I stayed there for eight years before going to university. It was a lonely, an awful time in my life that I try not to think about.'

Jeanie took his hand.

'They just abandoned you?'

'No, I spent the summer holidays in Oldport and the other holidays with my mother. But the in-between bits were not the best part of my life.'

'Did you have a fag?'

'Of course not. This isn't *Tom Brown's School Days*.'

Jeanie smiled.

'I'm just teasing you.'

'I know.' He looked into her eyes. 'You're incorrigible.'

'Maybe… tell me about your summer holidays in Oldport.'

'There really isn't a lot to tell. I did a summer job working in Sid Nicholson's TV and video shop, selling stuff.'

'Were you any good at it?'

'Not really. In the end, he had me packing boxes in the back, didn't dare sack me for fear of upsetting my father.'

'And he kept taking you on, summer after summer?'

'No, I didn't go back. I told my father that it wasn't working out. He threatened me with Fred Harris' chicken farm, but I ended up in an estate agent's office filing. I was there for three summers in all. By the end of the gig I knew the price of every property in Oldport, but the value of nothing.'

'And you're still living in your dad's shadow?'

'Now who's getting judgemental? This whole town lives in my father's shadow, haven't you noticed?'

'Come on Ian. There's a difference between me telling you how to run your life and you judging me for mine. I'm just offering some friendly advice. It's time to cut the apron strings, though the thought of Harry O'Leary in an apron frankly revolts me.'

Ian laughed out loud, a joyous throaty laugh that rather surprised him.

'Do you make a habit of imagining elderly men dressed in women's apparel? Surely that's the job of your prostitute friends.'

'No, they don't imagine it, but they might dress their clients that way if paid enough.'

Jeanie was laughing now as the two of them allowed their imagination to run riot for a few minutes.

'And I can't think of anything more revolting than your father in an apron.'

'Maybe I should wear it.'

'No, it wouldn't look good in the Testarossa.'

'You know, you're going to have to explain that joke to me one day.'

Jeanie shrugged.

'If you're good, maybe I will. Are you sure you can't get your boss to buy you one? I do think you need a company car.'

'Are you obsessed with cars or just that one?'

'You've got to treat a girl right, Ian. Pander to her dreams. If you want a babe like me, you need a babe magnet.'

'If I had a car like that, I'd be fighting them off. Is that what you want?'

'I don't know. The jury's still out on that.'

Jeanie finished off her chocolate cake and drank the last dregs of coffee. She wiped her mouth with a serviette and picked up her handbag.

'Shall we go for a walk?'

'Where to?'

'I don't care. How about some window shopping? Maybe walk up to the park?'

Ian nodded.

'Sure, why not.'

'Do you have to be back to work?'

'Not for another hour or so.'

'Good, let's do it then.'

As they left the café Ian took her hand. They turned left along High Street and strolled from shop to shop. He was keen to browse in a record shop, Jeanie not so much.

They came to a shoe shop. Jeanie stood there fascinated by the choice on offer.

'What is it about women and shoes?' Ian asked.

'You can never have too many shoes. Why don't men see that.'

'Actually, I have a lot of shoes.'

'And some quite expensive ones at that,' she retorted. 'You do dress well. John Baker must pay you a lot of money.'

He grabbed her by the waist in a playful manner.

'What, are you gold-digging?' he joked.

She laughed.

'If I was gold-digging, I can assure you that I would not start in Oldport, Mr O'Leary.'

They reached the park and settled on a bench. They could see the harbour below, the Georgian-style houses, the offices and shops. The Prince Albert dominating them all, or so it seemed.

Behind them was Pym Hill, to their left the Millstream council estate. Jeanie strained to see if she could make out her home but as ever it was indistinguishable from the other houses.

Ian pointed to Inchfield Estate and the green fields leading down to the cove, the scene of their first date.

'I never tire of looking down on this town,' he said. 'Well you and your dad own it.'

'No, my father *runs* it, John Baker owns it or, so he thinks.'

'Harry's law…' Jeanie mused. 'Councillor O'Leary and his gang of merry men, running our lives, telling us how to behave and where to live. Have you noticed that they're all men?'

'Pardon?'

'The people running this town, they're all men. Where are the female councillors, the businesswomen, the female magistrates? It's no wonder the powers that be are looked upon as some sort of mafia.'

'I don't think that's completely fair. There are women in all of those jobs.'

'Yes, but the really important ones are all men.'

'Fair enough, what have you got against us men anyway?'

'Where do I start?'

'No, on second thoughts, I don't want to know. I don't want another argument; I want to enjoy our time together.'

He went to kiss her, but she averted her lips. He looked confused.

'One step at a time,' she said. 'I just want to enjoy the moment. And I still haven't decided which side of the barricades you'll be on come the revolution.'

'Do you always talk in riddles?'

'Perhaps! We're very different you and I, I'm not sure we

can ever bridge the gap in our upbringings.'

'You've said that before. It shouldn't really matter. If we like each other, then we can overcome obstacles like that.'

'I'm not a project, Ian. The gap may be more obvious to me than to you, it's a cultural thing. I just need time to get used to it.'

He sighed.

'So, shall we take it slowly then. Perhaps one kiss now, maybe two the next time?'

She laughed and allowed him to kiss her. They cuddled together on the bench, silently enjoying each other's company for ten minutes or so before he suggested they walk back into town.

'I really need to get back to work.'

As they got to the entrance of Baker's nightclub, Ian kissed her again.

'You do realise that you have now used up your allotment for our next date,' she said.

'Maybe I'll have to apply for credit then.'

Jeanie looked sceptical. 'I'll consider your application form in due course.'

They parted, and Jeanie started the long walk down to the harbour and the Prince Albert. She was elated but also confused, not knowing how she really felt about this good-looking, well-turned out, classy man.

She was also attracted to his naivety. She was a sucker for men who had not yet been spoilt by the big wide world. But she worried too about the people he worked with, and who ran his life.

She wanted him to grow a backbone and to tell them where to stick their job and their town. She was worried he might be sucked into their way of life, and was certainly was not going to take on a man who'd been moulded in their image.

She sighed, this relationship stuff was hard work, she thought. She'd be glad to be back to the certainties offered by the Prince Albert, no matter how rough and ready they might be.

The people in that pub were part of her extended family, even Billy, an innocent abroad.

She stopped suddenly as if struck by a revelation. Why was she thinking about Billy when she had just been on a date with a Don Johnson lookalike?

Billy could be exasperating as well. Sometimes she wanted to mother him, at other times she wanted to clout him. And yet he wasn't one to be pushed around. And he had a lovely smile.

Her head was starting to hurt. She reached the Prince Albert and stepped into the familiar madness that formed her second home.

20
Looking the Part

The late summer of September 1987 had started to fade and there was a distinct chill in the air. Oldport's High Street was hardly bustling. Billy counted barely half a dozen shoppers as he rushed towards Thomas Bros gentleman outfitters.

He had arranged to meet Jeanie there and he was late. Early mornings did not suit him, but they only had a limited amount of time, so he'd had to compromise. Frank had teased him as he left the Prince Albert. He had suggested that the pub might start serving breakfasts to local businesses if Billy was going to get up so early each day.

As he turned into High Street, he saw Jeanie outside the shop. She was looking at her watch and shivering a bit. She had clearly not anticipated it being so cold and had failed to bring a coat with her.

As Billy approached, she glared at him.

'What is it about you men that you can't be on time for anything?'

'I'm sorry. It's a bit early and I hadn't realised how long it would take me to get here.'

She raised her eyes to the cloudless sky.

'Couldn't pull yourself away from Amber more like,' she teased. Billy went on the defensive.

'No, honestly, she didn't come in to see me this morning. I think it was a bit early for her.' He paused in brief contemplation and then turned towards her accusingly: 'Wait a minute, are you jealous?'

Jeanie let out a loud 'harrumph'.

'Don't get above yourself, country boy. You're lucky I came at all.'

'Yes, why did you come? I'm sure I'm perfectly capable of buying a suit on my own.'

Jeanie put on a look of deepest disdain and feigned

peering at him over imaginary glasses.

'Billy, you can barely dress yourself in the morning. Surely, you don't think you can be trusted to buy your first suit without the second opinion of an acknowledged style icon.'

'Oh, is somebody else coming along?'

'You're good, very good,' she mocked.

'Seriously, though it's always good to have a second opinion and we do have the reputation of the Prince Albert to uphold.'

Now it was Billy's term to look sceptical. He widened his eyes and half-sneered. They both burst out laughing at the same time. When they had recovered their composure, Billy moved towards the shop door.

'We'd better get inside before you change your mind and drag me to a shoe shop instead.'

Jeanie smiled, a happy contented smile.

'The thought had crossed my mind,' she said.

An impeccably dressed man stepped forward to greet them. 'How may I help you?

'He's here for a suit,' answered Jeanie.

The man looked Billy up and down, taking in the scruffy trainers, faded jeans, Bon Jovi T-shirt and black woollen jacket.

'I take it, sir, that this is your first one?'

Billy went to speak but Jeanie got there before him.

'You have to treat him gently, Mr Thomas. He's a country hick and needs to be initiated into the ways of us sophisticated townsfolk.'

'A hick eh? I'm sure we can accommodate you, sir. Is it a business suit you're after?'

Jeanie was determined to take over the process on Billy's behalf.

'He does, but nothing too stuffy. He's barely 19 years old. We don't want him dressed up liked a middle-aged businessman.'

'I *am* here you know. I think I'm capable of choosing my

own clothes,' Billy said indignantly.

'Don't be daft. Show us what you've got Mr Thomas.'

The tailor gave up trying to impress the odd couple who had come into his shop and instead escorted them to a rack of suits. Billy pulled out a pinstripe only to have Jeanie take it off him and put it back.

Eventually, they had two suits that Jeanie approved of and Billy was directed to the changing rooms, so he could model them for her.

'He'll need some shoes, some white shirts and a tie as well,' she said.

An hour later they emerged from the shop clutching a couple of bags. There was a self-satisfied smile on Jeanie's face, which Billy classed as rather smug.

'You've got to be fair, Billy, you do scrub up well. You'll look good trailing behind Harry O'Leary carrying his bags and opening the car door for him.'

'It's a job, Jeanie, a step up in the world.'

'If you say so, Billy, I prefer to think of it as an opportunity for me to have some peace and quiet in the pub.'

He smiled.

'Just you and the customers?'

'And Frank, don't forget Frank.'

'Of course.'

They stepped into a nearby café and ordered coffee. Billy put his bags down, sat back and yawned.

'Am I keeping you up? Or boring you perhaps?'

'No, of course not, I just didn't get my full eight hours last night.'

'Well if you can't hack it at your age, there's no hope. I can just see you in a few years' time sitting in front of the fire in your dressing gown and slippers, drinking hot chocolate before going to bed at ten o'clock.'

'Don't project your future onto me. I'm going to live a little before I get anywhere near that vegetated state.' Billy was enjoying this repartee and wondered whether Jeanie was, too. He was surprised when she diverted the conversation onto a more serious track.

'So, tell me something about yourself, Billy.' He hesitated.

'There really isn't much to tell. I grew up in the country. You knew that already. My Dad died five years ago, and my mum shacked up with some good-for-nothing drunk who used to push her around a bit. Not the full domestic violence you understand, just the occasional shove or slap.'

'Billy, that *is* full domestic violence. There aren't any halfway measures, you either respect your partner or you don't. If you hit someone then there's no respect and as far as I'm concerned, they should lock you up and throw away the key.'

Billy decided to draw a line and move the conversation on.

'What about you? Your family seems very stable.'

'Yes, I've been lucky. I have two loving parents and a decent, caring brother who's turned out well. Not bad considering the reputation of the Millstream Estate.'

'But you've encountered domestic violence.'

'I had an abusive boyfriend once. It wasn't a violent relationship, but he was controlling. Wanted to know everything I did, everybody I saw, tried to stop me going out with my friends. He stalked me even after I finished with him, until Frank had a word.'

'I bet that was messy.'

'In a satisfyingly good way, yes it was.'

She broke into a broad smile as she recalled the conversation between Frank and her ex. Billy had already concluded that Jeanie took no prisoners in her personal life.

'I'd better be careful not to cross you, hadn't I?'

'Too bloody right, country boy.'

'So, where's your brother, now?'

'He's at sea somewhere. I haven't seen him for months, but he writes to us regularly. I think his ship is due to dock in Southampton in a few weeks. You may get to meet him.'

'That would be interesting. Is he as mad as you?'

'You're really heading for a fall, aren't you?'

Billy smiled.

'A bit of banter never hurt anybody, isn't that what you told me?' Jeanie pulled the discussion back to her original interrogative intent.

'So, tell me, how did Simon end up here?'

'He left home eight years ago, I was too young to understand why or even what was going on. But he has done well enough for himself here, hasn't he?'

'Yes, like all the reporters, he's a regular. I get on well with him. He's not as cheeky as you, of course, or even as much of a yokel, but he's well-liked around here and that counts for a lot. How is he now?'

'He came out of hospital yesterday… still in a bit of pain but he seems to be coping okay. I offered to move in with him for a bit to look after him, but he wouldn't hear of it. I think he's planning to go back to work on Monday, but I suspect Jerome is going to veto that one.'

'Well if you need anything you just have to ask, you know that, don't you?'

'Yes, thank you and thank you for your support.'

'When're you going to see him next?'

'I thought I'd pop in tomorrow morning.'

'Would you like me to come with you?'

'Yes, I'd like that. Thank you.'

Jeanie finished her coffee and looked at her watch.

'It's time we got back to the Prince Albert?'

They left the café and turned down High Street. The temperature noticeably dropped as they turned a corner into a cold wind blowing in off the sea. Billy saw that Jeanie was shivering a bit, so took off his coat and wrapped it around her shoulders. She nodded her gratitude.

'You country boys do have very good manners,' she said. 'But won't you be cold?'

'No, we're used to the cold in the country. Not like you soft townies.'

'Really, is that why you're shivering?'

'Your needs are greater than mine, Jeanie.'

She cuddled into him to share the warmth. As they walked into a side street, Billy put his arms around her to secure the coat on her shoulders and to benefit properly from her body heat.

Jeanie looked up at him and their eyes met. Billy suddenly leaned in and kissed her. She pulled away in shock. Billy went red.

'I'm sorry,' he stammered. 'I got a bit carried away.'

Jeanie put a finger on his mouth to stop him in mid-flow, turned towards him, pulled him closer and kissed him properly.

As they broke away from each other, Billy was a bit stunned.

'Can we do that again?' he asked.

'Don't be greedy,' she scolded.

'Whatever happened to work colleagues not getting involved?'

'Let's be clear, Billy, one kiss does not constitute an involvement. If I want to sample the goods every now and again, then that is my right, and besides you started it.'

She smiled broadly.

'Not a word to Frank,' she added. 'And let's not rush into anything. We work together.'

Billy was still too stunned to speak. She leaned in and kissed him again.

'Are there any more rules?' he asked.

'Yes, don't discuss this with Amber either. I'm not having her teasing me.'

'It's almost as if you're ashamed of me.'

She took his hand and pulled him closer. Her face softened as she spoke.

'No, that isn't it, Billy. I like you a lot. I'm just not sure what I want. I need time to sort my head out.'

'Okay, I understand, I think. But there is one condition.'

'What's that?'

'You kiss me again.'

He moved his face towards hers, and they kissed passionately. Afterwards they held each other tightly, until finally, she disentangled herself.

'We need to get to work. And we need to behave normally,' Jeanie said firmly.

Billy nodded. He went to hold her hand, but she pulled it away.

'Normally, Billy. The Prince Albert is just around the corner, people will see us, and I value my privacy. I don't want somebody seeing us and telling the whole pub. We'd never hear the last of it.'

'Okay.'

'And besides I have a date on Sunday.'

Billy looked stunned at this news. She put her hand on his arm.

'This is not something I planned, Billy. I just wanted to be up front with you. I've been seeing somebody else, but it hasn't got very far and to be honest I don't know how far I want it to go. I just need some time to decide what I want to do. You do understand, don't you?'

'I think so.' He was confused and anxious. Jeanie tried to reassure him.

'Just give me some space. We've plenty of time to get this right. And you need to decide what you want as well.'

'Can I ask who it is?'

'It's Harry O'Leary's son, Ian.'

Billy stood back in horror.

'Seriously? You lecture me about working with Harry and you're in a relationship with his son.' Jeanie kept her cool, patiently outlining her position to him.

'It's hardly a relationship, Billy. We've been on two dates and they didn't go that smoothly. He's a bit posh for me but there's something about him that attracts me. I can't explain it and I'm not going to try.'

Billy went silent. He didn't know how to react. He felt jealousy surging inside him. If Ian O'Leary had been nearby, he may not have been responsible for his actions. Jeanie could see that he was upset and tried to smooth things over.

'Just give me time, Billy. I'll find my way. And if you want to go on a proper date then that's okay as well.'

'I've never been that good at sharing, Jeanie, but if that's what you want then I guess I will learn to live with it.'

'Good.'

She took his arm and walked out of the side street and into the tree-lined road that led to the Prince Albert, pulling away again as the pub got closer.

'Now let's go and serve some customers.'

21
Licensing Committee

It was Monday morning and Billy felt like a million dollars as he walked up the town hall steps in his new dark suit, white shirt and plain burgundy tie. He had even had his hair cut especially.

He had spent the Saturday afternoon hiatus between opening times at his brother's. Jeanie had joined him as she had promised.

It had been a difficult few weeks for Simon. He was still in some discomfort but keen to get back to work, and he was not going to miss an opportunity to tease the nascent couple.

'Well, this is a turn-up for the books,' he smiled as he opened the door to Billy and Jeanie. 'Have you come to ask my permission to get hitched?'

Jeanie's face reddened slightly, but she wasn't going to let Simon get away with anything.

'If you're not careful I'll be hitching you to a horse and cart and sending you back to the countryside where you belong,' she said menacingly.

Simon smiled and invited them to sit in the two armchairs, carefully removing some dirty washing first, and went to the kitchenette to put the kettle on. He seemed genuinely pleased to see them.

'So, what have you been doing with yourself?' Jeanie asked. 'The pub's been empty without you.'

'Yeah, Frank's been complaining that his takings are down since you were attacked,' Billy added.

'Reading mostly,' Simon responded. 'when I'm not being rudely interrupted by Billy calling round to see me.'

'Charming.'

'Don't get me wrong, Bro, your visits have been very welcome. Seriously, I've been going stir-crazy. I can't wait to get back to work.'

He handed them a mug of tea each and settled on the

edge of the bed. He started to interrogate his brother for gossip.

Jeanie inspected the bedsit as the two brothers talked, it was far more basic than she would have been comfortable with. She took advantage of a lull in the conversation to confront the issue.

'Have you ever thought of employing a cleaner, Simon? Or even buying a hoover? I'm sure Frank could lend you one.' Both brothers stared at her simultaneously.

'Jeanie...' Billy started indignantly.

'What? I'm just saying. This place needs a woman's touch. Whatever happened to that nice girl you were seeing, Simon? Hannah, I think her name was. She'd have sorted this place out.' Now Billy was curious. Simon was a bit taken aback.

'It didn't work out. We wanted different things.'

'You mean she wanted marriage and you didn't?'

'Yes, if you like. Can we change the subject please?'

'Wasn't there a girl back in Thane Bridge?' Billy asked. 'Just before you left. Yes, that's right, what was her name again?' Sophie wasn't it?'

'So, my love life is a mess,' Simon said, 'tell me something that's news. In fact, what *is* going on with you two?'

'We're just friends and work colleagues,' Jeanie said, rather too quickly. Simon gave a knowing smile. Jeanie changed the subject.

'Just how big is this village you both come from?'

'Oh, it's small,' Simon said. 'No more than a couple of hundred people. Basically, it has a post office, a pub, a telephone box and less than a hundred houses. Lots of outlying farms, the nearest school is a half-hour bus ride away and the nearest supermarket a mile further on. You'd love it, Jeanie.'

'If you can't get a pint of milk a ten-o-clock at night, I'm not interested,' she responded.

'We could teach you how to milk a cow,' Billy said.

Jeanie snorted. 'Honestly, you two. You should thank us

townies for introducing you to civilisation.'

The two brothers laughed. Simon winced with pain.

'Is it still hurting?' Billy asked.

'Only when I laugh.'

Jeanie filled him in on the gossip from the pub and Billy followed that up with news of his latest sartorial purchase. Simon soaked it all in, seemingly glad of the company.

Jeanie finished the last of her tea and looked at her watch. There was still plenty of time, but she didn't want to wear Simon out. He may feel he was ready to go back to work, but he was clearly still struggling.

'We had better get back. We need to set up for the evening session. It's been good seeing you, Simon. Take care of yourself. Look forward to seeing you in the Prince Albert soon.' They embraced.

Simon and Billy followed suit.

'Look after yourself, Bro.'

'You, too, Billy... and try to keep your hands on the pumps and away from Jeanie, or Frank might just have something to say on the matter!'

* * *

Standing outside the council offices, Billy felt that he could pass for any one of the council employees stepping into the building to start their week. It was almost as if he had a real job, instead of running errands for the council leader.

As he entered the antechamber to the leader's office, he saw Sue leaning over her typewriter seeking to correct an error in a typed document with the brush from a bottle of Tippex.

She applied the fluid, blew on it and sat back to let it dry. She looked across the room at Billy and did a double take.

'Good grief, boy, did you win the pools or something?'

Billy smiled.

'Do you like it, Mrs Evans. Harry told me I had to smarten up.'

'Well, you certainly succeeded there, young Billy. I'd

introduce you to my daughter except you have no prospects. She needs a good match.'

'Don't you trouble yourself, Mrs Evans. I'm most probably far too untrustworthy for your daughter,' Billy joked, not quite sure where this conversation was going. Fortunately, Sue moved the dialogue on.

'Yes, you could be right. Councillor O'Leary is expecting you. You'd better go in.'

Harry was sitting behind his desk reading a newspaper. He had what looked like a glass of whisky in his hand, but Billy dismissed the idea. After all it was just ten o clock, far too early to start drinking.

'Ah, Billy, excellent, you're here at last. Glad to see that Steve Thomas sorted you out with a suit, would have preferred a pinstripe myself but that one looks good on you. I hope you have the receipts. I need to claim the cost back from the council as an incidental expense.'

Billy handed him the receipts and the change.

'Good. I'll just pass these onto Sue, so she can do all the administration and then we can get down to business.'

Harry popped out into the antechamber, leaving Billy to take in his surroundings. He admired the glass-fronted, fitted mahogany bookcases, and studied the pictures of Oldport and past civic dignitaries. In one corner was a huge television, video recorder and a drinks cabinet.

'Right,' Harry said as he re-entered the room, 'this is a very important day. Later we have licensing committee and the decision on the new casino in High Street, but before that I have a series of meetings with officers to talk about the budget. Sue will be taking some notes, so I can concentrate on what they are saying. I thought you might benefit from sitting in.'

'In the meantime, have a seat. We have half an hour or so before the first meeting. Tell me what you know about this casino.'

'Well, I've only seen the posters like everybody else. They're putting in pole-dancers I believe.'

165

'Ah, no boy, that plan has been abandoned. Too many people were objecting. This is a very conservative town you know. And we have councillors who think it is their job to look after our morals, bloody busybodies that's what they are.'

'Is that not their job then?'

'No, absolutely not, it's their job to uphold the law and to use their judgement accordingly. It's my fault, I suppose, for allowing them to call it a Public Protection Committee. The only thing the public need protecting from are the councillors.'

Billy could see that he was deadly serious. He wondered why supposedly dangerous councillors might be allowed such responsibility.

'Have they stopped developments before, then?'

'Oh yes. We've even banned films… adult films, as if we have the right to tell grown men and women what they can and cannot watch.'

'Which films?'

'Well, The Exorcist for one. Have you heard of that film?'

'No, I haven't'

'Well what was worse was that the Public Protection Committee had to sit through a screening. It was a dreadful film, but that was no reason to ban it.

'We had legal advice that we had to watch it before we could pass judgement. I'd only been leader for a few years and was still the youngest member on the council. My instincts were to leave it be.

'I remember sitting next to a female councillor. She was a bit of a battle-axe, in her seventies. She fully embraced the whole concept of protecting the public from the horrors of pornographers and others.

'If the only way to ban the film was to watch it then it was her duty to make that sacrifice. Anyway, we got to this scene where the girl projectile vomits over a priest.

'The whole committee sat open mouthed, except for this

old battle-axe who couldn't take it anymore. She turned towards me and threw up in my lap.

'I had to go home to change. By the time I got back the committee had voted to ban the film by one vote. I still think to this day that she did it deliberately to make me miss the vote.'

Billy laughed.

'Every word true, Billy,' he said taking another sip from his glass as the alcohol loosened his tongue.

'And they're going to do it again today?'

'No, I don't think so. The pole-dancing has been abandoned to get the application through. Some councillors are a bit jumpy about gambling but since they're not licensing that vice, they aren't allowed to pass judgement on that aspect of the development. Gambling licenses are a matter for the magistrates' court and the Gaming Board, not us.

'The only fly in the ointment is this drugs business. There are some very jittery councillors about since that article appeared in the Observer.

'Some of them think that turning down this application will save the town from a drug epidemic, even though the new place is aimed at a different clientele. They want to put down a mark, I s'pose. Others are just frightened of their constituents. But I think it'll be okay.'

'Will I be able to watch proceedings?'

'Of course, there's a public gallery, but we have work to do before that Billy. The town treasurer is due any minute.'

There was a knock on the door and Sue entered accompanied by two middle-aged men clutching two very thick folders. Harry invited them to sit at a table in front of his desk, Sue sat next to them notebook in hand as Billy looked on.

* * *

The licensing committee went as Harry had predicted, and the music and dancing license was granted for the casino by five votes to four. There was to be a small party in the office to celebrate afterwards.

Billy was pleased to be included until he discovered that he was required to serve the drinks. On his way in Sue handed him a couple of extra-large packs of crisps and peanuts.

'There are dishes in the cupboard underneath the minibar,' she said smiling. 'This is one job I'm more than happy to hand over to you. At least while you're here doing this I won't get groped as much.'

Billy looked shocked.

'That John Baker is a bit of a pervert. Don't say anything though. I really need this job.'

'You should join a trade union,' Billy said, filling bowls with nibbles.

He set up some glasses and found a couple of bottles of wine and some beer. As he put out coasters the four men walked in.

'Billy,' Harry boomed, 'meet John Baker, Gavin Phillips and Fred Harris. Billy is my new assistant. Today he'll be serving drinks. Give your orders over to him.'

Billy dealt with each of their needs in turn and then passed around the nibbles.

'Well, we're all systems go,' Baker said raising his glass. 'I propose a toast to Harry and Fred who have ensured that our casino will open on time.'

'And to John, who has led from the front in building up this town,' added Harry.

As the glasses clinked, Billy wished that he could join them in their toast.

'We should discuss the official opening,' Phillips said.

Baker laughed.

'Do you never relax, Gavin. We're celebrating putting the last of the licences in place. There's plenty of time to sort that stuff out. Besides I'm leaving that detail to you.'

'There isn't that much time, John, a few weeks at best.'

Harris intervened.

'Well whenever it is, I hope I get an invitation.'

'Of course, you will Fred.'

Baker tried to be reassuring.

'This casino is going to be very different from the nightclub though. For a start, it will have a members' section targeted at businesspeople, with executive dining and entertainment, if you know what I mean. We've already started to market it in Southampton and surrounding towns. There's been a lot of interest. And with more executive homes going up in Inchfield, we will be expanding our clientele.'

They all laughed.

'So, you're putting the pole-dancing back in after all?' O'Leary asked.

'I don't know, Harry. Maybe we'll opt for lap-dancing instead. I'm planning something much classier. We're going to have a minimum age limit and a dress code, nobody younger than 25 is going to be admitted. That way we can keep out the riff raff from the Millstream Estate.

'Your boy there will get in dressed like that, Harry.' Baker turned to look at Billy as he spoke. It was the first time that he had acknowledged Billy's presence since entering the room.

'No, he won't' Harry retorted, 'he's not yet nineteen years old.'

Phillips snorted.

'What do you think, boy? Is this the sort of club you'd want to go to?'

'I think I'd prefer to stay in Baker's, sir.'

'See, that's the way. Sort the wheat from the chaff,' Baker said.

'God, John where are your manners,' Harry demanded. 'Billy is standing next to you. You can't speak about people like that.'

'Yes, you're right, Harry. I'm sorry, son. I was out of order, maybe had a few too many drinks.'

Billy muttered his acceptance of the apology and topped up the glasses.

Harris tried to change the subject.

'Are there enough people in your target group to make this pay, John?'

'Well I'm counting on you and your chicken farm keeping me afloat. Fred. Those chickens must be made of gold, the amount you make from them. But seriously there is a 17% gross profit on casinos if they're in the right place and attracting the right people.'

Gavin added his two-pennyworth.

'We've done our research, Fred. We reckon that there's a growing business class in and around the area who will want to let their hair down at this new club. A casino, a good quality restaurant, appropriate live entertainment and some exotic entertainment in the bar is just what the doctor ordered.

Oldport is becoming a commuter town for highly paid executives, who don't want to live in the city, and we're confident we can attract customers from further afield, including Southampton, as John has explained.

'Besides, who doesn't like a flutter now and again. There will be plenty of people keen to end a good night out in the local casino.'

'Leaving Baker's as the local cattle market?' Harry intervened. 'Ian's told me what goes on at that club. It's basically a pick-up joint.'

Phillips smiled and put his arm around Billy's shoulders.

'They all are, Harry. Maybe you should try your luck there, boy.'

'Yes sir, I may do that.'

Harry bristled.

'Stop patronising the boy, Gavin.'

'You're very defensive, Harry.'

'Yes, well I may have sold my soul many years ago, but I got into politics because I care about people. That's the big difference between you and me.'

Harris chipped in.

'Harry's right, Gavin, the boy is here to do a job. Leave

him be.'

'Okay, okay. We got the message.'

'Listen,' Baker said, 'We may not have the official opening tied down yet, but any excuse for another celebration. How about if I host a party at my place on Saturday? Are you up for that?'

'Yes, that's an excellent idea, John.' Harris responded. 'Do you want me to bring my chickens?'

They all laughed.

'No, but you can bring your committee, well the ones who voted for the application anyway. The rest can whistle for their supper.'

'What are we doing for entertainment, John?' Phillips asked. 'Shall I have a word with Frank at the Prince Albert?'

'Excellent idea, Gavin, and Harry, bring your boy with you.'

Harry looked puzzled. Baker addressed Billy directly.

'How would you like to earn a bit more money, serving at my party?'

'I would like that sir, but I'm meant to be serving at the Prince Albert that night,'

'Don't you worry about that; Gavin will have a word with Frank and make sure you're free. You'll be able to keep an eye on Frank's girls as well.'

'If Frank's happy then sure, yes.'

'Good, then that's settled. I'll see you all on Saturday.'

22
Keys to the Kingdom

Billy was back at the town hall the next day having been summoned by Harry to help with his ward surgery. Harry had told him that he held these events monthly so his constituents could come and see him for help and advice.

According to Sue, Harry's ward included Pym Hill. She warned him that as Harry was the council leader, people from all over the town tended to turn up.

'Surely, they have their own councillors to go to for help,' Billy had said.

'Sure, they do,' Sue replied, 'but there are councillors and there are councillors. Some don't hold surgeries at all. Others couldn't even find the town hall if the likes of Harry weren't there to draw them a map.'

As Billy walked into the office Harry looked up from his papers. Unusually, he was not wearing a tie.

'Ah, good, you're on time. Here, you're driving,' he said, tossing a set of keys at Billy, who failed to catch them and had to pick them up off the floor.

'Well, we're not putting *you* in the council cricket team,' Harry retorted.

He stood and gathered up his papers, handed a notepad to Billy and put on his jacket. Billy waited for him to put on a tie, a gesture that provoked a puzzled look from Harry before sudden realisation crossed his face.

'Ah, no, I don't wear a tie for these occasions. Being too formal makes people uncomfortable. They like the smart-but-casual look.'

They headed out to Harry's car.

A few minutes later, Harry and Billy were standing in a small room off the main hall of a draughty church outbuilding in the centre of Harry's ward, which he rented for this purpose. Billy was instructed to set up a table and a couple of chairs, and to place chairs in the hall.

'The way this works Billy is that you arrange the constituents in order of arrival. You then bring in the first one, sit with me taking notes, escort them out when we've finished and then bring in the next one. Is that clear?'

'Absolutely, Councillor O'Leary are you expecting many people?'

'To be honest, Billy, you can never tell. I'm sure Sue explained that, being leader, I tend to attract the great unwashed in addition to my own constituents, so we'll just have to see. I suspect more of the former than the latter.'

Billy set to work putting out the chairs while Harry sorted through his notes. At 1pm precisely he opened the doors and let the first of Harry's constituents into the hall.

The first couple were quite elderly. The woman used a walking stick, while the husband supported her other arm. They lived in Pym Hill and wanted Harry's help to get a grant to install a stair lift.

Billy took down their details. Harry promised to talk to housing officers and get back to them. He asked Billy to show the couple out and return to the office before bringing in another constituent. When Billy returned, Harry was contemplative.

'It's being able to help people like that couple, which makes this job worthwhile,' he said. 'The only problem is that once we've worked our way through all the application forms, I suspect that they'll not be eligible due to their income being too high. This is a means-tested grant after all. I may be wrong, but we'll have to see. Who's next?'

Billy went out and brought back a middle-aged lady who was concerned about youngsters drinking into the early hours of the morning in the local park.

Harry listened intently, while Billy took notes. He promised to speak to the police and ask them to increase their patrols.

As Billy took the lady out, he noticed that a small crowd had gathered in the hall. They were clearly all together and not especially happy.

Billy escorted them into the room. There were only enough seats for two, so the rest of the group stood at the back, enabling the main spokesperson, an elderly lady, to eyeball Harry across the table.

'Councillor O'Leary,' she started, 'we're concerned about the growth of drug taking in this town and the dangers our young people are being exposed to in nightclubs.'

'Yes, we're astonished that permission was given to this new club and casino while inquiries are still underway into Baker's,' a younger man in his thirties added.

'What's the council thinking?' the lady added. 'Don't they care about the future of our young people?'

Billy thought that the whole scenario was a bit bizarre. Harry had clearly seen it all before.

'Of course, I share your concern,' he said. 'the council is working very closely with the police to try and contain this problem.'

'What about the new club?'

'As I understand it, the new club is a casino, restaurant and live music venue aimed at the over-25s. We've had some categorical assurances that it will be properly managed. But our legal advice was very clear. We were acting in a quasi-judicial capacity and we had to determine the application on strict criteria.

'If we had refused it then the courts would have overturned our decision. We felt it was better to retain control of the application and impose conditions rather than allow some unelected judge to pass it with no constraints on the way it operates.'

'That's all very well Councillor O'Leary but the drugs problem is getting out of hand in this town and we need some action to deal with it.'

Harry spent some considerable time discussing these concerns with the delegation and trying to find practical ways to assuage their fears. By the time the residents left he was feeling exhausted.

Billy came back into the room and sat down.

'That was fun,' he said.

'All part of the trials and tribulations of being council leader, Billy.'

'Did you really have no choice but to pass the licence for the club?'

'We could have turned it down. We might have ended up in court on appeal, we might not have done. The point was, of course, that the town needs this investment, just as it needs the extension to the Inchfield Estate. We can't stand still. Billy. We need to continue moving forward as a town or we'll stagnate and die.'

'And if people profit from these ventures at the same time, is that just incidental?'

'Billy! Are you a socialist? Of course, people make money. That's the way of things. If they didn't then nothing would get built.'

Billy conceded the point.

'Now, is there anybody else out there to see me?'

'Yes, there is a young lady and her two children. Sarah Wilson, her name is …she says she's come to see you about being rehoused.'

'Ah yes, she's been to see me before. She's a single mother currently living with her parents in Millstream. She's absolutely desperate for a council house and I think I've found her one.'

'That's really good news.'

'The only thing we need to resolve is the question of the key deposit. Can you bring them in?'

Billy went out and ushered the woman and her two children into the room. She was in her early twenties he thought, and very attractive. She was about five-and-a-half feet tall with dark curly hair and a slim figure.

The two children, he learnt later, were aged two and five, both were boys, and each had a different father. She was no longer with either man so needed suitable accommodation to raise the boys.

Sarah Wilson was nervous and hesitant. She shook

Harry's outstretched hand and gave each boy a colouring book before placing them in the corner, where they sat quietly. Harry looked thoughtful and nervous.

'There's no need for you to stay for this, Billy. Miss Wilson will be the last person I see today, so why don't you put the chairs away in the hall? Billy nodded and left the small room, leaving the door slightly ajar as he did so. He was curious as to why he was not being allowed to be party to this discussion.

He lurked outside hoping to hear the conversation as Harry conveyed his news to the woman. He could just see the two figures through the crack in the partly open door.

'Well, Miss Wilson you'll be pleased to know that I've found you a nice two-bedroom house in Millstream, with a lovely garden, not far from the local school.'

'Oh, thank you Councillor O'Leary. I'm really very grateful.'

'There is though the question of the key deposit. I think we agreed three hundred pounds.'

'We did Councillor O'Leary, but I don't have that sort of money.'

'Well,' he sighed, 'I'm sure somebody else will want this for their home.'

'No, please! We're desperate. I'm sleeping on my mum's couch and the kids are sharing a single bed. Things are bad. We really need this house.'

Billy could sense Harry hesitating as if the council leader could see the despair in her eyes.

'You don't even know if you'll like this house,' he said.

'Councillor O'Leary, at the moment, I'll take anything.'

'This is not a huge sum of money to pay for a home that can last you the rest of your life. Could you raise the deposit if you had a few more days?'

'No, I really have scraped together every penny I can put my hands on, including borrowing from my mum.'

'So how much have you got?'

'A hundred-and-fifty pounds.'.'

Through the crack in the door Billy could see her pull out a wad of notes and hand it to him.

'Look,' Harry said eventually, 'I like you. I'm sure we can…er…come to an arrangement here. This is what I'll do. I'll take your one-hundred-and-fifty and you can pay me the rest in kind, if you know what I mean.' Billy couldn't see Harry's face, but he imagined a rather creepy smile crossing it, a bit like Dick Dastardly from *Wacky Races*.

Sarah sounded frightened. Billy thought she knew all too well what Harry meant, though he wasn't so sure.

'Do we have a deal?' Harry demanded.

Sarah nodded hesitantly, and Harry put the money in his pocket. He handed her a piece of paper.

'Good, here's the address. We'll meet you there tomorrow at 2pm. Is that okay with you?'

'Yes, thank you,' she stammered.

'And don't you forget our deal.'

'I won't.'

As she gathered up the children and their books, Billy rushed to tidy up the chairs in the hall. When she emerged, he ushered them out of the building. As Harry had predicted nobody else had turned up for the surgery, so Billy had an opportunity to speak to her briefly.

'What did he mean by payment in kind?' he asked.

Sarah looked at him disdainfully.

'You're with him, aren't you? Don't pretend that you don't know?'

'No, I really don't know.'

She sneered at him. 'Well maybe you'd better ask him then, You men are all the same.'

She turned on her heels, taking the children with her.

* * *

The following afternoon, Billy drove Harry onto Millstream Estate. He followed directions to a quiet cul-de-sac of council houses. The area looked shabby and unkempt.

There was a large communal area just around the corner where some children were kicking a football, and a community centre nearby. Behind it, Billy, could just make out a burnt-out car.

'Why aren't those kids in school?' he asked.

Harry shrugged.

'And shouldn't the council tidy this area up?'

'We do our best, Billy, but a lot of the people here don't care enough to help themselves.'

Billy looked sceptical, but he wasn't going to argue with Harry about this, He was still trying to grapple with the notion of the 'payment-in-kind'. He couldn't believe that it was what he thought.

They pulled up outside the house. There was no sign of Sarah Wilson. Harry looked at his watch. They were five minutes early.

Ten minutes later there was still no sign. Harry was getting impatient. Suddenly, Sarah came running around the corner. She was out of breath.

'I'm really sorry, I had to leave the kids with my mum, and the youngest was playing up.'

Without replying or acknowledging her Harry pulled the keys out of his pocket and opened the front door. Billy and Sarah followed him inside.

It was a recently renovated house complete with gas central heating. There was a basic kitchen but no cooker or fridge. Sarah said that some of her friends could help her out with second-hand equipment and furniture.

There was a large overgrown garden at the back and a swing hiding in the undergrowth. Sarah approved.

'It's lovely,' she exclaimed.

'Excellent,' Harry said.

He passed her a tenancy agreement, which she signed and then handed her a set of keys but, thinking Billy wasn't looking, made a point of taking one off the keyring and putting it in his pocket as she watched.

'It's all yours. Here are the keys.'

Billy was horrified. Sarah just looked resigned. And then Billy decided on his act of defiance. As Harry and he walked out of the building, he pretended that he'd dropped something and went back inside for it.

He found Sarah sitting on a windowsill, looking disconsolate.

'I haven't much time,' he said. 'I saw what he did. I really don't approve. Are you free tomorrow? I'll meet you here at three o'clock and we'll fix this.'

She nodded, and Billy rushed out to chauffeur Harry away from the estate.

On arriving back at the town hall, Billy enlisted Sue in his little scheme. He really had no other choice – without her he no idea how to organise what he needed to do. She confirmed his suspicion that tenants didn't have to pay a key deposit for council houses.

Sue gave him the number of the council's maintenance department and advised him to tell them he was acting on Harry's behalf.

'These repairs can take days, so you need to tell them that it's an emergency,' she said. 'Tell them they need to be there at the time you specify. They'll do it if they think it's for Councillor O'Leary.'

Billy did as he had been instructed.

* * *

At three o'clock on the dot, a council van pulled up outside Sarah's house with Billy in the passenger seat. Sarah was waiting outside, alone.

Billy directed the council workman to the house and watched him change all the locks. When he had finished, Billy handed the keys to Sarah. She stared at him wide-eyed

'They're all there,' he said. 'I haven't kept any back and nobody else has a copy. Just so you know I wasn't party to this outrage. I'm determined that old letch shouldn't get away with it.'

Sarah kissed him on the cheek.

'Thank you,' she said.

Billy watched her lock up as they drove away. This was one battle Harry had lost.

23
Amber and Jeanie

The Prince Albert had been closed for half an hour and already everything had been washed and put away. The pub was set up for the following day's lunchtime session and Frank had gone upstairs to get an early night.

The girls were either with clients or out for the night. Jeanie was relaxing with a glass of white wine after a busy shift. She was enjoying the solitude for the first time that day.

Outside she could hear a group of men, slightly the worse for drink, kicking a can around the street. The lights of passing vehicles illuminated the darkened pub. There was only a solitary lamp switched on by her table, just enough for her to see where she had put down her glass.

Jeanie could hear the faint sound of classical music drifting into the pub from the living quarters upstairs. Frank was in the habit of putting on a record to unwind.

Beethoven, Tchaikovsky, Brahms, Schubert, it could be any one of them. She had long ago discovered that Frank was not really fussed what he listened to. He was just not into modern music and preferred the classics.

She often thought that she should offer to play for him, bring in the violin she was rediscovering at night school, and maybe have a go at some Vivaldi or, more likely, play some folk music on it, treating it like a fiddle.

Perhaps she should rattle out a tune on the pub piano, Some Chopin or Bach, or perhaps a boogie medley to excite the regulars. She was grateful to her mother for encouraging her to take up playing music again.

When she was younger, she had been bored by it. The practise sessions had been hard work and she wanted to enjoy herself. But now that she was older, she appreciated how a talent such as hers could open doors and win friends.

Jeanie sipped her wine and smiled. It was getting late and

her thoughts were beginning to sound delirious even to herself. Maybe she should order her taxi and go home.

Just then she heard voices. It was Amber escorting one of her clients out of the pub. She hadn't bothered to get dressed but wore a short nylon robe that showed off more of her legs than was decent in mixed company.

She led a middle-aged man to the door. He was wearing denim jeans, a T shirt and denim jacket. Jeanie noticed the wedding ring on his left hand. She shrugged and went back to her wine as Amber unbolted the door and then locked it again behind her client.

Turning around to head back upstairs, she was startled to see Jeanie sitting there.

'Are you alright, kid?' she asked.

'Yes, sure, just having a breather before I go home. Why don't you join me? We haven't had a proper chat for ages.'

Amber agreed. She sat down at the table while Jeanie filled a second glass with wine and topped up her own. Amber took a long swig. Jeanie sighed and handed her the bottle.

'Maybe we should finish it,' she said.

'Yes. What you been up to, Jeanie? I keep meaning to ask but then get distracted.'

'Oh, this and that, been on a couple of dates with a bloke, helped Billy buy a suit, visited his brother in hospital, been serving here.'

Amber focussed in on what really mattered.

'What bloke, and why haven't you told me this before?'

'I didn't really have a chance. His name's Ian O'Leary. He manages Baker's in town. Real smart, very expensive taste in clothes and do you know what Amber, he's the spitting image of Don Johnson, well, Don Johnson maybe fifteen years ago, anyway.'

'What?! The guy from Miami Vice? Noooo! How cool is that? Does he have a posh sports car as well?'

'Alas no, I keep dropping hints, but he never picks up on them.'

'How long have you been seeing him?'

'We've been on three dates so far. But I don't know. He's not one of us. Money and looks aren't everything.'

Amber took another swig of wine. 'They help.'

'Yes, they sure do. But I always get the feeling that he looks down on me, wants to change me, make me more like him.'

'Where's he from?'

'Now that's the point. His dad's leader of the council. He went to boarding school and university. What does he know about living hand-to-mouth on a council estate? You'd never find him in here, apart from if he was looking for me.'

'Yes, I can see that.'

Jeanie hesitated as if she were summoning up courage to ask for something important.

'Listen Amber… you and Billy? Are you… you know?'

Amber laughed.

'God, no! He's like my younger brother. We talk a lot but that's it.'

'How's Paul?' Jeanie asked, changing the subject.

'Not good, love. Eighteen is very young to go into an adult prison for a ten stretch.'

'I know. Is he holding up?'

'Not really. It turns out he had some drugs to sell, the week before he hit that bloke and killed him. Nobody knows what happened to them, not even Paul. Now the bloke who gave them to him wants paying. Two-grand in all, and he's got some people in the prison who are turning the screw.'

'What's he going to do?'

'I don't know. I went and saw him last week. He's desperate.'

'Have you thought of asking Frank?'

'I can't. You know what he thinks of drugs and dealers.'

'But he might do it for you?'

'I can't ask him, Jeanie.'

'Would you like me to ask?'

Amber cast her a pleading look. 'Would you?'

'Of course, give me a few days to catch him in the right mood.'

Amber reached over to hug her.

'So, why are you asking about Billy?' she said suspiciously.

'Oh, no reason, I just wanted to know… you know… what you two had going on.'

'Are you interested in him then?' she asked beaming, knowing she had Jeanie on the run.

'He's a nice bloke.'

'Yes?'

'Well… we sort of got it on a bit.'

Amber laughed, before assuming a mock tone of indignation.

'Jeanie Carter, I'm shocked! Preying on innocent young country boys like that. You should know better.'

Jeanie blushed but Amber wasn't finished.

'I thought you had a rule on not getting involved with workmates?'

'I do, but come on Amber, it's hardly been a temptation all these years. All the other people I've worked with behind the bar have been girls. There's you four and Frank. Unless I switched to the other side and started chasing girls, it isn't as if my workmates have been queuing up to shag me.'

'I'll do threesomes you know, if you pay enough.'

Jeanie threw a beer mat at her. It missed.

'So, tell me what went down?'

'Do you promise not to tease Billy about it? I don't want him thinking that we've been gossiping behind his back.'

'As if, I think he'd be surprised if we hadn't.'

'He's quite sweet. isn't he?' Jeanie asked looking for validation rather than a judgement.

'If you like that sort of thing; me I prefer big butch men with lots of money.'

'Are you going to take this seriously?'

'Sorry.' Amber was beaming again. Jeanie could tell she was really enjoying making her uncomfortable.

'Well, we went to buy him a suit for this job he's got with

the council. I went along to make sure he didn't come away with anything too dorky. And we got chatting. One thing led to another and we kissed. Well we kissed a few times.'

'Is that it? Who are you? Mary Poppins? Was there no ripping-off clothes and all-night shagging?'

'No, of course not, you know I like to take my time with these things. And for fuck's sake stop smirking.'

'Sorry, I can't help it. What about Don Johnson?'

'What about him?'

'Well are you going to keep seeing him? I hope you're not going to hurt my Billy by playing the field.'

She was only being half-playful. Jeanie knew how protective Amber was of her brother, and if Billy was a surrogate then the same rule would apply to him, too.

'No, I've been upfront with them both. Ian and I went for a walk along the harbour wall this afternoon. It was a nice day and I love listening to the waves rock the boats against each other, that creaking sound and the occasional clang of a bell always makes me think I'm in a movie. I told him about Billy then.'

'How did he take it?'

'Not too well, actually – said it was my decision and all that, but I could see he wasn't happy. He'll just have to live with it. I just need time to sort my head out. I'm not going to be pressured into making a decision.'

Amber stroked Jeanie's arm. 'Don't you worry chick; it'll work out. And I'm here for you, especially if you've got some good gossip.'

Just then there was a sound at the side door as somebody tried to open it with a key. Amber looked at Jeanie.

'Is Billy out?'

'I don't know, but there's nobody else who has a key.'

Amber went to look and came back with Billy.

'Look at what the cat has dragged in,' she said. 'Do you want a drink, Billy?'

'Sure, why not.'

Amber went and got a glass and poured him some wine.

As she put the bottle back on the table, Jeanie indicated that she needed to adjust her robe. Amber smiled and did as she was bidden.

'Where have you been?' Jeanie asked.

'With Harry O'Leary at some function or other, God knows why he needs me there. I think I'm some sort of trophy, "look at me, I've got an assistant" thing.'

'Was it boring, love?' Amber asked massaging his shoulders.

Jeanie threw her a dirty look. Suddenly she felt a surge of jealousy. She couldn't help herself, but nor could she understand why. Amber responded by deepening her massage and sticking her tongue out behind Billy's back. Billy eased his shoulders back as she kneaded them, clearly enjoying it.

'Yes, it was tedious; he even had me passing round the bloody nibbles.'

'Ah, that's evil,' Amber said massaging his shoulders even more intently.

Jeanie stared at her disapprovingly

'So, what have you two been gossiping about?' Billy asked.

Jeanie jumped in quickly.

'Nothing, nothing at all, just catching up really.'

'Oh?'

'Jeanie has been telling me that she supervised your suit buying.' She stood back to take a good look at him. 'I have to say it's really smart. Have you ever thought of modelling, Billy?'

Jeanie was getting quite annoyed now.

'If you two are going to keep flirting like this, then I think you need to go upstairs. It's positively indecent.'

Amber gave her a wicked smile. Billy seemed oblivious.

'In fact, it's getting quite late, I'd better order my taxi,' she added, heading to the back room. Amber stopped massaging Billy's shoulders and went and sat opposite him at the table. She finished off her glass of wine and adjusted her robe again.

'So how is our beloved council leader?' she asked.

'The man is a lecherous pig,' Billy asserted.

Jeanie came back into the room.

'Is Harry O'Leary giving you hassle?' she asked.

'Sort of, I'll tell you both about it again. I'm quite tired now, and I've got a lot on tomorrow.'

Jeanie's taxi arrived. She embraced them both and made her escape. Billy finished off his wine and turned towards the stairs. Amber stood up too and rested her hand against his cheek.

She spoke softly and with a hint of sadness in her voice.

'Are you coping, country boy? It's a rough old world out there and some of the people are fucking dodgy, not least in that council office.'

'Tell me about it. What about you Amber? You seem a bit down lately.'

'It's nothing, lover… nothing that can't be sorted.'

She hugged him.

'Are you finished for the night?' Billy asked.

'Yes, time to get some sleep I think.'

They walked together into the living quarters and up the stairs. They came to Amber's room first. She hugged him and went to go inside, thought better of it and turned around to face him.

'Listen Billy, about Jeanie...'

'Yes, what about her?'

'Give her some space. Don't hassle her or come on all possessive. She'll see sense eventually and choose you over the posh guy.'

'To be honest, Amber, I just want to hit the other bloke. Every time I think about him with her, I just grow even more confused and angry.'

'Well, don't. She won't appreciate it. Listen to your little 'sister'. If you play this cool, then it will work itself out.'

'Do you think?'

'Yes, I do.'

She walked over and kissed him on the cheek. He stared after her, as she went into her room and closed the door behind her, before ascending the stairs to his own room, deep in thought.

24
Party Politics

Despite being late in the season, the Saturday of John Baker's party proved to be one of the best days of the year. The sun was shining, and people were walking around town in shirt sleeves.

Billy arrived at Baker's house at midday as instructed. He was shown to the pool area where there was a makeshift bar set up. Gavin Phillips was supervising the party arrangements, he handed Billy some money.

'I think this is what we agreed for your afternoon's work. You'll be based out here ensuring everybody is kept plied with drink,' he told Billy. 'Guests should start arriving from around two o'clock, so make yourself at home. Familiarise yourself with the house so that you can serve wherever you're needed.'

Billy acknowledged the instruction, the opportunity to look around this big house was a bonus he hadn't expected.

To the rear of the pool area was a separate building that turned out to be a huge games room complete with full-size snooker table, pool table and a card table, all overlooked by a large wooden cross.

A large set of French doors allowed access to the pool area. He headed towards them and into a substantial sitting room. An enormous sideboard adorned with china ornaments took up almost the whole of one wall.

Opposite hung yet another cross, but this one was massive, complete with a lifelike enamel statue of Christ, head bowed down, blood pouring from his side. Billy thought it might look more at home in a church than somebody's sitting room.

He wandered through a whole series of rooms, each dominated by similar iconography. The whole house was a homage to the Catholic faith. Billy would need to go to a monastery to see so many similarly decorated rooms.

He noticed a downstairs toilet and decided to check it out; sure enough, it featured yet another religious icon. This time it was a statue of the Virgin Mary…there to observe the wine turning back into water no doubt.

He went upstairs. There were five bedrooms and one large bathroom, which was the size of his brother's bedsit. He peeked inside one of the bedrooms. It contained a huge four-poster bed overlooked by another statue and cross. Billy could just make out the entrance to an en-suite bathroom.

At the end of the corridor was one last door. It was locked, maybe a cupboard, he thought. He went back downstairs and into the study. Baker was sitting behind the desk, writing.

'Oh, sorry I was looking for the way back to the pool area.'

He looked up.

'Billy, isn't it? Welcome to my home. The pool area is through the sitting room. Turn left and through the second door.'

'Thank you.'

'You may want to go through the first door, however, it's the kitchen. You can pick up ice there and some mixers.'

'Thank you, Mr Baker.'

But Baker wasn't listening. He had gone back to his writing.

Billy went into the kitchen to pick up a bucket of ice and a collection of mixers. He placed them into a small fridge by the makeshift bar and sat down to await the first guests.

Half an hour later, Harry turned up. Gavin Phillips had gone to fetch him; Baker had insisted on it due to Harry's known drink problem. They were closely followed by Councillors Eamon Jacobs and Sam Healy.

Billy was kept busy serving drinks as more guests arrived, local businessmen Sidney Nicholson, Stephen Thomas and Councillor Fred Harris. Then, much to Billy's irritation, in walked Ian O'Leary and Inspector Oliver Anderson. They didn't look as if they were together.

He had not counted on both of his nemeses turning up. Fortunately, O'Leary junior had clearly forgotten who he was. Oliver Anderson ignored him completely, which was a relief.

Billy wondered if the inspector even remembered him; he rather hoped not. But he was a policeman and the chances were that he could recall every minute of their last encounter. Billy's cheek tingled as he relived the blow he'd received at the policeman's hand.

Another cohort of councillors turned up. Billy recognised them from various meetings and events he had attended with Harry. They all had a thirst on them that only a free bar could cure.

He was so busy serving drinks that he didn't notice the girls arrive. Amber, Kitty, Heather and Serena tumbled into the pool area like a series of whirlwinds. They were laughing, chatting, greeting each of the guests like old friends.

It was then that he realised that it was an all-male affair. None of the guests had brought any partners with them. Clearly, it wasn't just drink and food that John Baker was treating them to.

Some of the men had already stripped down to swimming trunks and were soaking in the pool. It was a hot afternoon and Billy half-wished he could join them.

The four girls queued up at the bar for a drink. Heather and Serena pecked him on the cheek, Amber winked and hugged him.

'I see that Jeanie's other fella is here,' she said. 'He really does look like Don Johnson. For fuck's sake, Billy, don't say anything to her, she'll think you're snitching on him. As far as you're concerned, he was never here.'

She took her drink and joined the other girls who were flirting with the guests. Heather was sitting on Fred Harris' lap. Kitty was dancing with Jacobs who, for a man in his mid-seventies seemed remarkably sprightly.

Billy saw that Anderson was in the pool alongside Ian O'Leary and Gavin Phillips. The inspector was signalling to the girls to join in. Amber cast a glance his way and then rounded up the other three.

The four girls then stripped off their clothes and jumped in. There was a great deal of splashing and laughter as the swimmers larked about. It was the first-time Billy has seen any of them naked.

As the afternoon wore on, more and more guests joined the girls in the water. Others sat and chatted at the poolside. Harry was in deep conversation with Baker and Sidney Nicholson. He stayed there fully dressed, in his suit, pouring drink after drink down his throat.

Some of the girls disappeared with chosen guests, only to reappear half an hour later. Billy saw Anderson leave with at least two of them, only to reappear after a suitable interval smoothing his moustache and demanding more alcohol.

The party was turning into a marathon, a Roman-style orgy for the rich and powerful. Billy was relieved when the catering company turned up with food, giving him a chance for a break.

The four girls, now all wearing robes, joined in with other guests in demolishing the extensive buffet that had been laid out for them. Billy grabbed some sandwiches, a pasty, a greasy leg of chicken and some fruit and went back to the bar area to consume it. Amber joined him.

'Can't stay long, chick,' she said. 'I'm being paid to service the guests not the hired help.'

Billy smiled at her.

'That's okay, love. You need to do what you do. I hope you're getting paid well to look after these zombies.'

She kissed him on the cheek.

'Don't you start to get jealous now, your time will come. These middle-aged has-beens cheating on their wives don't deserve your contempt.'

Fred Harris came over and took her hand.

'Come and join us over here,' he said.

Amber stroked Billy's arm as she stood up, took Harris's hand and joined a group of councillors. Minutes later she was sitting on his lap and feeding him pieces of fruit.

Billy poured himself some tonic water, added plenty of ice and loosened his collar. Baker must have had a direct line to the weather gods to enjoy such lovely weather so late in the year, he thought.

As the evening drew on, it grew dark and the party moved indoors. The pool was now deserted, and Billy was operating the bar from the drinks cabinet next to the sideboard in the living room, constantly conscious of being overlooked by the huge portrayal of the crucified Jesus Christ.

There was no sign of the girls. Harry was slumped in a corner, much the worse for wear. His son was sitting next to him chatting to one of the councillors.

Billy didn't know whether Ian had availed himself of female company. But then why would he, looking like that? He was probably fighting off girls. He had no need to pay for them or share freebies with others.

In need of the toilet, Billy decided to use the upstairs bathroom away from the eyes of the Virgin Mary. He was rather shocked when he discovered that this facility too, also had its fair share of icons.

As he left, he noticed that the door at the end of the hall was ajar. Billy's curiosity was aroused. He padded quietly down the hallway. Standing outside, he could hear a man moaning.

Looking through the crack in the door he could just make out Baker standing naked, feet rooted to the floor against a wooden post, both hands secured to a cross bar in the form of a cruciform shape.

Kitty was kneeling, naked in front of him, his manhood in her mouth. Billy looked away quickly. This was not an image he wanted to take away with him. He had thought that the religious iconography in the house was there to underline Baker's faith, but now he could see there was a sexual angle as well.

Still a bit stunned by this insight, Billy went downstairs in search of Amber. He wondered whether she was in one of the bedrooms but didn't dare risk looking for fear of what else he might find.

Ian was helping his father into a taxi. Billy nodded to him as he went past but the greeting went unacknowledged.

The pool area was deserted but he could hear voices from the games room. Entering, he could see Amber and Heather wearing robes and not a great deal else, surrounded by a group of councillors.

Amber, snooker cue in hand, was taking bets as to whether she could pot a red at the far end of the table. Heather was sitting on Sam Healy's lap, his hand inside her robe, fondling her breast.

Amber stepped up to the table, expertly cued up the white ball and sent it hurtling down the table. It hit the target red ball, which rocketed into the left-hand corner pocket. She let out a little whoop and raised her arm in triumph.

One of the councillors hugged her, lifting her robe as he did so, fondling her naked body beneath it. Billy had seen enough. He turned and went back into the pool area.

As he got to the French windows, he was conscious that there was somebody behind him. It was Amber.

'Hey, country boy, what's up?'

'This place is fucking awful, Amber. These men are meant to be upright citizens, trusted to run the town, but they're bunch of perverts.'

She sat him down next to the pool.

'That's the way it is, Billy boy. It's the way of the world. The power goes to their heads and they think they can get away with anything. So far they have.'

'It isn't right. Is it like this everywhere?'

'How the fuck would I know, Billy? It's how it is here. It's how Baker keeps the council in line. I wouldn't be surprised if he was filming the whole thing to blackmail them later.'

Billy looked around. He couldn't see any cameras. He

thought that a blackmail attempt was unlikely given Baker's own sexual peccadilloes.

Some guests were starting to leave. Kitty and Serena had returned downstairs and had put their clothes back on. The party was beginning to break up.

'Where are your clothes?' he asked Amber.

'I think they're indoors,' she answered. 'The robes were waiting for us in the downstairs loo, so we left our clothes there.'

Billy took her hand and led her indoors, she let him watch as she got dressed. There was no point in her assuming any false modesty after the afternoon's shenanigans.

'I'll come back with the four of you to the Prince Albert,' Billy announced. 'My work here is done and the sooner I'm away from this place the better.'

As they walked past the office, they heard voices. The door was slightly ajar, and Billy could make out the figures of Anderson and Phillips inside. He squinted to see better through the gap between the hinges.

Seeing what he was doing, Amber squatted down so she could watch, too.

The conversation between the men was becoming heated. Anderson was insisting that he could no longer have his officers ignore irregularities at Baker's nightclub. Phillips was insisting that he take instructions from him and Baker on how the establishment was policed.

'The thing is Ollie, you're already in too deep to walk away,' Phillips insisted. 'We're grateful for what you've done so far in helping us manage bad publicity, but we need your co-operation with the casino as well. We can't have you looking too closely at any drug dealing going on around the club in case we suffer more embarrassment and the new place is damaged in the backlash.'

'You mean that you don't want my men to cut off your alternative source of income,' Anderson insisted.

'I don't know what you mean.'

'Oh, come on, I know some of your bouncers are working with the dealers and that they wouldn't be able to get away with it unless you're taking a cut, too.

'That young boy you've got in charge of the club couldn't tell ecstasy from aspirin but even he would see something was wrong, if it wasn't for you covering the bouncer's tracks.

'And I think the odds are strong that you were behind the assault on that journalist as well. The alibi you gave for the bouncer was hardly convincing.'

Phillips had gone white. He didn't try to contest the charges.

'I'm betting, too, Gavin, that John has no idea what you're doing. You're acting the good cop in front of him, while ripping him and your customers off behind his back.'

'You're a fine one to talk about good cops,' Gavin shouted.

'Maybe, but unless you meet my price I'm going to walk away and leave you to it. No more protection, and maybe I'll drop hints to John if he asks why my officers are no longer turning a blind eye.'

Phillips was furious but said nothing. Instead he opened a drawer in Baker's desk, pulled out a large wad of notes and handed it to the policeman, who counted the cash and put it in his pocket.

Anderson smoothed his moustache and held out a hand.

'Nice doing business with you, Gavin.'

Before Billy could see or hear any more Amber was dragging him away.

'Come on,' she whispered urgently. 'You don't want them to see you.'

They managed to duck into the living room before the two men emerged. The other girls were waiting there for them.

'I've ordered a taxi.' Heather said. 'It should be here any minute.'

At that moment a horn sounded outside. The five of them headed for the front door. As they emerged from the living room, Billy saw Anderson saying his goodbyes to Baker.

The inspector looked up, saw Billy and glared. Billy nodded and followed the girls out to the waiting car.

25
Wake-up call

It was mid-morning the day after the party, and the sun was as bright and as strong as it had been the previous day. Harry had stirred once and then returned to his bed with a terrible headache.

The bedroom curtains were proving to be inadequate in restraining the bright sunlight, and he was finding it impossible to get back to sleep. He got up and pulled on a dressing gown.

The long wooden staircase was a bigger challenge, but he somehow negotiated it and found his way into the kitchen. Ian was sitting there reading a newspaper, a pot of coffee simmering on the stove. He put his newspaper down and poured his father a mug of black coffee. Harry grunted his gratitude and found a couple of aspirin to take with it.

'I hope you're feeling better,' Ian said. 'You were in a terrible state last night.'

'What of it?' Harry demanded.

'Nothing, nothing at all, I was just enquiring after your health.'

'Well, I am perfectly well as you can see. It'll be some time before you get your hands on my money, don't you worry.'

'God, you're grumpy this morning. What's come over you?'

Harry swallowed about half the coffee as he took a long hard look at his son. Ian got his looks from his mother's side of the family. Harry saw far too much of his ex-wife in Ian's face to be entirely comfortable in his company for too long.

'Why are you here, Ian? Your home is in town is it not?'

'Yes, it is Dad, and it's good to see you, too. I brought you home last night and stayed to make sure you were alright.'

Harry grunted again. He couldn't remember much of the

previous night at all.

'Oh, well, thank you for that.'

He reached for the coffee pot and poured himself another mugful. He was starting to feel human again.

'Why are you so grumpy anyway?'

'I don't know, Ian. Sometimes I just feel as if I've been around too long.'

'Sometimes Dad, it looks exactly like that.'

'And with that answer, I repeat my question, why are you here?'

'I'm here because I care for you, Dad, and I don't like the way that things are going in this town.'

'Really? You've got a good job, good contacts and if you cultivate John Baker properly, you'll go a long way.'

'I work for him, Dad. I don't owe him anything more than a day's work for a day's pay and nor do I intend to give him any more than that.'

'So, what's brought this on?'

'Seeing you last night; you and me at that disgusting orgy at Baker's house; watching all those councillors prostrate themselves at his altar; just the complete lack of dignity on the part of grown men who should know better.

'This town is a complete basket case, Dad, dominated by a corrupt elite. What's more, working at that club night after night and seeing some of the lowlifes who patronise it, I'm rapidly coming to the conclusion that you deserve each other.

'I came back here in good faith, I'm grateful that you got me a job, but I don't know how much longer I can stick it out.'

Harry emptied his coffee mug and walked over to the stove to refill it. It often took three or four cups to revive him after a heavy night. He was starting to feel a bit more alert. He decided to ignore his son's rant for now.

'Do you have plans then?'

'No, no plans at present. However, the club's getting out of control. I may be the manager but I'm not running it.

Baker's henchman, Gavin Phillips, is undermining me at every turn. The whole situation is becoming intolerable.'

'What's going on there then?'

'I suspect that a blind eye is being turned to drug dealing by certain bouncers in return for a cut, and that Phillips is protecting them.'

'Does John know this?'

'I don't know. My guess is that Phillips is ripping him off as well, but I can't prove anything.'

'That could explain why Gavin was so opposed to the council introducing a registration scheme for bouncers,' Harry said. 'It would have better regulated them and kept them under control. No wonder, if he's profiting from dealing.

'You should take your concerns to John.'

Ian was having none of it. He felt that his father was happy to just allow the abuses and corruption carry on uninterrupted, that it was too much trouble for him to change things. He also wondered just how deeply Harry had sunk into this cesspit of corruption.

'Do you think he really wants to know? He's far too pre-occupied with this new casino. He needs Phillips to oversee that for him. Given the choice between his right-hand-man and me, he'll choose Phillips every time.

'But if I have to try then I will. I'm not wedded to this job. If I decide to walk away from it then I'll go out with a bang and stir things up a bit. The rot is so deep in this town that it's beyond redemption anyway.'

Harry was determined not to bite. Instead, he tried to be sympathetic.

'It really isn't that bad, Ian.'

'Isn't it? You've just said yourself that you've been around too long. Do you really feel in control?'

'Ian, it isn't about control. Running Oldport is about partnership, about working with others. But that doesn't mean that the democratically elected council has handed over the town lock, stock and barrel to John Baker.

'If I want to say no to John then I will do so. But the decisions I take are made for the right reasons, in the best interests of Oldport.'

'And in your best interests as well.'

'I think you'd better explain that comment.'

'I will, it brings me to the other reason I'm here, the Inchfield Estate development.'

'What, that again? We've had that discussion already, Ian, there's no point raking it up again.'

'Far from it, Dad, I'm still upset at you using my name as a director.'

Harry stood up and started rooting in the fridge.

'Do we have any food in stock, I'm famished.'

'I don't know Dad; I don't live here remember.'

'I could have sworn there was a rasher of bacon left and some eggs. Ah, yes here they are.'

Harry went over to a cupboard, pulled out a frying pan and lit the gas stove. He poured some olive oil in the pan and started to swill it around over the flame.

He was aware of Ian watching as he placed the bacon in the pan and broke a couple of eggs next to them. The process only took a few minutes, but he hoped it was long enough to change the subject.

'Would you like something to eat?' he asked his son.

'No, thank you. I ate earlier and no amount of fussing over those eggs is going to make me change the subject.'

Harry addressed the issue directly.

'You signed the papers, Ian. You're a grown man. I was rather hoping you might take responsibility for your own actions.'

'And I do, but those papers were for a holding company, to manage the common areas on the existing Inchfield Estate. You told me that I was looking after your interests and enabling you to keep them at arms-length. I wasn't expecting a full-scale assault on the countryside in my name.'

'What can I say? John felt that it was easier to use the existing company rather than reinvent the wheel.'

'And you didn't see fit to inform me?'

'That wasn't my job, Ian. I'm not a director of the company remember. In any case, what's your problem? It's a business deal, you'll get a share of the profits.'

'Will I? My understanding was that I am your nominee.'

'Yes, you will, because I will give you part of my share in payment for you looking after my interests.'

'Okay. But that's not really my point.'

Harry scooped the bacon and eggs onto a plate and started to eat them. He spoke in between mouthfuls.

'What *is* your point Ian?'

'I just think that the people protesting against this development have a strong case.'

'You've signed up to the green lobby, have you?'

'And why not, Dad? Do you know, I went for a walk the other week with a girl I met at the club? We went down to Inchfield Cove. What a beautiful area.

'She'd never been there. She was born and brought up in this town and has barely left its boundaries. She's never walked the coast or the hills and fields around us.

'And I found myself thinking that if I can open her eyes to the natural beauty around us just by going on one walk, then others could have their eyes opened, too.

'But no, because by the time they set out on their walk of self-discovery, it will be covered in houses and tarmac roads. We won't have anything left for them to discover.'

'It's a small extension to the estate, Ian. We're not recreating New York out there.'

'It may not be the end, but it's the beginning of the end. Tomorrow you build fifty houses, the year after another fifty and then a hundred and before you know it, Oldport is a minor city with two hundred thousand inhabitants and all our green spaces, the hills and the fields will be built over.

'Our streams and rivers will be culverted underground and coves like Inchfield will have a new concrete promenade and a shop selling ice creams and inflatable rings.

'Where do we stop? Isn't it the job of the council to place

limits on this sort of thing? Aren't they meant to have a masterplan which protects our natural environment?'

Harry went to speak, but Ian was in full flow.

'The answer is yes, they should. But our councillors are too preoccupied with making a fast buck and getting their end away with a couple of prostitutes at John Baker's mansion to care about such things.

'Oldport Council is letting this town down, Dad, and I'm embarrassed to have my name on those company articles. For fuck's sake, I'm embarrassed to have my father as leader of a council which behaves like that.' He sat down and stared directly at his father, more out of sorrow than anger.

'Have you finished?' Harry asked. He was tired of this conversation, of having to justify himself to people, most of all his own son, and he was losing patience with those who were trying to undermine his grand scheme for the town.

'Yes, I've had my say.'

'Look Ian, you're young and idealistic. I was the same at your age. As you get older, you'll see that the world doesn't operate like that.'

Ian was outraged.

'Is that the best you have? *Your* world may not operate like that, but other towns do. That's what I mean. Oldport is a small town with a small-town mentality.

'People like Baker stay here because they are big fish in a small pond. He can control things in a way he couldn't do in a city like Southampton or Portsmouth.

'And your council is letting him get away with it.'

'It's progress, Ian. We live in the 1980s now, the country is starting to come out of recession. People need jobs and places to live and if we don't give it to them then they'll go elsewhere. Can't you see that?'

'Yes, I can but there are other ways to achieve your aim without trampling over our natural environment and without handing people like Baker the keys to the council.'

Harry could see that he was not going to convince his son of his point of view. Besides, it was a Sunday, he had a hangover, albeit one that was fading, he needed to get dressed, read the newspapers and go to evening Mass.

'You've made your point Ian. I've listened and we're going to have to agree to disagree.'

'I wasn't expecting to convert you to my point of view, Dad. I just wanted you to understand why I have to leave.'

'When are you leaving?' Harry tried to disguise his surprise.

'I don't know. It will be soon. I'll come and say goodbye first.'

'And what about this girl, won't she want you to stay and help her explore more of our natural beauty?'

Harry was grasping at straws.

'I don't know. I'll give her the option, but I don't think she's that interested in me. We're very different people and she's seeing somebody else as well. She has to decide she wants to be with me before she has the right to ask me to stay in Oldport.'

'I'm surprised, Ian. You said you met her in the club, but just before that you were berating your customers as 'lowlifes'. What's the attraction? Aren't you too good for her?' Ian snorted.

'Yes, ever the politician, twisting my words. Jeanie's special, she's not like the rest. She's got a brain as well as looks. I believe that I can help her rise above her upbringing.'

'So, you want to change her? Do you know how many relationships have foundered on that rock? Perhaps you need to take a long hard look at yourself before you start condemning me, my friends and the town you were born in.'

'God, you're a real piece of work, aren't you, Dad? Don't start making this all about me. I'll live the life I want to, just leave me out of your schemes in the future.' He moved towards the door. Harry stood up as if to try and prevent him leaving.

'Just one thing before you go.' Ian stopped and turned back to look at his father. 'Please don't let these things come between us. You're still my son and I love you, imperfect as both of us may be.'

Ian, nodded, and the two men embraced.

'I'll let you know when I'm ready to leave,' he said.

Harry put his dirty plate in the sink and went back upstairs to shower as his son let himself out.

26
The Backlash

It was Simon's first day back at work and he had been assigned the late shift. After receiving the good wishes of the other staff, along with some gentle ribbing, he had been called in to the editor's office, where Jerome had made it clear to him that the late start was not a concession to Simon's need to ease his way back in.

'There's a public meeting on the Inchfield Estate', he said between drags on his cigarette, 'and I want you there to report on it.'

'Are we expecting trouble?' Simon asked.

'Only if Harry O'Leary turns up.'

'I can't see that happening, but what's the point? Surely, it's already settled. The planning permission has been given, there's no way back.'

'Yes, I agree, but the locals think differently. I've had the chairman of the residents' association on the phone to me. He says they're going to try and have part of the site registered as a village green. If they're successful, then they'll kill the development stone dead.'

'That'll be interesting. Can they do that?'

'Who knows? I'm not a lawyer, but they think they have a shot so we're going to report it.'

'They're not letting this go then. It could get really messy.'

'If it gets that far, yes, but let's see what transpires. They're well organised, have legal advice and funding, so it may well be a goer.'

The afternoon flew by as Simon caught up with the office gossip, and fielded inquiries about his health. He was still a bit sore and was being careful not to make any sudden movements.

When the time came, he headed for the Inchfield Community Centre. The place was packed. There were well over 200 people present, including the ward councillors and the local MP.

All the instigators of the development were absent. John Baker, Gavin Phillips and Harry O'Leary were nowhere to be seen. Simon thought that for once they had decided to keep a low profile.

He moved to the front of the room to get a good view and had started to settle in the third row, when he saw a familiar face. It was Billy. There was a seat vacant next to his brother, so he took it.

He turned to him and whispered, 'What the fuck are you doing here?'

Billy was delighted to see him.

'Hey Si, how are you? I hadn't realised you were coming back to work so soon.'

'I'm much better Bro, but why are you here? This is a long way from the Prince Albert.'

'Yes, I know. I'm spying for Harry. He daren't show his face here, so he sent me to take notes.'

'Well for fuck's sake don't let on to this lot, they'll lynch you.'

'Yeah, well I'm not going to own up to being with Harry, am I?'

'Hey, how's Jeanie? Are you two getting it on yet?'

Billy laughed, 'We're taking it slowly. Why do you ask?'

'Well she clearly likes you otherwise she wouldn't have come with you to see me in the hospital and at my bedsit. You could do a lot worse.'

'They sat up as the meeting started, both brothers scribbling away furiously as the MP and then the ward councillors addressed the audience.

Billy noted that this was the third or fourth such meeting. The others had been held in the run-up to the planning committee. A local resident explained that Inchfield Acre, which was the main part of the new development, had been used for years for informal football games, dog walking, blackberry picking and many other pursuits.

He said that this might be enough to register it as a village green under the 1965 Commons Registration Act.

A couple of the audience members got a bit carried away, alleging corruption in high places and questioning why Harry had been allowed to take part in the decision when his son was a director of the company.

The resident tried to calm things down by suggesting that this was a matter for the local police. He attempted to focus the meeting back onto the application for a village green.

'I think I'm going to have to be careful how I report that rant,' Simon whispered to Billy.

'Yeah, I'm just giving Harry the edited highlights,' Billy responded

As the meeting broke up the MP made a point of seeking out Simon to ensure that he would be quoted. He then joined the councillors in chatting to as many residents as possible.

Billy had hung back to get an opportunity to talk to his brother properly. Simon strolled out clutching his notebook and slapped him on the back.

'Do you fancy sharing a taxi to the Prince Albert?' he said. 'I feel like I haven't had a drink in weeks.'

Billy beamed.

'No need,' he said, 'I've got Harry O'Leary's car.'

Fifteen minutes later, Billy had parked outside the pub. As the two brothers walked in, they were greeted by several of the regulars, pleased to see Simon back on his feet.

'It's good to see you back,' Frank said, refusing to let him pay for the drink he just ordered. 'Perhaps we should arrange an escort for you so that you get home safely tonight.'

'I'm sure that won't be necessary, Frank. In fact, I may steal Harry O'Leary's car while Billy has his back turned.'

Frank laughed.

'It's a very nice car.'

'Yes,' Simon said, 'a Rover 800, two litre-engine, leather seats and five gears. It was a very comfortable ride back here.'

'Never really got into cars myself,' Frank responded. 'But I know a good ride when I see one.'

Just then Jeanie appeared at the bar. She had been serving other customers and hadn't had time to join in the greetings.

'Well you took your time coming back here,' she scolded. 'You've been out of hospital for over a week-and-a-half and only now you come in to see us. What's the attraction of that scuzzy bedsit of yours that you couldn't try and be a bit more sociable?'

'Well, I do apologise, Ms Carter. Have the Prince Albert's profits taken a nosedive while I've been away?'

'And some,' Frank interjected.

Jeanie kissed Simon on the cheek.

'It's good to have you back among the living,' she said.

Simon took a long slow swig from his pint and wiped his mouth with the back of his hand.

'Now that's more like it. Believe me Jeanie, you may have missed me, but I missed this place more. Thank God, I can drink again now I've finished with those painkillers.'

'Good, then we can expect to see you back here regularly.'

'You can, and I now have an extra incentive.'

'Oh, yes?'

'Well, I need to keep an eye on you and my little brother,' he teased.

Jeanie bristled a bit and then smiled.

'Why Simon that bump to the head did more damage than any of us imagined. You appear to be hallucinating. Allow me to assist you to your seat.'

She indicated in Billy's direction. Simon smiled knowingly. He started to move over to Billy when Jeanie called him back. She was holding half a pint of lager.

'Aren't you forgetting something?' she asked. 'Your brother hasn't got a drink.'

'Do you think that's wise?' he asked, taking the glass. 'After all, he has to drive me home in Harry's car.'

Simon joined Billy at a table near the door and handed

him the half pint. Billy looked up and took the lager from his brother.

'Just got one thing to say Simon, stop teasing me and Jeanie.'

'Of course, sorry if I went a bit too far. So how is working for Harry O'Leary going?'

'It's interesting.'

Billy wasn't giving anything away.

'Is that it, just interesting? This is Mr Oldport we're talking about here, a man who can shape the destiny of an entire town, a giant in town hall politics.'

'I'm not allowed to talk about it,' Billy said. 'Besides aren't you off duty?'

'I'm never off duty, Bro. Come on you can spill the beans, you know you want to.'

'Not while you have your reporter's hat on, no.'

'I guess you've been party to some interesting conversations,' Simon tried to press the point.

'I may have been, but I've also signed a confidentiality clause, so I really can't talk about it.'

Simon took another drink of beer, Billy followed suit.

'So, how are you feeling, Si, after your first day back?'

'I'm feeling quite tired actually, and I still get twinges of pain in my ribs, but otherwise I'm up for it.

'Do you know, I actually missed going to council meetings when I was laid up.'

'Well you're welcome to them. I tried to sit through the licensing committee for the new casino but had to leave in case I started snoring.'

'How is that place coming along?'

'I heard they're planning a big opening in a few weeks' time. Will you be there with your Press hat on?'

'I don't know. It isn't normally my beat, but Jerome may send me anyway just to keep them on their toes. Will *you* be there?'

'That depends on Harry. That bouncer may be around, and Gavin Phillips. You should keep away from him. He's one very dodgy bloke.'

'Yes, I discovered that for myself. I still think he was behind the attack on me.'

'You're not the only one. I was working at a party at John Baker's house on Saturday and I overheard a conversation between Phillips and Inspector Anderson.

'Anderson virtually accused Phillips of orchestrating the attack on you and providing an unconvincing alibi for the bouncer.'

'Did he admit it?'

'No, of course not, but he did hand Anderson a wad of money, hush money most probably.'

'So, Baker and his henchman have not only bought the council but the local police as well.'

'Yes, it very much looks like that.'

'The bastards!'

'Can you use any of this in the paper?'

'No, not without proof, and why would Jerome risk it? He knows what's going on as much as we do but he's tied down by solicitors, and the owners are twitchy about losing council advertising revenue. But give me the right story and I'm sure we'll run with it.'

'Maybe you need to concentrate on doing that then,' Billy said sharply.

'I wish. What do you think I've been doing for the last few years? Anyway, what does it matter to you? You've hardly been in this town for two minutes and you're working for the enemy.'

'That may be so, Si, but it's getting personal. That bloody policeman is a thug and what they did to you isn't on.'

'What about Harry O'Leary?'

'Do you know I started off thinking he was a victim, but he's as guilty as the rest of them. He abuses his power, both to enrich himself and to mistreat others.'

'This town is built on the abuse of power, Bro. O'Leary and Baker have been doing it for nearly twenty years according to Jerome.'

'Yes, and they've pulled in most of the other councillors into their schemes.'

Simon was conscious of another figure behind him, He turned around and saw Jeanie. She was holding half a lager and smoking a cigarette.

'I'm on a break,' she said. 'What are you two talking about?'

'The abuse of power,' Simon said, 'or how O'Leary and Baker have fucked up this town.'

'Sounds heavy, time to change the subject.'

She walked past Simon and sat on Billy's lap. He looked a bit surprised.

'What would you like to talk about?' Billy asked.

'Well, my sweet, it's Frank's birthday in two weeks' time, so I thought we might have a little celebration.'

'I see that this is becoming a private conversation,' Simon said.

'Don't be silly,' Jeanie retorted. She got off Billy and pulled up a chair.

'Now let's talk about a party.'

27
Make or Break

Jeanie had come to a decision.

She sat in their usual High Street café drinking coffee and eating chocolate cake. There was no need to torture herself by waiting for Ian to turn up before ordering the cake, so she had taken the plunge as soon as she sat down.

The cake also proved a useful distraction; it stopped her from clock-watching. Nevertheless, she looked up every now and again to check the time, fifteen minutes and counting. He was late as usual.

At that moment, the door opened and Ian entered, breathless. He had been running. Jeanie frowned at him.

'You'll be late for your own funeral,' she scolded him.

'I'm sorry,' Ian said. 'I got held up at the club again.'

The waitress came over and took his order, a coffee, and a refill for Jeanie. He leant over and kissed Jeanie on the lips.

'I don't have much time I'm afraid. I need to be there to supervise the refurbishment of Baker's. It's a really busy time.'

'Yes, I'm sorry to drag you away.'

'Don't be. I'm glad to be able to get out for a bit. And you're always a sight for sore eyes.'

She smiled and then put on a more serious face.

'We need to talk,' she said.

'Oh God! That old chestnut. I was half expecting it.'

She placed her hand on his arm.

'You're a lovely bloke, Ian, but it isn't working for me. No, that isn't it. I'm starting to talk in clichés. The thing is, I fancy the pants off you but we're too different. You know you could never cope with my world and I certainly can't relate to yours.'

'And then there is Billy?' he asked.

'Yes, I feel I'm getting much closer to him. It wouldn't be fair to him or to you to keep up this arrangement. I had to make a choice.'

Ian looked upset. She took his hand,

'It really isn't you,' she said.

'Yes, I know. I'm sorry. The truth is I've been thinking about leaving Oldport, but that doesn't lessen the shock. I'm very fond of you.'

'You've been thinking of leaving Oldport?' Now she was intrigued.

'Yes, I've had enough of this place. I had it out with my father on Sunday. I told him what I thought of his council and the way they run this town.'

'Wow, what did he say?'

'Oh, the usual bullshit, but the point is that I told him to his face. You helped to open my eyes that day in Inchfield Cove when you said I had to stand up to him and to Baker, and all the others who are ruining this town.'

She grasped his hand tighter.

'The thing is, Jeanie, we let these people walk all over us, we don't confront them because we're afraid of what they'll do to us but there's more to life than this town and the men who run it.'

She leaned over and kissed him on the mouth.

'What's that for? I thought you're breaking up with me.'

'I am, but just for a moment there I remembered why I started to go out with you in the first place. Can we stay friends, Ian?'

'Of course, but unless you're going to come with me it's going to be a long-distance friendship.'

'That's fine, we'll take it as it comes.'

'So, tell me more about the other bloke.'

'He's sweet, and a bit innocent. I like that in a man.'

He laughed.

'No wonder you're breaking up with me,' Ian said.

'No, you both have that in common actually. You're not so innocent, but you're an idealist and that's very attractive, too.'

'You think you can mould him?'

'Not at all, I just like him. He's a nice bloke and we get on very well.'

'Well, I wish you both the best, I'm sorry but I really have to get back. It would be nice if we could catch up before I leave Oldport.'

'Yes, that would be good.'

Ian stood up and they embraced. He gave the waitress some money and then left. Jeanie finished her coffee and followed him out of the café.

Half an hour later she was back at the Prince Albert, helping Frank set up for the lunchtime session. Heather and Kitty were upstairs with clients, Serena and Amber were out somewhere.

It was mid-week, so Billy wasn't needed to help. He was at the town hall with Harry O'Leary. Frank was checking the optics as Jeanie put out beer mats and rearranged the glasses behind the bar. There was still half an hour to go before opening time.

She went into the kitchen and put the kettle on. Frank followed and sat down as she poured two cups of tea and joined him at the table.

'I've been meaning to talk to you, Frank'

'Really, is it about you and Billy?'

'God, you don't miss a thing, do you? No, it's about Amber.'

'What's she done now?'

'Nothing, in fact she's been as good as gold and you know it.'

'Yes, she's bearing up well, considering.'

'It's about her brother, Frank. He's in trouble and she needs help to sort him out.'

'Well, he's going to have to find help elsewhere. You know he was responsible for getting her on drugs in the first place. If he hadn't hit that boy and killed him, he would have been found dead in a gutter by now, the victim of some gangland killing.'

'He was a victim, too, Frank.'

'No, he wasn't, he was dealing, Jeanie, and he was feeding heroin to his sister. Don't you go defending him. You know what a mess Amber was in when we picked her up and put her back together. It was touch and go for a bit and I'm sorry that she's still in touch with that useless piece of humanity.'

'Come on Frank, you know that it was only because she was so close to Paul that we were able to motivate her to make the effort. If we hadn't been able to convince her to clean herself up for him, she'd be dead now.'

'Yes, and I suppose he thinks that she must be there for him still… well I don't.'

'Can I at least explain the situation to you?'

'If you must,' he said stifling a sigh.

'Amber told me that in the week when Paul killed that boy, he was holding on to a couple of thousand pounds worth of drugs. Paul was locked up and the drugs disappeared. Nobody knows what happened to them.

'The dealer who gave the drugs to him to sell has got some help inside and is putting pressure on Paul to pay up. Amber's worried that Paul might get beaten up, or worse. I'm worried they might come after Amber.'

'Well if they come here, they'll get what's coming to them.'

'The thing is Amber wants to pay them off, to protect Paul. She was wondering whether you could help.'

Frank looked hard at her as if he couldn't quite believe what he was being asked to do.

'Two thousand pounds is a lot of money.'

'I know.'

'Listen Jeanie, I understand you're very close to Amber. You brought her to me in the first place and we cleaned her up together. I didn't mind doing that at all. I did it because you asked me. Your father is a good friend of my family, and I look after my friends.

'I did it, too, because Amber was young, and she was a victim of a shitty system that chews up vulnerable young girls like her and spits them out.

'But her brother used her. He doesn't deserve her loyalty or her love.

'What you're asking me to do now is of a different order. You're asking me to get her scumbag brother out of a jam, worse than that you're asking me to do it by giving a substantial sum of money to a drug dealer.'

He paused as if deep in thought, struggling to find the words to pass a verdict on her request.

'I'm not doing it, Jeanie. You know how I feel about drugs. As it is, I'm only discussing this now and giving you the benefit of the doubt because I don't think you've thought this through properly.'

Jeanie was disappointed, and she allowed it to show. But she understood Frank's reasoning. She put her hand on his.

'Thank you for listening and considering my request.'

Frank's face softened.

'You know you can always ask me for anything. But you must understand that I can't give you everything you ask for.'

Jeanie put her hand on his and sought to change the subject.

'What about you, Frank? How are you doing? We never really sit down and talk properly.'

'I'm fine, Jeanie… really I am. The pub is doing well, and I've got my friends to keep me company.'

'Don't you want more? There's always somebody out there for everybody if we look hard enough.'

Frank laughed. 'I'm not so sure many women would want to be seen with me dressed like this,' he said pointing to his red dress, high heels and brown wig. 'But you never know, maybe I'll get a dog, always fancied one of those Labradoodles.'

'Really? Well go for it. I'll walk it for you.'

He smiled. 'Let's not rush into anything. Now, we'd better get this pub open or they'll be hammering down the door.'

Jeanie went out to the bar, unbolted the doors and welcomed some of the regulars who'd been waiting outside for some time. One of them pointed at his watch.

'You're two minutes late, Jeanie love.'

'I'm really sorry, Jim. Is it cold out there? Come in and have a pint, that'll sort you out.'

She got to work, serving drinks while Frank put the television on, so the regulars could follow the afternoon horse racing.

Looking up, Jeanie just caught Amber come into the pub. She was with a client and they went straight upstairs without even acknowledging Jeanie's greeting. She shrugged; business comes first.

The pub started to fill up as workers from nearby businesses came in for a drink and a sandwich. Frank had taken to stocking up on these 'convenience foods' as he liked to call them.

He made them himself, fresh each morning with a sliced white loaf, some cheese, ham and various bits of salad. Nothing fancy, he would say, and none of that brown bread with chewy bits.

Even so, some of the office workers had started to ask for brown bread and Jeanie had made a point of buying in a few loaves to accommodate them, much to Frank's disgust.

'If you don't give them what they want, they'll go elsewhere,' she'd told him.

'Where else can they go Jeanie, we're the only pub in the old harbour area?'

She had pointed out the cafés that had started to spring up, attracted by the increasing number of small businesses setting up shop in the old Georgian houses.

She also pointed out Sid Coogan, who had invested his redundancy money in a mobile snack bar and often drove down to the harbour at lunchtimes to sell food to the hungry workers.

Sid was a real character, born and bred on the Millstream Estate and well-known to Jeanie and her family. He was

217

living in a rented flat just a few streets from the Prince Albert, where he had moved after breaking up with his wife. As a result, once he had sold all his sandwiches and rolls, he left the van outside his home, walked to the pub and spent all the profits.

It was halfway through the lunchtime session when Amber reappeared. She left her client at the bar, where he ordered himself some ham sandwiches and a pint of Guinness. Obviously trying to recover his strength, Jeanie thought.

Amber went to sit with Heather at their usual table. Jeanie came over with a glass of wine and placed it in front of her. Amber grinned.

'Thanks love, you know me well.'

'Thought you might need fortifying,' Jeanie said. 'I spoke to Frank just before. I'm afraid he said no.'

Amber looked utterly downcast.

'Cheer up, love, we'll work it out somehow.'

Amber nodded and then looked determined.

'Maybe I'll get that cop to pay, the one who attacked Billy. He's got lots of secrets he won't want to get out. How much is my silence worth?'

'For God's sake, Amber don't do anything stupid. We'll find a way without having to resort to blackmail.'

Amber reluctantly agreed, but Jeanie could see a steely determination in her eyes that she hadn't observed before, it worried her.

Just then a couple of men came into the pub, beckoned at Amber and Heather and went upstairs with them. Amber looked back at Jeanie as she left the public area and winked. Jeanie smiled, but she was not completely at ease with her friend's state of mind.

At that moment, Billy appeared, dressed in his grey suit, smart polished shoes, white shirt and a plain blue tie. Jeanie wondered where he had got a second tie from. Still, he was looking particularly smart and she was proud to be associated with him.

She looked up at Frank and indicated that she wanted to take a short break. He gave her a thumbs-up, so she walked over to Billy, who smiled broadly, clearly pleased to see her.

She took his hand and marched him into the kitchen.

'What's going on?'

'Shush,' she said, placing her finger on his mouth, and then before he could react, she pulled herself up to his level and kissed him. He responded in kind.

'What was that for?' he asked as they broke apart. She put her arms around him and placed the side of her head on his shoulder.

'I'm just marking my territory,' she said cheerfully. 'From now on, you're mine exclusively and you don't have to share me, if you want it that is. And if I catch you flirting with Amber or anybody else then you're toast.'

'You broke up with Ian?'

'We agreed that it was for the best that we become just friends, yes.'

A big grin came over Billy's face.

'That's great, I mean obviously, I feel for Ian, but yes, shall we try that.'

She kissed him again and then fingered his tie.

'Where did you get this from?' she asked with a mock jealous grin.

'Harry gave it to me. He said he was fed up seeing me wearing the same one all the time.'

'As long as it wasn't from another woman,' she scolded.

'Are you going to be that jealous type who locks their man up and won't let him out unsupervised?' he asked indignantly.

'And if I am?'

'Well get your own act in order first,' he said grinning. Jeanie smiled.

'You're getting good at this banter lark. Who's been coaching you?'

'That's for me to know and you to find out.'

'I'm on it. Don't think I'm not. Now, I have to get back

to work.'

'What are you doing afterwards?' Billy asked.

'Why, what do you have in mind?'

Billy gestured towards the stairs.

'One step at a time, country boy, one step at a time.' She said smiling and with that she was gone.

28

Esther

Harry stood in front of the full-length mirror in his bedroom and adjusted his new suit. It was Sunday and he was looking forward to attending morning Mass for the first time in some weeks.

Church for Harry was more than a religious obligation, it was an opportunity to network with other movers and shakers in the town, and a chance to interact with his constituents and listen to their concerns.

The service itself was secondary to all that, a necessary evil in some ways but one that he had endured his entire life.

The church was a ten-minute walk from his home and as usual he set off in good time. He greeted some of his neighbours on the way. Many of them were tidying their gardens to stay ahead of autumn, others were walking their dogs or, like Harry, on the way to church.

John Baker's car swept past him and pulled into the church car park. He was wearing one of the Armani suits he had taken to putting on for formal occasions. Harry was not sure what had brought on this sudden bout of sartorial elegance. He just wished he could afford to emulate him.

He walked towards the car and greeted his business partner of two decades.

'How are you, John? I trust everything is on schedule with the new club.'

'Yes, thank you, Harry. Baker's is re-opening tomorrow. We've a few surprises in store to pull in the punters. The casino is also on schedule.'

'Excellent. I trust Ian is pulling his weight.'

'Yes, of course. He's proving to be quite an asset. How are things at the council?'

'Well, as you know the good citizens of Inchfield are threatening to place our housing development onto the back burner through a village green application. However, the council's lawyers say they don't have a leg to stand on. It will all fizzle out in a few weeks.'

Baker grinned. 'Better and better, we'll need to get on with the detailed planning application and get some diggers on site. The sooner we start, the quicker we can take our profits.'

The two men walked together towards the church, greeting other locals along the way. As they approached the vestibule, Harry saw a familiar figure.

A slim woman, in her fifties, but looking younger, Esther O'Leary wore a smart red jacket and skirt combination over a cream blouse, matching red shoes and a floppy red hat. She was talking to Ian.

Harry didn't know whether to be more surprised by the reappearance of his ex-wife or the fact that his son had come to church for the first time since he'd returned to Oldport. Inevitably, the two events were related.

'What's this?' he said. 'Are you two staging an ambush?'

'It's good to see you, Harry,' she said, kissing him on his cheek.

Ian shook his hand. He was wearing a designer grey suit and a burgundy monogrammed shirt but no tie. Harry wanted to ask him if he had been tutoring Baker in the fashion stakes but bit his tongue.

'That isn't what you said the last time I saw you, Esther. Can I infer from your sudden appearance and your friendly manner that you're after something?'

'Harry, that is very ungracious. Can't a mother visit her son when she wants to?'

'Of course, but it gets suspicious when you then drag him to church, an institution he's not seen the inside of for at least seven years to my knowledge, and then lie in wait for me outside.'

'You haven't changed one-bit, Harry,' Esther said through gritted teeth. 'Still as difficult as ever I see.'

'Yes, well we'll see how difficult when I find out why

you're here.' He turned to Ian. 'Shouldn't you be getting that club ready for the big day tomorrow?'

'It's all done, Dad, isn't that right, John?'

Baker nodded. He was keen to get away from this little family reunion as soon as possible.

'I'm going to go inside, Harry. I'll catch up with you in there. Ian, Esther, it was a pleasure to see you again.'

He scurried into the church.

'I see John is still as big a bull-shitter as ever,' Esther said.

'It takes one to know one,' Harry retorted. 'Is that the sort of language somebody should use outside a church? Your father would be spinning in his grave.'

'Don't you bring my father into this; I came here to attend Mass and to have a civilised conversation with you. There's no need to be so hostile.'

Harry was just about to launch into a reply when Ian intervened.

'Dad, Mum, this isn't the place. You need to remember where you are, Dad, and the position you hold. Shall we go inside and then continue this conversation afterwards in a more private location.'

Harry and Esther glared at each other but didn't say anything further. The three of them went into the church and took their seats, Ian and Esther at the back; Harry near the front next to Baker, who turned to him as he took his seat.

'Not getting married was one of the best decisions I ever made,' he whispered. 'Even when you get rid of them, they come back to haunt you.'

'Thanks, John, you're such a comfort.'

Harry turned his head to look at his ex-wife and son. He could see that she still had her looks, but that had never compensated for the fierce temper and low cunning she had inherited from her father, the late Councillor David Kennedy OBE KSG, a former Town Mayor and council deputy leader.

He knew that if she was back in Oldport then she was after something. He spent the whole service wondering what it was. Even afterwards, as he greeted and chatted to the many constituents who came up to talk to him, he was distracted by her presence.

As he started walking back to his home, Esther caught up with him. There was no sign of Ian.

'You don't get away that easily,' she said.

'Oh, so you do have an agenda after all. Where's Ian?'

'He's gone back to the club, had some work to do apparently. In any case, it's for the best.'

'Why is that?'

'We need to talk.'

'I knew my instincts were correct. You're so predictable.'

'Shall we go inside?'

They had reached Harry's house. They went in and he put the kettle on. She sat in the kitchen and watched as he poured tea for them and then joined her at the large pine table that formed the centrepiece of the room.

'I'd offer you a biscuit, but I appear to be all out,' he said.

'Don't worry, I'm on a diet anyway.'

'Oh? I was thinking you were looking a bit anorexic.'

Esther stared hard at him.

'I'm not here to argue, Harry. But I need your help.'

'Go on.'

'I've got a small business in London, selling stationery. We've just had a massive hike in rent and a rates revaluation, and I need a cash injection.'

'Well go to a bank then.'

'I have, they're not interested. We're already mortgaged to the hilt. I don't have any collateral.'

'What makes you think I'll invest in it?'

'I'm not looking for an investor, Harry. I'm looking for a no-strings attached, non-repayable bail-out.'

He laughed out loud.

'Really Esther, you have to do better than that. You can't walk back into my life after thirteen years and just ask for money. We're divorced, we had a financial settlement. Ian is grown up and working, I no longer need to pay maintenance. In short, I don't owe you a penny and I'm not giving you anything.'

'That's what I thought you'd say.'

'Well then, you've had a wasted journey. Do you need me to get you a taxi?'

Harry started to tidy up the crockery. He filled up a bowl with soapy water and began to wash the breakfast dishes. Esther sat unmoving, watching him work, nursing her tea rather than drinking it.

He looked over towards her as if anxious to take the mug off her and wash it, but she was not giving it up easily.

'Yes, I will have a second cup of tea, thank you.'

Harry shrugged and reached across for the teapot. He poured her another cup and handed her the jug of milk. She looked up at him.

'I have my father's diaries, Harry.'

'That sounds interesting. Are you going to publish them?'

'I don't think you'd want me to somehow.'

'Why's that?'

'Because he kept a note of everything; of every transaction, of every conversation, of every sordid little deal.'

Harry went pale. He felt a sudden urge to sit down. Esther was now focussed intently on going in for a kill.

'You've come here to blackmail me?' Harry demanded eventually.

She didn't answer. Instead she fished around in her handbook and pulled out a sheaf of papers.

'They're copies,' she said as she handed them to him.

Harry took the papers and read through them carefully. She sat watching him, sipping her tea.

It was all there, the inducements to pass planning applications and licenses, the cash David Kennedy had received for allocating council housing and the way he had tutored Harry to do the same, and the business arrangements that should have been declared but were hidden away so he could vote in his own interest.

'What the fuck was your father thinking putting all this down on paper?' Harry asked.

Esther shrugged.

'He always was meticulous, Harry. Perhaps he just wanted to keep track of things. Maybe it was his picture in the attic.'

'Pardon?'

'You know, Oscar Wilde, Dorian Gray. Didn't you have an education, Harry?'

'School of hard knocks,' he said proudly. 'If you recall we compensated by sending Ian to school instead.'

'He kept a picture in the attic that exhibited all the signs of his excesses, while he retained his youthful looks and energy. I was suggesting that maybe these diaries were my father's conscience, neatly locked away in a drawer so he could go about his business without any feeling of guilt.'

'Well whatever the reason, it was a bloody stupid thing to do.'

'Maybe, but whatever his reasons were, I have them and I'm considering what to do with them.'

'You're not going to put those diaries into the public domain.'

'Well, if you give me the funding, I need then no, I won't'

'Let me put it this way Esther, if you publish those diaries it will trash your father's reputation. He was a Papal Knight for fuck's sake. And what about Ian, do you think anybody will employ him if both his father and grandfather are publicly disgraced?'

'You have it in your hands to stop that, Harry.'

'No, Esther, it's in *your* hands. I'm not going to give you a penny. You must decide what you do next, but you should remember two things. I run this town, so you're going to have to choose who you give it to very carefully and secondly, if you do put those diaries in the public domain you'll be destroying the reputation of your own family and you'll still not have the money you need.'

Esther looked downcast.

'You always were good at calling my bluff, Harry.'

'Look, I'm desperate, the business is sound, but the cash-flow problems are insurmountable without a decent line of credit.'

'And you know I don't have that sort of money.'

'Yes, I suspected as much.'

'But I'll try to help. If you can produce a business plan, I will put it in front of John Baker. Maybe he'll be interested in becoming a sleeping partner.'

She looked doubtful.

'Take it or leave it, Esther. If you want to survive in this world sometimes you need to sup with the devil. But next time you want something, just ask me, won't you? I can't take all this stress. I'm getting too old.'

'I'll take it,' she said. 'But I'm not going to sup from the same dish, and if I just asked you out straight you would have said 'no'.'

'Maybe. Give me a ring when you're ready. In the meantime, can I drop you somewhere? I would like to enjoy the rest of Sunday on my own.'

'I'm staying with Ian. Can you get me a cab?'

29
Comings and Goings

It was opening night for the refurbished Baker's nightclub and Ian had never been busier. The club now operated on three floors with a bar and disco on the two lower floors and a stage for live bands at the top of the building.

He had booked a well-known local rock band for the big night and already people were queuing outside. There were special offers on drinks too, which was also adding to the attraction.

Monday was normally set aside for students from the nearby college and many of them were outside waiting to be let in at a discounted rate. Ian had also put on buses from nearby university towns as a one-off and this had proved to be particularly popular with the students, if not with the venues they were deserting to be in Baker's.

He could hear the musicians carrying out sound checks upstairs while the technicians undertook last-minute tweaks to the systems in the two disco areas.

On the first floor, Phillips was putting the bouncers through their paces. They were all in dinner jackets, some more tight-fitting than others. Baker himself was due to make an appearance at some stage during the evening and it was important that everything was in place for him.

As the clock hit 10.30pm Phillips sent the bouncers to their places and the doors were opened for the hundred or so people shivering outside. Ian never ceased to be amazed at how few clothes the punters wore, even on cold evenings.

As the music blasted out on each level, he paced the various floors making sure everything was in order. He had worked hard to get this opening right and was determined that nothing would go wrong.

At 11.30pm, Baker arrived, He greeted all the bouncers and bar staff individually and stood and watched the band for a short time. The noise was so loud on each floor now that it was difficult to hold a sensible conversation.

Satisfied with what he saw, he congratulated Ian on a job well done and headed out to his car. Phillips walked out with him deep in conversation. Ian returned to pacing the floor. As he did so he became aware of a clean-shaven young man with blond hair, wearing a black T-shirt, chinos and a white jacket moving amongst the crowd selling drugs.

He watched the man expertly work the throng, pocketing notes as he slipped tabs to each of his customers. Ian kept out of sight, so he could see if it was true that the dealer was in cahoots with one of his bouncers.

Sure enough, the bouncer who had been accused by the reporter of working with the drug dealer, was lurking near the dance floor, almost as though he was overseeing the operation.

Ian noted the distinctive earring and tattoo on his thick neck as well as his long brown hair. He followed them from a distance as they met to share the spoils and then confronted his errant employee, inviting him into the office. Phillips was already in there.

'What do you think you're doing?' Ian demanded, becoming furious when there was no answer.

'You've been collaborating with drug dealers in this club and taking a share of their proceeds. As far as I'm concerned that is gross misconduct. You'll collect all of your things and leave the club immediately, never to return.'

The bouncer looked towards Phillips, who stood up.

'Can I have a word, Ian?'

Ian looked confused.

'When I have dealt with this, Gavin.'

Phillips nodded towards the bouncer who opened the door and left them to it.

'What's going on?' Ian was both angry and disconcerted.

'Look Ian, you're young, you haven't been at this game for very long. Drugs are an integral part of this scene and the bouncers learn to tolerate it. They work with the trustworthy ones to protect the punters from dodgy drugs. It's called the real world.'

'You're so full of shit, Gavin. Is he sharing the profits with you, too? You know that John wants zero tolerance of drugs in this club. It's my job to enforce that wish.'

'Oh, come on, Ian, John's an idealist. He doesn't know what goes on and nor does he need to. If he succeeded in banning drugs from this club altogether then he'd have no punters left. He has to be protected from himself.'

'I'm sorry, I don't accept that. I have a job to do and I fully intend to do it.'

'No, that isn't how it's going to work.'

'Pardon?'

'It's simple,' Phillips said, stepping closer and lowering his voice. 'I'm overruling you. Nobody is getting fired and we're going to continue to run the club as it should be run.'

'I don't accept that, Gavin. I'm in charge and I say how this club should be run.'

The voice grew more clipped and harder. 'Not when you try to upset the natural order, you don't. I answer directly to John. I'm his eyes and ears in this club and I say that you're not firing that bouncer. If it helps, you can give him a warning but that's as far as it goes.'

'Well, I'm sorry, but I don't accept that. If I need to, I'll go directly to John, but my decision stands.'

'You can go to John if you like, but put it this way who do you think he's going to listen to? I've been John's right-hand-man for over ten years and your father's agent for as long. You're a wet-behind-the ears boy who's seen and done nothing.

'If I tell John everything is in order then he'll believe me. Have you ever taken ecstasy? No, of course you haven't. How would you know what's really happening out there on the dance floor?'

Ian was stunned by this outburst, but he was determined not to lose control of the situation.

'Yes, I thought you might play that card. Okay, we'll do it

your way. Get the bouncer back in here. I'll give him a final warning and then tomorrow, I'll go up to talk to John and we'll see who he believes,'

Gavin shrugged.

'Have it your own way. We'll see tomorrow how this works out.'

* * *

The next day Ian drove to Baker's Pym Hill mansion, Phillips was already there, closeted in the office. Baker stepped forward to shake Ian's hand.

'Ian, it's good to see you. I understand there were some problems last night.'

'Yes sir, there were problems. I caught one of the bouncers working with a drug dealer and taking a cut for himself. I tried to sack the man, but Gavin here intervened and prevented me doing so.'

'Well Gavin tells me that you were mistaken. The bouncer was removing the dealer from the club.'

'I can assure you, John, that I was not mistaken. Not only am I sure of what I saw but this was the same bouncer who was observed by that reporter just three weeks ago, doing the exact same thing.

'Once I had caught him myself, I had no choice but to dismiss him on the spot. Unfortunately, Gavin took a different view, which leaves me with a question.'

'Oh?'

Ian tried to control his mounting anger. 'Who exactly is in charge at Baker's? Because if it's me then I'm going right back and I'm going to give that bouncer his cards.'

Baker took a deep breath and then pulled himself up to his full height. At well over six feet, the tactic nearly always worked. His reputation for getting his own way, and his wealth helped too.

'The answer to your question, Ian, is that I'm in charge of Baker's, Gavin looks after my interests there and you manage it.'

'That's no answer, John, that's a recipe for chaos and confusion.'

'That's the answer you're going to get.'

'Fine, if that's the case then you've left me with no choice. I can't have my authority as manager undermined and I'm certainly not going to tolerate officially sanctioned drug dealing on any premises I'm responsible for.

'I'm giving you due warning that I'm quitting the job. I will let you have it in writing this afternoon. I believe that I need to work a month's notice. That's fine. It will give you a chance to find a new manager.'

With that Ian turned on his heels and left Phillips and Baker standing there. He got into his car and headed for town. There were a couple of other jobs he needed to do before he called it quits for good.

As he sat drafting his letter of resignation, he was conscious that he was being watched. It was the bouncer he had disciplined the night before. The man had already drawn his own conclusions from the fact he was still in a job.

'You leaving, boss?' he asked.

'Yes, you'll be glad to know that you can carry on your dubious activities unhindered by me for the foreseeable future, in fact for as long as you want.'

The bouncer nodded and left him to it.

Ian stuffed the letter in an envelope and drove to his flat. His mother was there, packing.

'When are you leaving, Mum?'

'I'm catching a bus in a few hours, love. Why are you home already? I thought you had a meeting?'

'I've given notice that I'm quitting my job, and I think I'm going to be leaving town as well. Maybe move back to London if you'll have me while I find my feet.'

Esther stopped packing her case and hugged him.

'I told you this town was rotten,' she said. 'I'm glad that you're getting out while you can.'

'I've got to do some things first,' Ian said. 'For a start, I want to catch-up with a friend, tell her what's happened and then I need to arrange divesting myself of this flat. I think I need to give a month's notice, which is fine as that coincides with my remaining time at Baker's.'

'Are you okay for money, love?'

'Yes, I'm fine. Besides you're hardly able to help out.'

'No, but I'm sure your dad would if you asked.'

'I don't know, we didn't exactly part on the best of terms the last time we spoke.'

Esther laughed.

'That makes two of us. What a pair eh?'

'I promised him that if I left then I would go and say goodbye to him, so I'll honour that commitment.'

'You're a good boy, do you know that?'

'Mum, I'm twenty-five years old. I stopped being a boy quite some time ago,'

'You'll always be a boy to me, Ian.'

He grabbed his coat. It was starting to get cold.

'I'll be back to see you off,' he shouted as he picked up his car keys and slammed the door behind him.

Twenty minutes later he was standing outside the Prince Albert. It was the first time he had ventured this far into the harbour area; he didn't know why it had taken him so long. Ian thought that the building had seen better days but nevertheless couldn't help but be impressed by the way it dominated the area. He stepped into the porch and pushed open the door.

Nothing had prepared him for the scene that presented itself. For although the interior itself was rather old-fashioned with solid oak tables, padded benches and a very substantial bar, and although he knew what to expect, he was still taken aback at seeing the six-foot-plus landlord in high heels, a beard and prominent tattoos, wearing a blue dress, a blonde wig and big earrings.

He looked across to a table where three prostitutes were chatting over a few glasses of wine. One of them stood up to greet a client and disappeared into the back of the pub with them. Ian felt that he had stepped into another world.

He walked up to the bar. Frank came over to greet him.

'Good evening, what can I get you to drink?'

'Can I have a dry white wine please?'

Frank pulled out a bottle of wine from the fridge and poured Ian's drink.

'Is Jeanie here?' Ian asked, handing him the money.

'Sure, I'll get her for you.'

Frank went to the other end of the bar and attracted Jeanie's attention. He whispered something to her, and she laughed. She was still smiling when she got to Ian.

'Why are you laughing?' he asked.

'It's Frank,' she said, 'he told me that Don Johnson was here to see me.'

'What?'

'Seriously, has nobody ever told you that you look like a young Don Johnson? I told you that you should've got yourself a Ferrari Testarossa. It would've completed the look.'

Ian grimaced.

'Who's Don Johnson?' he asked sarcastically. She could see that he knew the answer.

'Never mind, what brings you to this den of iniquity?'

'I came to tell you that I quit my job and I'm moving to London.'

Jeanie looked shocked.

'I hope that this isn't down to me.'

'No, absolutely not, my position at the club was becoming intolerable. You were right, Jeanie; this town is a sewer of corruption and criminality. They were trying to pull me in, but I wouldn't play ball, so I quit. I'm serving my notice and then I'm going to London to make my fortune, or something like that anyway.'

She hugged him.

'I'll miss you. Will you keep in touch?'

'Of course, and when I get my Ferrari Testarossa, you will be the first to be offered a ride in it.'

She laughed.

'It'll be a total babe magnet. It was nice of you to come and say goodbye to me. Come and see me before you leave.'

'Of course. I'll be around for a few more weeks yet. I just wanted to keep you up-to-date.'

'Well then, I certainly expect to see you before you go for good.'

'Count on it,' he said.

Jeanie kissed him on the cheek and watched as he left the pub.

30
Consequences

It had been a busy week and Billy was exhausted. He had not got to bed until late the night before and so was in no hurry to get up. Fortunately, he was not needed by Harry until the afternoon, so he had the opportunity to snuggle up in his bed a bit longer than usual.

Nevertheless by 9am he was wide awake and contemplating going downstairs to make some breakfast. Just then there was a knock on his bedroom door. He waited in the hope that whoever it was would go away.

There was another knock and the door opened. Amber's head appeared.

'Are you alone, country boy?'

'Of course, what did you expect?'

She came into the room, wearing just her usual short nylon robe. It was tied loosely at the front so that a considerable amount of flesh was on show.

'I thought Jeanie might be in here,' she said.

'No, we haven't really had much time to ourselves to get to that stage yet. Mind you, if she finds you in here showing everything you've got there will be hell to pay. She already thinks I'm screwing you.'

'Oh Billy,' Amber mocked, 'I didn't think you cared. You should make time for her, she's more than worth it.'

She came and sat on the bed, making no effort whatsoever to cover up. Billy made a show of covering his eyes.

'Do you mind putting your boob back inside your robe?' he said.

She laughed and obliged him by securing her robe properly so that it covered her breasts. In doing so, she revealed yet more of her legs.

'It's not as if you haven't seen it all before,' Amber said playfully.

'Indeed, but as Jeanie keeps reminding me, attractive as your body is my life is at risk if I lay eyes on it more than is strictly necessary.'

'She's a hard taskmaster that girl. Who'd have thought she was the jealous type,' Amber joked.

'Do you know Amber; I can't tell whether she is being jealous or just winding me up. I suspect she's teasing me; she knows we're just friends.'

'Yes, and Jeanie is my best friend so there's no way I'd touch you, even if I were interested.'

Billy was part-relieved and part-offended at this back-handed rejection. But this was a brother-sister type relationship and so he took her joshing in good part.

'Good, now we've established that, yet again, what do you have planned today?'

She put on a serious face and looked at him intently.

'Tell me, Billy, do you have any money?'

'Good God, no not a penny to my name, why do you ask?'

She shrugged.

'No reason, it's just that my brother's in trouble and needs some quick cash to get him out of a jam.'

'I thought he was in prison?'

'He is but the sort of people he owes money to have connections and they can get to him there.'

'Have you asked Frank?'

'Jeanie asked him for me, but no-go. I didn't expect you could help but I thought it was worth a try.'

'You know I'd help if I could, Amber'

'Yes" she said leaning over to kiss him on the cheek. She sat back up, carefully readjusting her robe again so as not to embarrass him with another exposed breast.

'You really need a bigger robe,' he said smiling.

She laughed.

'I'm only wearing this one for your benefit. I wouldn't bother normally.'

Billy blushed. She laughed again and then put her serious

face on.

'Listen,' she said. 'I'm going to try and get the money I need elsewhere.'

'How do you mean?'

'I have information, which I can use to get the cash.'

Billy was concerned.

'What, blackmail? I really think you should talk it over with Frank and Jeanie before you try this on,' he said. 'This sounds very dangerous. What if they refuse to pay, and harm you instead?'

'It'll be fine, Billy, don't you worry about me, I can look after myself. Besides, I'll do it in a public place, where nobody can hear us, but with enough people around to stop the bloke doing anything stupid.'

'I'm sorry, Amber, but please don't do this. You saw what happened to my brother. You stick your neck out in this town, and threaten to reveal secrets, and you end up in hospital. Who is it? Is it that policeman?'

'I'm not going to tell you anymore for your own protection. But you're my insurance. You know what I'm about to do. If I tell them that other people know what I'm doing they'll leave me be. They won't dare touch me and they'll have to pay up.'

Billy was now very worried indeed.

'Seriously, Amber, you don't have to do this today. Let me talk to Jeanie. Maybe we can find another way of getting you the money.'

'No, it's the only way left to me, and Billy, I need you to not tell anyone about this, not even Jeanie. You've got to promise me. This is between me and you only. Nobody else needs to know.'

'But....'

'I mean it Billy, just you and me. Swear it to me.'

He was very reluctant to give his word. The blackmail didn't feel right to him and he feared for her safety. But she insisted over-and-over again until, worn down, he agreed.

'Good, I'm glad that's sorted,' she said hugging him.

'Now I've got a punter coming in soon, so I need to get all glammed up.'

She paused at the door and turned around.

'You're a lovely bloke,' she said. 'If only my brother had been like you.'

With that she was gone. Billy tried to gather his thoughts but found it hard to make any sense of events. Instead he got out of bed and ran a bath. An hour later he was dressed in his suit and shaved.

He went downstairs to grab some breakfast. Jeanie was not in yet and Frank was pre-occupied with his accounts, so he set off for the town hall.

As he entered the anteroom to Harry's office, Sue looked up.

'He's in a mood,' she said, 'tread carefully. It may be because he found the bill for that little bit of lock-changing you organised. I kept it from him as long as possible. But he was grumpy even before that.'

Billy nodded, knocked on the door and went in. Harry was sitting behind his desk poring over some papers. He barely acknowledged Billy's presence. Eventually he looked up.

'Oh, Billy, I didn't realise you'd come in. Grab a seat. I need to ask you about something.'

Harry sorted through the papers on his desk until he found what he needed.

'Yes, this is the one. Apparently, I authorised a locksmith to change the locks on a council house occupied by a Miss Sarah Wilson.'

'She was the one who came to your surgery Councillor O'Leary. If you recall, we took her to her new home the next day.' Billy was determined to get his explanation in first.

'Anyway, she rang in shortly afterwards and said that there was something wrong with the locks. You weren't around so I used my initiative and sorted it out. I knew you wouldn't want her, and her kids put at risk on that dodgy council estate.'

Harry looked a bit taken aback by this explanation but didn't feel able to challenge it.

'Oh, right, very commendable, good use of initiative and all that, thank you Billy.'

He put the paper back on top of the pile in front of him. He seemed distracted, so Billy reminded him that they were due to be at the opening of a new leisure centre in quarter of an hour.

Harry thanked him, put on his jacket and passed Billy his briefcase to carry.

'Don't lose that,' he said. 'It's full of budget papers I need to go through later. It also contains my speech.'

They went out to the front of the town hall and climbed into the official car. Ten minutes later they were standing in front of a brand-new leisure centre. Harry stood to one side, chatting to residents and volunteers.

A local marching band in full uniform came around the corner headed up by a drum major. The watching crowd applauded enthusiastically at the spectacle.

The town mayor was also present, wearing an expensive-looking ceremonial chain. Following the ribbon-cutting ceremony, Billy and Harry hung around grazing at the buffet and chatting with guests, before, heading back to the town hall, where they found Ian waiting in the anteroom chatting to Sue.

After father and son had greeted each other, Billy offered his hand.

'We've met here before,' he said, 'I'm Billy, your father's assistant.'

'Of course, yes, I remember you now. You work at the Prince Albert as well, don't you? Jeanie has told me a great deal about you. Congratulations, you're a very lucky man.'

The two O'Leary's went into Harry's room and closed the door behind them. Sue looked at Billy puzzled.

'It's a long story,' he said.

'I've got all the time in the world,' she responded expectantly. Billy told her about Jeanie and the little love triangle he had been caught up in.

'I do like a happy ending,' Sue said.

Their conversation was cut short by the sound of raised voices coming from Harry's room. They could not make out what was being said but the argument raged for a good ten minutes before the door opened and Ian emerged looking flustered.

He stopped to get his breath and then turned to Sue and Billy.

'I'm leaving town in four or five weeks-time,' he said, 'so just in case I don't see you again, can I thank you for all your courtesy to me while I've been here, Sue.'

'It was a pleasure Mr O'Leary.'

'Please call me Ian. The pleasure was all mine.'

He hugged her and then turned and shook Billy's hand.

'It was also a pleasure to meet you, Billy. Please look after my father and take good care of Jeanie.'

'Of course,' said Billy, stumped for words.

'What a lovely man,' Sue said as she watched Ian leave. 'Don't you think he looks a bit like Don Johnson?'

'I wouldn't know, Sue,' Billy answered rather sulkily. 'But yes, he seemed very pleasant.'

She looked at him with a twinkle in her eye.

'Now Billy, you don't need to be jealous, after all you got the girl.'

'And I've got the car, too,' he said holding up Harry's car and house keys in his hand. 'I've got to go up to Pym Hill to pick up a cream suit for tonight. We're going to a Hawaiian evening at the hospice and he doesn't want to look too formal.'

'Don't forget to get him a Hawaiian shirt while you're at it!' she joked.

'I can't see that, can you? Harry will do a lot for his constituents, but I don't think he'd stretch to that!'

A few hours later Billy and Harry were in a restaurant enjoying the attentions of the patrons of the local hospice. As they arrived some of the local ladies placed a Hawaiian

Lei over their heads.

Billy was astonished at how much pineapple there was and how it seemed to be included in every dish. He wondered if they had researched the menu or just decided that was the way it should be.

He picked up a record sleeve to identify the music being played. There was a good mix of what was billed as authentic Hawaiian music ranging from Elvis Presley's *Hawaiian Wedding Song* to something called *Ka Uluwehi O Ke Kai* by somebody or some group called Hapa.

Not being able to drink, Billy clutched a glass of lemonade as Harry, already the worse for wear, alternated between glasses of Californian wine and American lager. It was obvious that the evening was going to be shorter than anticipated.

Billy watched closely in case he overreached himself in his drunken condition. He often got touchy-feely in this state, which wouldn't go down well in such exalted company.

Harry seemed to have a liking for pineapple as he was gorging on the stuff. There was pineapple and cheese for starters, followed by chicken and pineapple and pineapple and cream for dessert. Billy could only just stomach the main course, which he classed as a culinary crime.

Harry stood up to dance with one of his hosts but stumbled and had to support himself on a nearby table. Billy decided it was time to go while his boss was still conscious. At least then Harry would be able to put himself to bed.

It was coming up to nine-thirty in the evening and there was a strong wind blowing outside. As he drove onto Pym Hill, Billy could see the trees swaying, leaves and small twigs blew across the road in front of him.

He pulled up outside the house and helped Harry inside. Billy left the house keys on a table just inside the door and got into the car to drive back to the Prince Albert.

It was earlier than he had expected, and he was looking forward to seeing Jeanie and having a drink with her. He was astonished therefore, to find the Prince Albert closed and in darkness. He parked the car and almost ran to the side door.

As he entered, he saw Jeanie and Frank sitting together at one of the tables. Frank looked devastated; Jeanie was crying uncontrollably. On another table, Heather, Kitty and Serena were comforting each other.

Jeanie looked up and on seeing Billy ran over to him. He put his arms around her as she hung onto him, crying on his shoulder.

'What's happened?' he asked, fearing the worse.

'It's Amber,' she sobbed, 'she's dead.'

Billy felt his legs go weak. He could barely hold himself upright. If Jeanie had not been clinging to him, he would have fallen to the floor in a heap. He didn't know what to say or think. He held Jeanie tight, overwhelmed by a feeling of loss and numbness.

31
Weathering the Storm

Jeanie was still sobbing. Billy helped her into a chair beside Frank and sat down next to her. He felt sick as he put his arm around her shoulder so that she could ease into his.

She sat up to take a sip of brandy and then rested her head against Billy's suit jacket.

'What happened?' he asked Frank.

'The police say that it was a heroin overdose. They found her body in an alley behind Baker's early this evening.'

'I spoke to her this morning,' Billy said. 'There's no way she was going to slip back into old habits.'

Frank nodded. He was clearly distressed, but he also seemed determined to take charge and calm things down

'It's something we can consider in the morning,' he said. 'In the meantime, we need to get some rest. Can you take Jeanie home?'

'Of course.'

'I'm not going home,' she said. 'I'm staying here with Billy.'

Frank indicated to Billy that he should take her upstairs. He then walked over to the three girls on the other table and hugged each of them in turn. They could not stop sobbing. He sat next to Heather and started to reassure them.

Billy led Jeanie to the stairs. Once they were in his room, he removed his suit jacket and tie and hung them up. He unbuttoned his shirt and sat down on the bed next to her.

He suddenly felt hot and flustered as if somebody had turned up the heating. He was shaking, and his nerves were jangling.

Jeanie had stopped crying and was sitting in silence staring at the closed bedroom door. Her eyes were red. Billy carefully stroked the tears off her cheeks with his hand. She turned to look at him and kissed him on the lips, pulling his shirt loose as she did so and putting her arms inside, hugging him tightly. He pulled her closer to him. They sat in that position in silence for what seemed like hours but was just a few minutes.

Jeanie sat herself upright and slipped his shirt off. He kicked off his shoes and socks and gently kissed her on the forehead.

She stood and moved in front of him slowly pulling her top over her head and unhooking her bra. She removed her skirt and unrolled her stockings. Finally, she slipped off her pants and stood naked in front of him.

Billy sat transfixed, unable to speak. He watched as Jeanie walked towards him and unbuckled his belt. She unzipped his suit trousers and pulled them off him, dropping them on the floor besides her and then eased his boxer shorts down his legs.

She leaned over and kissed him passionately, forcing him back into a horizontal position. He rolled her over so that he was on top of her and kissed her neck and breasts, but she was having none of it.

Instead she pushed him onto his back and climbed on top of him. Billy placed his hands on her hips to steady her as she moved urgently over him, as if her every movement could expunge their distress. They climaxed together, and she fell forward, smothering him in a desperate, grief-filled embrace.

She held him so tightly that he could hardly breathe. They lay like that for over an hour, wide awake and naked, just a single sheet covering them as the wind whipped up white caps on the sea outside.

They lay listening to the gusts grow stronger, until a storm raged and made the window rattle. Tiles crashed down to the paving stones below. Objects clattered around in the street, blown about by the gale. The wind was so strong it felt like it would blow Oldport away altogether.

He placed his hand into the small of Jeanie's back and spoke softly to her.

'Are you okay?'

'I will be.'

She clung to him even tighter as if their closeness could reset time and bring Amber back. The warmth of her body was comforting but he couldn't hold back an overwhelming feeling of loss nor the warm salty tears that flowed down his face into the corners of his mouth.

Jeanie kissed him. Now it was her turn to wipe his tears away. He returned the kiss and they made love again, slowly, exploring every inch of each other's body.

Neither of them could sleep, instead they held each other as the storm raged, each reflecting silently on their memories of Amber and the events that had destroyed her short life.

Eventually, Jeanie moved so that her face was directly in front of his.

'Frank tried to persuade all the girls to come off the game, you know, not just Amber, but none of them would,' she said quietly. 'They were earning more looking after horny punters than they could behind a bar. If only they'd listened, if only I'd been stronger in backing him up, Amber might still be alive.'

Billy kissed her. 'Oh, Jeanie. Don't blame yourself. You did all you could.'

'I know, but you can't help thinking what would have happened if...' her voice trailed off into quiet sobbing. Billy pulled her closer to him and held her tight, stroking her hair.

After a few minutes she settled down and gave him a determined look.

'What you said last night,' she said. 'I think you're right. I just don't buy into this story that Amber killed herself through a heroin overdose. She was clean. She's been clean for years. Why would she go back to that way of life now? It doesn't make sense.'

'I agree,' Billy responded. 'I think it stinks and I believe I know who may be responsible.'

Jeanie sat up, pulling the sheet up over her nakedness to protect herself from the cold.

'Are you going to tell me what she said to you?'

'She was obsessing about some money her brother owes and sounded quite desperate. She said she was going to blackmail some bloke to try and get the money off him. She wouldn't tell me who, but I am almost certain it was that police inspector.'

'No!' Jeanie almost shouted out the word. 'And you let her go?'

'Honestly, Jeanie, I did my best to talk her out of it. I pleaded with her not to try it on, to talk to you and Frank first, but she insisted.'

'You could have told me?'

'She swore me to secrecy, but in any case, I didn't see you until I got back and by then it was too late.'

Jeanie sat in silence, looking furious. Billy felt the need to apologise again.

'I'm really sorry. I did my best please don't be upset with me.'

She turned towards him and kissed him.

'I'm not angry with you, Billy, I'm furious with myself. She hinted that she might do something like that last week after Frank had refused to give her the money. I should have taken her more seriously.'

Billy put his arm around her and pulled her closer.

'It wasn't your fault, Jeanie; it wasn't' anybody's fault. She was desperate, and she wasn't listening to either of us. I don't think you, me, Frank or anyone else could have stopped her from going ahead with this blackmail plan.'

'But do you really think that it was Anderson – that a policeman is capable of murder?'

'I think that copper is capable of anything. But if you're asking me whether he killed Amber or not, I don't know. I can't even be sure that it was him she was after. And if it was, then remember, there are other people involved.'

'What do you mean?'

'Well, the bouncer who assaulted Simon was being egged on by Phillips. It was Phillips that Amber and I saw paying off Anderson. I wouldn't be surprised if he was involved somehow.

'The point is, Jeanie, we don't know what happened. We have to rely on the police to find out for us.'

'But if Anderson *was* involved then they'll cover it up and just write it off as an accidental overdose, another junkie who overreached herself.'

'Yes, we need to find a way to get to the truth.'

They fell silent and Jeanie started to cry again. Billy tried to comfort her, but she was inconsolable.

'I'm sorry, Billy, it's just that I'll miss her so much. I can't believe she's gone.'

'I know, she was like a sister to me. I'll really miss our early morning chats and her cheeky banter.'

Outside the wind had subsided and an eerie silence had fallen on the harbour area. Billy could hear voices in the street below, but he was too tired to look to see what was happening.

Instead he cuddled up under the sheets with Jeanie and started to doze. She had cried herself to sleep. He thought that she looked peaceful, almost serene, without a care in the world, not a hint of the tragedy they had both endured, nor of the upset that had rocked both their worlds.

When he opened his eyes a few hours later, it was still dark. Light from a nearby streetlamp was shining through a gap in the curtains onto the ceiling above them. Jeanie was sitting up, wide awake. He ran his hand down her back and allowed it to rest for a few minutes on the curve of her arse.

She kissed him tenderly on the lips. He responded in kind and she rolled over on top of him. They made love again; urgent, vigorous, passionate love-making that still could not quite wipe out the feeling of emptiness they shared. Later, Jeanie rustled in her bag to find a packet of cigarettes. She lit one and sat back using Billy as a prop to support her body.

'We need to hold a council of war,' she said.

Billy was confused.

'What do you mean?'

'I mean we need to gather up all those interested in

sorting this town out and find a way of getting some justice for Amber.'

'Who do you propose?'

'Well there's you and me for a start, there's Frank, and I think we need to involve Simon. We may need to use the Observer to flush them out.'

Billy smiled. He was discovering that he liked it when she took charge.

'You have a plan?' he asked. 'How can you think so clearly?'

'I'm just determined someone pays for Amber's death.'

'Do we need more help? If my time with Harry O'Leary has taught me anything at all, it's that the corruption in this town runs very deep.'

'I'm not proposing to bring down the council,' she said. 'but I'm going to ask Ian to come along as well.'

'I was afraid you were going to suggest that.'

She turned around and kissed him.

'You don't need to feel insecure, love. I chose *you*. Ian is just a friend, somebody with principles who told John Baker where to stick his job. As far as I'm concerned that makes him a valuable ally.'

Billy sat there in silence. She kissed him again.

'You're so insecure,' she said.

'I'm sorry, I've never met anybody like you before and I don't want to lose you.'

'I'm going nowhere, love. You don't have to worry about me. We do need Ian though if we're going to do this.'

'I know, that's fine, I'm as determined as you to avenge Amber's death.'

'Good, then that's settled.'

Jeanie kissed him again and then stood up. She fished around on the floor for her underwear and started to dress.

'Where are you going?' he asked.

'It's half-past-six in the morning, if we're going to do this we need to get started.'

Billy stood up and took her into his arms.

'We don't need to do this just now, Jeanie. Everybody will be asleep. Come back to bed.'

She snuggled up against his naked body, holding him tightly. She was crying again.

'I'm sorry,' she said. 'I can't stop thinking of her. I feel I must do something now. I can't just lie in bed doing nothing.'

'We don't need to rush things. If we're going to get to the bottom of Amber's death, then we need to do things properly.'

He unhooked her bra and slipped her pants down over legs.

'Shall we take a bath together,' he said, 'have some breakfast and then we'll get started?'

She kissed him.

'Yes, let's do that.'

32
Picking up the Pieces

Billy helped Jeanie into the front passenger seat of Harry's car. She was still fragile but as determined as before to get justice for Amber.

He looked around at the detritus from the previous night's storm. Broken tiles littered the street. It was a miracle that the car had not been hit. Just a few hundred yards away in the harbour two small boats lay on their side, wrecked by the force of the gale.

As he drove Jeanie to her home, he passed long-established trees uprooted in nearby streets. Council workmen were busy sealing off roads so they could repair the damage and remove trunks and shorn branches.

Billy had never seen anything like it. It was as if some apocalyptic force had visited Oldport in the night specifically to avenge Amber's death. The damage to the town could of course be put right, but there was no going back for his friend. She was lost to Jeanie and him for ever.

Turning a corner towards Jeanie's home he saw that a large tree had crashed down onto her neighbours' car. The owner of the car was in his dressing gown surveying the damage, a bewildered look on his face. He was not going to get to work that morning.

Billy left Jeanie in the capable hands of her mother. Mrs Carter (she had insisted that he call her Phyllis) had been at bingo with Amber's mother when she had been told the news, and Phyllis had gone with her to identify the body.

It was Phyllis who had phoned the Prince Albert to tell them what had happened. Frank told her not to worry, that Jeanie was being comforted and that he would get her back home safely when she was ready.

As Jeanie walked through the door, her mother stepped forward and embraced her. Jeanie sobbed a little bit. She had decided in the car that the time for crying was behind her, but it was proving harder to hold back the tears than she had thought.

Phyllis suggested that she should stay at home for the rest of the day, but Jeanie was having none of it, she was going back to the Prince Albert to work her lunchtime shift as soon as she had changed into some clean clothes. She said she was determined not to be mollycoddled.

'Does Harry need you today?' she asked Billy.

'No, he isn't expecting me in at all. I'm just going to drop off the car and then walk back to the Prince Albert. I'll give you a hand with the lunchtime trade.'

'Don't be too long,' she said, kissing him, 'we've got things to do.'

Billy drove to the town hall. For once it was a hive of activity as council vehicles were despatched to attend to blocked roads and officers took calls from concerned residents.

Sue was in her usual place in the anteroom. The inner door was open, and Harry was seated inside directing operations on the phone. The Town Clerk and Chief Engineer were with him.

Billy walked in and handed Harry his keys. As he put them on the desk Harry looked up. He had finished with his briefing for the time being, so he released the two chief officers back to their work.

'Billy,' he said. 'I wasn't expecting you in today.'

'I just came in to return your car, Councillor, I'm not staying.'

'That's fine. The place is in chaos. Half the trees on Pym Hill appear to have come down, though actually it's more like fifty. My phone's been red hot. I was lucky the council car could even get to my house this morning.

'According to the news, the death toll across the UK is in double figures, and a channel ferry has blown aground at Folkestone. It would have helped if that weatherman had given us the heads-up, instead of telling us it was safe to go to bed.'

'It's a fucking disaster. Worst storm for two-hundred-and-fifty years and it had to hit my town. How are you? You look very pale. Was it all those pineapples?'

Billy hesitated.

'No, I didn't eat that many. A friend of mine died last night.'

Harry stopped fussing about and focussed all his attention onto Billy.

'Oh Christ, I'm sorry. Who was it? What happened?'

'It was Amber, one of the working girls from the Prince Albert. She was at the party at Mr. Baker's house two weeks ago, a blonde girl, very slim. The police say it was a heroin overdose.'

'A prostitute? They're all into drugs Billy, hasn't Frank told you that?'

'Not this one, and the girls at the Prince Albert are clean, Frank makes sure of that.'

'Well, I'm sorry and all that but these girls are two-a-penny Billy.'

Harry's attitude irked him intensely. Despite being a Councillor and a pillar of the community, he wasn't above using prostitutes when it suited him, or treating single mothers like shit so he could take advantage of them. Did he really think these people were beneath him?

'She was a person, Councillor O'Leary, a living, breathing person like you or me.'

'Of course, you're upset. She was your friend. I understand completely.'

Harry put his hand on Billy's arm as he was speaking to try and reassure him, but Billy was by now quite agitated.

'We think she was murdered,' he said, regretting the words as soon as they were out of his mouth.

'Murdered? Good grief. Do the police have any suspects?'

'No, not yet, we still have to convince them of foul play.'

'Well then, you don't really know, do you. It doesn't pay to jump to conclusions in these things Billy, no matter how upset you may be. Why would anybody murder a common prostitute?'

'I don't really want to go into that at present.'

Harry snorted and went back to reading reports on the damage caused by the storm. Billy didn't want to let it go. He knew that he was letting his emotions get the better of him, but he was past caring.

'They found her behind Baker's nightclub, we think she was trying to blackmail somebody.'

Harry looked up startled.

'Pardon? What are you trying to imply, Billy?'

'I'm saying that there are some very dodgy people in this town, Councillor, and that some of them are not above using violence to get their own way.'

Harry almost spluttered his response. He was not used to being talked to in this way by employees.

'I hope you're not including me or my friends in that description young man.'

Something snapped in Billy's head. He was past niceties by now.

'I may not be including you, Harry, but I'm certainly including your friends. This is your town. Over the last twenty years you've re-made it in your own image, and it's lost its way.'

Harry looked furious, but Billy hadn't finished.

'You and your friends operate on the assumption that you can run the lives of others for your own benefit. I can't stomach the arrogance anymore, the corruption and all that goes with it. And now because of what you and others have done a precious human life has been lost. How many others have you wrecked? You should all be ashamed of yourselves.

'I quit. You can stick your job and your council where the sun don't shine.'

He turned on his heel and walked out of the room, leaving Harry open-mouthed as he slammed the door behind him.

Sue had heard it all. She saw that he was close to tears

and stood up to embrace him.

'Well done, boy. You told him. I'm so sorry about your friend. I hope that you'll be alright.'

Billy kissed her on the cheek.

'Look after yourself, Sue,' he said heading back to the Prince Albert.

The walk to the harbour area took longer than usual because of the carnage that littered the streets. A couple of shop windows in High Street had been shattered by a falling tree.

Council workmen with chainsaws were removing branches from a hundred-year-old oak that had finally succumbed to the elements. Further on, a car had driven into somebody's front garden as it sought to avoid yet another falling tree.

As he got to the Prince Albert, he noted that the pub had opened early. A group of locals were holding a meeting in a corner with some insurance assessors. Frank was keeping them well-oiled with beer and spirits.

Jeanie was behind the bar but on seeing him she put down the glasses she was washing and rushed over to hug and kiss him. He could see the sadness in her eyes, but she was doing a good job of hiding it behind her usual chirpiness.

'My mum thinks you are a lovely young man,' she told him. 'My dad, on the other hand, has got his shotgun out and is going to force you to marry me.'

Billy looked startled.

'What? What did you tell him? I didn't even meet him.'

Jeanie laughed.

'I'm so sorry I couldn't resist that. You fall for it every time.'

'Don't joke about these things for Christ's sake. Shotgun weddings are a real thing where I come from.

'You seem a bit more cheerful by the way.'

She kissed him.

'Got to get my act together for Amber's sake, how're you

feeling?'

'Tired and emotional, I've just let rip at Harry O'Leary and quit working for him.'

'What happened?'

'I just saw red. He was so dismissive about Amber, I told him that I thought she'd been murdered and that it was him and his pals who were responsible.'

'Oh love, are you okay? You've had a shock, too.' Jeanie hugged him again.

'But we can't let on what we suspect too soon and certainly not until we have some proof, otherwise they'll have covered their tracks and get away with it.'

'I'm sorry I couldn't help myself. I wasn't thinking straight.'

'Well I don't reckon Harry was involved, so hopefully there was no harm done.'

She took Billy by the hand and led him behind the bar.

'As you have no other work to do you can help me,' she said taking him to the sink and a stack of glasses which needed washing. Frank joined them.

'How are you two feeling today?' he asked. 'I advised the girls to take the day off. They're still very upset. In its own way, this storm has been a blessing, it's enabled Jeanie and me to concentrate on other things.'

Billy looked over to where Heather, Serena and Kitty were sitting together drinking. They were more modestly dressed than usual, in jeans and jumpers.

Jeanie took Frank and Billy by the arm.

'Right you two, I've been busy. I've set up a meeting here tomorrow morning, us three, Simon and Ian. We need to plan what we're going to do about Amber.'

Frank looked doubtful.

'If we're going to do this, we need to be one hundred per cent certain,' he said. 'Once we start pulling at the threads that hold this town together, the whole place could come apart. And there'll be consequences for the Prince Albert, too.'

'In what way?' Billy asked.

'Well if Anderson was involved, as you two think and we can prove it, then we may lose our protection. Things will change, Billy. My fear is we'll be the ones who'll suffer the most while the likes of Harry O'Leary and John Baker carry on as they've always done.'

'Surely, if we're able to expose them for what they are then Harry and Baker will suffer, too?' Billy asked.

'I don't think you fully understand how deep things go in this town,' Frank responded. 'They're in control at every level. At best we may get some underlings, but we might get lucky. Let's see how it works out. I'm prepared to take the gamble if you are.'

Jeanie kissed him on the cheek. Billy shook his hand.

'We're all in this together,' Jeanie said. 'For Amber's sake, we're going to find a way to put this right.'

33
Council of War

It was Saturday morning and Jeanie had awoken early. She was in Billy's bed in the Prince Albert, he was lying naked next to her. She turned over and spooned him. At least she would not have far to go to get to work today, she thought.

She had not been able to sleep much during the night, and not for any good reason. Her mind had been racing with thoughts of Amber. Jeanie had gone through every conversation they'd had over the last few days, desperately trying to find something she could have done or said that might have averted her friend's death.

She snuggled closer to Billy, soaking up his warmth. How is it, she thought, that men could sleep through anything, even the most profound upset?

She needed to be up and active, but there was nothing she could do until the others gathered in the pub later that morning. It wasn't yet six o'clock, and it was dark outside.

She kissed Billy gently on the nape several times. When that did not work, she shook his shoulder in a further attempt to wake him. He groaned quietly but gave no indication of impending consciousness. Jeanie pushed a bit harder and whispered his name a few times. That did the trick. He opened his eyes and turned his head towards her.

'What time is it?' he asked.

'About six o'clock.'

'Urghhh, it's really early.'

She shook him again, pulling her body closer to his as she did so. She needed to talk through her plan of action with him again, and it couldn't wait. Billy misinterpreted her signals.

'What, you want to go again?' he said turning to kiss her.

That hadn't been her intention, but now that he mentioned it…. She returned his kiss and slowly ran her

258

hand down his back. He responded in kind, kissing her neck and her breasts.

She decided that the conversation could wait and climbed on top of him.

A few hours later they walked down to the kitchen together to find some breakfast. Frank was already there, fully made up and wearing the ginger wig he always wore in times of crisis. Jeanie knew that no matter how hard Frank tried he had never been able to break the habit of early starts from his time in the Navy.

'I'm going to have to start charging you rent,' he said to Jeanie as he broke a couple of eggs into a frying pan and added two rashers of bacon,

She smiled.

'I'll have two eggs please, Frank.'

'Well it looks like you're having Billy's eggs then, which is a shame because I think the boy needs to keep his strength up.'

'Nice one, Frank,' she said sarcastically. 'I'll settle for just the one egg then.'

'You can have my egg if you want,' Billy said.

'You are so sweet,' Jeanie said, kissing him, 'but I insist.'

'Give me a break,' Frank said, groaning, 'it's still early in the morning.'

As they finished their breakfast there was a knock on the door. It was Simon. He joined them at the table for a cup of coffee.

'So,' he said, 'Jeanie has briefed me on this. If it's okay I've asked my editor to join us. He'll be with us later. Sorting out this town is a bit of a lifelong mission for him and my life wouldn't be worth living if we took on the town's establishment without him.'

'This is becoming a bit of an ensemble,' Frank said. 'I suspect that Baker and his cronies will be shaking in their boots.'

'Should I conclude that you are not entirely convinced by this enterprise, Frank?' Jeanie asked.

'Oh, don't get me wrong, love, I'm fed up of living in the shadow of those bastards as well, I want my town back for the sake of all the honest, hard-working people who live here. And I'm prepared to risk a great deal to get justice for Amber, or at least to find the truth behind her death. Amber was family, and nobody messes with my family. But I've lived here a long time and these people are well dug in. They won't be easy to shift.'

'Frank's right,' Simon said. 'This won't be easy and I for one am not entirely clear what we can do. Moreover, I'm not sure about involving Ian O'Leary in this. Will he be happy if we start targeting his father?'

'We're not going after his father,' Jeanie said, 'I don't believe Harry had anything to do with this.'

'Well that's settled then,' Simon said. 'What's the plan?'

At that moment, there was a knock on the door. Frank went over to let Ian in.

'Mr O'Leary,' he said, 'we were just talking about you.'

'All good, I hope?'

Jeanie hugged him and then conducted the introductions.

'You've already met Frank and Billy, this is Simon, Billy's brother. He's a journalist.'

'Mr Jones,' Ian said, shaking his hand, 'we've spoken on the phone. It's a pleasure to meet you. I hadn't realised you were Billy's brother. For that matter, I don't think my father knew either. Well played.'

'It wasn't a conspiracy,' Billy said. 'I didn't see how it was relevant.'

'No, of course, sorry I'm not trying to imply anything.'

'Shall we start?' Jeanie said impatiently. 'I'm determined that Amber is going to be the last victim of those bastards.'

'Could we start by reviewing the circumstances of her death?' Simon asked. 'It was a drug overdose wasn't it?'

'Yes,' Frank said. 'but she was clean, had been for years. It's just inconceivable that she would have gone back onto it. We would have seen the signs.'

'I'm not an expert in these things,' Ian said, 'but are you

not in denial? Is there anything that points to it not being a heroin overdose?'

'She placed herself in danger,' Jeanie responded, 'going against all our advice, crossed all the wrong people, violent people at that. And now she's dead. I call that bloody suspicious, don't you?'

'Okay, okay, let's hear what you propose,' Ian said.

'We need to flush them out,' Jeanie said, 'and that's why I've asked Simon. It's about time that we opened up their little world to public view.'

'I'm more than happy to do that,' Simon said, 'but as Jerome will say when he gets here what we publish needs to be legally defensible.'

'And it will be,' Jeanie said, 'because we have witnesses here in this pub to their sordid little world, people who will back up what you write. And having exposed them we can use your credentials as a journalist to open doors to make sure Amber's death is properly investigated and not just written off as another drug death.'

Billy took Jeanie's hand and squeezed it. She reciprocated before continuing.

'The party at Baker's house should be our starting point. Let's put the secret life of those who run Oldport on show.'

'Hold on,' Ian said, 'I was at that party, as an employee of Baker and to keep an eye on my father. If this is going to embarrass my family, then I don't want anything to do with it.'

'Ian,' Jeanie said firmly, 'you've said yourself that this town is rotten, that Harry has lost your respect. Well it's time to grow some balls and help us.'

He sat back deep in thought. Jeanie turned to Simon and Frank.

'Are you in Simon? What about you Frank? Can we rely on the girls to back up our story?'

'The girls are as cut-up about Amber as we are, they'll put their necks on the line to get the truth.'

Simon was not so sure: 'Happy as I will be to have that exclusive, don't we need some hard evidence as well. After all, newspaper headlines are tomorrow's chip paper. I want to see the likes of Phillips and Baker in court, being sent down for twenty years or more. I think we need to set about proving their guilt.'

Frank looked sceptical, but Simon pressed on.

'Look, we can do this. I can talk to my editor to get what we need to put them on the record and in prison.'

He looked around at the others, waiting for someone to say something. It was Ian who broke the silence.

'Mr Jones...sorry, Simon, is right. Let's target the real criminals. For all our disgust at what's been going on in this town, a terrible crime has been committed, and we need to ensure that justice is done.'

There was a knock on the door. Frank went to see who it was. Ian sat there deep in thought, Simon was making notes. Billy turned to Jeanie and whispered.

'You taking charge like this is really turning me on.'

'Later,' she said, 'just control yourself in the meantime.' She was smiling.

Frank returned with Jerome Wilson. The editor was dressed in one of his trademark large-checked woollen suits and red bow tie. The contrast between the two men was stark. In his high heels and ginger wig Frank towered over the portly editor.

Jerome stood there taking in the scene.

'What's this,' he said, 'the famous five for adults?' All you need is Timmy the dog.'

'That would make six,' Ian responded tersely.

'Whatever,' Jerome said, 'this looks interesting. All the best conspiracies start in back-street pubs.' He pulled out a pipe, stuffed it with tobacco and teased a lighted match over it.

'Who are you calling a back-street pub?' Frank demanded only half seriously. Jerome ignored him.

'So, Simon has briefed me. Apparently, you're all

planning a revolution that will put the establishment of this town up against a wall where they'll be summarily shot. You can count me in on that for certain.'

'You only got it half-right,' Simon said.

'No, I live my life in a world of eternal wishful thinking and not one of you is going to shatter that lifelong dream for me.' Jerome was clearly having a ball.

'We're here to find out the truth about the death of Amber,' Jeanie said.

Jerome pulled out a note and read from it.

'Jennifer Daisy Ford, aged 22, commonly known as Amber, found dead from a heroin overdose in an alley at the rear of Baker's nightclub, worked as a prostitute out of the Prince Albert.'

'Except that she'd been clean for a year and had shown no signs of lapsing into bad habits,' Simon said.

'So, I understand. What is it that has cast suspicion on this explanation?'

'She was trying to blackmail someone, we think Inspector Anderson, regarding a bribe he took from Gavin Phillips,' Simon said.

Jerome whistled softly and pulled up a chair.

'Now that *is* interesting,' he said. 'Are we suggesting that the police officer bumped her off?'

Frank put a hand on Jerome's arm.

'Take it easy,' he said softly. 'There are some very upset people here.'

Jerome acknowledged the rebuke.

'We suspect that she was murdered, yes,' said Jeanie, 'but who did that is still open for discussion.'

'Jeanie and Billy have given me material for stories that will open up some of the stuff that has been going on in this town,' Simon said. 'And we have witnesses who are prepared to back them up. You may be getting your wish Jerome. We can peel away the veneer and expose what's really going on in this town.

'However, I want to go further. I want to use the

Observer's resources and work with the people in this room to get some concrete evidence.' Jerome looked thoughtful.

'You do know that we are a newspaper and not a detective agency, don't you Simon?'

'Er…yes, of course…'

'But fear not, I have contacts. I can get you what you need. So, what are we are sitting here for? Haven't we got work to do?'

'Give me a chance Jerome, I'm still taking notes. I also need to come back later to interview the girls. There's a lot of detailed work to be getting on with.'

Jerome stood up and walked towards the door.

'Well my work here is done. I will see you back at base, young Simon, I think you're going to have a busy weekend.'

Ian and Simon stood up to leave as well. The other three walked with them to the door. They shook Frank's hand. Simon embraced his brother.

'You've got a good one there, Bro,' Simon said. 'She's strong. I'm not sure I could have set this up if I'd been in the same position.'

'Oi, stop talking about me when I'm here,' Jeanie said. 'We women run this world. You'll all find that out one day.'

'She's not wrong,' Frank said. 'And this one *is* special.' He gave Jeanie a hug.

'Get out of here all of you.' Jeanie said smiling. She was struggling to hold back tears, once more.

Billy took her hand and led her away as Frank escorted Simon and Ian from the building. He kissed her.

'You're amazing,' he whispered.

'Hold me,' she said.

34
Casino

It was Saturday and Baker's new casino had been opened for just a few hours. Gavin Phillips was pacing the floor making sure everybody was happy.

He was delighted at how many gamblers and members of the great and the good had come to the launch and were spending their money. Fred Harris was splashing the cash alongside Eamonn Jacobs and Sidney Nicholson. Downstairs on the ground floor, the restaurant was booked up with customers.

On the first floor, a more informal cabaret area was being set up with tables for the exotic dancers. Phillips was looking forward to this part of the club opening later in the evening.

Baker was showing the local MP around following his cutting of the ribbon earlier. It had been quite a turnout for that ceremony, with many councillors and businessmen coming along to be seen by the media.

Many of them had gone home to get their partners and to put on glad rags to return later. There had been a concerted marketing campaign and so far, it seemed to be paying off.

As Phillips walked into the cabaret area, he noticed that the cocktail bar was open. Baker was treating his VIP guests to the drink of their choice, while the waitresses moved among them with canapés.

Phillips felt equally at home in this company as he did with the bouncers and the young people in Baker's. He chatted easily to the guests about the state of the economy and the revitalisation of the town while sipping a whisky and soda.

Baker disappeared with the MP, the MP's wife and some select guests to the restaurant for a pre-arranged meal, leaving Phillips in sole charge. He wandered up to the casino in search of Fred Harris and found him playing at the roulette wheel. Harris was just ahead but knew that it couldn't last for long.

As Phillips approached, he gathered his chips and walked to the bar. The two men sat together drinking whisky and picking at peanuts from a bowl on the table.

'It's worked out well then,' Harris said, 'quite a classy place. It will really put Oldport on the map.'

'Glad you like it, Fred. It's been a marathon getting it right on time, and we couldn't have done it without you and your colleagues.'

'I hear you had a bit of trouble a few days ago, at Baker's.'

'Do you mean that prostitute they found round the back?'

Yes, sign of the times I'm afraid. Heroin is becoming quite a problem in this town.'

'It worries the fuck out of me, Gavin. I've got two teenage kids; I don't want them ending up like that young girl.'

'You're right, of course, but what can you do? The police need to get a grip; there has to be a crackdown on these addicts, and on the people, who sell them the drugs.'

'Is it just heroin you're opposed to or all drugs, Gavin?'

'What do you mean?'

'Well I've been in Baker's, I'm not stupid. I've seen those kids using ecstasy and its quite clear that some of those pills are being sold in the club.'

'We've had that discussion, Fred. My bouncers are not working with the dealers.'

'Yes, that's what you told John. He must believe you because otherwise he'd need to act and lose his right-hand man. Some of us are not so easily fooled.'

'What're you after, Fred?' Phillips asked, leaning in.

'Nothing, nothing at all Gavin, just making some observations, but you can't pick and choose with these things. These drug dealers may be selling ecstasy today, but they're selling heroin tomorrow. If you sup with the devil be sure to use a long spoon.'

'I can assure you everything here is above board.'

Harris stroked his beard thoughtfully.

'The way it looks to me, Gavin, is that you've been hiding quite a few things from John; no doubt making a few bob out of it at the same time. What he doesn't know can't hurt him, eh?'

'Those are very serious accusations Fred; I hope you can back them up.' Not even the nightclub's muted lighting could hide the flare of red that suffused Gavin Phillip's face as he listened to the words.

'I'm not making accusations, just stating it as I see it. Oh, don't worry, I'm not going to tell on you. I just thought we should understand each other if we're going to do business in the future.'

Phillips eyed him with barely disguised malevolence. 'I'm intrigued as to what business you think we're going to be doing, Fred.'

Harris sipped his whisky before continuing. 'You know I'm not going to be chair of licensing forever. Harry's been in charge for a long time. He's getting tired, losing his grip, it's only a matter of time before I take over. I'll need John's support, and the key to that lies with you.'

'I'm flattered,' Phillips said, 'but I don't think you'll need me to get John's backing. He's very grateful for what you've done already.'

'Still, it doesn't do any harm to have all your ducks in a row, and I find that the sort of understanding we have can often be very productive.'

Phillips picked up his drink and knocked the dregs back in one. He looked at his watch there was plenty of time before he had to open the club to the general public. He debated whether to have another drink or not. However, Harris beat him to it by indicating to the waitress that they wanted refills.

'I really need to be getting on,' Phillips said.

'Come on, have another drink. You've got plenty of time, besides everything is going like clockwork. You've done a good job here, Gavin.'

'I'm not sure that Harry is going to move over so easily,' Phillips responded. 'He seems well entrenched to me, and John certainly finds him useful.'

'It does look like that doesn't it, but that's why I'm in politics and you're not. Things can change very quickly in my line of work and sometimes the fault lines are not as obvious as you would think.'

'I'll have to take your word for that.'

Harris adjusted his glasses and drank some more of his whisky.

'I'm glad we've had this conversation, Gavin. It's good to understand each other's business. A bit of advice though, now you've got this place it isn't going to be so easy to hide the dodgy stuff going on in Baker's, even with Ollie's help. And John's not going to tolerate the rumours forever. Clean up your act and we can make a lot of money together.'

Phillips bristled. He was not comfortable with this conversation at all, but he could see advantages in continuing to court Fred Harris, so he tolerated the bluntness.

The two men stood up and shook hands. Harris headed back to the casino tables. Phillips went to look for the cabaret act.

As he got to his office, he could see that the door was ajar. He went in to find Ollie Anderson standing in front of a framed, glass-covered poster admiring his reflection and smoothing his moustache. He was out of uniform, dressed in jeans and one of his customary brightly patterned shirts.

As Phillips walked into the office, Anderson turned around. He was furious.

'What the fuck, Gavin.'

'Have a seat,' Phillips said unperturbed, closing the door behind him and moving a chair to accommodate the inspector. Phillips settled into a large leather armchair. He swung it around to face Anderson and moved it closer to the desk.

'You have a problem, Ollie?'

'Too right I have a fucking problem. When I came to you to ask for help with the whore who was trying to blackmail me, I meant pay her off, not kill her and dump her in an alley.'

'You have a very vivid imagination, Ollie.'

'It comes with the territory, but that doesn't answer my question.'

'The girl killed herself from an overdose before I could get to her.'

Anderson shifted in his seat and fixed Phillips with a stare.

'I'm a police officer, Gavin. I'm not stupid. The girl had no other signs of recent drug use, she'd clearly been clean for some time. It was a bit of a stretch don't you think that she should suddenly start using again just hours after she'd demanded money with menaces?'

'These things happen.'

'Do I look like a fucking idiot, Gavin?'

'You look like a police officer up to his neck in shit, Ollie. Did you think that girl was going to go away just like that? Did you think she was going to settle for two grand and then disappear, that she wasn't going to come back for more?'

Anderson put his head in his hands and rocked back and forth groaning. He seemed to be having some sort of breakdown. After a few minutes, he sat back up. He was deathly pale, and his usually impeccably styled hair was ruffled.

'I can't believe you, Gavin. You're a real piece of work. You've just blown away two decades of policing for me.'

'For fuck's sake Ollie, pull yourself together. Has there been any blowback? It's been two days now and everybody accepts that she topped herself in some tragic accident. Nobody cares about her.

'She's a whore, a piece of street trash with no family to speak of and, according to the local press, a brother in prison for drug dealing and murder. As far as we're concerned, it's problem solved, now move on.'

Anderson glared at him with a look of horror.

'You don't have any kids do you, Gavin?'

Phillips shook his head.

'I've got three. None of them are even in their teens yet. I've seen so much in this job, people who've thrown their lives away, victims of circumstances, people who exploit others and then discard them, that I fear for my children's future.

'When I looked at that girl's body I thought – "what if that had been my daughter, how can I prevent her ending up like this one day?"

'Whatever her circumstances, that girl was somebody's daughter, somebody's sister, somebody's friend. Her life was wasted just when she had started to get it together at the tender age of just twenty-two.

'And now, because of your actions I'm implicated in that wasteful death.'

Phillips clapped his hands together loudly, stopped and did it again.

'Bravo, Inspector, that was a noble speech, but the reality is that if that whore hadn't stuffed herself full of drugs then you and I, and John and possibly half of the council could be up on corruption charges by now.

'And what would have happened to your precious family then? Do you think your daughter would still admire you?

'Could any of your children have looked you in the eye when the money to pay for their private schooling and their luxury holidays had dried up, and your wife was getting by on benefit while you rot in solitary confinement on the Isle of Wight?'

Anderson stood up and leant across the desk. Phillips didn't flinch.

'I've fucking had it with you and Baker,' he said quietly. 'We're through. I've made sure that nobody looks too deeply into the death of that girl but that's the last favour you're getting from me. From now on you're on your own.'

Phillips got out of his chair and squared up to the

inspector.

'Don't let your pride and your bleeding heart get in the way of what you need to do, Ollie. You'll be back. You know you will be. I know it, too. I'll be seeing you around.'

He opened the office door and gestured for Anderson to leave.

35
A Reckoning

Ian sat quietly in his office, enjoying a few peaceful moments before the rest of the staff arrived to open up Baker's. He still had three weeks left before he finished working in the club for good, but already his head was elsewhere. He was just going through the motions, while his deputy and possible successor, Jim Evans, picked up the slack.

Ian was waiting for Phillips, having invited him back to the club to discuss the handover. He wasn't looking forward to the meeting – the man disgusted him.

There was a knock on the door and the drug-dealing bouncer with earing and tattoo entered. Ian regretted having not learnt his name.

'Mr Phillips is here,' he announced resentfully, as if he'd been cut out to be more than a doorman.

'Of course, send him in.'

Gavin Phillips barged past the bouncer into the room. Ian stood to greet him, but Phillips waved his arm to indicate that it wasn't necessary. He looked back at the bouncer.

'There was no need to announce me, Tony. I know my way around.'

The bouncer nodded but didn't move.

'What's wrong, Gavin, do you need protection, now, when you come and see me?'

Phillips dismissed the bouncer and closed the door.

'So, what's this all about? There's plenty of time to arrange things before you leave.'

'There would be if you told me who's taking my place.' Phillips sighed and sat down.

'For the time being Jim Evans will look after the place. He used to be a bouncer, he knows the business inside out and that way we can guarantee some continuity. We'll see how he does before deciding if he stays or not.'

'Good, and will he be doing something about the drug dealing that's still going on here?'

'Don't start, Ian, we've been through this already. Whatever happens after you've gone is none of your concern.'

Ian smiled at Phillips' defensiveness, and probed further.

'Come on Gavin, it's just the two of us here now. You've obviously persuaded John that everything is hunky dory, so what do you have to lose?'

Phillips frowned, looked around the room and lowered his voice.

'I think you already know what's going on around here, Ian, so don't pretend you don't. Yes, drug dealing is going on in the club, and yes, my bouncers are involved with that. It's the only way to control it and keep the really nasty stuff out. If you were half clued-in to the real world, you'd know that by now.'

Oh, don't come the philanthropist with me, Gavin. You control it so you can make money from it.'

'And what if we do? It's our reward for keeping the drugs trade at a manageable level.'

'Until somebody dies, of course.'

'Not on my watch.' Phillips laughed. 'You're such an innocent. This whole town is on the take... one hand washes the other. We pay off the police inspector to turn a blind eye, everybody gets their share. But you'll never prove any of it. If I was you, if you know what's good for you, I'd forget everything you've seen and heard in this club and go running back to mommy in London. You're out of your depth. It's time you realised that college boy.'

He stood up to leave, but Ian had one last question.

'Just one more thing, Gavin. That prostitute who was found dead behind the club a few days ago, do you know anything about her? After all she worked in the Prince Albert, don't you and my father drink there all the time?'

Phillips hesitated, sensing a trap. 'I knew of her, of course I did. Anybody who uses the Prince Albert is familiar with the girls there. But the last time I saw her she was on Inspector Anderson's knee. That's a matter of public record – there were plenty of witnesses. Why do you want to know? Are you upset that you missed out? There are plenty of other girls to take her place,' he sneered.

Ian laughed, refusing to take the bait, but determined to get as much information as he could.

'Good grief, no. I just thought it was suspicious that she was found here, when she worked out of the Prince Albert. As far as I know, she's never worked this area, but I suppose that's a matter for the police. Just as long as we don't have prostitution to contend with in here as well as drugs.'

Phillips was getting irritated by this line of questioning.

'Would you even know a prostitute if you fell over one, Ian? Have you even set foot in the Prince Albert? I shouldn't think you'd find many of your posh friends there. But as you ask, I'm told the police think she came here to score – end of story. Now, I really need to get back.'

There was a knock on the door and, as if on cue, Tony the bouncer entered.

'You're needed back at the casino, boss'

Gavin acknowledged him and turned towards Ian.

'Whatever our differences,' he said, 'good luck in whatever you do next. I can't say we'll miss you, but for your father's sake I hope you find something more suited to you. Try and clear your office in good time.'

He held out his hand. Ian took it reluctantly and watched as the two men left. He sat back in his chair and grinned. Phillips would find out soon enough not to mess with "college boys".

* * *

The Prince Albert was just about to close for the afternoon, when Oliver Anderson walked through the door. He was in a hurry and looked flustered. He stopped just inside the bar and scanned the room, spotted Heather and went over to meet her.

She was wearing a short leather skirt, a flimsy top without

a bra and fishnet stockings. Her hair was bleached blonde with darker roots starting to show at the top, and she wore a dark purple lipstick. She was thin and short but made up for her lack of stature with two-inch stiletto heels.

They walked to the back of the pub together and up the stairs to Heather's room. Anderson watched appreciatively as she slowly removed her top and stood briefly topless in front of him. She unzipped her skirt and slid out of her knickers – only her stockings remained.

He pulled out his wallet, placed some money on the bedside table, undressed and advanced towards her It was obvious that he worked out, but middle age and alcohol had taken their toll on his body, which was starting to look flabby around the hips, and a prominent beer gut was beginning to develop.

She picked up a condom, took it out of its packet and offered it to him. He rolled it over his penis and pushed her onto the bed.

She had been told by Amber that the inspector liked to play rough but was unprepared for the ferocity with which he held her down, crying out with pain as he secured both her arms in a vice-like grip.

Heather struggled to loosen his hold on her, but only succeeded in provoking him to hit her across the face with the palm of his hand. Instinctively, she stopped struggling and allowed him to thrust hard and painfully inside her. It was as if he was using sex to exorcise all his demons – and a visceral hatred of women

After it was over, he sat up on the edge of the bed, breathing heavily. His body glistened with sweat. Heather placed a hand on his shoulder, concerned that he might expire then and there.

'Can I get you anything,' she asked. 'A glass of water, perhaps?'

'He shook his head, still panting. She pulled her legs over the side of the bed, positioned herself next to him and put both arms around his body.

'What are you doing?' he demanded.

'I was worried about you, thought you might like a few extra minutes before you go.'

'I'm not giving you any more money.'

She smiled. 'There's no charge. It's just nice to have some company for a bit. To be honest, we're all a bit jittery since we lost Amber.'

His expression softened. 'Yes, I was rather fond of that girl. It's a shame she lost her way before she died.'

'What do you mean?'

'Came to me demanding money. I sent her packing of course. Told her to go and see Gavin Phillips, but I guess her addiction to drugs was too strong, and she ended up dead before he saw her.'

'Is that what happened?' Heather asked innocently. 'I didn't know she'd got back into drugs.'

He stood up, pulled his pants on and started to button up his shirt.

'You fucking whores are all the same out for what you can get, only looking for your next score. Well, your pal over-reached, and she ended up dead.'

He grabbed her by the chin, pulled her to her feet, and placed his face just inches from hers – snarling: 'Just keep your fucking nose out of my affairs, or you'll end up like your friend.'

He threw her back onto the bed and stood briefly in front of a mirror, smoothing down his moustache and rearranging his hair. He glared in Heather's direction as if he was going to hit her again but thought better of it. Instead, he, slipped his shoes and socks on, grabbed his jacket and walked out of the room without speaking another word.

Heather sat on the bed rubbing the red marks on each arm where he had held her down. She inspected her face to see if his blow had done any damage and used a tissue to dispose of the discarded condom.

Still naked she walked over to an old oak chest of drawers. A small microphone protruded from a partially opened drawer. She picked it up, traced the wire back to a cassette recorder and pressed the off switch.

* * *

It was just after closing time and the pub was deserted, apart from a determined-looking group of people sitting around a table just inside the main entrance. Frank, Simon and Billy were supping pints of lager, Jeanie, Heather, Serena and Kitty were drinking white wine. Ian was nursing a large brandy.

They were sitting in rapt attention as a tape of Ian's conversation with Gavin Phillips was played back. Simon was looking pleased with himself.

'There's enough here to hold up a story about drug dealing in Baker's, including the active collusion of Phillips and his bouncers,' he said. 'I'm sure Anderson's bosses will be interested in the admission of bribery, and with Heather's tape I think we also have enough to prompt an investigation into our local inspector and Phillips for Amber's murder.'

'What happens now?' Billy asked.

'Well, I've spoken to Jerome, and we're going to run a series of articles over the next week. By the time we're finished everybody will know what really goes on behind the scenes in this town.'

Frank grunted. 'This can't just be about your circulation figures, Simon.'

'No. you're right. We will, of course hand over all the evidence to senior police officers and ask them to open a formal inquiry. They'll want to take statements from all of us, I suppose.'

'I think we're all prepared to tell them what we know,' Jeanie said, looking to the others for confirmation.

'Good, in the meantime, I'm going to have to sit down with those of you who were at Baker's party, so I can get my facts straight. Shall we do that now?'

Frank nodded his agreement and looked to the girls. They were still upset at Amber's death and were more than willing to co-operate.

277

36
Fit to print

A light drizzle fell outside as Jeanie and Billy set up the bar for the first lunchtime session of the week.

Frank was with the girls. They had gone to see Amber's mother to comfort her and to discuss the funeral arrangements. He'd told Jeanie before he left that he didn't expect Amber's mother, Sarah, to be very coherent, and that he would end up doing all the work.

Jeanie knew Mrs Ford of old. The woman had never been particularly coherent even on her good days. When the police had told her about her daughter, she was playing bingo, having already consumed several glasses of wine before she had got to the club.

Phyllis Carter had helped them calm her down and left her with a neighbour. A few people on the estate had rallied around to support her. Others had found themselves paralysed by moral indignation at Amber's profession or the manner of her death.

Sarah Ford had herself been brought up on the Millstream Estate. Her husband had been an abusive drunk before she had thrown him out. She had subsequently found common cause with others in a similar situation but had slowly alienated many of them by her own drunken behaviour and the drug-dealing antics of her son.

Frank, Kitty, Heather, Serena and Jeanie had been Amber's real family in her later years and now they were reaching out to Sarah, albeit far too late to save her only daughter.

Jeanie still had to stop every now and again to steady herself. She kept imagining she saw Amber stalking her from room to room, except that when she turned around to confront her, Amber was not there.

Billy was checking the optics while Jeanie did a stock take of the mixers. She looked across to Billy in his jeans, T-shirt and trainers and smiled. She had been grateful for his support even though she knew he was hurting badly, too.

She went over and gave him a hug.

'What was that for?'

'No reason,' she said, 'just a thank you for being here for me.'

He smiled. Just then there was a knock on the door. Billy looked at his watch. It was just eleven o clock, a full hour before opening time. He walked over and slid the bolt back. It was Simon.

Without saying a word, he walked past and threw a copy of the Oldport Observer onto the bar.

Billy bolted the door and followed him into the pub. Jeanie came and joined them.

'Morning, Simon,' she said. 'What do you have for us today?'

He unfolded the newspaper, so they could read the headline: 'Leading councillors partied with prostitutes. By Simon Jones' Billy whistled softly.

'You'll be featuring semi-naked page three girls next,' he said.

Jeanie picked up the paper and started to read out loud.

'Senior Oldport Councillors partied with prostitutes at the home of a leading local businessman just days after passing a license for his new club, it has been revealed.

'The party took place at the home of club owner, John Baker on Saturday 3rd October. Council leader Harry O'Leary and Licensing Committee Chair, Fred Harris were in attendance along with local businessmen Sidney Nicholson and Stephen Thomas, and Oldport Police Inspector Oliver Anderson.

'Witnesses say that the prostitutes romped naked with guests in Mr Baker's swimming pool and games room. Some of those present spent time alone with the girls in one of the many bedrooms in the Pym Hill mansion.

'It is understood that the party occurred on the weekend after Oldport Council passed a controversial licensing application for Mr Baker's new club and casino in High Street. All the councillors who supported the application were present at the party.

'Mr. Baker, who is also a prominent developer, has been a controversial figure in Oldport in recent weeks after securing permission to extend the Inchfield Estate onto a conservation area just outside the town.

'That application is currently being challenged by residents who are seeking to register part of the site as a village green. If they are successful, the new development won't go ahead.

'Many of the councillors who supported that planning application also backed the club license and attended the party, including planning chair, Eamonn Jacobs.

'Inchfield Residents Chairman, Matthew Lawrence has called for an inquiry into the conduct of the councillors. He told the Observer that the close ties of councillors to Mr Baker called into question the impartiality of the process.

'Mr Lawrence said: 'Such a close relationship between councillors and the developer throws fresh doubt on the validity of the decision by the planning committee to extend the Inchfield Estate.

'We want our MP to demand that the Minister call the application in and overturn the decision. We will also be seeking a full inquiry into the way that Oldport Council is being run.'

'The Observer tried to contact Mr Baker and Councillors O'Leary, Harris and Jacobs for comment but at the time of publication had had no response from any of them.'

Jeanie put the paper down and smiled.

'That's a good piece, Simon. It's bound to have an impact.'

'It's only the first one,' Simon said. 'We're running another one tomorrow placing Amber at the party, and later in the week we will be using the information Ian got for us about Phillips being in league with drug dealers and bribing Anderson. But there's more.'

Simon opened the paper at the comment and letters page.

'Here,' he said. 'Editorial: The apparently incestuous relationship between local councillors and developers has long been a matter of concern to this newspaper.

'However, revelations today, of councillors and businessmen partying with prostitutes raises serious questions of propriety. It also casts doubt on the validity of decisions taken by the council on key planning and licensing matters.

'We support residents in calling for an investigation into the way that the council is being run.'

'That's it then,' said Billy. 'It's over.'

'On the contrary Bro, it's only just begun. Jerome has contacts with the police, he's passed on the tapes and my interview notes and he's going to get somebody high-up from outside Oldport to come and talk to you.'

'The case is not rock solid yet but the evidence of collusion between Baker and the council, the presence of Anderson at the party and the tapes are enough to get a formal investigation underway.

'They'll take what you have to say and look deeper. He may try to deny it, to discredit our testimony and the tape, but if Anderson has been careless in any way at all then they'll have him bang-to-rights.

'The key feature of this whole business is the arrogance of those involved. They've been getting away with it for so long that they think they're untouchable.

'If one of them *did* kill Amber then it was because he thought he'd get away with it.'

'Harry certainly acted that way,' Billy said. 'The way he treated that single mother, taking a bribe and keeping a key was outrageous.

'Unfortunately, I can't use that story as the woman doesn't want to speak to us on the record. She spoke very highly of you though, Bro. You hadn't told me that you went up to change the locks afterwards.'

'Ahhhh, he's a knight in shining armour,' Jeanie mocked,

kissing Billy on the cheek.

'I just did what needed to be done,' Billy responded.

'My worry,' Simon said, 'is that the likes of Gavin Phillips are not going to go easily, even with what we have on him. The more I hear about that thug the less I like him.'

'He certainly seems to be a nasty piece of work,' Billy said, 'but the bigger they are the harder they fall.'

'That's easy for you to say, Billy,' Simon said. 'but there are wider implications. For example, Jeanie what do you think is going to happen to this place?'

'What do you mean?'

'Well, you can't shake things up like this and not suffer consequences. The pub will survive, it may well thrive but there'll have to be changes.'

'I'm not sure Frank is in favour of much change.'

'Okay, let's look at it logically. So far, the girls have been able to operate from here because they have had protection from the powers that be. All of that is about to be undone.

'The girls have just alienated some of their best customers. Don't get me wrong, they've done it for a very good reason, but Baker and his cronies aren't going to be inviting them to any more parties.'

'That's if they have any more parties,' Jeanie interjected.

'Precisely, and if Anderson gets his come-uppance do you think his successor will tolerate a brothel on his doorstep?'

'I suppose not, but the alternative isn't worth thinking about,' Jeanie said. 'I don't want to see the girls back on the streets where they're exposed to drugs and are in danger of being beaten up or worse?'

'They don't care, Jeanie. As far as the powers-that-be are concerned the girls don't matter. They don't acknowledge the obvious, that men sometimes pay to have sex or that girls might choose to sell it to them for a whole host of different reasons.

'The two oldest professions in this world are prostitute and politician, but society only recognises the legitimacy of the politician even though many of those who enter that world in this town have worse morals than the girls who sell themselves for money.'

Simon had climbed fully onto his high horse now.

'Yes, there are victims, women are exploited, abused, demeaned, but isn't that an argument for legitimising the profession? The more we fail to acknowledge the existence of prostitution, the more we persecute girls who rely on it to feed themselves and their children, then the more victims there are.'

'And you think they'll force Frank to put the girls out on the street?' Billy asked.

'Not in that way, Bro. In the eyes of the law, I guess Frank is a pimp, but from his perspective he allows the girls to work from here for their own protection. He takes rent not a cut, he keeps them safe. At best, he might have to be more discreet about it. At worst, then yes, they may have to go and work elsewhere.'

Simon looked at his watch.

'I have to be getting back,' he said. He embraced Billy and Jeanie in turn. 'You know, Bro I was a bit wary of you coming here, but I'm glad you did. I'd forgotten what it was like to have a family.'

Billy walked him to the door while Jeanie went back to setting up the pub. Simon was right, she thought, the place would never be the same again, all her certainties had been swept away by Amber's death.

Now she had to rebuild her life, as would Frank, Heather, Kitty, Serena and even the town itself. Billy re-joined her at the bar. She turned to him.

'If I must start again Billy, will you come with me?'

He pulled her into his arms and kissed her gently on the forehead.

'Don't be daft,' he said, 'why would you need to start again? This is your town. They can never take that away from you. All we're doing is righting a wrong. Of course, Oldport may be different but if we succeed it will be for the better, and the town will be fit for decent, honest folk to live in once more.'

Jeanie looked uncertain. She could feel herself starting to lose it again. A tear slipped surreptitiously down her cheek. She dabbed it away with her hand and pulled herself together.

'Don't set your bar so high,' she said, 'I'll settle for getting to the truth behind Amber's death.

'It's as if part of me died with her. I feel lost, Billy, as if I'm drifting in a never-ending dream. You're the only thing anchoring me at present.

'And Simon is right, things are going to change. Ever since I started here, I've known where I belong. Now all that I can see in front of me is a huge black hole.'

Billy held her for a minute.

'I've already taken one leap into the unknown in coming here, Jeanie. I'm not afraid to take another and nor should you. Whether we stay here or move on, we'll do it together. The one thing you should know is that you're not alone in this.'

'You're right, Billy, and I'm not going anywhere. I'm sure things will settle down after the funeral. I belong in Oldport, they'll have to drag me from here kicking and screaming.'

'I can't imagine anybody even attempting that, Jeanie. They're all too scared of you.'

She smiled.

'Don't you forget it,' she said.

37
A Superintendent Calls

The next day Billy was sitting reading a book while Jeanie and Frank kept themselves busy tidying up after the previous night's session.

It was a Tuesday and Billy was not needed in the bar, so he was sat in the back room, studying a prospectus for Southampton University. When he had left home, he'd been on a gap year following A-Levels and was in the process of applying to study for a degree in English. Was it time to revive that ambition, he wondered?

He was so lost in the brochure that he didn't notice Jeanie come up behind him. She flicked the back of his head with a tea towel causing him to jump up with a start. She laughed.

'If you've got nothing better to do you can wash some glasses,' she said.

'I'll pass,' he replied. 'It's my day off and I'm doing some research.'

Jeanie shrugged her shoulders and left him to it. As she walked away there was a knock on the door. It was Simon.

'This is becoming a bit of a habit,' Jeanie said, letting him in.

'Yeh, sorry, thought you'd like to see the latest instalment and catch up on the news.'

Billy came into the bar and Simon went over to join him, while Jeanie went to fetch Frank. They returned with a pot of tea and some mugs. Frank poured as Simon read from the paper.

'The article is headed: 'Dead Prostitute attended Councillors' sex party.' A local prostitute found dead from a heroin overdose behind Baker's nightclub last Thursday, was romping with councillors at a party just two weeks previously, the Observer can exclusively reveal.

'Jennifer Ford was one of several prostitutes at the party

hosted by nightclub owner and developer John Baker, which had leading councillors as guests, including council leader Harry O'Leary, Planning Committee Chair, Eamonn Jacobs and Licensing Committee Chair, Fred Harris.

'However, less than two weeks later Ms Ford was dead, having overdosed on heroin.

'Friends of the dead woman have questioned the circumstances surrounding her death, claiming Ms Ford had not used heroin for many years and had shown no sign of doing so again.

'However, local police Inspector Oliver Anderson told this newspaper there was nothing suspicious about her death and that the case has been closed.

'The revelation that Jennifer Ford was at the party at the home of local businessman, John Baker, has intensified the pressure on council leader Harry O'Leary to resign.

'Opposition Councillor, Rupert James told the Observer that the existing leadership were bringing Oldport into disrepute.

''If these allegations concerning members of the council partying with prostitutes turn out to be true, then they are a disgrace" he said, 'while the alleged close relationship between those same councillors and leading businessmen raises serious questions about the way this town is being run and the legitimacy of several key decisions.'

'An inquiry must be held immediately to get to the bottom of these very serious claims – and a response from the council is definitely called for,' the councillor said'

'Councillor James has written to the Town Clerk demanding an extraordinary meeting of the council, so that Councillor O'Leary can answer questions about the allegations.'

'The Oldport Observer, once again, sought comment from the council on these matters, but none was forthcoming at time of publication.'

'Not bad,' Jeanie said. 'You're really putting the pressure on them.'

'Yes, but that's not all,' Simon said. 'We had news this morning that Harry O'Leary has had a heart attack and is in intensive care. His son is with him and he's expected to make a full recovery, but it is doubtful if he will be able to stay on as council leader.'

Frank whistled.

'It seems like you've had quite an impact, Jeanie.'

'That's all very well,' she said, 'but I wasn't trying to get at Harry O'Leary, we need to force the police to properly investigate Amber's death.'

'Oh, that's in hand as well,' Simon said, 'Jerome has been onto the Chief Constable. He's agreed to send a senior police officer to Oldport to investigate what's been going on here.

'The officer has a wide brief that includes investigating corruption, as well as finding out what happened to Amber. He should be calling around here today to talk to you all.'

Jeanie looked pleased.

'You've done well, Simon. Thank you for all your support.'

'It's my pleasure, and besides it doesn't do my career any harm either. There's much more to come. We're covering the drug dealing in Baker's tomorrow and using the tapes to report that Amber allegedly went to Anderson to blackmail him on the day she was killed. I'll be in Fleet Street before you know it,' he joked.

'Good on you Si,' Billy said. 'You deserve it. It's just sad that it took a tragedy like this.'

'Yes, I'm sorry, I didn't mean to make light of what's happened.'

'Don't worry,' Jeanie said stroking his arm. 'It's fine. You've been brilliant.'

Simon got up to go.

'I have to get back to the paper,' he said. 'Keep me informed of any developments.'

Billy escorted him to the door and was starting to push it closed when a hand appeared and held it open. He stepped back, and a man entered the pub.

'Sorry to startle you,' he said. 'My name's Superintendent Tim Adams. I'm looking for Billy Jones.'

He flashed a warrant card in Billy's face.

'That's me,' Billy said standing to one side, so the man could enter.

Superintendent Adams towered above Billy. He was almost as broad as he was tall with a square clean-shaven face and a good head of dark brown hair. He was wearing a light grey suit that seemed a bit tight on him, a white shirt and what looked like a rugby club tie.

Billy escorted him to the table where Frank and Jeanie were still sitting, did the introductions and pulled up a fourth chair.

Adams tried to disguise his surprise at Frank's appearance. It was almost as if he had not seen a pub landlord dressed in a full-length green dress, high heels and a brunette wig before.

Whatever, the superintendent thought he managed to quickly overcome his shock and get down to business.

'Jerome Wilson has briefed me on what you told him,' he said. 'and has passed onto me the tapes you made together with his reporter's notes. It's my job to get to the truth, so I would be grateful if you could tell me in your own words what exactly you saw and heard.'

'I think I should leave you to it,' Frank said. 'I've got work to do. Are you coming Jeanie?'

'Do you mind if I stay for a bit, Frank? I may be able to add some details to help get a complete picture.'

'I'd rather I spoke to you all individually, if that's okay with you,' Adams said. Jeanie acknowledged the request and joined Frank at the bar.

Billy outlined the details of the party and how he and Amber had overheard a conversation between Ollie Anderson and Gavin Phillips. He told Adams that they had then seen through a crack in the door the two men exchange a large sum of money

'And are you absolutely sure that this Gavin Phillips handed over cash to Inspector Anderson?'

'Yes, of course, but I understand that it's my word against his.'

'It is, but we have the admission of Phillips on tape that he was paying off our inspector, and there are other things we can do to establish whether there is any substance to the charge.'

'Such as?'

'Well, for one thing, we can look at his bank accounts and lifestyle to establish whether he's living above his means. I can assure you that we will take this very seriously, Mr Jones and carry out a very thorough investigation.'

'What about Amber?'

'Yes, the prostitute. She was found dead from a heroin overdose less than two weeks after overhearing this conversation. Why do you think there was anything suspicious about her death? The local police have effectively closed the file.'

'I bet they have.'

'Are you implying some impropriety on the part of the local police?'

'Amber had been clean for nearly two years,' Billy protested. 'She had no reason to start using heroin again. But she did need money, and in the last conversation I had with her she told him that she was going to try blackmailing Inspector Anderson. Your inspector even admitted on tape that she had come to him asking for money.'

'I pleaded with her not to do it, but she wouldn't listen to sense. And a few hours later she was dead. I think that's suspicious, don't you?'

'It could be a coincidence, of course, but I'm reviewing all the circumstances of the girl's death as well as the various relationships around the matters you've raised with me, and I'll make sure everything was done properly. Is there anything else you want to tell me?'

At this point Jeanie came back with a cup of coffee for

Adams.

'You could tell me what's happening about the corruption in the local council,' she said.

'I'm sorry, Ms Carter, I'm not in a position to do that. That investigation is being taken forward and it would compromise our work if I were to discuss it with outside parties.'

'Well I'm sure Billy could help. He worked for Harry O'Leary for a bit, before quitting over what happened to Amber.'

She squeezed Billy's arm.

'Thank you, I'll be sure to pass that onto my sergeant, who is dealing with that side of the investigation. She'll want to talk to you, Mr Jones.'

Adams stood up and straightened his jacket.

'Here's my card,' he said, handing one to Billy. 'You can contact me on this number if you think of anything else. I'll make arrangements for all of you to come in and give formal statements over the next few days.'

He shook both their hands and left them to their work.

As he departed, Billy turned to Jeanie.

'I wish you hadn't volunteered me to give evidence against Harry,' he said.

'Why, didn't you think you'd need to? It's all or nothing now, Billy. This is the real world. There's no room for misplaced loyalties, especially after the way he's treated you and this town.'

'He was quite decent towards me actually,' Billy protested, but Jeanie was having none of it.

'He and those bastards have spent twenty years ruining this town. They've trampled over everybody who's got in their way, without any regard for feelings or even what's best for the community they represent, and ultimately, it's their arrogance and their cruelty that led to Amber's death.

'I can't forgive any of them for that, and I'll do all I can to bring them down, and to make them pay for what they did.'

'You must do what you have to do, of course,' Billy said, 'and I'll support you in that. But please don't lose touch with who are, don't become bitter and twisted. We want justice, Jeanie, not revenge.'

'I'm sorry,' she said, pulling away from him, 'I apologise for volunteering you, but let's get one thing clear, I want revenge as well as justice. I've ignored what's been going on here for too long, now I want to do something about it.'

Billy stood looking at her as she wiped the tears from her cheeks. He wanted to cosset her, to protect her from all the dangers that the world threatened them with.

But he was struggling to know what to do for the best. He put his arms around her again.

'I'm here for you, Jeanie.' He said simply, even though he was unsure what it was he was committing himself to.

38
Front Page News

It was one of the busiest Friday night sessions the Prince Albert had seen for some time. Frank was not sure if it was because it was payday or that people were just having a blast before the November run-in to Christmas.

Oldport Council, many of the local firms, and the college paid their workers on the last Friday of the month rather than the last day, so the pub was packed with people intent on drinking their wages.

The three girls were also busy, servicing a growing clientele of cash-rich customers, who by Sunday night would be back to counting the pennies until the next pay day.

Frank noticed that the journalists from the Oldport Observer were out in force and for once had been joined by Jerome Wilson, who was regaling them with tales of his legendary forty-year career as a stringer, local government correspondent, columnist, sub-editor and editor at the Observer.

He had placed his jacket on the back of his seat and was standing in front of his audience in white shirt, his customary red bow tie, and red braces that stretched across his substantial belly and secured a pair of grey-checked suit trousers.

He was waving a cigarette in his nicotine-stained right hand, occasionally puffing on it as a form of punctuation before embarking on the next section of his story.

Several of the journalists had heard it all before and were engaging in separate conversations, but some of the younger members of staff sat engrossed. Simon and Sally were sitting slightly to the side having their own private discussion.

Jeanie and Billy were rushed off their feet serving customers, so Frank did a tour of the pub to collect glasses. He picked up half a dozen empties from the Observer table, nodding to Jerome as he did so.

'Frank,' the editor boomed, 'it's good to see you. I've got some news for you and your band of outlaws. Can I hang around after closing time to update you all?'

'Yes, you can Jerome. Which particular outlaws did you want me to assemble?'

'Oh, the usual suspects, you and your two sidekicks. I'll bring Carl Bernstein here,' he said gesturing towards Simon.

Simon responded by raising his glass to Frank and then emptying its contents.

'It's your round, Jerome,' he said. 'Sally will have a glass of white wine.'

Frank sighed and took the glasses back to the bar.

An hour later he was calling last orders, and ushering people into the rain. Many of them were heading on to Baker's. Simon kissed Sally goodbye and hung back with Jerome. Frank handed them a tea towel each.

'As you're staying, you'd better make yourself useful,' he said.

Jerome held the cloth in front of him with a look of disdain on his face.

'Surely this is woman's work,' he said.

Billy, who had just walked into the bar, laughed and took the tea towel off him.

'You appear to have strayed into the wrong century, Mr Wilson,' he said.

'Yes, yes, whatever you say boy. Shall we get down to it, so that we can leave you to your ablutions?'

'Sit down there and behave yourselves. We'll be with you in half an hour,' Frank said. 'Billy, would you mind getting some tea and coffee for our guests?'

He headed back behind the bar, where Jeanie was washing and stacking glasses.

Forty-five minutes later they were sat around a table drinking coffee and eating left-over sandwiches from a container on top of the bar.

'Here's the thing,' said Jerome, indicating towards Billy, 'events have moved swiftly since Superintendent Tim interviewed Deep Throat here.'

'Jerome,' Frank interrupted, 'we all know you're obsessed with Watergate but some of the people here were still in school when your journalistic heroes toppled Nixon. How about we all stick to the present day.'

'Of course, Frank', Jerome said, hesitating as he tried to adjust his narrative. 'As I was saying, events have moved on since Superintendent Tim's visit to speak to Captain Ivanov here on Tuesday.'

Frank glared at him with an intensity that could have frozen the surface of a small sun. Jerome coughed and got on with his story.

'Yes, of course, well, following young Billy's testimony and a proper assessment of all the other evidence you gathered, the superintendent pulled all of Inspector Ollie's financial records and found that he's been living beyond his means for quite some time, financed by substantial cash payments.

'Long story short, they pulled the vain bastard in and turned the bright lights on him, thumb screws at dawn apparently, within hours he was squealing like a stuck pig. He gave them everything, names, dates, amounts and the lowdown on the death of the prostitute.'

'Working girl,' Jeanie said.

'What?'

'She was a working girl.'

'Yes, so she was, anyway, in the meantime, Superintendent Tim had got one of his underlings to pull all the physical evidence on the girl's death. Turns out they'd not done any forensics just tucked it into a box and filed her death as misadventure on Inspector Ollie's say-so.

'These people really thought they were indestructible. They were so arrogant they'd stopped covering their tracks.'

He paused to light another cigarette and take a sip of coffee.

'So, they found a smoking gun. The syringe didn't have the girl's fingerprints on it. The natural conclusion was that she was not the one who had administered the fatal shot.

'Instead there was a partial thumb print on the plunger, which turned out to belong to Gavin Phillips, agent to our beloved but incapacitated council leader, consigliere to casino boss John Baker, and chief briber of Inspector Ollie.

'They are undone my beauties. Read all the gory details in tomorrow's Observer. I thought about doing a supplement, but I've had to hold back until the trial, law of natural justice, innocent before proven guilty and all that bollocks.'

Jeanie looked stunned. Frank noticed that she was holding Billy's hand so tightly that it was turning white.

'So, have they arrested the murdering bastard?' she asked.

'Yes, they have him in irons in the dungeons of Oldport Police Station,' Jerome said. 'Bread and water are the order of the day; gallows being built as we speak.'

'Well if they're going to hang him, we may need to organise a lottery to pick the executioner. I think there'll be a long queue,' Frank said,

'It's just a shame that they really have abolished hanging,' Jeanie said grimly. 'It'd be too good for him.'

'Indeed, my dear, but we could always line the buggers up against a wall and shoot them.' Jerome said.

'I never took you for the hang-'em, flog-'em brigade, Jerome,' Frank said.

'What me? Lifelong liberal dear boy, believe in the power of redemption and all that, but I make an exception when it comes to this lot. Oldport is my town, born and bred here, and they've ruined it. Justice is what we need, and justice is what we're going to get.'

'The question,' Simon said, 'is what does justice really look like? I think it's clear that Anderson and Phillips are going down for a long time, and it's well-deserved. But I'll put money on it that the rest of the council will get off scot-free, while Baker continues to run this town from his house on the hill.'

'The boy speaks sense,' Jerome said.

'Why's that?' Billy asked. 'Haven't we got enough on them?'

'Not really,' Simon said. 'Nothing that will stand up in court, at least I don't think so. We may have to depend on the voters to deliver the clear-out that we all need.'

'We should wait and see what transpires,' Jerome said. 'You'll get your clear-out one way or another, though I agree with Carl Bernstein here that the police will have a hard time putting most of the councillors in jail.

'But we have the possibility of a ministerial intervention and a full inquiry into the way the council is run. This play is going to work its way to a conclusion one way or another.

'And another thing, this story will be in the national media. Oldport will be shamed before the nation for its choice of civic leaders. That's not a bad thing. It means that whatever happens now, there is no way it'll be business as usual.

'Things have to change; the council has to change...'

'Or else the bastards will get better at hiding it from the rest of the world,' Simon interrupted.

Jerome fixed him with a stern look of reproach.

'Don't you be getting above your station now, my boy. We'll save all the crystal ball gazing 'til later shall we? I think we've sorted enough of the world out for one night as it is.'

'There's one more thing,' Simon said. 'On the basis of Ian's tape, they put some undercover cops into Baker's and caught the dealer and his bouncer pal red-handed. Couldn't happen to a nicer bloke.'

Jerome got up to go and signalled Simon to follow. Billy escorted them out while Frank and Jeanie carried on clearing up. Frank thought Jeanie looked particularly pensive.

'Are you alright, love?' he asked.

'Yes, I think so. It's a lot to take in and I can't stop thinking about poor Amber. I'm not looking forward to the funeral at all.'

'It was a terrible price to pay, but you've really made a difference here, Jeanie. You've helped to crack open Oldport and expose the corrupt way it's being governed. You've also got justice for Amber. It's a remarkable achievement.'

'So why do I feel so deflated?'

'It's natural, Jeanie, you're grieving. Nothing can make up for the loss of your closest friend and you should never forget her, but you'll need to move on at some stage, you know that don't you?'

'Yes, maybe it's the thought of moving on that's scaring me.'

Frank reached into his pocket, pulled out a packet of cigarettes, lit two of them, and then handed one to her.

'Do you know,' he said, 'change never comes easily. Look at me. I was at sea for twenty-three years, hardly visited Oldport at all. And then one day my father died, and I took a decision to take a leap in the dark.

'I came back here, took over the Prince Albert and asserted my right to dress and act as I wanted. That wasn't easy. People mocked me, they whispered behind my back but in the end, I won their respect, well the ones who mattered anyway.

'I stood up for what I believed was right. I cleaned up the pub and got rid of the drugs. I tolerated the politicians and the crooked businessmen because at some stage you must compromise, but I didn't like it.

'You, you're young, the world is lying at your feet waiting for you to pick it up and run with it. I envy you that. Now you've got justice for Amber maybe it's time to see a bit more of it.'

'Are you pushing me out, Frank?'

'No, of course not, I'm just saying the world's a bigger place than Oldport. Maybe you need to embrace that.'

Jeanie stubbed her cigarette out and looked directly at him.

'Okay, Frank, spill, what do you know?'

'It's not what I know, Jeanie, it's what I've observed. It's up to you, of course, but that boy of yours has got itchy feet. He's a clever one and my guess is that he wants to go to college. You know that he's been looking up university courses between shifts?'

'Yes, of course, we've discussed it briefly. He's always got his head in a book.'

'Well, if he goes, will you be going with him?'

'I don't know.' Jeanie was confused. 'We haven't buried Amber yet and you're asking me to make decisions on my future.'

'No, I'm asking you to make room in your head that you might have a future away from Oldport. And I'm saying to you that if you love Billy and you want to keep him, you need to think about that.

'I know you've said before that they'd have to drag you out of Oldport by the heels, but maybe you should reconsider. It's not impossible you know. I did it, your brother did it. You should allow that you might do it.'

Jeanie walked over and hugged him.

'Thank you for looking after me. You're right, I have a lot of thinking to do but let me get the funeral out of the way first.'

'Sure. I'll miss you; you know that don't you, Jeanie?'

'Yes, but you don't get rid of me that easily, Frank.'

Just then Billy walked in.

'Are you two slacking again?' he said.

Jeanie flicked a beer mat at him.

'Don't get above yourself country boy, it's about time you did some work.'

39
Black and Amber

When Billy awoke, he was alone. He fumbled about for a few minutes trying to find Jeanie and then opened his eyes to confirm that she was not in the room. He reached over to look at his watch. It was seven o'clock.

He remembered that she had spent the night at her parents so she could support Amber's mother and travel with her in the family car.

As Frank had predicted he'd had to make all the arrangements. He'd also paid for the funeral and was hosting a wake at the Prince Albert.

Amber's brother, Paul, was being allowed out of prison for the day to attend the funeral. He would be at the crematorium handcuffed to guards but would not be allowed to attend the wake.

Billy dragged himself out of bed and had a bath. Jeanie had hung his suit up for him and bought him a new black tie. He put it on and went down to the bar.

Frank was already up setting out the bar and directing the caterers. The funeral was scheduled for 11am, so they would be back for a buffet lunch. Billy poured himself a coffee, toasted some bread for a quick breakfast and then gave Frank a hand preparing the wake.

Heather and Serena came downstairs, dressed in identical plain black dresses that could have done with being two inches longer. Both had black fishnet stockings on and black high heel shoes. Kitty joined them shortly afterwards in the same outfit. They were all wearing slightly too much make-up.

'Christ', Billy thought, 'although they looked much classier than usual, anybody who knew them might think they were going to be turning tricks amongst the gravestones.' He smiled at them but kept his thoughts to himself.

Billy was going to the crematorium, but he would be in charge of the bar during the wake. It was a working day for him.

Frank had arranged a taxi to the crematorium, which arrived on cue at 10.15am. The five of them poured into it. Half an hour later they were standing outside the main building waiting for the coffin and chief mourners.

Billy was astonished at how many people were there and the attention the funeral was getting from the media. He saw a group of Jeanie's friends and quite a few regulars from the Prince Albert, but there were also several others, who had come from town, who he had never seen before. They had obviously come to gawk.

Frank was dressed in a plain black dress, black coat and gloves and a short wig. He knew many of the people who were there and moved easily amongst the crowd greeting old acquaintances and friends. Billy saw Simon and Jerome. The editor was dressed in a smart grey checked suit with a black tie and black braces.

Behind them was a TV camera crew and a few journalists from out-of-town. Amber's murder and the subsequent arrest of a police inspector and political agent had attracted national attention as Jerome had predicted. Many regional and national media outlets had sent people down to report on the aftermath.

Billy went over to greet his brother. As he did so he got his first look at Amber's brother. Paul Ford was standing between two prison warders in a suit he had clearly last worn for his court appearance. He was thin, almost scrawny but clearly hardened by hours in the prison gym. His head was closely shaved, and he had a nascent goatee. Billy thought he had a haunted look as if he was constantly looking over his shoulder. He remembered what Amber had said about the threats being made to him inside.

As they stood there Paul caught Frank's eye and nodded. Frank turned away and refused to acknowledge the greeting.

On schedule, the funeral cars crept up the drive towards

the crematorium and some smartly dressed men pulled the coffin out and carried it into the building followed by Amber's mum, Sarah, Jeanie and her mother, Phyllis.

All three wore plain black dresses. Sarah was wearing a hat with a net veil covering her face. She leant heavily on Jeanie as she entered the chapel. Frank, Billy, Paul and the other mourners followed them, the camera crew stayed outside but the journalists stood at the back, notebooks and pencils to hand.

Billy, Frank and the girls positioned themselves in the second row behind Jeanie and Phyllis. As the congregation sang the opening hymn, Billy could see that Jeanie was crying. He put his hand on her shoulder to reassure her. She acknowledged the gesture by placing her hand on his.

After the ceremony, Jeanie stood with Sarah and her son as the mourners lined up to offer their sympathies. Frank kept an eye on the journalists, making it clear that they should not approach.

Simon and Jerome ambled up to Billy and shook his hand. Billy spoke to them while keeping a watchful eye on Jeanie and Mrs Ford.

'Well, my boy, it's been quite a turnout,' Jerome boomed. Simon put his hand on Billy's arm.

'Are you okay, Bro? I know you were close to her.'

Billy forced himself to gulp back his tears. Simon could see that he was struggling to stay in control and hugged him. Jerome pretended to look elsewhere.

Frank joined them.

'Your colleagues in the media are scavengers,' he told Jerome. 'Don't they have any respect?'

Billy noticed that the camera crew had packed up and moved on but that many of the remaining journalists were taking photographs of the chief mourners as they headed towards their vehicles, a black Rover for Jeanie, Phyllis and Sarah, a prison van for Paul.

'Sorry about that,' Jerome said genuinely shocked, 'I'm afraid journalism took a turn for the worse in 1970 when

Murdoch started publishing pictures of naked girls and has been declining ever since. Me, I'm old school. If you can't sell a paper with a good story, then don't bother.'

'Yes, I've noticed,' Frank said wryly.

'Still,' Jerome continued, 'the good old Oldport Observer has come up with the goods once more. As of 9am this morning Harry O'Leary has ceased to be leader of the council. Grounds of ill-health apparently, but if he hadn't jumped, he would have been pushed.

'And our local MP has been on the blower to tell me that the minister will be standing up in the House of Commons tomorrow afternoon to announce a full inquiry into how the council is being run. And he will be sending in a team of inspectors to carry out a full audit.

'I call that a result, don't you, old boy?'

'I think that is the least he could do,' Simon said.

'Ah, you're still young,' Jerome said. 'Just getting them to their feet in the Commons chamber is a major achievement these days. We really had to stir the shit to get this outcome.'

Frank looked at his watch. A taxi was making its way up the driveway to take them back to the Prince Albert. Heather, Kitty and Serena were already standing at the kerbside waiting for it.

'Will you be coming back to the pub?' Billy asked.

'Love to,' Jerome said, 'but your boy here has to write up the latest developments and I need to kick the printing presses into life. We'll be in this evening.'

'Sorry,' Simon said. 'Look after Jeanie will you, she needs you more than ever right now.'

'Don't worry Si, I've got that covered.' Billy said as Frank pulled him towards the taxi.

The three girls were subdued and had been crying. None of them had a handkerchief so Billy lent out the clean one Jeanie had laid out for him with his suit.

Heather handed the mascara-stained cloth back to him.

'No, keep it,' Billy said, 'I'm sure I've got another one back at the pub.'

When they got back, the temporary staff Frank had hired for the day had already opened-up and were serving several of the mourners. Billy joined them behind the bar and started to put the food out on the counter.

He looked around for Jeanie. Eventually he saw her sitting at a table with Sarah Ford, her mother and the three girls. Mrs Ford had removed her hat and veil and he could see her clearly for the first time.

She was in her late forties but looked ten years older. She had permed brown hair and her face wore the unmistakeable signs of a life of hardship and torment.

She was crying and being comforted in turn by Heather and Serena, pausing between sobs only to sip at a glass of gin and tonic. Jeanie came over to the bar to get some more drinks. Billy went to serve her.

'How are you feeling?' he asked.

'Pretty shook up, I've never lost somebody before.'

'I know, it's pretty hard, I remember when we buried my father, I didn't know how I was going to cope. I missed him terribly. Amber was special to me, too. We're both going to miss her.'

Jeanie took his hand and he kissed her on the cheek. They hugged, and Billy helped her carry the drinks over to her table. She introduced him to Sarah Ford who was already a little tipsy. He gave his condolences, but as he spoke tears came flooding out. Jeanie pulled him away and went into the kitchen with him.

'Where's your handkerchief?' she asked.

'I gave it to Heather,' he said. She pulled out a tissue and dabbed at his cheeks.

Billy held Jeanie tight. He knew that he had to hold himself together for her sake. After what seemed an age but was only a few minutes, he decided that he needed to broach a subject he had been avoiding since Amber's death.

'Listen, Jeanie, I've been meaning to talk to you about this for some time. When I came to Oldport, I was on a gap year before going to college. I had to leave home early

303

because of what happened there, and the plan was to spend time here before moving on next year.

'But all that's gone a bit ape shit in the last few months, what with meeting you, Amber dying and all the things that have happened. I've been torn over what to do.'

He stopped. She was looking at him expectantly, her eyes brimming with tears. He took her hand.

'Don't worry, Jeanie, I'm not going anywhere without you.' He kissed her forehead.

'But Billy, you can't abandon your dreams, your plans for my sake.'

'That's just it, Jeanie, I don't want to, I want you to come with me.'

She looked stunned; she went to speak but he put a finger on her mouth.

'Let me finish. I've applied for a place at Southampton University starting in September next year. We could move there together, get some bar work or something else, stay together through it all.

'I know you said that they would have to drag you kicking and screaming from Oldport, but I don't want to lose you. There's a bigger world out there, we're young, maybe we should explore it together.'

'And what if I don't want to go,' she said softly, 'if I decide that I want to stay in Oldport with my friends and family?'

'Then I'll stay with you.'

'Oh Billy,' she almost sighed the words. 'I can't make you choose between me and your degree.'

'You don't understand, Jeanie, I've already chosen. I've chosen you; all we're debating now is how and where we live in the future.'

'And do I need to make a decision now?'

'No, absolutely not, there's almost a full year before I have to decide whether to take the college place or not. All I want is for you to think about it and when you've made up your mind then we can act on it.'

She put her arms around him and placed her head against his shoulder. It had been an emotionally exhausting day and he was beginning to doubt the wisdom of even raising the matter with her. But it had been preying on his mind for some time and he felt it was the right thing to do to get it out in the open.

'Let me think about it,' she said. 'Give me some space to work out what I want to do with my life.'

He kissed her, and they walked back into the bar, hand in hand.

40
Succession

It was a new week, a new month and a new era. Fred Harris stood outside the door to the leader's office trying to decide if he had done the right thing in taking on the job.

It was hardly going to be a piece of cake following the scandal that had swept Harry O'Leary away and placed the council under siege from residents, government inspectors and the minister himself.

He opened the door and stepped inside. The office was much the same as it had been the last time he was in there with Harry. The main difference was that the desk was now cleared of all the paperwork.

The glass-fronted fitted mahogany bookcases were still there, as were the plain mahogany panels and the pictures of Oldport and past civic dignitaries. Harris walked over to the corner housing the television, video recorder and drinks cabinet and helped himself to a tonic water from the fridge.

It didn't do to get into the habit of drinking alcohol too early, he thought, that had been part of O'Leary's downfall.

He was conscious of somebody standing in the doorway, He turned around. It was Sue.

'Good morning, Councillor, is there anything I can get for you?'

'No, that's fine, thank you Sue. I was expecting a big pile of paperwork.'

'There's a large volume of correspondence,' she said, 'plus several reports for you to sign off. I have them back here. I didn't want to overwhelm you too early by leaving them on your desk.'

'That's very good of you, Sue. You'd better wheel them in so I can get started. Do I have any appointments today?'

Yes, I'm afraid the diary is quite full. You have a meeting with the inspectors at 10am. That will take up most of the morning. You have a lunch meeting with the Chamber of

Trade and then at 2pm you are scheduled to meet officials from the minister's office.'

Harris swallowed hard.

'So, an average day then?' he half-joked.

Sue didn't respond, instead she disappeared into the anteroom and reappeared a few minutes later with a large pile of papers. Harris gulped down the rest of his tonic water and settled in at his new desk to get started.

'You'd better get me a supply of black coffee please, Sue. This lot may take some time.'

He started to pull out the individual letters and make notes for Sue to use in composing replies. Many of them were from individuals in Oldport demanding action to purge the council of corrupt practises. Others were asking the council to re-open various planning and licensing decisions which the writers alleged had been compromised by the taking of bribes.

There was a knock on the door and Sue reappeared.

'Mr John Baker is here to see you,' she said.

He waved the visitor in.

'Fred, let me be the first to congratulate you on replacing Harry as leader.'

Baker was effusive in tone but chastened in manner. Harris could see that he'd had a hard time of it over Phillips' arrest and the revelations about his parties and the influence he exercised on the council.

'Did anybody see you come in here?' Harris asked, only half-joking. He'd been named as being at that party as well, and his role in granting the licence for the casino had come under intense scrutiny in the press and in the council.

It was only by calling in favours from various cronies, who had equally benefited from Baker's largesse and who, in some cases, had received a small gift from the businessman to persuade them to vote the right way, that Harris had won the leadership.

He may have been tainted, but then there were no credible rivals who weren't also tainted.

Nevertheless, he had to present his leadership as a fresh start and that meant that for the first few months, while everything settled down and he dealt with all the external interventions, he needed to keep his distance from Baker. He thought that the businessman had understood that.

'That's no way to greet an old friend,' Baker responded. 'I just came to convey my best wishes and to try and establish an understanding about how we should work together in the future.'

'I've got to give you this John, you ain't subtle and you ain't no diplomat.'

Harris liked to be blunt, it fitted well with his physical presence. After all nobody was going to argue with a six foot four-inch-tall man weighing eighteen-plus stone and resembling a ginger yeti in appearance.

He stroked his thick beard. He had let his hair grow in recent months as it gave him a fiercer appearance. He had recently seen a film about the conflict between the Romans and the Picts' beyond Hadrian's wall, and had been so impressed by the way the barbarians intimidated their opponents that he had adopted some of their so-called style.

'What, can't a man keep in touch with his friends?' Baker seemed put out.

'Why, of course you can, John, but not here and not now. We've just had our business dealings splashed over the national media, we have inspectors and government busybodies crawling all over us, and we're fighting half a dozen attempts to undo decisions that have given all of us the lifestyle we enjoy so much.

'If we're going to recover then we need to manage the situation carefully and that means discretion and keeping things low key.'

Baker hesitated. Harris thought he looked a bit lost. He'd had his world torn apart and he didn't appear to be coping very well.

'Look, John we're going to come back from this, but it will take time. For once in your life you're going to have to be patient.'

'Patience is not what I do, Fred.'

'No, I'm aware.'

'My main concern now, is to secure the future of the new casino. I believe the license is being challenged. Does that challenge have any prospect of success?'

'Give me a chance John, I've been in this office for literally half an hour. But no, I've seen a legal report that says the decision is watertight, irrespective of how many prostitutes the committee shagged. It would take a judicial review to turn it around and there are no grounds.'

'The committee followed all the correct procedures and there's nobody around who is going to pay to take it to court. So, for fuck's sake, relax.'

'That's good, so the tricky one, the Inchfield Estate extension... Is this village green application serious? Do they have a case?'

'To be honest, I have no idea. The lawyers are still looking at it. The informal advice I've seen is that they don't have evidence of a clear twenty-year use for recreation as of right. And thinking about it, that makes sense.

'The estate is not twenty years old yet, and this field only started being used for games by the residents once they occupied their homes. But the evidence is still coming in, so we can't say for certain and this thing goes to an independent arbiter anyway.'

'That sounds hopeful, but I need you to keep on top of it, Fred.'

'Do you now? Well you should know that I'm not Harry. I'm my own man and if you want my help then I need to know what my incentive is.'

'Of course,' Baker replied. 'You know that Harry had a direct investment in this development, which he protected by making his son a director. I can give you a share of the profits if you can help me overcome this village green challenge, so I can get the thing built.'

Harris thought for a bit.

'You've got yourself a deal, John. Now we need to get you out of here. I've got inspectors coming in very shortly and I don't want them finding you here.'

Harris ushered him towards the door; The two men shook hands.

'Listen John, we've got a long history behind us, so relax and leave things to me. We just need to get over this hump and we'll be back to business as usual. In the meantime, you get on with consolidating what you've got. I'll be in touch.'

'Business as usual is what I'm looking for, Fred. I'll await your call, but don't leave it too long.'

Harris left it to Sue to escort Baker from the building. He sat down to work his way through the mound of paperwork on his desk. As he got into one of the reports there was a knock on the door.

Ian O'Leary poked his head in.

'Ian, how good to see you, please come in, how is your father?' asked Harris, inviting him to sit down.

'He's recovering slowly, thank you Fred. He's still very weak and needs nursing, but I think he'll be able to come home tomorrow or the day afterwards. I'm planning to stay as long as I can, but we'll be employing a private nurse to help out alongside the support being put in place by the social services.'

'I'm glad to hear it. I'd like to visit him once he's at home.'

'Yes, of course, I'll let you know when he's strong enough. I just wanted to call in to congratulate you on your election as leader.'

'Thank you. What are you up to now?'

'Well, I was going to join my mother in London, but Dad's heart attack has held that up. I think I'm going to have to stay in Oldport for some time to come.'

Fred stroked his beard thoughtfully.

'You know what Ian, maybe we could find something for you. I was appalled at the way John Baker treated you. You were just doing your job and that thug Phillips should have been sacked on the spot. I think John showed some very poor judgement.

'Can you give me a couple of days? We're a bit under the cosh here and it looks like the minister is going to set up an intervention board to oversee the running of the council. If we're going to emerge the other end of that in one piece, we'll need somebody to project-manage our response. Would you be interested?'

'Yes, I would. It'll enable me to spend some time with my father while putting right some of the mess he made here.'

'Don't be too harsh on him, Ian, he was always doing what he thought was best for the town.'

'But he was on the take, Fred. He was profiting personally from those decisions.'

'That's one way of looking at it. You know, Oldport is a small town, a close-knit community. If we're going to grow, then we need to work together. The business community and the council can create jobs, bring prosperity to the town and put Oldport on the map.

'There are no clear dividing lines. To suggest that there are is naive at best. People need to be incentivised.'

'I'm sorry, Fred, I don't agree. You can do that hands-off. You're not here to enrich yourselves.'

Ian was talking calmly and quietly.

'What has been missing from Oldport for some time is the principle of public service. Councillors are elected to serve, to represent everybody, not just one interest group, and they're meant to set an example.

'Oldport Council has fallen down on every count for many years and I'm ashamed to say that my father was as guilty of that as are all the other councillors who assumed leadership roles. The likes of John Baker shouldn't have been allowed to subvert the political process. He should have been kept at arm's length. The errors of judgement and the greed that the whole town has witnessed over the last few years, is no way for any council or councillor to behave.

'What's worse is that the rot has spread to encompass all

aspects of public life, the police through Ollie Anderson, even some magistrates, and the business community. It must stop.

'I'll take your job if you still want to give it to me, Fred, but I'll do so because I want to put right the mess my father made, to clean up the town where I was born and brought up.

'It may be too late for my father, for Baker, maybe even for you, but I think it's important that the generation of public servants who follow you do so for the right reasons.

'Get in touch if you still want me but remember, those are my terms and I'm not going to compromise on them. The future of Oldport lies in the balance. It's time to choose which side you're on.'

Ian stood up, shook Fred's hand and left, leaving the new council leader staring dumbfounded in his wake.

41
Epilogue

It was a fine August day. A small crowd gathered in Oldport's bus station. Frank was wearing his best summer dress and a short brown wig. He was flanked by Simon and Jerome.

Behind them Billy and Jeanie were saying their goodbyes to the girls. Jeanie was hugging Serena and Kitty, while Heather was trying to hold back her tears as she embraced Billy.

She pulled back from him, both hands on his shoulders, eyes fixed intently on his as she dished out her advice.

'Remember country boy,' she said smiling, 'Southampton is a big city. You keep close to Jeanie if it starts getting too scary for you.'

Billy grinned.

'Don't you worry Heather; I've had my baptism of fire here in Oldport. Southampton will be a breeze after that.'

Heather turned to hug Jeanie as Serena and Kitty took turns to kiss Billy on the cheek. All four girls were crying now.

It wasn't just that they were losing Billy and Jeanie, but their whole way of life had changed, too. The Prince Albert no longer operated as a brothel. The new police inspector had seen to that. Instead, and with Frank's help, the girls had moved on. Serena was working as a barmaid with Frank, Heather and Kitty had found jobs in Baker's. Amber's death and the clamp down on the pub operating as a brothel had been the impetus they needed to get out of the sex trade once and for all.

As Simon had predicted, it had proved almost impossible to put together a solid-enough case to prosecute councillors for corruption. The intervention board was still in place however, and Fred Harris had found his room for manoeuvre severely limited. There were no more parties at

Baker's mansion, at least for the time being, and the businessman had been warned off visiting the town hall.

Billy shook Frank's hand.

'Thanks for everything. It's been a real pleasure. I'm sorry to leave you in the lurch like this.'

Frank put on a mock grimace.

'I can cope with losing you, Billy, but I may never forgive you for stealing the best barmaid I've ever had.'

He looked up as a middle-aged couple hurried towards them. The man was carrying a suitcase which he presented to Jeanie. Frank went to greet Dave and Phyllis Carter as they were hugging their daughter goodbye.

Jeanie was reassuring her parents that everything would be fine. 'We have accommodation sorted, and we both have jobs. And Billy has his student grant.'

Phyllis handed her daughter a violin case. 'I know you've enrolled in the technical college there, but you never know you might find time for this. I checked, Southampton University, it has a music degree course.'

'Thanks Mum,' said Jeanie, raising the violin case and brandishing it in her mother's face as she continued.

'One of the advantages of being in Southampton is that I'll be able to see Matt more easily when he's in port. We can all get together; it isn't that far away.'

Dave Carter shook Billy's hand as his wife embraced Jeanie. It was as if he was engaging in a traditional handover of his daughter, father to boyfriend.

They chatted for a bit and then Billy said his goodbyes to Simon. The brothers embraced, before Billy turned his attention to the Oldport Observer's editor.

'Thank you for coming to see us off, Mr Wilson.'

'It's my pleasure, though I'm more focussed on making sure young Simon here doesn't sneak off with you and defect to a bigger newspaper.'

'I think it may well happen, Mr Wilson now that he's been nominated for a regional newspaper award. I suspect Fleet Street will come calling very soon.'

'Yes, yes, and he deserves it, but you won't blame me if I put off that day for as long as possible.'

'I couldn't have done it without you, Billy,' Simon said.

'Oh, I think that you would have got there,' Billy responded. 'But we did what we set out to do, we got justice for Amber.'

'Yes, and shook up Oldport in the process,' Jerome said.

'You know I wonder what did really change,' Simon added thoughtfully. 'We got rid of Harry O'Leary and got Fred Harris instead, just more of the same as far as I can see.

'I'm sure that whatever Ian says, Baker's still pulling strings from behind the scenes. His two clubs are going strong and the bulldozers are moving in on the Inchfield Estate after the village green application failed.

'We've skimmed the scum off the top but beneath the surface it's just the same-old, same-old.'

'Oh, I wouldn't be too sure about that,' Jerome said. 'It may look like business as usual, but the arrogance and complacency has gone. They know that we're watching them. And the government inspectors have done their bit.

'Fred Harris and his pals are working with one hand tied behind their backs and John Baker has been warned off. The cronyism is still there at all levels of course, but it's far less effective and is producing fewer rewards.'

'We'll see,' Simon said.

At that moment, the bus to Southampton pulled in and passengers started to disembark. Dave Carter picked up his daughter's bag and carried it over to the luggage compartment. Billy followed with his bag.

There was another round of goodbyes as they climbed aboard the bus. Billy sat next to Jeanie. She put her head on his shoulder, hardly daring to look the others in the eye in case she should break down.

The bus slowly climbed up out of the town. As it got to the brow of the hill, Billy looked back. He could see the harbour area below with the Prince Albert standing proudly above it.

They rounded a corner and the town disappeared from view.

Billy leant over and kissed Jeanie on the cheek. He was putting the pain of the past behind them. She was his future now.

* * *

Harry was shaken from his thoughts by the door to his private room opening. An orderly entered carrying his breakfast.

He hated being ill. One stay in hospital was bad enough, but to be back here because of his own carelessness was incredibly frustrating. He had drunk too much and fallen, knocking himself out in the process. His cleaner had found him and driven him to St Theresa's. He calculated that he'd been unconscious for a few hours, and was still groggy when she arrived, blood pouring from a huge gash on his head.

He had expected to be patched up and sent home, but doctors were worried about concussion and his high blood pressure, and admitted him, hooking him up to all these infernal machines, again.

He gingerly touched the bandage around his head. It was itching but he couldn't get in to scratch it. It was day three of this so-called monitoring, and as if to add insult to injury Ian had messaged to say he was rushing back from London – yet another lecture on his lifestyle.

What was the point of having a healthy lifestyle, if he had no life? What was left for him?

It was almost as if he were a pariah in his own town. His power had gone, his so-called friends had abandoned him, his family were nearly a hundred miles away and he'd had to endure hours of interrogation from the police.

His solicitor had told him that even now they were still digging. When would they leave him in peace? No wonder he was so stressed that he could only find comfort from drinking.

He starred at the muesli that had been left for him. He couldn't eat this crap. Pushing the tray to one side he reached for the button to summon somebody to take it away – it was too far away. He fell back, exhausted from the effort.

The heart monitor beeped repeatedly in the background. He looked around – no flowers, not one get-well card, just a copy of the Oldport Observer with the latest news on Fred Harris' self-proclaimed crusade to clean up the town – the hypocrite.

Harry put his head in his hands and started to cry, the tears turning to heaving sobs that shook his body. His chest felt heavy and he was finding it more difficult to breathe. A shooting pain ran down his left arm; the beeping on the heart monitor grew more rapid. Harry gasped as tears streamed down his face, the pain was excruciating. Somewhere in the distance an alarm was sounding.

Where was the nurse, where was everybody?

It was to be Harry O'Leary's last thought before the monitor changed to a single, continuous tone.

About the Author

Peter Black is a graduate of Swansea University, a former member of the Welsh Assembly, Deputy Minister for Local Government in Wales from 2000 to 2003, and has been a Swansea Councillor since 1984. Awarded the CBE for service to public life, he was Lord Mayor of Swansea for the civic year 2019-20.

Previous works include The Assassination of Morgan Sheckler. He blogs regularly on political matters at **www.peterblack.blogspot.com** and writes the occasional article for the South Wales Evening Post. These can be read at **www.peterblack.wales**.

Peter can be found on Twitter @peterblackwales and on Facebook at peterblack.wales. He is also on Instagram, where you will be able to find many pictures of his cats.

The Assassination of Morgan Sheckler by Peter Black

When Morgan Sheckler is elected Mayor of the Cardiff Capital Region in Wales, he finds himself at odds with his own staff, not just because of his policies but also because of his brash, bullying manner.

Sheckler immediately sets his sights on dismantling plans for a new power plant in the region -- a move that puts him on collision course with some unsavoury American backers who will do anything necessary to have it built.

Caught in the middle is Dawn Highcliffe, Sheckler's director of development, who must do as the mayor orders but yet also, somehow, please the Americans, who have blackmailed her into cooperating with them.

A world of corruption and intimidation is revealed that brings Dawn to breaking point and sees her facing the prospect of a lengthy prison sentence.

But there's hope, because Sheckler's past is coming back to haunt him and a group of those he wronged are circling, and they're looking for blood...

Available now on Amazon

Reviews

'Loads of sex, murder? If this is what Welsh local government is like, how do they find time to collect the bins?' **Sunday Times 12 April 2020**

'This is great entertainment, a pleasant and fast paced read that doesn't feel like a first novel. This will please thriller fans as well as mystery lovers.' **Christoph Fischer**

Local politics and a murder mystery 'An intriguing tale of murder and corruption set in a backdrop of dog eat dog local politics. The story twists and turns until reaching its unexpected conclusion. A real page turner and a great read. ' **JanetMcB on Amazon**

Murder, political intrigue and a romance too. 'If you enjoy House of Cards (and who doesn't?) there's a good chance you'll like this book too. It's a murder mystery full of political intrigue and corruption but also intertwined with a love story. I couldn't put it down, so ended up reading it in less than a day (although I may have stayed up half the night as well!)' **Mellifluous on Amazon**

A book of political intrigue and interesting characters. A different story with a female lead. Sexy and violent bits. A story that obviously starts with the assassination and works back to why it happened with a sting in the tales. A real page turner. **Mr M W Thomas on Amazon**

Printed in Great Britain
by Amazon